I0562520

FRANKIE B.
& OK BILL

THE TALE OF TWO FRIENDS FROM DIFFERENT CULTURES IN 1888 AMERICA

Conrad R. Dreas

Cover illustration by John F. Dreas

copyright © 2025 Conrad R. Dreas
ISBN: 978-1-959700-56-2

Hoot Books Publishing
Owner, Victoria Fletcher
851 French Moore Blvd.
Suite 136 Box 14
Abingdon, VA 24210

Dedication

This book is dedicated to all generations who, like me, have a fascination with the old west and how cowboys and Indians learned to live side by side after many years of killing each other.

Acknowledgments

I would like to acknowledge my family and friends. They play many of the characters in the story; but only they would know. Hopefully they will enjoy the storyline along with many others.

My great-grandson Frankie inspired me when he was born to get going with a project I had been thinking about doing for some time. I don't know how it fits together, but it does.

Characters & Places

OK Bill - Ahatahkakood, Apache, friend & ranch hand,
    horse named Friend then second horse from
    Crow named Stranger
Frankie B.- Frankie Butler, cowboy,& ranch hand,
    cattle herd point man, horse named Star
Angelina – Chananget, half-breed Comanche, 18
    years old, horse named Alice
Chief Bengalese – Comanche, a tribe in Eastern,
    Oklahoma, Chickasaw nation
Prairie Flower - Toh-Tsee-Ah, Comanche, mother of
    Angelina, horse named My Friend
Carlyle Coeburn - Grandpa of Angelina, mountain
    man
Michael C. Andreas – Doctor, friend of Shoshone
Jacob Wentland - Doctor
Constance Sikorski & daughter Antonina -
    kidnapped by Logan Belt gang, sold to
    Comancheros in southern Illinois, son Hansie in
    Illinois
Margaret Edwards & daughter Grace - Arkansas,
    kidnapped by Comancheros
Butch & Wilma Evens - parents to Mary & Gloria
Mary & Gloria Evens - Oklahoma, kidnapped by
    Comancheros
Red Socks - Juan Gonzalos, Comanchero
José Lopez - Comanchero
Captain Louis Milroad - in charge of a fort
Sheriff's Outpost Saloon
Chisholm Trail

Episcopal creek - Arroyo Episcopal
Doc Jim Clark – Stillwater, Oklahoma
Dolphus Dickenson, Cattle & Double DD ranch
    owner, former Texas Ranger
Harve Sunny - former slave, cowboy, & ranch hand
Miss Shirley Chung
Dance Mead – cowboy, gunslinger, & ranch hand
Tommy Holbrooks – cowboy, gunslinger, & ranch
    hand
John Johnson - cowboy, ranch hand
John Davis - cowboy, ranch hand
Tim Shiloh - ranch hand
Señorita, Señora, Señor, sombrero, Comancheros,
    banditos - Spanish words
Long John Lowther - ranch foreman, cattle drive trail
    boss, former Texas Ranger, horse named Easy
    Rider, a sister Kate, friend April
Stephen C. Fuller - Captain, Texas Ranger
Red Fox - Comanche, Cu la al ke, point man, good
    with cattle, works well with Ok Bill, horse named
    Night Spirit
Taters Barnett - cook & horse shoer with the herd,
    former Texas Ranger
Sheriff Stanley K. Malawy – Granite, Oklahoma
Marshall Tony Malawy - the Territory
Deputy Herman Malawy- Granite, Oklahoma
Bill & Felix Dunaman & their green bandana's gang
Orlies and Clarius – Glada's sisters
Gabriel the dog
Phyllis Evens - mother of children Joseph & Agatha
Clem Wilson - husband, saloon owner, all around bad
    guy in Higgins, Texas
Tracker Jack - Apache with the Rangers
Lieutenant Sergeant Reading, Sheriff Ray Jones,
    Deputy Randy Smith, Marshall Bill McCoy, Judge
    Macintosh, Mayor Dick Haverman - Lipscomb,
    Tennessee
Jim Moore - government man in Lipscomb
Miss Clarius – rides a horse named Peaceful
The Comanche chief in Oklahoma

Tim Shiloh & Phyllis – Higgins, Texas

José, Margaret, & Grace - the law in Higgins, Texas, for six months

Major General Kaczmarek - procurement army, cattle, Helena, Montana

Diane L. Binks – Helena, Montana postmaster

Captain James Styles - army, receives the cattle in Helena

The Sunday Record - Independent Record - Helena weekly record

Crabtown named after John Crab, miners from Missouri called it St. Helena

Sheriff Jacob Grzeszkiewicz – Dubois, Wyoming

Doc Isaac

Captain George Pinter - Dubois, Wyoming

Rose Caldwell - saloon girl in Denver, Colorado

Cuerno Verde - dangerous man, a Comanchero's leader in Colorado

Old Chief- Crow, came to die

Like a Deer- Grandaugher of Old Chief

Louis Vertie- Cañon City doctor

Beaufort Powers- Cañon City sheriff

Cedric Tillman- Mayor of Vici

Bill Waselman- Sheriff of Vici

Preacher Lefty Ledford

Table of Contents

Chapter 1

Frankie, a young cowboy, is separated from the rest of the cowboys and the herd of cattle in a sandstorm. And his good friend, an Apache named OK Bill, searches for him in some of the worst weather conditions. Most sandstorms make it hard to see but this one was worse than most! Frankie's horse stumbled and broke a leg. He did what anyone would have done in 1888. He knew that a horse with all its weight could not stand on a broken leg and would surely die a merciless death from wolves or other wild predators. He hated to do it, but he shot the horse, took off his saddle and his gear, and started walking. Having no idea where he was, he settled in for the night, made camp in a wooded area close to a creek. Late after sunset, as he was about to doze off, he heard some noise. Looking up over a fallen tree he was near, he saw a band of wild horses, five to be exact, at the creek. He guessed he was no more than a hundred feet from them. Not wanting to scare them away, he just lay still hoping they wouldn't smell him and run. By now he was getting the idea of maybe catching one and breaking it to get out of his dilemma. After all, he thought he had some experience with horses, never really breaking one himself but being around horses and seeing them being broken all his life, he figured it would take a couple of days to get things done right. Frankie was remembering all the men on the cattle drive. There was Dolphus Dickenson; he was the owner of the ranch and was along on the drive. Taters was the cook and also was especially good with horses. He wished he could get some tips on how to catch and tame one of the horses. He knew that was his way out of this dilemma. All the other men kept coming up in his mind. Frankie had only been with Mr. Dickenson a couple of months, but hoped he would catch up on the skills to stay on the ranch and have a good job and place to live; but now that he got separated from the crew in the storm, he wondered if the men would even look for him! One thing he knew for sure, if he was ever going to catch up with the herd, he had to start in the morning doing something about it. He had some dried meat and bread in his saddle bag, and he might kill a rabbit, if he could, for food, then he would concentrate on the horses. He would have to find out where they spent most of their time. He had a long rope. If he could wait till they came for water, it might be the best time and spot the one that looked more catchable. *Okay*, he thought, *I'll scout around for the horses while it's light and maybe I'll get lucky.* Frankie kept thinking about what the guys might do if they were in his place. OK Bill, the only Indian on the drive, was always good to him. He would know how Indians catch horses. I think they'd sneak up on them and try to hobble them, maybe even at night. OK Bill is a full-blooded

Apache. He called him Frankie B. Guess he just thought it sounded good because Frankie's last name is Butler.

Now was the time to get on his feet and look around, find something: hoof prints, horse crap, crushed brush. He fills his canteen from the creek and gets moving. He checked his gun and ammo, holstered his pistol, and grabbed his rifle. As he walked, he watched the surrounding area and off in the distance for anything, plus watched out for critters. This scrub land could have anything, also the Indian tribes in this area are very unpredictable; however, the one person he wouldn't mind running into is a white man that lives with the Indians by the name of Carlyle Coeburn. Stories were told about him helping whites in distress; sounded pretty good right now. Just then, Frankie smelled a horse. Carefully looking all around, he spotted the five he thought were the ones he saw yesterday, not that it mattered. A horse is a horse. He figured if he could get close enough to throw a lasso, he might get lucky, and he was down wind, so they shouldn't be able to smell him. Laying his gear down, he crept slowly. Just then a covey of quail startled and flew up. The horses looked up and then went back to eating the patches of grass they found. Now was his chance to get closer. He also thought, *I better remember where my rifle and gear are. Don't want to lose the gear.* Looking around to size up the area, he guessed he could find his way to it. Right now, he needed to concentrate on horses and getting close enough to throw a rope. Thinking he was close enough, he threw the rope and missed. The horses bolted, but not very far. Throwing again, he got the rope on the horse's head just below the ear. The horse shook it off. By now he was thinking, *Do or die, I got to get this done.* He pulled back the rope, coiled it up, and started walking slowly to the horses. Surprised they didn't run off; he touched the one he tried to rope. It looked up but continued to eat its grass. Now if he got the rope on the horse, it could bolt and drag him half to death.

He reached out and got it over the head. It let him rub its neck, the others stood there and looked at him. He thought they must be half way used to humans when all of a sudden, the four ran, leaving him standing there with the brown horse. Can I walk this horse back to my camp and tie it up? I don't think this horse is going to cooperate with me, but he started to walk. The horse came along without holding back. I guess if I just walk and not jerk on the rope, this young horse might go along with me. Frankie went to his gear and rifle, picked it up, and continued the walk back to camp. All the while, the horse came right along with him. He stopped at the creek and let the horse drink, then crossed the creek to camp and tied the horse to a tree where there was plenty of grass. He couldn't believe his luck or maybe God was looking out for him after all. This was rough country. He would pet the horse every once in a while as he got himself something to eat; some stale bread was all he had left. Remembering he saw fish in the creek, he tried his luck with a spear sharpened from a branch. Almost giving up, he caught a pretty good-sized one, cleaned it, and got it on a flat rock in the fire. All the while, a young wolf or wild dog of some kind watched his every action from a distance, which also made the horse very nervous. Frankie chased it away a few times and just gave up. He didn't think it would be much of a problem. The horse kinda settled down, too. After eating his fish, he reckoned it to be about three in the afternoon. There were a few more hours he could get the horse used to him before he tried to put his saddle on it tomorrow. As it turns out, that wolf was a big dog from an Indian camp not too far from where he was. He only found that out when two Indian boys came looking for the dog. They saw the horse tied up. Now what will happen when they tell back at the camp? Frankie didn't know what kind of Indians they were: Comanche, Arapaho, and Apache raided in the Oklahoma territory. Frankie tried to remember what he had heard about that white man, Carlyle Coeburn. If it were possible, could he be in the area? As luck would have it, Coeburn was close by; not in the camp near Frankie, but the next camp over. Being Comanche left a little to be concerned about, peaceful some of the time and on the warpath other times, depending on what the Whites pushed them into. Carlyle Coeburn living freely among them was a good thing. Coeburn had a son that married an Indian maid named Toh-Tsee-Ah, meaning Prairie Flower. They were only married a short time when Coeburn's son got himself killed in a raid to another area. Prairie Flower had a baby girl less than nine months later that she named Chanannget. Don't know what it means in American. Carlyle Coeburn, being the child's grandpa, didn't like the name Chanannget, so he called her Angelina. She loved her grandpa. He took her everywhere with him. The girl is about eighteen now. Frankie tried to keep his mind on

13

what he had to do and not worry too much about what the Indians might do, but that was hard at the moment. He went over to the horse and rubbed it. He heard a noise. It was the Indians. They came to see what this white man was doing here. They were on horseback and had their rifles in hand but not in a threatening way. About six of them. All of a sudden from the back, out walks a big buckskin-clad White man with a rifle in hand stopping a distance away from Frankie, and demanded, "What are you doing here? I'm Coeburn, Carlyle Coeburn, these people are my friends."

Frankie was glad and afraid at the same time and said, "I have heard of you. Maybe you can help me. I'm trying to get back to my cattle drive." He told him the whole story and why he needed a horse.

Coeburn said, "These are kinda the Indians' horses. I will ask the chief if you can have a horse. I will let you know in the morning. It might be a good idea to spend the night in the Indian camp. They are not hard to get along with if you treat them fair." Coeburn took the rope loose from the tree and turned, leading Frankie's horse off, following the Indians as one Indian gave him the reins to his horse and said, "This way." Frankie started to put out the fire, dump out the coffee, and gather up his saddle and all he had. He knew he had a fair piece to walk to the camp when he heard in broken English and in a low voice, "Frankie B." Turning around fast, he saw his friend OK Bill, the Apache that worked for Dolphus Dickenson, the ranch owner. OK Bill got off his horse, leading it out from the trees where he had been watching everything that had gone on with the Indians. "I no sure how they treat me, so I stay in trees," he said. "I be here for time. Boss tell me find you. Track you no easy, wind cover tracks. Find Frankie B.'s dead horse, bullet in head. Know you in trouble. Good see you."

Frankie said, "You have no idea how glad I am to see you OK Bill. Are you hungry or thirsty? I was about to dump the coffee."

"I take coffee," OK Bill said. They both stooped by the fire as they sipped their coffee.

"We need to talk about how we are going to do this. We should be able to go into their camp without trouble, but not sure."

He asked, "OK Bill, have you heard of Carlyle Coeburn, the white man that lives with the Comanche."

OK Bill said he had heard some. He said it was a good thing and maybe the Comanche would be fair with him, being an Apache.

"Let's get going. We should get to their camp before dark." They loaded his gear and saddle on OK Bill's horse, and both got on, heading for the camp. This is better than walking. We can get there a lot faster. Frankie said, "Let me go in to camp and get a hold of Carlyle Coeburn before you come. It might set off the Comanche when they see you."

OK Bill was a tall, commanding figure. His clothes were Apache for sure. The camp was pretty much in the open, so when they got close, Frankie got off the horse leaving OK Bill away from camp. In the open walking into the camp, they were okay with Frankie. Most knew he was coming. The sun was setting and light was limited. He asked around for Carlyle Coeburn. Finding him in a tent, he lowered his head, took his hat off, and went in. The two did a limp handshake.

"I have a friend waiting for me outside camp with all my gear. He's an Apache and looks like one, too. I want to be sure it won't start something. How do the Comanche feel about the Apache?"

Coeburn said, "They accept me. They have to accept him."

"He is a good friend. He came looking for me," said Frankie.

"Let me talk to the Chief. Should be okay but let me check."

"How about I go with you," said Frankie.

"Let's not wait too long. It's getting dark. Might make things worse."

"Yeah, let's go see the Chief."

"You wanna leave your rifle here."

"Yeah."

They walked over to the tent where Chief Bengalese was, ducked, and went in. Frankie took his hat off and bowed his head. The Chief crossed his chest with his right arm in a peace gesture. While sitting by a fire with a blanket over his shoulders, Carlyle Coeburn started right in talking to the Chief. "This man is peaceful, no war, no lies, good White man, needs horse, nothing to trade, got lost, horse died in sandstorm. If you say okay, he will break horse and leave in maybe two or three moons. One more thing Chief, he has friend waiting outside camp. He is Apache, no war, no trouble, he just tracked his friend Frankie after the storm. They will leave together. The Apache will come into your camp only if you say okay."

Chief Bengalese stood up fast, and looked hard at Frankie right into his eyes, as if to see good or bad intent, and said, "I will see this Apache. Now, take his guns and knife, bring him to me."

Frankie and Mr. Coeburn went to where OK Bill was, told him what the Chief said, the conditions.

At first, OK Bill, shook his head, "No take guns, no take knife." It's easy to see why he would feel that way. He was a very proud man with a navy colt stuck in a waist band, a pistol in a holster, a knife in a scabbard on his right hip, another knife in a leg band, and his rifle standing stock straight up in front of his Mexican, military saddle and a proud looking horse if there ever was one— just like its master. OK Bill wants a peaceful stay with the Comanche if they can have one, but he is not going to let them take him prisoner. "I keep small gun. You tell Chief I come talk."

Frankie didn't push the subject. He said to Mr. Coeburn, "That's how it needs to be." Grateful for small miracles, the Chief was okay with that.

The Chief was friendly with OK Bill, they understood each other's words and hand signs pretty well, although not all, some they had to do over and over, Mr. Coeburn and I were in the tent with the two Indians of different traditions and customs, neither got mad at the other; they really seemed to try to get along.

OK Bill tried to tell the Chief why he is named OK Bill. He said when he first started tracking and scouting for the Whites, he would always want to know when it was payday. He liked counting the coins they gave him. They gave him a piece of paper with his name on it. They called it a paybill. He would go to the men and show the paper and say, "OK Bill (no one could understand his name), so OK Bill got to be his name."

"It makes sense I guess," Frankie said.

"I didn't know." OK Bill told the Chief his name is Ahatahkakood which means star blanket. Next, they tried to get the horse settled for Frankie.

The Chief said, "If Frankie B. can break and ride the horse around the camp for all to see, he can have it." OK Bill agreed on Frankie's behalf.

Mr. Coeburn said, "You better get a good night's sleep. Looks like you have to prove yourself tomorrow."

Morning came early in the camp. Frankie was up before light. He walked out to the edge of camp to relieve himself and take in the air of the morning thinking, *I didn't sleep very well but I can't worry about things. I have to get it done.* Walking down to a branch of water to wash up a little, he spotted some of the young Indians getting water in skins and buckets. One caught his eye— a girl about eighteen with long, almost black hair, dressed in buckskins. He wondered if she was Chanannget, the granddaughter of Mr. Coeburn. As she turned back to camp, he noticed she was fair skinned. He said to her as she walked by, "Are you Angelina?"

She nodded and said, "Yes. I'm also named Chanannget." She touched her heart with her right hand and said, "My grandpa— he is my heart." She spoke good English but with a slight accent. He felt something at that moment he couldn't describe. Frankie, being a young man of twenty-two, had at that moment to keep his mind on what his job was and only his to do. By then, all the camp was active.

Their women getting food prepared (not sure what they ate) but whatever it was he needed some. He thought, *Something smelled like bread*. He walked around. Stopping at a cook pot, he saw some kind of paste-looking meal. The squaw saw him and motioned for him to stick his hand in the pot. So, he did. It tasted pretty good. She saw that he liked it, so she fixed him a dish with some bread like food on top. He ate it all with some water. Mr. Coeburn came over to him and asked if he wanted some coffee.

"Yep, I'll have some. Where is it?" he asked. "Over by my tent. Come on, have a cup. My granddaughter is getting it ready. There she was looking up. She didn't say a word. So, Frankie said morning to her. Mr. Coeburn saw he was staring at her and so he started to make conversation with Frankie.

"How you gonna break that horse? You know you kinda got a time limit."

"I know. The Chief wants it done quickly or not at all."

"I'll get it done." He drank his coffee, tipped his hat with his finger, looked one more time at Angelina, and walked through the camp to where the horse was tied up. OK Bill was already there.

"Have a good night," he asked. OK Bill was just swallowing something and taking a sip of coffee. He said, "Frankie B., you can ride horse. You talk to horse real good. He like you rub him." Frankie looked around for his saddle.

"It by my horse. All stuff."

Frankie put the bit in the horse's mouth and bridle on his head without any problem, then took his saddle blanket, rubbed the horse all over slowly. He would jerk and raise up a little, all the while Frankie talked in a low voice calling him My Boy. He laid the blanket on the horse's back, which My Boy quickly shook off. He picked up his jacket from the pile of his gear, wrapped it around the horse's head covering his eyes and tying it with the sleeves. The horse stood still. He put his saddle blanket over the horse's back. So far so good. The camp was watching by now, including the Chief standing with Mr. Coeburn, a fair piece away. *I'll try the saddle, see what he does,* he thought. He threw it over the blanket as gently as he could. A few jerks and stomps but the saddle was still on. He reached under to grab the strap and all hell broke loose— saddle and blanket went flying. He did it over and over till he got the saddle strapped on. Frankie walked it around, talking all the time to the horse calling him My Boy. OK Bill stayed away but yelled, "Give him some grass." So, he walked him into a grassy area near some trees, picked up a handful of green grass, rubbed it on his nose saying, "Come on, My Boy, have some grass," and he ate it. "Okay, can I take the jacket off? Let you see what's going on?" He hugged him and rubbed him on the chest. I better walk him around more before I let him see. Frankie went all around the camp.

Mr. Coeburn cupped his hand around his mouth and yelled, "Keep it going. You can do it boy."

Frankie gave him a smile, walked back to where OK Bill was leaning against a broken tree, and tied the horse there.

OK Bill said, "See you get on horse?"

Frankie said, "Yea, I'll leave my jacket on his head, tie him close to the tree, and try." He stepped up on a stirrup and just leaned against the horse. So far so good. Threw his leg over, just sat there, both legs in stirrups, nothing happened.

OK Bill said, "You take off coat, he throw you. Walk him some more. You take off coat later." That's what he did. He got off, walked him all around, through the camp, wanting to get a glimpse of Angelina. He saw her. She was standing by her horse in a corral rubbing its head, a nice-looking pinto. He stopped by her to see if she would talk, rubbing his horse like she was doing all the while. He took off his hat and said, "Hi."

She looked up at him and said, "You a good rider."

"I hope I am. I need this horse." He told her what happened to his other horse. She sighed and looked back at her horse.

"Gotta go. Before I do, will you rub this horse to gentle him down? It might help."

She came over and did just that and put her face against the horse's head and whispered something in Comanche. The horse whinnied and shook its head. I know the horse understood what she said.

"Thanks," he said, "I will see you later, okay?" No answer. He went back to where OK Bill was, he tied the horse up, and sat on him again. *I think I will take the jacket off.* As soon as he did, he went flying. He hit his right elbow and landed on his left shoulder. It hurt pretty bad. I need a break and so does My Boy.

OK Bill said, "Let's sit and talk. What you want to talk about— young squaw on your mind. Not now. Horse now. Get medicine man look at Frankie B., blood on elbow. Put horse in fence, take off saddle."

OK Bill meant that was it for today. The horse was

21

going to have to wait till tomorrow. Hope the Chief would be alright with that.

Mr. Coeburn came by. "I want you to stop crowding my granddaughter, you hear me boy?"

"Yes Sir, but…"

"No buts, she is young and don't need a feller yet. You get back to your herd and we'll see what comes down the road. You hear me boy?"

"Yes Sir."

"So, how bruised up are you, can you ride him tomorrow? Let's take a look. Take your shirt off. He said, "You are bleeding on your elbow. How does the shoulder feel?"

"Hurts."

"Let's see."

"Can you wrap me up? I'll be alright."

They put some grease on the elbow and wrapped up his shoulder extra tight.

Frankie and OK Bill went into their tent. Frankie needed to rest. OK Bill would get some food for both of them. He came back with some cooked meat and meal with a pot of coffee. Frankie was asleep when OK Bill got back. He wouldn't sleep long, his shoulder woke him. He was in pain.

OK Bill put more wood on the fire in the middle of the tent. He said, "I talk to Chief, have medicine man look at you. You rest, be back soon. You hear me?"

"Yeah, okay."

OK Bill left the tent, ran into Carlyle Coeburn on his way. OK Bill told him what was going on.

"Okay, you talk to the Chief. I'll see if anything is broken."

He found Frankie awake. "Let me take a look at your elbow and shoulder."

"Okay."

He checked him over pretty good and couldn't find anything broken; just strained, swollen, and elbow cut, but not cut bad or deep. It didn't need stitches.

"Moving my shoulder is where most of the pain is."

"You think if you had something to kill the pain, you could move it all right; enough to hang on to that horse."

"Don't know for sure."

"Hope so, otherwise you might be stuck here for some time and might not get your horse. You know the pain will get worse and there'll be more swelling. I think if you are to get it done at all, it has to be tomorrow. Maybe we can get you something from the medicine man to kill the pain as long as it don't make you too soft in the head.

A few minutes went by, and OK Bill and the medicine man came through the opening. "Medicine man say to smoke pipe tonight and morning," said OK Bill.

Mr Coeburn said, "Yes, that should kill the pain. Nothing more needed," Mr. Coeburn added, "Will he be able to concentrate on not getting bounced on the ground?"

OK Bill looked at the medicine man. He nodded. "If strong in head." He threw his arms out and said, "If big important him, head will keep in there."

Mr. Coeburn said, "Okay, let's find a soft place in the grass in the morning. You will be thrown off at least once, you know that."

"I'm sure you're right," Frankie said.

The medicine man mixed up a pipe full, lit it, and gave it to Frankie.

Frankie took a couple of puffs and coughed his head off, then started to relax.

"That's what we want. Now you just lay back and sleep. OK Bill will wake you in the morning."

"Frankie B., I get you up, you eat, you smoke pipe, break horse. Next day, we go Dolphus Dickenson cattle herd."

Frankie answered, "Yes," already half asleep.

Morning came pretty fast. OK Bill woke Frankie up like he said he would. The sun was just coming up. He had a pan of water to wash up a little and some Indian flat bread to dip in a batter with a piece of deer meat.

"This is good. I'll take that coffee."

They each poured a cup.

"Good, this is the way I like it. Okay, where is my pain killer."

Mr. Coeburn came through the opening with a pipe lit. "Here Frankie," he said. "Not too much. Just enough to slow the pain so you can move your arms without the pain, you hear me boy? You tell us when you think you're ready and can lift your saddle."

"I can do it. I'm ready. Let's get it done."

They went to the horse pen. Frankie went in and right up to his horse, rubbed him, and talked a little to the horse, grabbed his bridle, put the mouthpiece in and over the head to make sure it was in place. He put his jacket over the head, tied the sleeves, and looked over at the men. "You find a nice soft place."

"Got it," was the reply.

The saddle went on without any trouble. "You think I can let him see now?"

"Don't know. Guess you gotta get it off."

He did and the horse stood still. He led the horse out the gate. Still no problem. A thunderstorm was coming up fast with light rain and lightning, giving the horse something else to be concerned about other than Frankie, which in this case was good. The horse was definitely afraid of the lightning. Frankie got up on the horse. The horse whinnied and snorted and started walking on his own. *Okay, here we go,* thought Frankie. He pulled back on the reins, he stopped, he kicked him a little and he moved. All of a sudden, he took off running and Frankie nearly fell off, but he hung on. The horse kicked up once in a while as he ran. The whole tribe watched in amazement, while the sound of thunder all over the place and the lightning surely kept the horse running. Suddenly stopping, the horse was breathing hard, like he couldn't move another step. Frankie reached down and smacked him lightly on the neck and said, "Good boy." Frankie pulled the reins left, then right, then to stop. The horse responded really well. He got off and walked him a little, got back on, turned, and headed back to the pen. The thunder had finally stopped, but the lightning kept on. *This horse might not be totally broken but I think I can ride him now and he will break in on the trip back to the herd.* He got off when he entered the village. He got a lot of looks from the Indians; seemed friendly looks— at least he hoped so. The horse walked behind him. Every time Frankie stopped, it stopped. OK Bill and Mr. Coeburn were waiting by the horse pen. "How'd it go," Mr. Coeburn asked.

"Not bad, I think the storm helped. He was more concerned about the storm than he was me. He kept me on his back the whole time, ran till he couldn't breathe anymore, and just stopped. "Wonder if he would let either of you take my saddle off him?"

"I get," OK Bill said. "I brush him if I find a brush."

"I think I might know someone that has one," Frankie said. "You mind if I ask Angelina?"

"Sure, but remember what I said, don't crowd her. She is shy and young."

OK Bill said, "I will get him some grass and water. How's your pain?"

"Not too bad. I think I'll be okay riding. Frankie found Angelina and asked her if she had a horse brush he could borrow.

"I do. Can I help you brush your horse?"

"Why yes, can we do it now?"

"Yes, I'll get it," Angelina said.

"Can we put the two horses in together?"

"I think so. My horse and yours, I'll ask my Grandpa."

"Okay, it might relax mine."

"Good idea."

It was okay. They spent some time together brushing the horses and Frankie did most of the talking. He said he would be leaving tomorrow if things went well with the horse. "What is the horse's name?"

"I just call him My Boy."

She laughed. "That's no name."

"I know. I haven't thought much about it. What's your horse's name?"

"Alice. Grandpa has a sister named Alice. I like the name."

"Okay," Frankie said. "What would you name mine?"

"How about Star? He has almost a star on his forehead."

"Yeah, that would be fine. If I come back in six months or so, can I see you? By the way, can I ask you how old you are?"

"I will be eighteen in three months. How old are you?"

"Twenty-two."

"If Grandpa says okay and my mother says okay, then I will agree."

"Is your mother here in the camp?"

"Yes, you want to meet her?"

"What is her name?"

"Prairie Flower, in Comanche is Toh-Tsee-ah. I will ask if she will meet you. You wait here, I be back little bit."

Frankie agreed and kept brushing his newly named horse Star. He was hurting in his left shoulder and some in his right elbow. Mr. Coeburn and OK Bill checked to see how he was doing. "I'm okay, just hurting some," he said.

"You be ready go tomorrow?"

"Yes," he said.

"How early?"

"Morning if this horse will cooperate. Do you think we need to get him shoes?"

"Yes, carrying the weight: you, your saddle, and your gear. First town we come to should have a blacksmith."

"That will do. Suppose we should turn in early, right? Mr Coeburn, if I can get back in about six months, can I court Angelina? If you and her mother agree, she said it's okay with her."

"I don't want you taking her off to Lord knows where. I'm uneasy about that but I won't stop her from doing what she wants. Don't forget, she is a half breed. I won't let anything hurt her. Don't forget that. Keep those words in your mind. She is my heart. Here she comes now with her mother, Prairie Flower."

All the while, OK Bill kept quiet, leaning on the pen rail. He straightens up when the two women come near.

Angelina said, "Frankie, this is my mother."

He turned and looked at them, and thought she was a very handsome woman, no wonder Angelina is, too.

"Mother wants to know what you do."

He took his hat off. "Pleased to meet you, Prairie Flower."

She nodded.

"Mother don't speak English much."

"I have my first job on a ranch in Texas. I hope to do ranch work. I came from Illinois with my parents when I was a boy. My mother died in Texas about five years ago. My father is still in Texas. He is a doctor in a town near Mr. Dolphus Dickenson's ranch."

Carlyle Coeburn asked, "What is your full name?"

"Franklin Robert Butler," Frankie said.

"That's why OK Bill calls you Frankie B."

"That's it."

Angelina spoke up. "Mother said I would have to live in both worlds— Indian and White. Whites won't accept me if we marry."

Frankie said, "Whites would have to deal with me."
"That's not good enough," Carlyle said. "You would be fighting a lot."
"What else can I do?"
"I don't know."
Frankie thought to himself, *OK Bill looks like he was overcome with the love bug when he looked at Prairie Flower, like I was when I first saw Angelina.*
OK Bill said, "We get ready leave tomorrow." He walked over to where Prairie Flower was standing and said softly, "You go with me tomorrow and daughter go too with Frankie B. to cattle drive. We bring back when we through work. What you say?" He said a lot then in Apache and hoped she understood. It must have been something very loving and kind because she smiled and looked like it pleased her.
Angelina was shining too. "Mother, Mother," she said. She ran to her grandpa and hugged him long and hard.
Carlyle said, "I trust these two more than anyone I ever have, but still, it's a hard thing you are asking." Turning to OK Bill, he said, "If you will agree to bring them back when you finish up your work and agree not to push the two women into marrying, then if they do decide to marry you, you will wait till you get back here before marrying. Where will the women live when you get to the ranch?"
"I can't say off hand, but we know how to respect their wishes. I will ask Mr. Dickenson if we can put them up in one of the buildings on the ranch.
Prairie Flower was kind of shaking her head at what OK Bill said to her.

She said, "Ask Chief what he say." Then she said, "If we go, no marry yet. We think about it. I like OK Bill, but he Apache. What Comanche think? Ask Chief."

OK Bill was very quiet, letting her get all her emotions out. Then he said something in Apache again and she must have agreed.

She said, "We talk when we eat, okay?"

They all agreed, so the women set off to prepare some food while the men went to get their gear together for tomorrow.

"If we do this," Frankie and OK Bill agreed, "we will need two more horses. Really what we should have is a pack horse, too. The Chief will have to okay all this going on.

I will ask Chief what he say about taking the women on a trip, Frankie thought. Apache's sure work fast. Prairie Flower didn't seem too surprised though. I guess Indians don't waste any time when it comes to getting together. Maybe Prairie Flower was waiting for just such a man to come along. With her husband dead, she is sorta needing a man.

OK Bill came back from Chief. "Him say we go with women, but we die if they are stolen or killed. Sometimes other tribes or Comancheros or bandits take women to sell. We might have to get some extra guns. Maybe even for them. Can they shoot, do you think?"

Frankie said, "Where we get more guns?" They went to Prairie Flower's tent to eat and talk more. Walking along, Mr. Coeburn caught up and went into the tent with them. Prairie Flower said, "Sit, eat. It was meat roasted on the fire, cornmeal, and coffee too.

Mr. Coeburn was the first to speak, "I have an idea. How would you all feel if I came along? I have nothing else to do and I want to help if I can."

"Grandpa! Yes and yes," Angelina said. Her mother followed with a yes. They all looked at the two men.

"We could use an extra gun," said Frankie.

OK Bill said, "Yes, more power with gun."

"Okay then," Mr. Coeburn said, "I have another idea. Can we wait one more day to get things together?"

It was OK Bill who spoke first, "Yes, can we get more guns. I have several. And knives. I got a horse and a pack horse, too."

"I know where we might get more guns, but it's dangerous. Let me explain. About a month ago, a military wagon loaded with rifles and ammunition went over a cliff about five miles from here and not all was recovered because of the high cliff. We can take a look. If so, let's go early morning. If we can get just a few rifles and a lot of ammo, that should do us. What you think?" Carlyle asked.

OK Bill said, "We can wait. While we are doing that, the women maybe get a lot of food made up and we should be ready to pull out day after." OK Bill walked over to Prairie Flower and put his hand on her shoulder. She touched his hand in an 'it will be okay' kind of way. It brought a smile from the others. Which one of us has the climbing skills to get down? We will see in morning."

"Apache good at climb," OK Bill said.

"I can climb, too," Frankie said. "I did some climbing in Texas."

"Okay, we're good. I'm ready for some sleep, how about you all?"

"Yes, was the reply. We will get the longest ropes and as many as we can find and head out in the morning. Good night everybody."

"Good night, Grandpa," Angelina said. "Grandpa, I love you."

"I love you, too, sweetheart."

Frankie said, "How come the army didn't get the guns all out?"

"I'm telling you, it's almost impossible. You'll see."

OK Bill was pondering the whole thing: *need two rifles for a man, one rifle for a woman, as many pistols as you can hide on you, all ammo can get.*

"If we run into bad Indian, will need to fight to live, save women," said OK Bill.

"Can women shoot?"

"Yes, they both have had to shoot at raiders from other tribes a few times."

"Okay, each woman one rifle, two pistols, plenty ammo. You think all down there?"

"Don't know what's there. If we can get down, we can get whatever is there. I know there's rifles for sure, the army said so. Hope not all busted up. I'm going to bed. See you early. Night everybody."

Chapter 2

All were up early. Carlyle told the women to get together as much food as they can, plan on wearing some clothes that's comfortable riding and not flashy. I want you both to look older and not so good. In other words, the worse you can look, the more likely you will stay alive. I think you know what I mean. We need to check your horses today, too. They're not shod, are they? I mean shoes."

"No."

"Okay, might not matter. You need a way to carry a rifle on horseback and two pistols in your clothes somewhere that you can get to fast and not shoot yourself and the ammo fast, too. Hope we get some pistols. If we don't get killed in the process, I know we'll get rifles."

OK Bill and Frankie were up early and washed up a little. They grabbed a bite of hot bread and meat and talked as they ate.

"Hope my horse, Star, is up to it today. What you think?"

OK Bill said, "Me think he will not be trouble. We go saddle up and wait for Carlyle."

Carlyle showed up with plenty of rope and a large sack, a shovel, and pick. Can't think of anything else, can you? One Indian brave wants to go with us. He said he can climb. Might need him, so I said okay."

"What kinda saddles do the women have," Frankie asked.

"Angelina's is western. Prairie Flower's is Indian."

"You mean blanket," asked Frankie.

"Yeah, blanket and wood."

"Can a person sit on one all day?"

"I guess so. Indians been riding them a long time."

"Okay, if we have to, we'll get her a saddle somewhere. Let's get saddled up. I think I should take my pack horse with me in case we really get lucky. Let's go."

"Okay, we're ready."

Things went well with Star. He didn't buck. Frankie got on. They moved out. Carlyle led the way. Half hour's ride and they were there. Looking over...

"Wow, that's a long way down, let alone up on a rope. All four sides are the same. Gotta lower you down. Make a loop around your waist and legs. You know how to do that."

"Okay, who's going down?"

"I will," Frankie said. "I'm going down. I'm probably lighter weight and, no offense, younger too."

OK Bill didn't like any of it. He said, "Okay, you go, I pull rope. How's the brave from camp?"

"I go down too," the brave said.

"We probably don't need two people down there. One can check it out and fill the bag. Can anyone see anything that looks like boxes in one piece?"

"No, the wagon is on top of everything. Frankie, put this bar in your belt, get tied up, we'll let you down.

Get the bag, too. Keep your pistol handy. Might be snakes. They like places like that."

"Okay, I'm ready."

"We'll have to tie ropes together. No place to tie or wrap the rope around. Might have to use a horse."

Frankie was in the rope and going over the edge. Down, everything going well... down, feet not even touching the rock side, just straight down. One rope ran out, the next rope tied on.

"How you doing, Frankie," Carlyle yelled.

"I'm fine; nervous as hell, otherwise okay. I can see something. Boxes. I hope so. Another hundred feet. Keep going. Okay, Im here. I'll look around. Dead horses and two dead men. You want to take them up?"

"Probably not. Too much decay. Get their pistols and holsters, knives, whatever they got."

"I've got to move the wagon if I can. Rifles, ammo, yeah. I can see boxes. I'll pry them open. Yeah, good stuff: rifles and ammo. Got about a dozen rifles. Pistols and holsters and plenty of ammo. Okay, got everything in the bag. If not too heavy, you can pull it all at once. Okay, take it up."

They pulled it up. Let's see what we got: dozen rifles, dozen pistols, holsters, plenty of ammo.

"Frankie, we need more ammo. Can you put a couple more boxes in your shirt?"

"Yes, pull me up."

Okay, here we go. Up, up, up. Seemed like a long time. No problems. Almost there. The two Indians grabbed Frankie and yanked him up.

"Whee, I'm glad that's over. Let's see what we got, compliments of the army: rifles good, pistols good, ammo good. Let's get back to camp to see what we got and what we don't need, we'll leave with the chief. I think he should hide everything. If the army finds out about it, they will raid the camp and maybe end up killing everyone. You never know. The army from the fort didn't want to get it out and work in the heat for it, so I think they lied to General Miles and told him they couldn't get to the supply wagon. Well, it was hard but not impossible."

"OK Bill, tell this brave if he wants a rifle, don't let the army know. He probably shouldn't keep one anyway."

Getting back to camp, they needed to check out every part of the guns to make sure nothing was broken. They could have been from the hard fall. We each have our own rifles. We should each carry another one and all the pistols you can hide on you and get the two women checked out with a rifle each."

"Okay," said Carlyle.

"Right," said Frankie, "you check with the women and make sure they can handle a rifle and pistol, Carlyle, and give them each a pistol or if they can handle it, give them two each and plenty ammo."

"That's what I will do. We need to be very quiet about what we did. Nobody needs to know outside this camp."

"How about Red Fox? Can he be trusted?"

"We don't know. He went with us. You think maybe the chief sent him to spy on us?"

"Anything is possible. See what the women think about him. I think they would know."

"OK Bill, what you think about Red Fox?"

"I watched him, no see anything bad. I think he is just young and wants to impress a squaw. In camp, I saw him with a young one the other day."

"Carlyle, can you run things? You have a lot more experience than I do. If it was just OK Bill and me, it would be different."

"I would like to see OK Bill take the front and lead, scout, and watch for tracks, and you act as sort of leader. What you think, OK Bill?"

"That good with me. We all watch out for the women, Carlyle."

"Okay, we can all work together. I will try to do what's best for all of us, but the women come first. I think we can all agree on that."

Frankie said, "Right."

OK Bill said, "Right."

The two women didn't have anything bad to say about Red Fox. He's just young and trying to be a man.

Carlyle said, "Frankie, get everyone together now."

"Okay, here come the women dressed like men in loose buckskins and hat with their hair tucked up in their hats with a chin strap."

"That's good. Okay, come close. Here's what we will do. The horses are ready. Men, one rifle in scabbard front of saddle, extra rifle stuck in saddle strap, two pistols loaded in saddle bags, extra ammo, pistols on you. Women, listen to me. You each take one of these rifles and show me you can use it."

They both grabbed a rifle and pulled the lever back, aimed at a branch, and fired. They hit what they aimed at.

"Good," Frankie said. "Wow, I won't want to make them mad."

Carlyle said, "You keep these rifles with you at all times. Pick up a pistol. Show me the same thing."

Frankie said, "They need to know what is at stake."

"I think they do."

"Make sure all your guns are loaded and put a couple in your saddle bags and two on you somewhere you can get at fast. Everybody gets a knife. Say your goodbyes and we are ready to go. OK Bill, take the lead, Frankie next, the women next, and I will take the rear. If I yell stop, everyone stops. Keep an eye on OK Bill at all times, If OK Bill puts his arm up, we all freeze. OK Bill will be our best front man. We will be going through Indian territory where they don't much like anybody coming through. They might even hate OK Bill even more than Whites and the women they would like to have. Keep all that in your minds."

They all said their goodbyes. Frankie and OK Bill thanked the Chief and said they would be back. They mounted up and headed west. It was about noon. They left in the order they had decided on. As they rode, they discussed things about the trip.

"You know we have about three hundred to four hundred miles before we get to the so-called Chisholm Trail coming up from Texas," Carlyle Coeburn said, and he is pretty smart about the west. He made a few trips on drives and knew what to expect, where the bad parts were, which was good. When they get into Crow territory, that's when they'll probably be in the worst of it. If we make it in 18 to 20 days, we will be doing great. Don't forget, some land is flat, and some is rough with

38

gullies and mountains. The Crow nations don't like anybody crossing their land. Let's keep going till we lose daylight. I'll ask OK Bill to keep moving till we lose light and pick a spot to pitch camp. Anybody has to stop to relieve themselves, just let us know. Watch where you're sitting your butt."

"How you doing, Angelina?"

"I'm okay. How are you, Frankie B.? I like that when OK Bill calls you Frankie B.. It sounds like it fits you real good."

Frankie asked her, "How many pistols do you have on you?"

"Two in saddle bag and two on me."

"Good, I'm worried about you and Prairie Flower."

"She might look weak, but she is not, and she is not afraid to use them."

"How is her saddle?"

She said, "It's okay, but I think you should look to get a White's saddle. I've rode Indian saddles, and they are not too good on long trips."

"Okay, we will soon. I'm getting Star shod at the first town we come to."

"How's he doing?"

"He seems like a regular horse. I'm dropping back to talk to Mr. Coeburn."

"Carlyle, hey," yelled Frankie.

"Yeah, what?"

"I think we need to get a western saddle for Prairie Flower."

"I was thinking that too."

"How long to the first town?"

"Tomorrow afternoon if we keep moving."

"What we doing for dinner tonight?"

"Well, we got plenty of bread and corn meal. How 'bout I go ahead and get at least one rabbit?"
"Good, but don't fire a shot if you can keep from it."
"How am I gunna do that?"
"Well, I have seen Indians run 'em down with their horse. Try it."
"Okay. I'm going up to talk to OK Bill. Talk later."
"Okay, are we moving fast enough for OK Bill?"
"I think we'll do better after a few days."
"OK Bill, see me coming on your left side?"
"I see you. Everything okay back there?"
"Yeah, we are fine. Carlyle said to go till you lose light, then pick a campsite when you think best."
"Okay. Frankie B., you know someone is tracking us?"
"No, I didn't know."
"I think it is Red Fox. One horse. He will wait till we get couple days further, so we no send him back."
"What should we do?"
"What you want. Ask Carlyle what him think."
"OK Bill, be safe my friend."
"I try, my friend Frankie B. See you in camp later."
"Carlyle, did you know we are being tracked?"
"Wasn't sure, Frankie."
"Yes, OK Bill said one horse, probably Red Fox. He will follow for a couple days, then come in so we won't send him back."
"I guess we could always use another gun. What is your Boss Dickenson gonna say?"
"Don't know. We are already getting crowded. If Red Fox is a good person and good worker, might

be good. Just don't know. Mr. Dickenson, I believe, is a fair man."

The night was uneventful: all rested up, food was good with roasted rabbit on the fire, everybody got their fill with bread meal and coffee. They can see a fire off in distance— the follower.

"We will keep an eye on him. Must be what OK Bill said, unless it's another brave."

"That's right, it could be another Comanche." Carlyle talked to OK Bill. They agreed OK Bill would go out in the dark and see if he could get close enough to see who it is. OK Bill was gone a short time and back with news.

"It's Red Fox, alright. You think maybe we should just bring him in tomorrow."

"OK Bill, can you work with him or is there too much distrust between Apache and Comanche?"

"Don't know. I will talk with him, see how he feels about Apache, and why he want come with us."

Carlyle said, "He seemed okay when we went after the guns. Let's get some sleep. I'll take the first watch. Frankie, you do next. I'll wake you about midnight, okay? How the women doing?"

"Just talked to them, they seem fine."

"Let's stay close together at night and keep a gun handy. I'm not taking any chances. If you hear anything or see anything, wake us quietly."

Up in the morning first light with coffee, bread rolls, and leftover rabbit. Good mood amongst everyone.

"Prairie Flower, how is your saddle? Are you sore?"

She said, "Okay, I alright, but maybe worse to come."

"Let's see if we can pad it a little," Frankie said. "I will roll up some of my clothes to sit on."

41

"Okay for now."

"Will look into it when we get to a town. Carlyle, how far to a town?"

"Maybe tomorrow afternoon."

"Okay, let's get going. Saddle up."

OK Bill said, "I get Prairie Flower's horse saddled." Frankie said, "I'll get Angelina's saddle on." Then they broke camp. In a short time, they were all in the saddle heading west.

Carlyle said, "I'll lay back and wait for Red Fox. See what he's up to. Go on. I'll catch up. Do I have all your agreement on Red Fox? Do we let him join us?"

All agreed that he could.

Carlyle waited in a low spot with his horse and the pack horse went on with Frankie. It wasn't long before Red Fox came over the hill and saw Carlyle. He stopped. Carlyle motioned him on over to him. Carlyle got on his horse, and they rode together.

"Red Fox, what do you want?"

"I want go with you. Need to go somewhere."

"If you are looking to rob us, you won't make it. We will all be watching you till you prove to all of us you mean us no harm. And if you bother the two women, I will kill you myself."

That made the impression he wanted.

"Mr. Coeburn, I just want get away. We are going to go through hostile Crow territory in about two days. They will try to kill us, and you will have to fight for your life and the rest of us, too."

"If you want to go on with us, you have to promise me right now that you will not run out on us."

"I no run. I not afraid. I Comanche warrior. I fight before with Crow. Look, I have two rifles and many pistols. I wanted plenty guns. I got guns you not take from me."

"Okay, can you get along with OK Bill?"

"Apache okay, much warrior."

"We are going to meet up with a cattle herd in about twenty days. You sure you want to do that. We might have to fight for our lives against the Crow Indians, kill some food every day, ride hard every day. Not easy. You want to do all that and maybe not sleep much at night, guarding the women and our camp?"

"I want do."

"When we get to the cattle herd, you want to work with Whites. They might not want you. I don't know if they will want any of us except OK Bill and Frankie. They already work for Dolphus Dickenson. He is the boss. Then we intend to go back to Comanche camp in half a year."

Red Fox seemed to understand what Coeburn just said. Anyway, he'd hoped so.

"Okay, let's catch up to the rest. You go up to OK Bill and stay with him till I say."

"Okay," Red Fox said.

Coeburn said, "I'll tell the others, and you eat while you ride till evening. You got food?"

"I got food and water, too."

So, another day started off with another Indian. Maybe it will work out for the better if he will fight with us, if need be. They rode as fast as they could with OK Bill and Red Fox in the lead. Red Fox has a western saddle. He is young, about Frankie's age. Indians are able to push harder than Whites, so we shouldn't have any problem slowing down. If Prairie Flower and Angelina can hold up, we shouldn't have any trouble making good time. Time passed. Everyone would stop once in a while to pee and stretch, then they would catch up. We are making good time. In the distance, we could see what looks like a town. Carlyle sent Frankie up to OK Bill to let him know that before we get too close, we should stop and talk. Frankie asked OK Bill how it was going with Red Fox.

"Okay, we say we will be friends. I watch him anyway."

"Okay, let's stop and wait for the rest to catch up. Have Red Fox keep watch for anybody coming at us. We want to know if the town has spotted us."

When they were all together, Carlyle spoke up, "What do you all think? Frankie wants to get his horse shod. We could use a saddle for Prairie Flower. Anybody need anything. Before we say no, let's think this over. Do you two women think you would rather ride on a wagon instead of on horseback?"

They both said, "No, we good."

"Okay then. Here's another thing, I don't think we should all go into the town. The less the people know about us the better, so I say we stop here and rest up. Frankie, you go into town, get your horse shod, buy a saddle. Let's make a list of anything we can think of. How's our water? Take the pack horse in and get the water bags filled up."

"Now wait a minute."

"Just take the water bags on your horse. If people ask you a lot a questions, answer as carefully as you can. I am not sure how to explain the Comanches and an Apache with you. Don't give any information unless you have to. Hope the blacksmith isn't the nosey type. Good luck. Off you go."

Frankie took the water bags and headed for the town. The blacksmith was on the edge of town. He thought that was good; not too many people walking around. He headed straight to the blacksmith, stopped, and dismounted. The blacksmith was black.

He said, "Can I help you?"

"Can you shoe this horse. It's not been shod."

"Yeah, it'll take a little longer. Gotta trim the hooves more, Mister."

"Okay, can you do it right away?"

"Sure."

"Okay, get started, will you? Do you have a saddle to sell?"

"I got a used one."

"Let's see."

"Over there," the blacksmith pointed.

Frankie looked at it. Not too worn out. He asked, "How much for the whole rig: saddle, blanket, bridle, and saddle bag?"

"$5.00."

"Okay, I'll take it. Where can I fill up these water bags?"

"Front of the store, there's a well. Watch out, Mister, for the Dusty Saloon, couple bad ones rode in today. Been drinking couple hours. They always look for trouble when they're in town. They work on a ranch north of here."

"Okay, I'll get my water and a couple things from the store and Il be back. I don't want to stay long. Here's the $5.00 for the saddle"

Frankie took one water bag and walked to the well. He could see it from where he stood. He filled up the bag, took it back to the smith, set it on the ground, went back with the other water bag and filled it up, set it on the steps of the store. He went in to get some flour, bar soap, and some matches. All of a sudden, gunfire rang out. It was what he was just warned about. The two from the saloon were in the street firing their guns at nothing in particular. Frankie hesitated, then thought, *I'm through here. I'm going.* Just then a stray bullet hit the leather water bag and water went all over the place. Frankie was outside by now looking at the bag and looked up at the two. He said, "You boys owe me a water bag."

"We what?"

"One of you owe me for a water bag. Storekeeper, what do you think a water bag costs."

"Don't know. Indians make them. No Indians here."

"Then how about one of them water barrels?"

"$2.00."

"Okay, one of you boys owe me $2.00!"

"We don't owe you a damn thing. You shouldn't have it laying there."

"I should be able to lay it anywhere I want to." So, Frankie walked towards them. They were standing their ground. The sheriff was watching the whole thing from across the street. Frankie might not look tough, but he can be when need be, and he is very fast on the draw. They both started to draw, and didn't even clear the holster. Frankie's gun was aiming right at them. Even the sheriff was taken aback and said, "Wow!"

"Now, I'll take my $2.00 if you don't mind."

"One of them went for his gun."

Frankie put a bullet through his hand. "Now, I'll take my $2.00. Wrap up your hand and give me my $2.00."

Just then a hand touched Frankie's shoulder. It was Carlyle. "You okay, Frankie?"

"Yeah."

Carlyle said, "I heard the gun fire and thought I'd better check on you."

"Then you can see what happened."

"You gonna let the sheriff take care of these two?"

"Yes, I'll holster my gun when the sheriff moves these two guys off the street. Sheriff, it's your next move."

"Alright, it's over everybody. Move on. You two can sit in jail and cool off. Let's go." He locked them up and came to the blacksmith's where Frankie and Carlyle were packing up. They had everything on the two horses.

Carlyle said, "Good thing I came into town. You couldn't get all this stuff on one horse anyway."

The sheriff spoke up, "Hey, fast shootin' boy."

"Just doing what's right."

"Here is your $2.00 plus another $1.00 I got from the other one."

"How's his hand?"

"It will be fine. Somebody needed to teach those two some manners. I guess it was you."

"I didn't come into town looking for trouble. I just needed a few things, Sheriff."

"I know. I saw you ride in. Where you two heading?"

"We work on a cattle drive west of here."

"Okay, you boys know the Crow won't like you crossing their land."

"Yeah, we heard."

Frankie wanted to talk to the blacksmith. He asked, "How'd he do?"

"He did okay. Good patient. Had a lot to trim off. Should be more comfortable for him. He might not like the shoes at first, but he'll get used to them. Be careful when you get on at first, he might buck."

"I owe you anything more?"

"Na sir, I all paid up."

Carlyle, you get the saddle and water barrel. Let's get over to the store and get my pack horse. Everything is on him."

"Sir, you watch out for those two. They might make trouble for you."

"That sheriff, is he working for the town or is he working for the big rancher."

"Don't know for sure. He kinda goes both ways. Just when you think he's working for the good of the town, he ain't. I guess he will relay everything that happened here today to the ranch foreman. They're real close and he can be a badass, so I'd watch out for a couple days. They might track you all and cause trouble. You're going through Crow territory. They might leave you alone."

"Okay, we'll watch out."

Frankie got on his horse and reached down and shook the smithy's hand. Carlyle did too. They got their pack horse and headed out to the others. OK Bill and Red Fox were waiting with a rifle in hand.

"Didn't know what coming next," OK Bill said. "We're good for now. Let's get this saddle on Prairie Flower's horse and see how it fits."

48

"How is your horse," Red Fox asked.

"He's good. He bucked a couple times. He's okay. There's a rifle scabbard with her saddle. Prairie Flower, you can get your rifle in it."

"Okay. I see how saddle feels." She mounted up. "Okay, good, better, now hand me rifle, I put in scabbard. Rifle okay, too." She got down. "We eat now."

Angelina handed them both a cup of coffee.

"Ah, that's good," Frankie and Carlyle said almost at the same time.

Frankie looked at Angelina. "Are you okay?"

"I worry about you when I hear shots."

"Yeah, well I lost one water bag to a couple drunks. Can you patch two bullet holes?"

"Maybe, let see. I think we can."

"We should get a few miles away from here today so let's eat fast and get going," Carlyle said.

All agreed. Frankie squeezed Angelina's hand. "Good to be back."

OK Bill said, "I ate. I go on horse. Red Fox, you go with me, we go."

"We go," said Red Fox.

OK Bill continued, "We ride slow. You catch up. Mr. Coeburn, we be ready in a few minutes.

"Frankie, you ready?"

"You all get going. I'll put this fire out and be in the saddle. I will catch up. How much daylight we got left?"

"About four hours."

"That's good," was the reply.

They rode hard for the next two hours then kinda slowed a bit but kept heading west, the two Indians in the lead. Dark was coming down fast. Guess we made about ten miles from trouble. They ain't following us in the dark.

"I wouldn't think so. What you think Frankie?"

"Yeah, you really don't know about people. I put a bullet through that one's right hand. His boss might come after me. We need to be ready at any time. Let's stop for the night and get an early start in the morning."

"Okay, get everybody gathered round. Get that coffee started and what else we got?"

Frankie waved to OK Bill and Red Fox. They both came in. Frankie said to Red Fox, "You got bow and arrow." He said he did. "Okay, can you kill a rabbit or something?"

"I try."

"Don't shoot a gun if you can help it. Crow might not be too far off and keep the fire low to ground so not to make much light. Everybody, let's get something straight. Here's what I'm thinking: if we should get overrun by hostiles, whether Crow or Whites, let's tell them Prairie Flower is your wife OK Bill, and Angelina is my wife. Maybe, just maybe, that will mean something to them. It is worth a try. What do you all think?"

Carlyle said, "It might."

OK Bill said, "Might help."

Carlyle said, "Let's get a watch going."

Prairie Flower said, "I will watch the back."

Red Fox said, "I will watch the west."

"Yeah sure, okay, don't stick yourself out, stay hidden. Wake us up quietly."

"Wake you at about midnight."

Angelina said, "I'll watch too. I know listen for any noise and movement."

OK Bill said, "I'll watch. I'll watch east."

"Okay everybody, I'm turning in."

Up in the morning to coffee and fried rabbit. Red Fox got two last night with the bow and arrow. Didn't take long to get them in a frying pan for leftovers this morning with hot biscuits. The Indian women make good biscuits, even get a gravy of sorts from rabbit. Good food. Some Indian food, too.

"Red Fox, if you see a turkey or quail, get it for our supper but only with the bow and arrow."

Riding along, nothing happens, but things are about to change.

Over a rise were five horse men. They looked like Indians. One dressed like Army. They came close and stopped, gave us the peace sign. We all came together and pulled up.

"What you want," their leader said.

Carlyle said, "We are going to a cattle drive, coming up from Texas."

"What name cattle drive?"

"Dolphus Dickenson is the boss."

"You come to fort, talk to Captain McCoy."

"Why do we have to do that?"

"Captain say everybody stop at fort to see him."

"Okay, we will obey. Don't want trouble."

The leader looked at OK Bill and Red Fox and said, "What Indian you?"

OK Bill said, "Me Apache, him Comanche."

"What, you no Crow? We Shoshone. This our land. We no want Crow. They not from here."

They went to the fort to talk with the Captain. He stuck out his hand. "Hi, I'm Captain T.J. McCoy."

Carlyle shook his hand and said, "I'm Carlyle Coeburn. This is Frankie Butler. We are all kind of related. The young Indian girl is Frankie's wife and my granddaughter. Her mother here is OK Bill's wife. Red Fox is kinda a chaperone for the women. We want no trouble. We just want to get back to Dickenson's herd."

"I understand what you're saying," said Captain McCoy and I just try to keep the peace between Shoshone and Crow and any Whites going through. The Crow are migrant. They stay in an area for a while and claim it. The Shoshone have been here for a long time. The Crow will fight anyone that comes through."

Carlyle asked, "How far are we from the Chisholm trail. That's where we expect to run into the Dickenson herd."

"You're still about 200 miles," the Captain said. "Stay the night, freshen up if you want, and leave whenever you want. This Fort is like a town. If any of you want a bath, we got bathtubs.

"What about Indians? These people have any problem with Indians staying in the fort," Frankie asked."

"I don't think you will have any trouble with my people here in the fort," the Captain said.

"I know I'd like a bath," Frankie said.

Carlyle said, "Me too. Can we have a couple rooms to settle into?"

"Yes, you can. Sergeant, take these people to building C. There is a bath house next to it: one side for men and one side for women. Sergeant, I will expect you to see to it they get all the privacy they need. Is that understood, Sergeant?"

"Yes Sir, it is."

"Mr. Coeburn, you can take your horses to the corral and your people to the building."

"Thank you, Captain McCoy. I think we all will appreciate the chance to clean up."

Frankie said, "Let's see what the women want to do. I don't know their habits."

Frankie turned to the women. "Prairie Flower, would you and Angelina like to bathe. The bath house has a tub and all the hot water you need."

"Yes, we would like it very much."

"OK Bill, you come with me. Red Fox, you go with Carlyle. Is that okay with everybody?"

"Yes it is," they all agreed.

"I'll get the Sergeant to restrict all the army personnel from bothering us. Okay, let's do it so we don't hold up the bath house too long."

The area was secured and we all got to get the trail dust off and wash our clothes, which was a welcome treat. We had a good dinner with the Captain and had a good night's sleep.

Up early in the morning. "Let's get our people together," Carlyle said to Frankie.

"Okay, I'll do it right now. Okay, everybody here?"

"Yep," was the response from all the group.

"Okay then, I think we should get moving. What do you all think?"

Everyone agreed.

"Get all your gear together, get your horses saddled and ready to ride, check all your guns and ammo, and don't leave anything behind. While we are here, don't show off your guns. No one needs to know all the guns we have. Get something to eat and let's ride. OK Bill and Red Fox will take the lead like before. Then I will go next. Prairie Flower and Angelina next, and then Carlyle."

Stopping by the Captain's quarters, Carlyle said, "We appreciate everything you have done for us. Thank you, Captain McCoy. We will be on our way."

"Carlyle, you will probably run into hostile Crow Indians. The Shoshone Indians will probably meet up with you too, but they shouldn't be a threat if you tell them you're just passing through and mean them no harm."

"Okay Captain, I'll remember what you said. I'll let my people know, too. Thanks again, Captain. Maybe we'll see you on the way back in about six months."

"That will be fine."

Off they went heading west. Carlyle pulled up to Frankie and told him what Captain McCoy said about the Indians and said to pass it on, even to the women. Tell them to be very alert, ready at a moment's notice and watch for my signal or yours. Let OK Bill and Red Fox know the same. We will watch both of them for signals too. The next couple of days were quiet, nothing but sky and scrub land. We stopped a couple of times to rest up; otherwise we just kept riding west. On the third day at about noon, a band of Indians come up from our rear. I guessed there were about twenty.

Frankie said, "They don't look friendly."

Carlyle yelled, "Everybody, fast to those big rocks where OK Bill and Red Fox are. Make sure you hang on to your horses, tie them up if you can. We are in a fight. We don't want to lose our horses. Grab your rifles. They must be Crow."

The Indians started coming faster and fired as they got closer. We got in the rocks just in time. "Angelina, grab all our horses. The rest of you make every shot count," Frankie yelled.

And we did too. We were knocking them off their horses. They would ride by yelling and firing in the rocks, not hitting a one of us, but we were killing them.

Carlyle yelled, "They're gonna try and get around us. We can't let that happen. Red Fox, get to the far side of these big rocks and hold them off. We need to spread out and cover the whole ground. Prairie Flower, how you doing?"

"I'm fine."

The horses were jerking on Angelina from the noise, but she was holding on to them just fine. The firing stopped and the Indians pulled back. "What you think they gonna do, Carlyle?"

"Don't know. Where's OK Bill?"

"He's over there."

OK Bill said, "We wait. They mad now, will talk."

Carlyle said, "They got seven dead on the ground. We had nobody hit, right?"

"That's right," Frankie yelled.

"How's Red Fox doing?"

"Red Fox, how you doing," he yelled.

Red Fox yelled back, "Me fine. They all pulled back to the east of us."

Carlyle said, "I'll see if I can talk to their leader." Two of them are riding this way holding their rifles in the air. Guess they wanna talk. OK Bill, you come with me. We will go out to meet them."

The two of them rode out in open ground and stopped. The Crow came closer and stopped. Carlyle asked, "You speak White man's tongue?" One of them said, "Yes."

The Crow brave said, "This our land. We stop you. You pay or you no go through."

Carlyle said, "We mean you no harm, but we will fight if you come after us. This is not your land. It's Shoshone land. We had talk with Shoshone yesterday. They said we could cross over the land."

"No," the Crow said. "You give us pack horse and young woman, or we will fight again."

Carlyle said, "No pack horse, no woman, we will give you nothing. If you want to fight, we will fight. We will leave this place in the morning going west. You can leave us in peace, or we can fight again. We will not shoot first. Pick up your dead and leave this place. They died for nothing."

OK Bill and Red Fox kept watch while the rest settled in for the night. They made a fire and heated up what meat they had left and some bread. Most of all, the coffee was extra good after a trying day.

Frankie said, "Okay everybody, check your guns and ammo. This is a good time to clean your gun barrels. We don't want any misfires; a misfire can get you killed. Angelina, how you doing?"

"I'm okay. It was hard to hold all the horses. The pack horse almost got away from me, but I hung on. Bullets were flying all over the place, bouncing off the rocks. One hit my sleeve; no blood, just a scrape," she said.

Frankie said, "Let's see the scrape. You're right. You want me to wrap it? Let me clean it and wrap it, okay?"

"It's fine now. I'll give the horses some water and find some grass. I'll leave the saddles on for the night! We might have to make a quick run for it."

"Everybody get some sleep. We'll leave early and see how far we get before the Crow follows us. If we're lucky, the Shoshone will get wind of the Crow fighting us and come out to help. If not, we're on our own."

Off in the morning, everything quiet, just light enough to see where we are, sun coming up behind us to the east.

"Angelina, how is your arm?"

"It's fine, Frankie B."

"Okay then, I'll check with the others. Prairie Flower, how are you?"

"I good, Frankie B. Rifle cleaned, ready to shoot. I watch for Crow."

"Good, I'll check ahead with OK Bill and Red Fox." They were good, too.

Watching all around for anything, Frankie said, "I'll drop back with Carlyle. Be safe my friends."

"You be safe too, Frankie B."

"Carlyle, anything?"

"No, nothing new. I don't think they will let us go. They will look bad to their people with seven dead and nothing to show for it. They will try us again. We might have to huddle together in the open and shoot our way out if they pick a better spot than they did yesterday. If they do as bad as they did yesterday, be good for us and bad for them. You still got plenty of ammo? You need more from the pack horse?"

"No, I'm good."

We rode on for hours and all of a sudden, there they were spread out to get around us. We were in the open.

"Get all together, pull your horses down," Carlyle yelled. "Huddle in close and make every shot count. Don't just fire; fire only when you got a target. Fire from a circle, and we will get a lot of them. We're down in the grass. It's all the cover we have. Try not to panic. We're together. We will get through this." Bullets started hitting close. "We are holding them off; keep killing them," Carlyle yelled, as he got hit in the left shoulder.

OK Bill got a bullet in the side of the head. Frankie B. was hit in the right arm. Prairie Flower was hit in the arm, too. We all kept firing. All of a sudden, the Crow quit circling. We got help. The Shoshone drove off the Crow. Frankie yelled, "Thank God, or we'd be dead soon."

They crawled out of the low spot and tried to stand up. The Shoshone Chief got off his horse along with a few others to see how we were.

"I guess we're alive. That's about all. Most of us been hit. Can you help us," Frankie yelled.

The Chief came over and said, "We help. That is Shoshone way. We help our friends."

Carlyle was bleeding pretty badly.

"Gotta stop it."

They pulled him out of the low spot and got him on a horse. His horse was dead. OK Bill needed the blood stopped, too. His horse was also dead. Red Fox was okay. Not hit. His horse was okay. Angelina was okay as well as her horse. The pack horse was okay. Prairie Flower wrapped her arm.

Her horse was okay. It was hit but it just went through the skin in the neck, not bleeding bad.

"OK Bill, let's see how bad you're hurt."

"I not bad; just a graze. Not go to bone."

Frankie asked the Chief, "Can you have your people get our live horses and all the saddles and gear to your camp? Can you grab a couple of those Crow horses standing over there? So, what we got is two dead horses, four people wounded. Is your camp far, Chief?"

"Not far. We go now. We will get two Crow horses and get White doctor. Him come to Shoshone camp from small town."

"Red Fox, you okay to go to Shoshone camp?"

"Yes, they are our brothers."

"Carlyle, we got a doctor coming to the Shoshone camp to help us. The Chief said we can rest as long as we want.

"Frankie, can we just go? I need a doctor soon. I'm bleeding a lot. I might pass out if I don't get help soon," Carlyle said.

Prairie Flower checked Carlyle's bandage, then checked OK Bill's, and touched her heart with her right hand."

"Okay everybody, let's move out to the Shoshone camp," Frankie said. "Let's ride. Chief, lead the way. We are indebted to you and your people. Thank you."

Chief said, "You are my brothers. We go to the village. We need to get you patched up."

The doctor was already waiting for us when we rode in, clearly a friend of this people. Lucky for us. Carlyle needed to get a bullet taken out and who knows what else. He had lost a lot of blood; that can't be good. Angelina was by his side holding his hand while the doctor worked on him. Carlyle did pass out. Just as well, the doctor had to dig deep to get the bullet out. Carlyle didn't feel a thing. OK Bill needed stitches on the side of his head, but the bullet went through. Prairie Flower had a flesh wound on her arm. It wasn't too bad. My arm was just a flesh wound, also. Thank God for this doctor. The doctor's name was Stephen C. Andreas, a remarkable man. The Shoshone loved him. I can see why. Whenever the Shoshone need him, he comes to help them. I heard he likes one of the Shoshone women. He is a widower. His wife died a few years ago. The Shoshone woman likes him, too. Just a matter of time and they will marry. He patched us up pretty good. He's got Carlyle doing real good. Another couple days, we hope Carlyle will be able to ride.

"What do we have to do about these two Crow horses, OK Bill? You think they will be any problem. When you feel up to it, I'd like to see if one of them will accept your saddle and the other one Carlyle's saddle. Can you see well enough with one eye patched?"

"I good, Frankie B. We go now if you want."

"Okay, we'll try."

OK Bill's saddle is a big Mexican saddle, but we got it on the horse without any problem. It is a bigger male horse. Should be just right for OK Bill.

"You feel like getting on him to see how he feels with you on him?"

"I do right now," OK Bill said and mounted up and rode around the penned in area without a bit of trouble. So we're thinking him will be alright. We saddled up the other one with Carlyle's saddle and had no problem with him either.

"Good, we got these two things out of the way. With all that we had gone through, it's good that we don't have to break wild horses. These two Crow horses shouldn't take much to train our way. We will forever be grateful to our Shoshone friends for their help and generosity letting us stay with them while we heal and get our strength back."

"You're right Frankie. I sure hope we never have to fight these people," Carlyle said.

Frankie asked, "You think we are rested up and healed up enough to ride out in a couple days?"

"I think so, but let's see what the doctor says. He's supposed to be here tomorrow."

I guess we stayed four days with the Shoshone. We were able to heal up pretty good with their help, and the good doctor. We talked among ourselves, and we are all ready to move west. The doctor said Carlyle was healing fine and that riding horseback shouldn't bother him too much. OK Bill's head was healing, too, and if we wanted to leave, we would have to take out the stitches ourselves in maybe a few more days. So, on the fifth day, we all said our goodbyes and headed west not knowing what lie ahead. Carlyle and OK Bill rode their new horses. Prairie Flower and I still had our arms wrapped but no pain. I worried about my gun hand. If I needed it, how would I do? My wound could slow me down. I hope we'll be alright. We still carried extra pistols on us. Angelina seemed fine and in a good mood. Red Fox took the lead with OK Bill and Angelina took charge of the pack horse which was good. It gave me a chance to be more vigilant and watch out all around. The first day, we didn't push too hard, and we stopped early and made camp. Red Fox got us a couple of rabbits for dinner. The women got dinner ready while we got the horses taken care of for the night. "Carlyle, how you doing?"

"Oh, I'm fine."

"OK Bill and Red Fox, how you two doing?"

"We fine."

"Anybody need their bandages changed?" Angelina asked, "I'll look after my Grandpa."

Prairie Flower said, "I'll check OK Bill."

"Alright," Frankie B. said. "I'll get more wood for the fire. Let's talk about guard duty for the night. I'll take the first watch. OK Bill, you go next. Carlyle, you follow OK Bill."

"Yep," they all agreed.

The rabbits were ready to eat. We settled into a restful time and small talk.

Frankie B. said, "Do you want to have those two Crow horses shod?"

"Not much of a problem the way there are," Carlyle said.

"How about you, OK Bill?"

"Good horse, no problem."

"Okay then, we can wait till we get to the herd in another hundred miles or so. Mr. Dickenson's cook, Taters is a pretty good blacksmith. He can shoe them if you want. We got a town coming up soon. Anybody need anything?"

Carlyle said, "I'd like to have a doctor take a look at my shoulder. It's hurting me some."

"Okay, if you look hard enough you can kinda see the town? Should we all go in or do like we did last town?"

"The hell with them. We are as good as they are," Carlyle said. "We'll probably get into trouble either way."

"Okay, but everybody be careful. Be on guard at all times."

Chapter 3

As they got closer, they could see people starting to look up and pay attention to them. They rode into town and pulled up in front of the general store. Carlyle got off his horse and asked a man in front of the store, "Is there a doctor in town?"

"Yes," he said. "Down the street you'll see the sign."

"Thanks." They turned their horses and headed down the street. Carlyle walked his horse. They were met by a few townsfolk that didn't look too welcoming.

"What are those Indians doing here," a big voice said coming out of the saloon.

"They're with us," Frankie said.

"Yeah, I can see that. Maybe you better get them outta here before you start asking for a doctor."

The doctor came out of his office and said, "Never mind him. You all come in here. Let's take a look at you."

They tied up their horses and went in.

Doc said, "What we got here?"

"Well, we were in a fight with a band of Crows about a week ago. We got shot up pretty bad."

"Yeah, I can see that."

"Check my friend OK Bill and Prairie Flower and Frankie, then me, okay Doc?"

"These stitches need to come out of the Indian."

"Okay, do it." He did and cleaned up the wound. Prairie Flower's wound was fine, Frankie's was a little red.

"You keep this salve on it and clean it often. It'll be alright. Now, let's see that shoulder."

Carlyle said, "It hurts me some."

"Who did the doctoring on you people?"

"Doc Andreas at a Shoshone camp," Frankie said.

"Oh, I've heard of him. He kinda lives with the Indians."

"That's right," Carlyle said. "He's a blessing for the Shoshone. They treat each other like everybody should."

"Well, he did a good job on your shoulder. If you're not careful though, you could start it bleeding again. I know you have to keep moving but keep it in a sling. That'll take some of the pressure off it. You might have to shoot with one hand. If I'm right, some of these liquored up crazies will come looking for trouble."

"What we owe you doctor, ah…"

"Wentland, Jacob Wentland," the Doc said. "If you got $2.00, I'll take it. If not, forget it."

"Oh, we got $2.00. We'd like to pay our way," Carlyle said. "Here and thanks. We will be on our way."

The crowd was still standing around outside as they walked to their horses.

Someone yelled, "Get those savages outta here."

They didn't answer, just mounted up and each one, even the women, pulled a rifle out and held it across their saddle. Never said a word, just slowly rode out of town. Frankie, being last, turned his horse around in one last act of defiance and kept moving. He caught up to the rest and said, "Let's move. Someone will come after us, no doubt." Being early enough we can still make some space between us and this town. Remembering what the doctor said to Carlyle, we didn't want to bounce him too much. Once we thought we were far enough from the town, we slowed up. That's when we saw the dust from the south. Looks like a few horses and probably a wagon.

"Alright everybody, listen up. Carlyle, take your bandage off. OK Bill, you too. We can't look weak. Rifles in hand, pistols close and ready. From a distance, I'd say their Comancheros. All they want is the women. They will try and kill us. When they get closer, they will stop, and a couple will come up to talk. Let's get in a position where we can fire without hitting one of us and shoot to kill. If six come up, that's one a piece. If two come close to you two women, kill them before they can touch you and we will kill the rest. OK Bill, Red Fox, and I will take off for the rest of them and kill them. There is no other way. They might have prisoners. Careful not to hit them. These men are the worst human beings there are. I see about eleven of them and a wagon loaded down. Anybody see more? Ok here we go, they are stopping, six are staying with the wagon, five are coming to us. Let me talk. If they move around, you move at them. Soon as the women fire, we fire."

The leader had a smile on his face. He looked like a Mexican.

"Hi, my friends, how are you today?"

Frankie said, "What do you want?"

"We want you to pay us something," he said.

"We can't pay you. We don't have any money."

"You give us those two squaws and you can go."

"Well, I really don't think the squaws would like that but now, you can ask them for yourself."

Two of them started over toward the women.

"Ah, you should come with us. We will let you live."

The women swung their rifles around and shot them dead. Before they hit the ground, the rest of us quickly fired killing the other three. As we headed for the wagon, they started to fire at us. It was no contest. We caught all of them off guard, killed them all. Voices were coming from the wagon, they had two young girls and a wagon full of stolen goods. As it turned out, they were not two young girls, they were a mother and daughter. They were crying so hard they couldn't talk.

Frankie told his people, "Gather up all the guns and knives in the wagon and tie the horses on to the wagon and let's get back to the others."

The woman said," I'm Constance Sikorski and this is my daughter Antonina," she said. "We were taken about a week ago, and my husband was killed, and one of my sons. We are from southern Illinois. I don't know what happened to my other son. He's sixteen. He escaped. They didn't bother with him."

"Okay, it's going to get dark fast now," Frankie said. "Let's get away from this area."

He asked the woman, "Can you drive the wagon?" She said she could.

"Okay then, all horses tied to the wagon, all guns and whatever else in the wagon. Anybody want to bury any of these, let's do it fast." They decided they would bury them, so they dug fast, rolled them and covered them up, said a quick prayer, "May the Lord have mercy on their souls."

"Let's go people. We are going as far as we can before dark."

It was strange having eleven horses fully saddled tied to one wagon, but we had them spread out on a long rope and it worked very well. The horses followed without any problem. Frankie asked all the others what they thought they should do with the horses and guns.

Carlyle said, "You think we could sell them in the nearest town, or do you think Mr. Dickenson could use them or would be glad to have them?"

"You know, Carlyle, I thought the same thing."

"I'd give the two women their choice or pick of horses or guns," Carlyle said.

"Right, I agree. OK Bill, Red Fox, what do you think we should do with the horses?"

OK Bill said, "Maybe Mr. Dickenson want."

Red Fox said, "Your boss, you know."

"Okay then, they're following really good the way they are, and they are not slowing us down. I say we keep them. They can be a kinda peace offering to Mr. Dickenson for all our extra people. Guns I don't know; maybe the same thing. Prairie Flower, Angelina?

"We keep for now," they both said,

"Okay, good."

"Mrs. Sikorski, what do you want to do?"

"I'd like to stay with your people, if it's okay with all of you."

"It is. If you or your daughter would like to ride a horse for a while, someone else can drive the wagon."

"We would like that."

"Let's stop for the night. Red Fox, do we have any rabbits?"

"Yes, two rabbits and two quail."

"Let's get them cleaned and frying."

The women, now four, worked well together. "Carlyle, you sit down and rest that arm. We'll take care of the horses."

They got the horses in a rope corral. The grass was wet from a light rain earlier, so that will have to do for watering the horses, maybe tomorrow we'll cross a stream. They all ate good thanks to Red Fox. There are extra supplies in the wagon: plenty bread, some potatoes, and a lot of dried meat.

"We'll put it to good use," Frankie spoke up. "Let's do the watch tonight like we've been doing and tomorrow, can someone drive the wagon and give Mrs. Sikorski a rest?"

"Sure," Prairie Flower said. "Angelina and I will drive wagon."

"Okay, fine, see you all in the morning."

Everything went well through the night. Morning came. Coffee was cooking, and some fried potatoes with leftover rabbit and quail.

"Mrs. Sikorski, can you handle a rifle?"

"Yes."

"And your daughter?"

"Not so good but she knows how."

"Okay, then pick a horse for each of you to ride and put a rife in the scabbard. First check it, make sure it's full of bullets. Put on a holster and gun. Check it too for bullets and put another pistol on yourself somewhere you can get to fast if you have to. That's the way we have stayed alive on this trip. We are all very well armed. Have your daughter practice with the rifle and pistol a little but don't fire. It could be the difference between her living or dying, and you too. You know what you have to do. \If it comes to killing, don't hesitate for one second. I mean it. It's very important. Can you do it if it comes to it?"

"Yes we can, Frankie. I can see if we would have been taught what you're teaching us, we might not have been taken, and my husband and son not killed. We can have an edge because men don't expect women to be armed and ready to kill if they have to."

"That's right, Mrs. Sikorski. Keep that in mind for the rest of your lives, you and your daughter. Have her put a pistol on her somewhere she can get to it fast. I mean, besides a holster and pistol. Angelina, you both keep your rifles with you in the wagon, where no one can see them, and how are your pistols? Make sure they are fully loaded and ready to go."

"We have Frankie B.," Angelina called, "Can you come over here?"

They're seated on the wagon. "Sure, what?"

"Come here, lean over." Angelina put her arms around his neck and kissed him on the cheek. "Frankie B., thank you, you have kept us alive." Prairie Flower leaned across Angelina and hugged and kissed him, too.

"Thank you, thank you."

"Okay, now we should go," Carlyle said. "They're right, you know. You are a good leader, Frankie. Your quick thinking probably saved our lives."

"Thanks, Carlyle. I hope we come across a water hole or a stream tomorrow. The horses need water. By the way, how's our water?"

"We are getting low but not out," Angelina said.

"Okay, tomorrow we'll look for water."

Everybody started to move out, all the horses followed the wagon without a problem.

"Mrs. Sikorski, how is your horse?"

"So far, so good."

"How's Antonina?"

"She's okay." She looked for a smaller saddle and I think she's fine."

"How about, can she handle that rifle?"

"I think she took you very serious when you told us we could die if we don't get tough. We almost did die because we just let those men take us because we didn't think we could do anything about it. You taught us that we could."

"That's right, you need a survival instinct, and you have a better chance on staying alive."

"Thank you," Mrs. Sikorski said.

"Okay, since you are good, I'm gonna check on the rest. Carlyle, how you doing?"

"I'm okay. I like what you've done for Mrs. Sikorski. Her and her daughter. You've scared them just enough to turn them into a fighting pair."

"Thanks Carlyle, that's what I was hoping for. I'm going up to see how OK Bill and Red Fox are getting along. Red Fox, where is OK Bill?"

"He looking for water."

"Can you let me know if he finds it?"

"Yes I will."

"I'm going to the rear to make sure nobody's following us." Frankie pulled off to the right and headed to the back, all the time looking near and far, nothing to get his attention. *That's good,* he thought. He stayed in the rear for a few hours, keeping a sharp eye out for anything that moved. Then Carlyle motioned Frankie up. Red Fox wants you.

"Okay, thanks."

"Frankie B., OK Bill found water far ahead, go talk to OK Bill."

"Okay." He caught up to OK Bill.

"Frankie B., there is a waterhole we need. Looks like we have company. Five men, look like Mexicans, camped at the water, one wagon. I think they are waiting for the Comancheros to bring them Mrs. Sikorski and her daughter. What we do?" Frankie told OK Bill, "Keep going like you are. We need that water. Our horses are going to drop if we don't get them water soon. I'll alert the others. Red Fox, watch out for an ambush. They probably know we're coming. Carlyle, Mrs. Sikorski, Antonina, pull your rifles out, lay across your saddle fully loaded, know where your pistols are. Prairie Flower, Angelina, rifles on your lap, pistols ready. We don't know what their reaction will be when they figure out we killed the Comancheros. Carlyle, take off your bandage, stay alert. When we get close, spread out a little, look all around for an ambush and turn your horses a little so your rifle is pointed at them. Okay, they see us now. Mrs. Sikorski, you and Antonina, if any of them come over to you two, and go for their guns or try to touch you, shoot to kill, because they will. They might figure out you two are the ones they are waiting for and might have already paid for."

"Buenos Dias, my friends, come have some cold water. We are waiting for a wagon. Looks like you have it. Where are the riders of those horses?" Frankie spoke up, "They are in the ground rotting two days back."

"That is too bad. We paid for some cargo. Where is it at?"

"What are you talking about?"

"Two women, like the two over there."

"These two are with us, and in our protection," Frankie said.

"What about that? We have a problem," the leader said.

"I thought," Frankie said, "you need to leave now so we can water our horses and move on. If you want your horses to join the others tied to our wagon, then go for your guns."

"Oh, you don't look so tough to me Señor," as two of them moved towards the two women. He said, "You two should go with us," and reached out to grab Antonina, but her and her mother moved fast and fired. The two were dead in an instant. OK Bill and Red Fox got the drop on the other three, they put up their hands.

"We quit Señor."

"Guns on the ground, off your horses. What's in that wagon?"

"Some supplies, Señor."

"Pull that tarp off."

"Okay, Señor."

"My God, more women." Four young women were huddled together. Frankie and the rest got off their horses and let the horses drink their fill.

"Señor, we worked for that one laying on the ground there. We were paid to take them to a border town, and we'd get more money. They were never hurt, ask them, Señor."

"I will. Let's get the women out of the wagon."

"Come on out of there. We won't hurt you. You're free now," Mrs. Sikorski said as she helped them to the ground. "Were you hurt in any way?"

"No, except they tied our hands a lot. I don't know why we couldn't go anywhere."

"Well, you can relax now. You want to wash up over there. We'll get some food going and you can tell us who you are."

Frankie said, "What do we do with these three? Who were you to meet at the border?"

"I don't know Señor but that one has a paper he kept looking at a lot, maybe it says."

"OK Bill, Red Fox, search these three. Take off their boots and tie them up to that tree for now." Carlyle said, "Do any of you three have wives and children."

"Yes Señor, we are married and have children."

"I think I'd like to have a talk with them," Carlyle said. "How would you feel if someone took your wives or children and made sex slaves out of them."

"No Señor, we would not like it."

"They probably wouldn't want you back if they knew what you have done, you think," Frankie asked.

"Well, maybe Señor, I don't know."

"I think maybe we should just shoot the three of you and your family will never know. What you think?"

"Ah, oh no, Señor. We want to live."

Mrs. Sikorski, had the paper from the dead one's pocket.

"What does it say?"

She said, "It has a couple of men's names and meeting places. We probably have all we'd need if we wanted to go after them."

"How's the supper doing?"

"We can eat," Angelina said.

"Okay, let's eat. Red Fox, can you grab something to eat and stay on guard. Someone will relieve you in a little bit. OK Bill, will you eat and have one of these three dig two graves and bury these two. Keep all guns and knives, put on our wagon. Take all belongings off them and see what they have. Can somebody take care of the horses? And someone relieve Red Fox. Mrs. Sikorski how about you and I have a talk with the women."

"Sure."

The women were still scared. "What are your names?"

"I'm Margaret Edwards, this is my daughter Grace. We are from Arkansas. My husband was killed three years ago when a bank was robbed. We were taken off a stagecoach a couple of weeks ago. These two girls were taken from another family somewhere in Oklahoma. Can you tell the man about yourself?" "Okay, I'm Mary Evens. I'm seventeen. This is my sister Gloria. She's sixteen. We don't know if our mom and papa are alive. They broke into our house at night and put bags over our heads and took us. I don't know how long ago that

75

was. Please help us." "We will. You are safe now," Mrs. Sikorski said as she hugged the two of them. "No one can hurt you now. These people are good people. We will do everything we can to help you. Can the four of you ride a horse, drive a wagon, and shoot, rifle and pistol?"

Mrs Edwards said, "I can ride, drive, and shoot."

"Okay, how about the girls?"

"My daughter Grace can ride a horse very well. I'm not sure about driving the wagon, but she can learn. She knows a little about guns."

"Okay, here's what we need. Each one of you four pick out a horse that suits you. It will be your horse for good, saddle and all. You will need to take care of it. Get a rifle out of the wagon, two pistols, make sure they are fully loaded. If you want a holster, we have plenty, put some extra ammo on you or in your saddle bags. You can have one pistol in a holster and one on you somewhere that doesn't show. If you don't feel comfortable with a holster, that's okay, then put both pistols on you somewhere that you can get at really fast. Do all of you understand?"

"If you want to change clothes to something more rugged like the other women, we have plenty. Men's clothes and boots. I want you to know one thing, we are in a fight. The men that paid for you will not give up. We will probably have to shoot it out again. When we ride out in the morning, you will be on horseback with a rifle in your scabbard. You should practice pulling it out and laying it across your saddle horn and ride like that every once in a while. Same with your pistols. Don't fire though, you can practice without firing. Do you all understand?"

"Yes Frankie B."

Mrs. Edwards said, "The three girls didn't look so sure but said they will try."

"It's very important. It might be the difference between you living and dying. Okay, can you do that now before it gets dark? One other thing, sleep with your guns close by. We'll leave early in the morning."

"Frankie B., I had a small handgun. One of the men took it from me. Can I look in all the saddle bags for it."

"Sure, Mrs. Edwards. I haven't seen it. I'll ask the three tied up."

"Yes Señor, the one with the paper in his pocket had it."

Frankie B. looked in the dead bandit's saddle bag and there it was. "Here Mrs. Edwards, here's your gun. I don't think we have bullets for it."

"I had a box. He took them, too. Look again."

"You're right, here they are."

"Thank you, Frankie B."

"Glad to help. Carlyle, I'm thinking about having two bandits drive the two wagons for us, all the women can ride horse back if they want. Put the third one on a horse, no boots. And tie his horse to a wagon and have someone keep a close eye on the three of them. We got about four days yet to catch up with the herd, that way not so many horses tied to one wagon. Also, make sure no guns and no boots. Make sure all the guns and ammo is in that big box on the wagon so they cannot get to them. I wish we didn't have them with us, but what can we do? What do you think? I don't know what we will do with them when we get to Mr. Dickenson."

"Frankie, I am like you. I wish we didn't have them to worry about. Tell you what, Frankie. Let's have a straightforward talk with them. Maybe we can let them go, maybe. Lot of maybes. I would like to think we can trust them, but I don't know. They might just want a job, or they might be good liars. Let's see if we can get something out a them. Let's get OK Bill and Red Fox with us and grill them. But first, let's talk to the four women that were in the wagon. What do they think about these three? They were around them for a long time. What do they remember about them?"

"Good idea. They should know if they're lying to us. Mrs. Edwards, get your daughter and the two girls. We need to talk. We want to know what you think about the three bandits. We need to make a decision."

"Okay, I'll get the girls and be right back."

The four women didn't seem to know much about them. They said they were not let out of the wagon much. These three were no different than the other two.

Mrs. Edwards said, "We were their prisoners. They all took turns feeding us and letting us out to relieve ourselves. None were any kinder than the others, no small talk from any of them. They didn't seem to care or feel sorry for us then. I don't think they're any better now. What do you girls think?"

One of the three was a little nicer than the others. He would say, "I have a daughter like you, your age. He didn't seem to like what they were doing. That's the only difference."

Mary Evens said, "I can show you which one. Not the one that keeps saying Señor and smiles all the time."

"Point out the one."

"The one with the red socks."

"Okay, I know which one. Let's walk over to where they are. Are you okay with that?"

"Yes, that's okay."

"You three listen up," Frankie said, "what do you think we should do with you three? We have a problem."

"What is the problem Señor?"

"There is three of you too many. We can either let you go with no saddle, no guns, and no boots to go back to your boss and tell him about us or we can kill one of you and the other two can drive the wagons for us, or we can kill all three of you. My two Indian friends here haven't stretched out anyone's intestines for a long time. They would like to see which one of you has the longer one. What do you think? You have mistreated these women, and probably others."

"Yes, Señor, we have done as you say. We have sinned against the Almighty God and women. We are sorry for what we did. We want to live, and we will do anything you ask."

"How many times have you captured women and young girls and ripped them away from their family, and what happened to these girls' parents while we are on the subject? You be still and let the other two talk."

"We don't talk too good English," one said, "but we tell you what we know."

"Okay, that's good," Carlyle said. "Talk, it's getting late."

"Him and me, we never do this before. The girls' parents were shot, not dead when we left, maybe dead now, don't know. The leader saw them in town, and we followed them to get the girls."

"So, who shot them?"

"Don't know for sure. Those two we buried went into the house, shots were heard, then they came out with the two Señoritas with bags on their heads, they put them in the wagon, and we left. I saw the two parents come out of the house screaming for their children."

"Did you already have the woman and her daughter?"

"No sir. Maybe two days later."

Frankie looked at Mrs Edwards.

"That's probably right," she said.

"Was anyone killed when you attacked the stage and captured Mrs. Edwards and her daughter?"

"One man killed and one wounded."

"Okay, who did the killing? Now you can talk Señor. You tell us who did the killing and who did the wounding."

"The leader did the killing, and I did the wounding."

"When you say wounding, what exactly do you mean? Okay, Red Socks, you tell us how he wounded the man."

"Yes Sir. He hit him with his rifle when the man tried to protect the woman, Sir. The man was bleeding from the head, Sir. I know I was wrong, but I did it and now you will kill me."

"OK Bill, what do you think we should do with them."

"You give them to me, Frankie B. Red Fox and I will have them beg for death," OK Bill said. "Everyone, tell them what you think."

"Prairie Flower, what do think?"

"They should have their wives and children sold into slavery."

Angelina said, "That would be the best for them."

Mrs. Sikorski said, "They should feel the pain that families feel when their women are ripped from them. It was bad for me but even worse knowing my daughter would be used and there was nothing I could do. But at least we had our revenge, when Antonina and I killed those two sons a bitches."

"Now Mrs. Edwards, you and the three young ones have to decide what you want."

"I wouldn't change what I did for nothing. I got my revenge. That's all I have to say about it. Whatever you all decide will be all right with me."

Antonina said, "Me too, Frankie B."

"Mrs. Edwards, what do you think?"

"Well, is there any way we can get Mary and Gloria Evens back to their homes to find out what happened to their parents. Just think how their lives have been destroyed because of what these three and the others did to them."

"Señor, Señoras, if you will permit me a way, and you won't have to kill us. We can take the two young ones back to their home."

"We don't trust you," Carlyle said.

Everybody kinda agreed to that.

"I would like to do something like that Frankie said. Do any of you three know the way back to their home? Where is it, Arkansas?"

"Yes, it is Arkansas, just across the border. Only one of you can take them back. Which one? Mrs. Edwards, which one would you trust enough to get them back safely." Frankie said. "Maybe we should just kill them and be done with it, and I'll take the girls back when we get everybody safely to Mr. Dickenson and the herd to Montana."

"Mr. Frankie," the quiet one spoke up, "would Señor Dickenson hire us to work for him, do you think?"

"I don't know, maybe, if you could prove yourself."

"If you will allow me, I will take the two Señorita's back to their family, and then meet you in the Dakotas, if you will trust me."

"What do you think, all of you."

"Ah," Mrs Edwards said, "only if I go too. Maybe that's the way. He goes only because he knows the way. I go with rifle and pistols, the girls too, him no gun, give him his boots and saddle and hat and water. We won't hurt him as long as he does what he's supposed to. If we see he's not doing what he said he would, we will kill him with no hesitation and find our way back to you. If we make it back to the girls' home and their parents are alive and they want to stay, José and I will leave them and catch up with you folks."

"That sounds good to me," Frankie and Carlyle agreed. "What do all of you think about that?"
All agreed.

"We can see that Mrs. Edwards will not take any crap from this guy or anybody else."

"Well, if that's true, that's because Frankie B. showed me I don't have to take any, as long as I can outsmart someone or get my hands on a gun or a knife, I won't be taken again. I will constantly be on guard. We'll leave in the morning. We'll take a horse each and some food. I'd like Grace to stay with you all."

"I'd like to be with you Mama, but I know you can't be looking out for me too, so I'll stay. Okay, Mr. Frankie B.?"

"Yes, that will be alright. You and Antonina can get more acquainted."

"I think we should all turn in for the night. We'll get moving in the morning. Night everybody."

"Carlyle, you think we made the right decision? I really think this will work. She turned out to be a really tough lady, that Mrs Edwards. She's just like Mrs. Sikorski now. I'm glad they're on our side. Okay then, what about the other two?"

"Well, I think they both can stay with us and drive a wagon each or let smiley Señor go to tell his boss we are coming after them with the army for kidnapping and enslaving women and keep Red Socks with us. I think we can get him to work with us. Okay, I'm turning in finally."

They set out their guards for the night and went to sleep. Morning came fast and after eating, Mrs. Edwards and the girls saddled up along with José. They said their good-byes and headed east.

"Good-bye Frankie B. I hope to see you in a couple of weeks."

"Okay, Mrs. Edwards. You girls mind Mrs. Edwards."

"We will, Mr. Frankie B. Thank you for everything."

"José, don't forget these women won't hesitate to kill you if you give them a reason."

"I won't, Señor Frankie B. I want a job with your Mr. Dickenson."

"Okay, we'll see."

Now back to what to do with the other two. Let's have another talk with these other two.

"Red Socks, would you work with us till we get to the herd and drive a wagon, and not cause any trouble because I will shoot you if I can't trust you."

"Yes, Señor Frankie B. I want a job also with the cattle man."

"Okay, no guns, no boots, in the wagon. Okay, now for smiley Señor, what do we do with you? If you were free, where would you go?"

"To my family, I think. I miss them."

"You didn't miss them when you were selling women and young girls. What happened?"

"I see now it is wrong to earn money that way."

"I don't believe you. I think you would go tell your boss where to look for us and help him kill us and keep selling women."

"No Señor, if I went to him, he would kill me. I don't have the money or the women, and the others are dead. He would really be mad at me."

"Where is your family?"

"Across the river from Del Rio, Texas, called Acuna."

"And where is the big boss?"

"In Centenaro, about 10 miles away from Acuna, Señor."

"Won't he find you— being so close?"

"I don't know. I hope not. He will surely kill me."

"So, what do you want to do? You want to stay with

us," Frankie asked. "Everybody hold on, we got company from the south! Alright people, listen up. Everyone get saddled up and check your weapons, checked and loaded, pistols checked and loaded, fire's out, water bags and barrels full, canteens full. Can anyone make them out? Look with binoculars, someone. What do you see?"

"There are sombreros, Frankie B."

"We might have to run for it, but not yet. Who are they Red Socks?"

"I do not know, Mr. Frankie B."

"Who are they Señor."

"Ah, they are the ones from Centenaro coming for the money and the women and me," said smiley Señor.

"Did you know they were coming?"

"No Señor but all the days have passed, we should have been there by now. That's why they are here."

"OK Bill, tie these two to that tree back there. Okay women, be ready like before, but don't look too tough. This is the time to look weak so you can catch them by surprise. Turn your horses to the side with rifles on the saddle and cocked, aimed at them. We will probably have to shoot our way out of this. Be ready. Heads up, they're almost here. Carlyle, Red Fox, OK Bill, with me to the side so the others have clear shot. If you have to shoot, get the five in front. The boss is in there. Looks like there are twelve of them. The five stopped within range of our lever action rifles. Can't tell what they got for rifles."

The leader yelled, "Buenos Dias, Señor. Where is my money and my property?"

Frankie yelled back, "What money and what property."

"Well, Señor, those wagons are mine and maybe those women. Someone has my money, too. Oh Señor, where are the men for those horses?"

"Oh, those horses, well, we killed them a few days back," Frankie said, "when they didn't leave when we told them to leave us alone and they kept bothering our women."

"Señor, you have the women sitting on their horses like they will shoot us. Do they know how?"

"Do you really want to take a chance."

"I don't think they can shoot, Señor."

"If you don't leave now and never bother us again, they will. I will count to ten. You have till then to turn your horses and go. What's it going to be? They will shoot. 1, 2 ,3, 4, 5, 6, 7, 8, 9, 10."

At the count of ten, the men hadn't moved, so the women swung their rifles into action. They fired and five hit the ground. Carlyle, Frankie, OK Bill, and Red Fox charged the seven and took them by surprise. They quickly put their hands up and yelled, "Don't shoot, Señor."

"Off your horses and guns on the ground. Pick up your dead and go back where you came from. If you come after us, we will fight you again. All of you and any more you send after us. Do you understand?"

"Si."

Frankie went over to where the two were tied to the tree and asked them, "Do either one of you want to go back with them?"

"No Señor," was the answer from both.

"Okay, this is your last chance," Carlyle said. Maybe smiley Señor should go back with them!"

"That's kinda what I think. You men, one of your friends is over there tied to a tree. See if you know him!"

They walked to the tree. "No, we don't know him."

"Okay, we kinda thought maybe you did. We'll take that empty wagon. I guess it came from your boss. You can put your dead in it and maybe you should take him with you."

"Señor, I don't know."

"Señor Frankie B. Maybe yes, maybe no. If they won't kill me, I would like to see my family. I will go."

"I don't think they have any reason to kill you," Frankie said.

"Okay, then I will go."

The smiley one left with them driving their wagon. "Adios Amigos."

Once again everything settled down and we were heading west. Carlyle, his granddaughter Angelina, her mother Prairie Flower that are Comanche, OK Bill the Apache, Red Fox the Comanche, Mrs. Constance Sikorski, her daughter Antonina, Grace Edwards, the daughter of Margaret Edwards who were the women rescued from the Comancheros, and Red Socks whose real name is Juan. He was one of the Mexican bandits that suddenly got a conscience.

"We'll have to keep an eye on him," Frankie said. "Between Carlyle and I, we keep things running. With only one wagon instead of two, we can manage better. Of course, Taters has his supplies in a chuck wagon. Red Socks will be the wagon driver with all our gear, extra guns, and ammo on it. We still have seven horses with saddles and the gear from the dead bandits. We won't be giving up these horses yet. The other horses came in handy when we rescued the women from the Comancheros," Frankie said.

Mrs. Edwards is on her way to Arkansas with two young girls they rescued, also. The girls want to find their parents; if they are still alive. José, the reformed bandit, said he could lead them to the parents' home where they were shot when the bandits kidnaped the girls weeks earlier. Things are going okay for Mrs Edwards and the two girls. They are well armed. And José is not armed. Mrs. Edwards said she wouldn't hesitate to kill him if she had to so he has that to keep him straight.

Back on the trail with Frankie, they were making good headway. OK Bill and Red Fox scouting and leading the group. Prairie Flower and Angelina, Carlyle, Mrs. Sikorski, and her daughter Antonina are all on horseback. Red Socks, Juan, was driving the team of horses pulling the wagon with most of their supplies. Some still on the pack horse tied to the wagon with seven saddled horses. Frankie, on horseback, scouting the rear and keeping an eye on Juan. Carlyle dropped back to talk with Frankie.

"I know of at least one town. I'm thinking two before the Chisholm trail. Maybe seventy miles yet to the trail. The town closest to the trail, we should hear whether the herd has come through yet. If we have to turn north and catch up or wait. How many in the herd, Frankie?"

"About twelve hundred head of cattle and a hundred horses; and not enough hands as you can see, two of his hands are here. That's why I think Mr. Dickenson can use all of us. I know he won't think these women can push cows, but I think they can if given a chance. He won't have any problem with Mexicans or Indians. If Red Socks and José are being honest and don't mess up, they will have a good job, and Red Fox, too, if he wants it. I'm not sure if Red Fox wants a job. He might head back with us. If OK Bill wants to marry Prairie Flower, and she will have him, then he probably will head back with us, too. At least for a while. And you know I'd marry Angelina, if she'd have me. We're making good time today for havin' a late start."

"Frankie, I need to ask you a couple of questions."

"Yeah, go ahead."

" I saw you outshoot fast guns and not blink an eye at killing, and I'm wondering who you are. I think you've been in a few gun fights before."

"We'll say I have. My grandmother was Polly Butler, the mother of Wild Bill Hickok. She raised me as much as she could. Wild Bill is probably my father. He always said, 'You better learn how to shoot. You'll need to when people find out who you are,' so I learned from him. I've had to prove I can draw fast and hit what I shoot at a few times. My grandmother gave me her last name, Butler. I suppose you could question what my name is but I like Butler. Carlyle, I don't go around looking for trouble, but I have learned how to stay alive."

The town of Duncan was coming up. All attention shifted. The greeting party came out to where Frankie B., Carlyle, OK Bill, and Red Fox were.

One man spoke. "Good afternoon! We are from the town of Duncan over there. We heard your party was getting close, so we watched out for you all."

Frankie B. said, "What can we do for you?"

"Well Sir, we heard that you all killed off a bunch of Comancheros that where kidnaping women and killing people in the process and stealing their property. Is that right, sir?"

"Well, that is right, but we think there will be more coming after us."

"Well, Sir, I hope not."

"I do, too, Mr. ah…"

"Paul McCoy, Sir, my name is Paul McCoy. I'm the mayor of Duncan."

"Ah, Mr. McCoy, have you heard anything about a cattle drive passing west of here?"

"No Sir, I've not but they might be closer to Fort Sill. Now, Fort Sill is about 30 miles from here, Mr. ah…"

"Frankie Butler is my name. This is Carlyle Coeburn, OK Bill, and Red Fox. We are going to meet up with the Dolphus Dickenson cattle drive coming up from Texas. Some of us are already part of the drive."

"Well Sir, Mr. Butler, we won't keep you all any longer. We just wanted to thank you for helping clean up the territory. Thank you all."

"Okay, I'm sure they've all heard you, if they didn't, I'll tell them."

The townspeople swung their horses around and headed back to their town.

"Okay, let's move. I'll talk to all of you as we go," Frankie B. said.

They turned their horses and headed west once more.

"We can keep going a few more hours, don't you think Carlyle?"

"I do. You want me to fill everyone in on what was said."

"That would be good. I want to talk to OK Bill and Red Fox. Nothing special, I just want to tell them we will have Fort Sill coming up in about thirty miles. The Mayor didn't say anything about another town, did he? I wonder if there is another town before Fort Sill. Probably not or I think he would have said."

"Okay, I'll talk to you in a bit." Frankie B. rode up to OK Bill and Red Fox. "Did you hear what they said? We got Fort Sill coming up in about 30 miles, maybe tomorrow or the next day. Do you feel like keeping going till just before dark?"

"Yes." He talked to them separately, they said, "Okay."

"Red Fox, can you get a couple quail and rabbits?"

"Yes I can, Frankie B. See you later."

Frankie B. turned and went back to see how the others were doing. He pulled up alongside Red Socks, Juan. "Juan, are you doing alright?"

"I'm fine, Mr. Frankie B."

"Were you able to hear we will have a fort coming up, maybe tomorrow or the next day."

"Yes. Are you going to turn me over to the army when we get there?"

"No, I wasn't planning on it. You just keep doing like you are and you can stay with us."

"I will, Mr. Frankie B."

"Mrs. Sikorski and Antonina, is everything okay with both of you?"

"Yes, Frankie B., we are glad to be with you and not a prisoner. Right Toni?"

"Yes Mama."

As they kept moving, Frankie B. spurred his horse around to talk to Prairie Flower and Angelina. He grabbed Angelina's hand and said, "Could you ever think of marrying a man like me," as they kept riding. She looked down with shyness.

"I don't know what to say, Frankie B. I think I could. Mother, what should I say?"

"Daughter Chananget, if you could be happy, I would be happy for you."

Frankie B. kissed her hand and let go of it. "I have to get back to work. I will talk to you later. If we keep pushing, we might see Fort Sill tomorrow afternoon."

They kept riding till evening, and Red Fox came to Frankie B. and said, "OK Bill is picking a spot to camp tonight, and I have quail and rabbit like you asked."

"Okay, Red Fox, tell him the camp will be fine, and thank you for quail and rabbit."

"Okay, Frankie B."

"Carlyle, are you ready to get off your horse?"

"I think so; he's a good horse, but I'm ready to get off a while."

"We should see OK Bill pretty soon. Okay everybody, follow OK Bill and get dinner going." OK Bill waved everyone into camp just in time as all were ready to get out of the saddle, wash the dust off, and eat something— warm or cold! The women got things going fast. They have had plenty of practice! Don't know, I guess we have been going west for three weeks now. We're almost there. Another day or two should about do it. The smell was overpowering. Smells so good: fresh hot biscuits, gravy, roasting quail and rabbit, green beans, and don't forget the coffee. Horses watered and settled in for the night. The watch around the camp was set. Everyone relaxing and cleaning up things after eating. Horses cooled off and rubbed down just a little so they could feel a closeness to us. We are all tired, but gotta keep going 'cause we're almost there. The long journey to catch up with the herd and then on to Helena, Montana. Don't know how long we will stay with Mr. Dickenson since our lives have changed— OK Bill's and mine. Frankie was laying there thinking, *The two women that have come into our lives. OK Bill hasn't said anything to me, but it's evident OK Bill cares for Prairie Flower, and I can see she cares for him. Here are Indians from two different tribes, one an Apache man and one a Comanche woman wanting to have a life together. It sure sounds good to me. And I want to have a life with Angelina. As long as we have the blessings of our friends and the Comanche chief, we should be okay. I know White people will make an issue of it, but the Indians will accept it much better. I need to get some sleep. I will be on watch in a couple hours.*

Night went just fine, no problems. The sun was coming up over the hills. Everyone was up early. Coffee was brewing. OK Bill, Red Fox, Carlyle, Red Socks (Juan), and Frankie were sipping their coffee, eating hot biscuits and pieces of quail and rabbit. Mrs. Sikorski came over and sat down with her coffee.

"You know, Margaret should be catching up with us anytime!" She was referring to Margaret Edwards.

"Hope everything went well for her," Carlyle said. "I think she can handle things pretty well, at least I hope so. Be nice if those girls found their parents alive and well."

OK Bill said, "She strong woman, she be okay. Be good to have her back, her daughter lonely for her."

Gracie, her daughter, was walking nearby. Mrs. Sikorski called her over.

"How are you, Gracie?"

"I'm okay, just wish my mom would get back. Isn't it about time?"

"Yes, it is, she should be catching up to us any day now."

OK Bill got up, stretched a little, and said, "Red Fox and I, we go start looking for trail head for Fort Sill."

Frankie stood up and asked OK Bill, "How's your new horse?"

"Him good horse. I keep Crow horse."

"Now you know you can always have one of the others. We got plenty of horses and saddles."

"Okay everybody, let's get on the trail. Juan, are you ready to pull out the wagon?"

"Yes Frankie B."

"Okay then, as soon as we get everybody saddled up and packed, we'll head out. I'll stay behind and make sure all the fires are out. Carlyle, can you get 'em moving?"

"I sure will, Frankie B."

"Mrs Sikorski, can you see to the other women?"

"Yes, I sure can."

"Gracie, you need any help with your saddle? Antonina, you need help?"

"No Sir. I'm good."

"I'm okay."

Frankie was the last one out of camp. He talked to his horse, Star, "You are a good one, My Boy." He stood there for a while and watched everybody heading west. His eye caught the eye of Angelina. They exchanged smiles across the way. He jumped on Star, turned a couple of times, and was off. The lives of all the men and women have changed. Frankie can remember not long ago how his life changed when he first saw Angelina. If you asked Carlyle, he'd say the same. His life was different, too, just living day to day in the Comanche camp without much of a care in the world. OK Bill, too, was content working close with Mr Dolphus Dickenson, and helping keep the peace between the Whites and Apache down in Texas. Now he is working his way back to the man that gave him a start, crossing over into the White man's world, but without a doubt staying a full Apache and finding love that seemed to elude him in the past. Prairie Flower is on his mind a lot. And she is thinking of him a lot, too. Red Fox had no idea he would be working out as a top scout and trailblazer. Now, heading west to find the herd and helping these people through some of the most hostile territory. He already had to fight off and kill some Crow Indians. The Crow Indians didn't much like the Comanche, and didn't get along much with other tribes either. The Crow were likely to attack them again. But they will be ready and are seasoned fighters.

Chapter 4

Mrs. Edwards got to the Evens' place in Oklahoma without any trouble, thanks to José knowing where he was going. The two young girls didn't know the way. The parents were alive, nursing their wounds. It turned out someone came by and took them to a doctor. Lucky for them or they would have died. They were Butch and Wilma Evens. When the girls saw them from a distance, they couldn't wait to get off their horses and run to them and hug them. The girls both talked at the same time.

"Mama, we were saved by some nice people. They killed some of the bandits. Mrs Edwards here was taken, too, with her daughter. We are all okay, we were not hurt. They would have sold us all to some bad men."

José and Mrs. Edwards got off their horses.

"Can we rest up overnight," Mrs. Edwards asked.

"Yeah, sure, over here is some water. Ya wanna clean up a little?"

"That would be nice," Mrs. Edwards said. "The girls can keep these horses and guns if they want. They used to belong to the bandits. They're dead. This man José was with them. Do either of you recognize him? He said he was outside and didn't hurt you."

"No, I don't. Do you, Wilma?"

"It all happened so fast, we didn't know what was going on. We thought we were going to be killed and never see our girls again. They put bags over their heads and left us for dead."

"Well, I'm glad to get the girls back to you," Mrs. Edwards said. "José and I will be leaving in the morning."

"Okay. Can we at least feed you and give you a warm place to sleep tonight?"

"That would be fine. We don't want to put you out."

"No trouble, it's the least we can do. Butch, do you want to take care of the horses?"

"I'll surely do it."

"I'm Margaret Edwards."

"I have to say, Mrs. Edwards, you look like you are ready for anything that comes along."

"Yes, Ma'am. I learned the hard way. I was taken too easily. No more. You would do good to do the same. Your daughters can probably show you a few things. I never want to be put through something like that again, seeing my daughter and your daughters, as well as myself, treated like a piece of meat that had no feelings and only worth a few dollars for sex. I will continue to be armed. The men that took your daughters might be dead, but the men that sent them and paid for them are still out there. If I were you, Mr. Evens, I would sharpen up your shooting skills and get Wilma to do the same. These horses and guns that I am leaving with you didn't help the ones they belonged to, but they can help you if you remember what I am telling you. They will surely be coming, and you have to be ready. Your daughters can fight, too. Well, I'd like to eat a little and lay down."

"I'll have some food ready to eat in a little bit. I got coffee on all the time if you'd like some now."

"Yes Ma'am, we would. Right José?"

"Sì, Señora Evens, coffee."

Mrs. Edwards went to the pan of water, took off her neckerchief, shook it hard a couple times, and put it in the water, rubbed it over her face and neck, shook her hair, and left her hat hanging on her back and headed for the barn. José rubbed his neckerchief over his face, neck, and hair much the same. Their horses were already in a stall with saddles off. Mrs. Edwards brought along José's holstered pistol and rifle, but as yet had not talked about them. José hadn't either. José is playing it cool. He could grab his rifle at any time, but he hasn't. They both looked at the rifle sticking up in the air from Mrs. Edwards saddle. José turned and walked to the house. Mrs. Edwards followed. She thought, *He could grab it anytime, but it wouldn't be wise. He don't need it now anyway. I think I'll give it to him tomorrow when we leave. He's smart and he knows what's going on.*

The coffee was great; in fact dinner was great. They all said their good nights and turned in. José and Mrs. Edwards headed to the barn. They opened their bed rolls, spread out on some hay, each in a separate stall.

"Good night, Señora."

"Night, José."

Mrs. Edwards was still well armed: a holstered pistol and two pistols on her besides it. They were kinda uncomfortable to lay on but she wasn't about to let down her guard. She took out her little pistol and held it in her hand and went off to sleep. They both have learned to sleep light. Every time a dog barks or horses makes a sound, they'd wake up for a second. A totally good practice living in an environment like they're in.

Frankie and his people rode most of the day, stopping only a few times for the usual reasons. Something is starting to show up on the horizon. They all guessed it was Fort Sill, or a town near the fort. Let's keep pushing and we can make it before dark. They also started to see movement in the same direction. Could be Army, could be Indians, or civilians from the nearby town. Frankie went up and down telling everybody, "Stay alert for anything. You never know what's going on. When we get closer, I'd expect the Army to send out a precautionary welcoming party. They can't be too careful, just like us."

OK Bill and Red Fox started to fall back so as not to stand out too far ahead of us and get themselves shot as hostiles.

Frankie circled around Carlyle and said, "We shouldn't have any problems with all of us staying together. I expect them to let us in the fort, don't you Carlyle?"

"That's right. But I've seen some Army officers that probably wouldn't with what we got for a party: an Apache, a Comanche, buckskin White like me, and White and Indian women."

"I know what you mean. We could seem a threat, but we can't change our appearance. I will tell whoever comes out to meet us that we have been through hell from Crow and Comancheros and survived. We are not looking for trouble, but we won't run from it either."

They kept riding all together: Red Fox, OK Bill, Frankie, Carlyle, then Juan driving the loaded wagon, and last, Mrs. Sikorski, Antonina, Grace Edwards, Angelina, and Prairie Flower. All had a rifle in front across the saddle, hand on the lever. Slowly, they got closer. And as they expected, a welcoming committee on horseback: two Indians and three Army came out to meet them. Their rifles in hand, aimed at them.

Frankie said, "Let's get up a little closer."

By then the Army was not moving. They were blocking the entrance to the fort and the gates were closed. A young officer spoke up.

"Do not come any closer till you identify yourself."

"Yes Sir." Frankie threw up his right hand and they all stopped. "Sir, I am Frankie Butler. This is Carlyle Coeburn. The two Indians are Red Fox, a Comanche, and OK Bill, an Apache. Juan is our wagon driver. Mrs Sikorski, her daughter Antonia, Grace Edwards, Angelina Coeburn, and her mother. Prairie Flower. Angelina and Prairie Flower are Comanche. Sir, we mean you no harm. We are trying to catch up with a cattle herd—the Dolphus Dickenson herd. Have you heard of them coming up from Texas?"

"Yes, as a matter of fact, I have! It hasn't got this far yet."

"Can we stay near the fort till it gets here?"

"That will be Captain Milroad's decision! Holster all your weapons and follow us into the fort!"

"Yes Sir! We are also waiting for a woman and her helper coming here to meet us with the herd. I believe she's coming from Arkansas."

"That's okay. Follow us."

"Yes Sir. We're right behind you."

The two Indians let us pass and followed us in. The fort was big. It had a big officer's quarters and a long row of barracks for the enlisted men, other buildings, and a stable with a large corral to hold a lot a horses. Once inside, they were asked to wait for the Captain to come out.

Captain Louis Milroad came out shortly. A very tidy looking man, probably in his forties, sharp looking uniform and boots that you could see yourself in.

"Which one of you is Mr. Butler," he asked.

"That would be me, Sir. Thank you for seeing us."

"What brings you to Fort Sill?"

"Well, Captain, we are hoping to meet up with the Dolphus Dickenson cattle drive. I and my friend, OK Bill, over there are working for Mr. Dickenson." The Captain got a nod from OK Bill. "I got separated from the herd in a dust storm about three weeks ago. OK Bill came looking for me. Captain, can we stay in or near the fort till the herd gets here? I would like to explain all of our stories to you, but for now, can we get off our horses and clean up a little?"

"Yes, by all means. Ah, Sergeant, show these people to that empty building and show them to the corral. Mr. Butler, I see you have extra horses and some Mexican saddles."

"Yes, Captain, we had a couple of shoot outs with Comancheros. We killed a few and kept their horses, and I'm proud to say we rescued some women: these three, pointing to Mrs. Sikorski, her daughter Antonina, and Grace Edwards, whose mother is the one we're expecting tomorrow. Do you have much Comancheros' activity around here, Captain?"

"No, we don't. I guess they try to stay away from the Army for their own good."

"Captain, before we go, I'd like to introduce you to everybody. This is Carlyle Coeburn, you may have heard of him."

"As a matter of fact, I have. How do you do?"

"Pleased to meet you, Captain."

"This is my Apache friend, OK Bill. This is also my friend, Red Fox, a Comanche."

"Indians are welcome at this fort. We want peace."

"That's good to know, Captain. And this is Mrs. Sikorski and her daughter Antonina. Captain, we had to kill some Comancheros to free her and Antonina. And this young lady is Grace Edwards. Grace and two young girls were captives that we freed when they attacked us the second time and we had to kill more Comancheros to save our lives and theirs. Mrs. Edwards, Grace's mother, took the two young girls to Arkansas to try to find their parents who might have been killed in the raid that they were taken in. When she gets them settled, she is supposed to meet us here while we wait for the herd. Captain, this is Angelina, Mr. Coeburn's granddaughter, and this is her mother, Prairie Flower. Captain, this is Juan Gonzalos. He is our wagon driver. Captain, if you have any questions, you can talk to any one of us at any time. I thought I would wait for the introductions but then decided it might be better for you to know who we are. Captain, if it's alright, we'd like to corral our horses and go to that building you mentioned."

"Yes, right, I'll get someone to show you the way." "Thank you, Sir. All right people, let's get something to eat and rest up. Everybody, don't let your guard down." Frankie rolled his eyes and said, "You never know. And right now, we have no idea how long we'll have to wait for the herd. I know one thing. Tomorrow I'm looking for a bath."

They all agreed with that. The building was empty, just like the one at the last fort. They were able to settle in away from everyone. The women cooked up something for a light supper in a cooking area near the building while the men took care of all the horses. After eating, they put things away. All used a couple outhouses nearby and cleaned up a little with fresh water from a nearby well at a washing table, and most rolled out their bed roll on the floor and fell asleep. OK Bill and Red Fox did not. Being the eyes and ears for the party and the cautious nature of Indians kept them awake. Carlyle Coeburn wasn't sleeping either. They would do their sleeping when they felt a certain trust, which at the moment they did not have.

OK Bill said to Red Fox, "You stay in here. I go out check wagon, much on wagon. Army Captain might want to take from us if he finds out what's on wagon."

Red Fox raised his right hand and nodded.

Carlyle said, "I'll go with you. I'll walk around the building while you check the wagon."

They went out into the evening air, not quite dark yet, not carrying a rifle to draw attention, if seen by anybody, but well-armed. Eyes searching everywhere, listening for any sound. The only sound was a dog, a collie wagging its tail and walking towards OK Bill. Musta smelled the jerky he was eating. He broke off a piece and gave it to him and petted his head. "Now you be friend forever."

At the same time that the Frankie Butler bunch was settling in at Fort Sill, Margaret Edwards was making her way through Oklahoma with José Lopez, the maybe reformed bandit like Juan Gonzalos. When they left the Butch Evens' place just across the border in Arkansas, Margaret had a talk with José as they rode side by side for a while. She said, "José, if I give you your guns, can I count on you to help me in a shootout with Indians or bandits and not turn on me, or anybody for that matter."

"Señora, I will help you no matter what."

"I am going to take a chance then. If you cross me, I will kill you José. Here is your rifle, not too many bullets in it. Here is your holstered pistol."

"Sì, gracias Señora."

"Now, let's ride hard to Fort Sill, and see if we can get a job with the herd."

Several days have gone by without trouble. Now that's about to change. Indians are approaching from the southwest.

"José, can you tell what kind they are?"

"I still can't tell. We need to be closer."

"Here is your bullet belt. Load your rifle, and don't use it on me."

"Señora, I know you have no way to be sure, but I tell you, I will not hurt you."

"Can you tell what kind they are now?"

"I will say they are Crow. It's good that there are not too many. Señora, let's head for that hilly area over there. Looks like five of them!"

"Hopefully, they are not well equipped!"

"That's right, Señora. They probably don't have lever action rifles like us. We have the advantage. They won't think a woman is any threat. They will only be watching you. Most likely, we'll have to shoot our way out. What do you think?"

"Keep your rifle on your saddle ready to shoot if they get to us before we get to that gulley."

"I wouldn't wait for them to start shooting. If they're Crow, they mean to kill us or kill you and take me captive."

Before they made it to the gulley, the bullets started to fly. José made it with his horse; Margaret got shot off her horse. She was hit in the side, and her horse was hit too. She was close to the gulley. She grabbed her rifle and saddle bags. She would need both if she were to survive and started to crawl.

Margaret has toughened up since she was rescued a few weeks earlier. She made it over the edge. Good thing there wasn't much water in the gulley or they'd be laying in it. The Crow stopped firing for the moment.

José looked over at her and said, "Señora Edwards, are you hit bad?"

"I can't tell, José. Can you take a look? It's in my side somewhere. Doesn't feel bad but I'm bleeding a lot. Are you hit?"

"No, Señora. If they circle around us, we'll have a hard time getting out of here. Let me take a fast look at your wound and then I have to see where they've gone to." José ripped open her shirt and saw the gaping wound. It looked like the bullet went through, which was good, but he needed to close it up long enough for them to shoot their way out of here. José took her bandana off her neck and squeezed it in the water and put it on her bloody side saying, "Hold this, Señora Margaret. I need to see what they are doing."

"Okay José. Before you go, pull my belt off and put it around my bandana to hold it on. I need to be able to shoot!"

"Si."

Looking up just in time, there they were. Two from the front and two from the back. José grabbed his rifle and fired and got one. The other one jumped on him with a knife, slashing him pretty bad on the arm. He managed to get the knife away and kill him. Margaret shot one and the other one fell over the one she shot giving her time to shoot him. So that left one more out there somewhere.

"José, your arm is bleeding pretty bad! We have to stop the bleeding, or you'll bleed to death."

"My bandana, Señora!"

She grabbed it and tied it on his arm, stopping the bleeding.

"I need to see where the other one is at!"

"Okay, I'll get this belt tightened up on me and I'll help you!"

They both very carefully stuck their heads up and looked all around. They couldn't see the fifth one. He has to be around here somewhere. They could see five horses standing close together.

"Where is he at," Margaret asked.

"I'm gonna get up and look, Señora."

"You be careful. He's probably waiting for you to stand up."

And he was.

Another bullet caught José in the leg. He fell back and on top of Margaret, not hurting her, but keeping him from hurting himself more.

"Did you see him?"

"Yes, he's on the ground crawling towards us."

"Is your leg bleeding bad?"

"No."

"Okay, you see what you can do for your leg, and I'll go up this gulley and see if I can get a shot at him."

"Si. Be careful."

"Okay, be back as soon as I can."

This gulley was God sent. Margaret was able to move fast in a crouch and not have to crawl. In fact, it got deeper as she went. She held her left side as she went. It began to bleed more and hurt some now. She figured she'd better get this Crow before she passed out. No where could she see him. Maybe he was hit with all the shots that were fired; maybe he was dead. *Na, I doubt it.* She made her way back to José. José was sitting with the Indian laying across his lap.

"He lunged at me, and I got him with my knife." he said. "That's all five. Let's get out of this water and see what we can do about patching ourselves up. I'll grab a couple of those horses."

"Before we do though," José asked Margaret, "are you okay enough to start a fire or are you about to bleed to death?"

"I'm okay. I'll do it." She tied up José's horse and grabbed two of the Crow horses and tied them up, too. She looked at all five Crow Indians to see if they were dead. We don't need one creeping up on us and finishing us off. While she was up, she grabbed all the guns and knives she could see and put them by the horses for later. Now she thought, *I need a hot knife to stop our bleeding.* José had a fire going as best he could. We'll add more wood to it and get it hotter. *José doesn't look too good,* she thought. Before I lose my mind, I'd better get a knife hot and cauterize our bullet wounds to stop the bleeding and stop them from becoming infected. José is bleeding more than I am with two bullet holes. I better get him first. She'd talk to him, and he wouldn't always answer. I guess he's losing consciousness. She wiped off his wounds with water so she could see them better. The bullet is still in his leg. I gotta get it out and I need a better knife. She found a better knife from one of the Indian knives and put it in the fire. Soon it was as hot as she needed. She started cutting the bullet out while José was still passed out. He didn't even move. She got it out without too much trouble, rinsed it with water, and pressed a hot knife into his leg to cauterize it. The arm wasn't too bad but bleeding a lot. Washing it out was all it needed before cauterizing. The bleeding stopped. She tore up a shirt and wrapped it good. Now, I got to do me. She stuck that knife back in the fire to get it almost red, washed her wound with fresh water, and looked at José. He was still out. I gotta do this, I don't want to. I can't wait. I will probably pass out, too. She grabbed the knife and pressed it to her wound on one side and quickly on the other, screamed, and passed out.

Luckily, the hot knife fell away from her side, or she would have had another wound to deal with. It must have been an hour before Margaret woke up. When she did, José was awake, standing up and looking over her.

"Are you okay, Señora?"

"I guess so. How are you?"

"I'm okay. Did you dig the bullet out of my leg?"

"Yes, I did, it needed to come out! You were passed out, so I dug it out while you were sleeping. You didn't even move, and I cauterized both your wounds and mine, too. I must have passed out when I did mine. Well, we stopped the bleeding and that's all that counts. Now we need something to kill the pain. Boy, mine hurts like the dickens. I'm sure yours does too, José."

"Yes, it does, Señora."

"Do you know of any towns around here?"

"Señora, I think there is one about a day's ride from us."

"Any plants we could use for a pain killer?"

"I saw Apache's use something a few years ago, but I don't know what it was."

"Then I think we will have to stay here and try to rest up and to heal for a couple of days. What you think."

"Señora, I agree."

"Okay, in case we get attacked again when the Crow start looking for the dead ones, we need to prepare. Can you walk enough to help me bury these five?"

"Si."

"If you start bleeding again, let me know. Make sure we got all the weapons together, and let's see if we can get my saddle on one of those Crow horses. The other one I thought we might use for a pack horse. We can make some kind of bag or whatever it takes to carry all our gear and extra rifles, pistols, and extra ammo. I think two of the Crow rifles were lever action! Now, where did they get them? Anyway, we will hang on to them and whatever else they had that we can use."

"Señora, let's make some things to eat. I'm sure you're hungry. I know I am."

"I am, José. What we got?"

"Well, some biscuits, dried beef, beans, and, thank God, coffee."

"Okay, but can we hurry. We need to get these dead in the ground. Before it gets dark, let's look around and get some more wood for the fire. It will get cold at night."

"Okay, let's get these guys buried before the coyotes and the buzzards move in. We don't have much time before it gets dark. We can see about your saddle tomorrow. I'll make sure the horses are tied up good. We don't want to lose them."

"Okay, José. I'll get the food warmed up and make the coffee."

Both still in pain, they pushed themselves. So far, no bleeding. Fire going good down in the gulley. Shouldn't be hard to see if the Indians come looking. They probably won't till morning, hopefully. They probably could smell it if they got close and the wind was blowing in their direction.

"You're right, José. What do we have to dig with?"

"Oh, we got to have something. Oh, I know. A frying pan or a Biscuit pan. The ground isn't too hard, I don't think. If it is, then we just can't do it."

"You know why I want to bury them, don't you?"

"Si. Respect for the dead."

"Yes. The Crow will be upset knowing their braves were killed. But really upset seeing them laying on open ground, half eaten by scavengers."

"That, Señora, is very right. Let's get digging and pile all the rocks on them we can find. If they see that we show respect for their dead, they could give up on us. I doubt it, but it's worth a try."

José and Margaret picked a spot near the gulley but not in it and dug with pans. They worked pretty well. They got the graves dug. They rolled the body in the blankets from the two horses. They cut the two in half and took half of one of their blankets for the fifth one. They piled all the rocks on top. They even said a little prayer.

"We got that out of the way. Are you bleeding any, Señora?"

"A little, José, how about you?"

"Yes, I am too."

"Okay, you check me, and I'll check you."

They redid each other's bandages, and settled in for the night, close to the fire. Night was upon them and was getting cold.

"Señora, we have to keep that fire going? For heat, wrap up in a blanket. Are you okay with lying close to me to keep warm. It will be warmer?"

"Yes, that will be okay. We have to sleep but we have to stay alert too. Rifles and pistols loaded and close enough to grab. I'm so tired I can't stay awake."

José thought, *I gotta get some sleep, too. We should be okay for the night. Tomorrow, we could be fighting for our lives.*

They both slept through the night without any problems. The fire burned down to almost nothing and as they got colder, they snuggled in closer to each other without knowing it. When they woke to the sound of a horse, it was starting to get light.

"Time to get up," Margaret said.

"Si, I guess so."

They stuck their heads up over the gulley, looked all around, nothing there.

"You know, Señora, I've been thinking we need to get away from here as far as we can. Your dead horse is going to bring all kinds of animals. And if the Crow come looking, this is where they'll come to. When we eat a little, and have some of that good smelling coffee, we should pack up the horse and get your saddle on the other one and move as far west as we can. I think we might try riding, or if not, we can walk."

"You're right. Are you bleeding any, José?"

"I don't think so. Are you?"

"Don't know. I'll take a look. Ah, my side looks a little wet. I'll wash it with fresh water, and you bandage me up again."

"Si."

"God, we're liable to die out here if we don't get to a doctor soon."

"Si, we don't have any clean rags to bandage with. I guess we just rinse out the ones we have and hope for the best. At least we have fresh water."

"José, let's move on like you said. Get as far away as we can. Help me put my saddle on this horse and see if I can ride. Okay. Saddle fit like it should. Put out the fire. Everything's on the pack horse." Margaret got on her new horse. It accepted her and the saddle without any trouble. José mounted up and away they went slowly, so not to bounce their wounds.

"I think I'll be alright. How about you?"

"Fine."

They rode pretty far. They could hardly see where they were.

"You know this gulley runs almost straight west. I think we should stay close to it. We'll have fresh water and cover with our fire like last night."

"Si, Señora."

Time passed, and they kept riding. Must have ridden ten miles.

"José, can you keep going?"

"Si. I can. We want to get as far away as we can from that dead horse. I'm starting to get a lot a pain in my side. Can't go much further."

"Okay, I think we did pretty good, better than I thought we would. We and the horses did good. Let's stop in that low area there, get a fire going, and boil these bandages."

"Good idea. Horses can stay saddled and packed up."

They got wood gathered up, fire going, coffee pot on.

"Señora, I'm going over there to do my thing. You gonna be alright."

"Sure. José hopped along with a stick and flushed out a couple of quail. Sure would like to get a couple of them. I don't want to shoot. Just by chance, he hit one with a couple of rocks and took it back to Margaret."

"Oh good, I'll get that bird cleaned and cooking."

"Okay, I still need to go do what I started out to do. We have some soap, don't we, Señora?"

"Yes, on the horse."

He got it and washed up a little. Took a chance and washed his leg and arm downstream. Hurts but not bleeding.

"Señora, cold but should help them heal. Maybe you should do it too."

"I think I will. And boil our bandages in the coffee pot after a cup a coffee. Here have a cup. We don't have anything else to boil water in, do we?"

"No. I wish we did. I don't want to use this coffee pot, but I guess we have to. Two cups of coffee each. Wash the bandages in the stream with soap, rinse, and in the pot to boil a while. That oughta kill off any infection. I'll get 'em out and hang 'em to dry. I wish we had something else to bandage them with while we wait for these to dry. Tomorrow, hopefully we can ride another ten miles or so."

"Si. I think we should get to a town sometime tomorrow and have a doctor take a look at our bullet wounds."

"I hope so. We're lucky we didn't get infected without ointment or something to put on besides a bandage."

"Si. Señora. How is our quail doing?"

"Just about ready to eat. You want some of these beans and bread?"

"Si."

Margaret had the fire going really hot to dry the bandages, hanging on sticks. All the while, her side was burning like fire. She would sip on hot coffee and tend the quail in a frying pan.

"Anytime you're ready, José, here's your quail and beans with a piece a bread. Your coffee, too, keeping hot on a rock."

"Smells good, Señora."

"Your leg looks swollen."

"It is, but it'll be fine."

"I don't see it festering, José. You think the Crow found the graves and the dead horse today?"

"I don't know, Señora. I was wondering the same thing myself. I would sure think they did. If they did, you'd think they'd come looking for us."

"I know. Strange, isn't it?"

"Si."

"Before it gets too cold, I need to clean up a little too."

"Go ahead, Señora, I'll take care of everything here."

"Good, cause I gotta go. Where'd you leave that soap?"

"On that big rock down a ways."

Margaret went off in the brush to do her thing. *Everything would be fine if my side didn't hurt so bad, but at least it's not bleeding. It's a little swollen like José's arm and leg. Sure hope we see a doctor tomorrow.*

When she got washed up a little, she made it back to the fire.

"Are those rags dry yet?"

"Si, pretty dry."

"Boy that cold water on my side was something. But it should help if the soap isn't too strong. It shouldn't be. I don't know about you, José, but I'm ready for some sleep!"

"Si."

"Hope tonight will be quiet like last night. You think the horses are okay?"

"Si, they are fine."

"If they stand around with the saddles on for days, it shouldn't hurt them, should it?"

"No, they're fine, Señora."

"If we find a doctor tomorrow, I hope we're not late with infection. What you think?"

"I know. I'm worried too. I almost feel like riding more tonight."

"You too, José?"

"Yes, Señora. I'm in pain."

"Then let's do it. I'm game. We'll get this fire out, bundle up, and ride! I think we have enough moon to see by."

"I think so."

So off they went. The moon was bright enough to see. They were used to the dark anyway. They went on and on dozing off a little as they rode.

José said, "Hey look, Señora, a little light."

It was a light. Must be that town you talked about yesterday. It's still quite a ways off yet. But we'll get there.

"It's either a town or a bunch a bandits."

"Yeah or Indians."

As they pushed on and it got closer, they could see. It was spread out like you'd expect a town to be.

The little town of Stillwater was coming up on the night horizon. Both feeling good, picked up the speed a little. More lights.

"We can make it, José."

"Yes, Señora. If the doctor is in bed, we'll just have to get him up."

"That's right, José. Little more, horse, just a little more." Margaret was talking to the horse as she patted it. It gave her an okay jerk of its head up and down. Now they began to trot.

"We'll be alright as long as we don't step into a hole and break a leg."

"I know, Señora."

They got to the edge of the town. They could hear music coming from a saloon. It was early yet so all the men were probably either playing cards or just getting started drinking. One or two were walking in or out the swinging doors. As they rode quietly down the street, a sheriff's office came up. They pulled up and dismounted, tied up the horses, and went inside. A sheriff's deputy was asleep with his head on the desk. José's spurs made enough noise to wake him up. Wiping his eyes, he was looking like something strange was in front of him.

"Where in the hell have you two come from? Can I help you?"

"Deputy, we have been through hell, so you're not too far off," Margaret said. "My amigo, José, and I need a doctor. Do you have one in town?"

"Uh, yea, sure, come along with me."

"Will our horses be okay out front, Señor?"

"Sure, they'll be okay," the deputy said. "This way. Not too long a walk across the street."

José had to hobble on the stick he had brought along. José and Margaret must have looked pitiful with dried blood on their ripped up clothes. The deputy knocked on the doctor's door. A woman came to the door.

When she saw them she said, "Come in, come in. I'll get my husband. He's upstairs asleep. Deputy take them to the patient room."

"Okay, Mrs. Clark."

"My husband will be right down. You two have a seat."

The deputy said, "I'm Hoss Jones. I'm gonna get the sheriff. He's gonna want to talk to ya."

"Okay," replied Margaret.

The doctor was down in a couple of minutes .

"Hi, I'm Doctor Clark, Jim Clark. Is it bullet holes on both a you?"

"Yes it is, Doctor."

"Okay Miss, I need you on this table."

"My name is Mrs. Margaret Edwards. And this is José Lopez."

"Okay, Mr. Lopez, you on this table and Mrs. Edwards, you on that table."

"Doc, can you help José? He can't hardly walk."

"Okay José, up you go."

José never made a sound but he was in pain. The doctor's wife came back in the room and put an apron on.

"Helen, will you cut away the bandages so I can get at the wounds?"

"Okay, Jim!"

"Either of you care to tell me who shot you."

"Crow Indians. Doctor, I guess it was two days ago or maybe three. Two or three days east of here, I'm not sure. Right, José?"

"Right, Señora. Two I think. I dunno either."

"Well, neither of you have any blood poison, just a little infection. When I drain each of your blood build up, I'll get some ointment salve 'rubbed into the wounds.' Helen will get you bandaged up. The swelling should go down in a couple of days. Stay off your feet José as much as you can."

"Doctor, I sure hope you got something to kill the pain."

"I do."

"We both need it."

"José, whoever dug the bullet out probably saved your life."

"Si. The bullet went through my arm. Señora Edwards dug the bullet out of my leg when I was passed out. I do not know how she did all that when she was in pain and bleeding herself."

The door opened and the sheriff walked in and said, "Hi, Doc."

"Hi, Sheriff. Sheriff Jim Wheeler, this is Mrs. Margaret Edwards and this is José Lopez. Give me a few more minutes. I haven't started on Mrs. Edwards yet."

"Okay Doc. No rush. José Lopez. José, will I find you on any wanted posters?"

"No, Señor."

"Mrs. Edwards, how about you?"

"No. Why would you ask us that question?"

"Well, because anybody as shot up as you two are, I'd wonder even if I wasn't sheriff. Who you been trading bullets with?"

"Well, Sheriff, five Crow Indians tried real hard to kill us two, maybe three days ride from here."

"Looks like they came pretty close."

"Yes they did."

"Sheriff, you can draw your own conclusions. We dug five graves with pots and pans and I'm riding one of their horses and packing some of our gear on another," Margaret said.

"So, they just attacked you for no reason."

"That is right, Señor. We took two young girls to Arkansas to their parents that were taken by bandits and were on our way back to catch up with our party on a cattle drive when the Crow attacked us."

"What cattle drive is that?"

"The Dolphus Dickenson drive on the Chisholm trail. By the way, Sheriff, are we close to the Chisholm trail?"

"No, not really. You're not close to any trail. There is a trail coming up from Texas going through the Fort Sill area, a couple days ride west from here. If that's what you want. I don't think it's called any name but drives come past Fort Sill quite a lot."

"Our people are probably in Fort Sill now. We need to catch up with them and the herd," Margaret said. "If we can rest here a couple days, then we'll move on. I guess we need some new clothes. Doc, can I lay in a bath tub with my side the way it is?"

"I think it might be good for it , Margaret. José, you too. It might be good for you to soak your arm and leg."

"Si. I think so."

"Well, I'll see you two later. Okay Sheriff. See you around."

"Bye Doc."

"Bye Sheriff."

"We don't have any money, Doc. We will need to trade something for some clothes."

"Now that I don't know, but your best chance with that would be at the general store a couple doors over from here. You can rest here till morning if you like. Here, take a couple sips of this. It will kill some of the pain and help you sleep."

"Thanks Doc."

"Si. Thanks Doctor."

"Oh Doc, could we tie up our horses out front of your office here?"

"Sure. That would be fine. José, use this crutch to get around."

"Thank you, Doctor."

"I'll get the horses, José. You just stay here."

"Okay Señora."

"I'll get our bed rolls and bring them in here." Margaret went outside and looked around for a watering tub to water the horses. There was one close by. She took the horses there to water them. *Wish I could feed them*, she was thinking. She was going back into the doctor's office just as the doctor's wife was on her way out.

Helen asked, "Would you like to take your horses around back. There's plenty of grass and you can tie them up?"

"Thanks, Mrs. Clark. I'll do that." She took them to the back. It was pretty dark back there, but she could see enough. She let them eat some grass in one spot, then moved them to the hitch rack and tied them up, petted each one, and said something soft to each one, and went back inside. José was just about to fall asleep. There was just one lamp lit at the time, but it was enough. The room had plenty of floor space, so they rolled out their bed rolls on it.

"This is a lot better than where we were last night."

"Sure is."

"How's your pain, José?"

"Ah, better, not too bad, Señora."

"Mine is better, too. José, if you need to use the little house before you go to sleep, there's one around back."

"Okay, Señora. I probably should. Whatever the doctor gave us for pain might really knock me out."

"You should be able to go out this back door. Be careful in the dark. Use your crutch the doctor gave you."

"Si."

"José, I'm going to sleep. See you in the morning. Good Night."

"Night, Señora."

Chapter 5

The morning came early at the doctor's house. José and Margaret woke up to the sound of people coming and going and the smell of coffee on the stove. The breakfast table was being set. Helen opened the door and said, "Are you ready for your coffee and some eggs?"

Margaret raised her head and said, "Oh my God, yes! It's been awhile."

José was still waking up, rubbing his eyes.

"You can wash up a bit in this room," Helen said and left the room.

"Okay, thanks."

Seated at a table, sipping coffee was something Margaret hadn't done since she sat with her daughter, Grace, the day before they were taken off the stage by the Comancheros, probably more than a couple of months ago. José was savoring his sips, too.

"Señora Clark, do you have some sugar?"

"Oh yeah, José, I forgot. Vaqueros like their coffee sweet."

"Si, Señora."

"Here you are. Are you ready for some eggs?"

"Yes Ma'am, Si Señora."

"How do you like them?"

"Any way you want to make them is okay."

"Is bread okay, José."

"Si, bread is just fine."

"Here you go. If you want more, just say and I'll fix 'em right up."

"Thank you so much for your kindness, Mrs. Clark."

"That's alright."

"Mrs. Clark, do you think we could get a bath and a change of clothes in town somewhere? We don't have any money."

"Señora, I have some pesos."

"Okay, José. There is a bath house on the other end of town. As far as clothes, I would think Chet Phillips at the general store would fix you both up with clothes."

"How about washing these clothes and sewing them?"

"Oh sure. Ask at the store. Don't worry about the dishes. Just go if you're ready."

"José, do you want to go to the store and see about some clothes?"

"Si, Señora. I really do have some pesos."

"They won't take them here, I don't think."

"Probably not."

"Let's see if Mr. Phillips will trade for an Indian rifle."

"Si. If not, then let's see if someone will wash and sew our clothes. Can you walk next door with me?"

"Si. How is your side?"

"Oh, it hurts a little. I don't care. I just want a bath and some clean clothes."

"Si. Me too."

They limped out the door and looked for the store. Just a few steps to the right, they opened the door and walked in. A few people were in there. They must have been a sight to look at. The looks they got were like they had leprosy.

"Mr. Phillips, Mrs. Clark, the doctor's wife, said you might sell us some clothes or trade for clothes and you might know where we might get our clothes washed and sewn. We have pesos or an Indian rifle to trade."

"Let's see the Indian rifle. Ah, not bad. Pick out what you want and we'll see."

José was quick to pick out a shirt and pants and some underwear. Margaret was another story.

Mr. Phillips said, "My wife will help you, if you want."

"Yes I would."

Mrs. Phillips walked over and said, "I'm Mary. I'll help you. What is it you're looking for?"

"Underwear and some kind of pants skirt and a top. Oh, and socks. My boots are okay, I guess."

"Over here are the blouses for women."

"I need something a little more rugged where we're going. I have to be able to ride fast and hard with a rifle in my hand to survive."

"Can you wear men's shirt and pants?"

"I probably can. Let me see. Yes, I'll do that and get my old stuff washed and sewn so I can wear them again."

"I have a washtub out back you can wash your clothes in. I'll show you, you and your man."

"How about under clothes?"

"Yes, right here. We got 'em."

"Okay, get me what you think I can wear with socks. José and I will get a bath and come back and wash out our old stuff, if that's okay with your husband."

"It will be okay."

"But let's see if the rifle is enough payment. Well, if it's not, I'll get another rifle."

"Okay, but don't say anything unless he does first."

"Okay, thanks Mrs. Phillips. Does anyone do any sewing?"

"Yes, there is a woman living at the hotel that sews for people. I'll see if I can get a hold of her while you're at the bath house."

"Mr. Phillips, do we have a deal for the clothes?"

"Ya. I think I can sell the rifle for more than the clothes are worth. So yeah, we have deal."

"Okay then, we will get our baths and be back to wash our clothes."

"I'll see if I can get hold of the seamstress."

"Okay, thanks Mr. and Mrs. Phillips."

"José, it's a long way to the bath house from here. I'll get the horses."

"Ah Señora, I'll go with you. I'd like to walk. It will make my leg stronger."

"Okay, but don't overdo it."

"Señora! You think we should leave tomorrow?"

"Probably! What supplies do we need! We should probably sell another rifle. We could buy some bandages and ointment, and maybe some of that pain killer medicine! How's our bullets?"

"Don't know."

"Okay, before we mount up, let's see what we got."
They walked around the buildings to the horses.

Horses looked fine, still standing where Margaret tied them up.

"Let's look in our saddle bags! Dried beef, can of beans, crusty bread, bunch of bullets, maybe fifteen or so in this bag."

"Can of beans, smoked meat of some kind, twenty bullets in this bag, Señora."

"Let's see what's on the pack horse. We got four rifles, a bag of bullets, two pistols, four knives, a bag of some kinda corn meal, two water bags, our canteens full of water, coffee pot, frying pan, and two tin plates."

"Okay, but right now I can't think of anything we need except maybe what you said: bandages, that ointment, and some pain killer. We could have a week before we catch up with Frankie B. and the cattle herd."

"José, for now, let's ride to the bath house."

"Si, Señora."

"Can you get up, José?"

"Si."

"Let's take the pack horse with us. We might need something."

"Si."

Riding through town gave them a chance to see what it looked like.

"There it is. I see the bathhouse. Does our packhorse look strange with that Indian blanket holding our supplies?"

"Probably, but there's nothing we can do about it Señora."

They tied up their horses and went inside.

"How much for a bath?"

"50 cents!"

"Will you take pesos? How about 100 pesos for both of us."

They were all Chinese working in there. They looked at each other and nodded okay.

"We wash clothes, too, for more pesos."

"Here's 50 more pesos. I have no more."

"Okay, we wash clothes and clean hats, too."

"Good! Margaret's hat could use a cleaning."

"And José's sombrero, too. Where's the boss?"

"I'm Boss, what you want?"

"I want to move our horses off the street."

"Okay, you take round back."

"José, I'll be right back."

"Sì, gracias Señora."

Margaret moved the horses and came back in. José was already in a hot tub on the other side of a curtain.

"Señora, is that you?"

"Yes it is. What did you do with your guns?"

"On the floor next to the tub."

"Okay, I'll do that too." Margaret had four pistols on her and didn't want to get too far away from them. José had three on him, also. Margaret emptied her pockets. A young girl came in and took Margaret's clothes to wash and said, "I be back to help you wash."

"Okay."

José was already out and getting dressed when the sheriff walked in the back door.

"Morning José."

"Señor Sheriff."

"What's in that blanket on the packhorse out back?"

"Everything we own and spoils of war with the Crow Indians."

"Like what?"

"Rifles, some knives." José s back was turned to the sheriff. He had his new shirt and pants on. He was tying his pistol and holster to his right leg, a pistol in his belt in front, and a pistol in his belt in back, a long knife in his right boot, and a bullet belt across his shoulder that was full. A tan sombrero was hanging on his back. When he turned, his spurs jangled. An impressive sight: clean shaven, hair washed and combed, and even his boots were cleaned and polished. He was leaning on his crutch but still was an impressive sight. The sheriff knew that this man and woman was as tough as they come and that they were nobody to mess with.

"Sheriff, we will leave tomorrow if you are worried about us causing trouble. Señor Sheriff, we don't start trouble."

Margaret was out and dressing by now, all scrubbed up and hair washed, hanging loose to dry. She was putting on her new clothes and a clean bandage on her arm.

"Sheriff, you seem to be concerned about us for some reason."

"Well, I am Mrs. Edwards."

When she came around the curtain, she was a sight not like most women of the time with her pistol and holster tied to her right leg, pistol in her belt in front, and pistol in back belt. Long knife in her right boot Her small pistol in her left boot. Her hat was hanging over her shoulder.

"My God, lady, you look like an army all by yourself."

"Sheriff, I am not taking any chances. I didn't know how to stay alive before I and my daughter were taken by the Comancheros, but I do now. I haven't given up being a woman, but I can ride and shoot like any man."

"Señor Sheriff, the Señora is not lying. She is tough."

"Sheriff, I had a husband killed when a bank was being robbed a couple of months ago. I have a daughter waiting for me. She is with a cattle drive. I intend to survive and get back to her. Sheriff, do you have any more questions for us?"

"Not at this time."

"Well, we will probably leave in the morning. I hope you didn't take anything off our packhorse. We know what was on him and in our saddle bags."

"No, Mrs. Edwards, I did not."

"José, let's get our clothes off the clothesline out back and get them sewn up. Talk to you later, Sheriff."

"Mrs. Edwards, José."

"Señor Sheriff."

They took their clothes off the line, rolled them up, and put them in their saddle bags and rode back to the store. The woman was waiting on a chair outside.

"You must be the seamstress."

"Yes I am. You must be Mrs. Edwards and José."

"Yes. How do you do?"

"Im fine, how are you?"

"Well, not too bad. How much will you charge to sew up our clothes?"

They rolled out their clothes for her to see.

"A dollar for both."

"Can we have them in the morning?"

"Sure."

"Okay, go ahead, right José?"

"Si Señora. I'll get another rifle off the pack horse."

"Okay José."

"Señor Phillips, would you like to buy another Indian rifle, same as the other?"

"Let's see the rifle. Uhm. Looks pretty good. I will give you 20 dollars cash."

"Okay. Now we need some coffee, bandages, some salve ointment, very small bag of sugar."

"What you think, Señora, little flour? Okay Señora?"

"Ah José, let's see what the doctor wants to charge us for his services and maybe get some more pain killer from him. And I'm getting hungry. How about you?"

"Si, I could eat something."

Mr. Phillips bagged up their things and charged them $2."

"Thank you, Mr. and Mrs. Phillips, for your kindness and help."

"That's alright. If we don't see you again, have a safe trip."

"Thanks."

They moved their horses in front of the doctor's house and knocked on the door. Mrs. Clark came to the door.

"Come in, Mrs. Edwards and José. The doctor is busy with a broken arm. He'll be out in a few minutes."

"Okay. You think it would be alright if we tied up our horses in the back again, Mrs. Clark?"

"It would be fine, you just do it."

"We will be leaving in the morning. We have to catch up with our people. I think we still have at least a hundred miles and maybe a lot more depending where the cattle drive is at."

The doctor came out of the patient room, let the people out the door, and came back and said, "You two look cleaned up and ready for anything."

"Well doctor, we hope not, but have to be prepared. We got about four or five days to catch up with our people. Uh, doctor, can we buy some of that pain killer you gave us yesterday? We still got pain coming and going! And if you have the time, would you take a look at the both of us? José, you need the doctor to look at your arm and leg?"

"Si."

"Come in this room and get up here. Let's pull that shirt up and take a look. Uh, looks okay, but whatever you do, don't hit that side. It's healing nicely and would do much better if you'd stay here a couple more days and stay off a horse. If it were to bust open and start bleeding again, you could bleed to death. Don't forget you had a bullet go through your side. There's more injury inside than you realize. I'll rewrap it. Okay, José, let's take a look at you. I'll redo you too, José. Uh, the same with you both. You need to stay off a horse as long as you can."

"We would like to, Doc. We can't do it."

"At least keep these dressings clean and change them once in a while. Here's a bottle of the pain killer, don't take it too often or you'll get hooked on it."

"Okay, Doc," Margaret said. "The people in town have been good to us. We kinda like it here, but we need to get going. Doctor, would you mind if we slept on the floor one more time?"

"Sure, that would be fine."

"Thank you so much for everything. We can pay you, just tell us how much."

"Maybe $3."

José handed the doctor $3.

"You need more, you just tell us."

"Na, that will be fine."

"Where is the best place to eat? We need to eat something."

"The saloon serves a good lunch, but they also serve up a lot a trouble. And you two would be like a magnet."

"You think so?"

"Yes. Why don't you try the hotel. They have an eating room where they serve food and it's not bad."

"Yes, Doc, we will. Oh. Where is the hotel?"

"About the middle a town."

"Señor Doctor, I will leave crutch with you now. Might not see you in the morning."

"Okay José. I'd let you have it if I had more of them."

"That's okay, Señor Doctor. I got a stick I can use."

"As soon as we pick up our clothes in the morning, we will leave town. So if we don't see you any more, thanks again for everything."

"When you're ready to sleep, just come in the back door."

"Okay Doc. Thanks."

Margaret and José left the doctor's house through the back door, checked on the horses, put the medicine in one of the saddle bags, and decided to walk to the hotel. It wasn't far. José grabbed his walking stick. Walking along, they got a few looks from people, nothing unusual, and a few tipped hats.

Probably just being friendly. In the hotel, it was the same. Seeing two people armed like they were should be an eye catcher. They just smiled at people and sat down at the table. Their meals were great: roast chicken, mashed potatoes, gravy, corn, rye bread, butter, apple pie, and coffee. Sitting there sipping their coffee, a stranger across the room was doing a lot of staring.

José said, "It would be a shame to bloody up this nice, clean floor!"

"I know, José. Maybe we should go."

"Ugh, I guess so, Señora."

Leaving a couple of dollars on the table, they went out the door. José leaned on his make shift cane and Margaret assisting him whenever she could. And to no one's surprise, the staring stranger was right on their trail.

Margaret turned and said, "What is your problem, young man. If you want to shoot it out with us, let's step off the boardwalk so we don't bloody things up."

"No Ma'am. Could you be Margaret Edwards? And you sir be José Lopez?"

"What is your business with us if we are?"

José was already gripping his revolver, and flipping off the leather strap across the hammer.

"Well, Ma'am, I'm Tim Shiloh from the Dickenson cattle herd and Frankie Butler sent me to fetch you and Mr. Lopez. Ma'am, Frankie B. was telling me about you two making your way to Fort Sill searching for the herd. Well, Ma'am, I'm supposed to get you to the herd."

"Where is Frankie B.," José asked.

"Well, Señor José, when I left them, they were at Fort Sill resting up. They would have sent someone with me but Mr. Dickenson is shorthanded as it is."

"Well Tim, how far are we from the herd, do you think?"

"Ma'am, the fort is about 150 miles from Stillwater. I was looking at a map in one of the towns I went through and if we go straight west, we could cut off about half of that and maybe run straight into the herd if they keep moving north."

"Señor Tim, it is good to see you. We are glad to catch up with Frankie B. and our friends."

"José, Ma'am, what happened to you?"

"Well, we got shot up by five Crow Indians and had to heal up and rest a few days in this town. We were pulling out tomorrow. Can you travel tomorrow or do you need a day to rest up?"

"No Ma'am. I'm good."

"Okay then, you take your horse around the back. Come on, we'll show you. I'll ask the doctor if you can sleep on the floor with us."

Margaret knocked on the back door. Mrs. Clark opened the door wide and said to come in.

"Mrs. Clark, I'd like to introduce you to a new friend that came looking for us from Mr. Dickenson's herd. This is Tim Shiloh. Tim, this is Mrs. Clark, the doctor's wife. Between the Doctor and Mrs Clark, they did so much more for José and I than just patch up our bullet wounds. We will forever be grateful. Mrs. Clark, Ma'am, would it be alright if Tim slept in the room with us tonight? We will still be leaving in the morning."

"He sure can. I will tell the doctor just so he knows."

"Thank you, Ma'am."

"That's alright. You three just settle in as soon as you're ready. The doctor is out on a call. He probably won't be back till after dark. In case you hear someone coming in the front door later, it will be him."

"Okay, Mrs. Clark. We will take care of the horses and turn in early. Tim, did you run into any Indians on your way here or bandits?"

"No Ma'am, I didn't."

"I don't know if you know it or not but the Crow claim this whole territory as theirs. And the Comancheros are active and taking captives, any women or young girls they run across. Sometimes they will take young men and boys to sell as slaves to mine owners."

"Ma'am, I did not know all of that! And how, may I ask, would you know all that?"

"Well, I will tell you something, and you listen good. Before I looked like this, just a short time ago, I was a house wife in a blue dress with ribbons in my hair. My husband was killed in a bank robbery. My sixteen-year-old daughter and I were taken off a stage by Comanchero bandits. We were stuffed in a low covered wagon with two young girls for days, scared to death, bouncing all over the territory while they looked for other victims. Lucky for us, Frankie B. and his bunch happened on us and killed most of the bandits. They saved us from a life of slavery. After going through that, my daughter and I learned how to stay alive. And what's more, my friend José here used to be a bandit, and we fought and killed five Crow Indians. That's why we are here in Stillwater. José got shot in the arm and leg. I was shot in the side! We needed a doctor. The doctor said we should stay off horseback for a while yet. But we want to get going."

"Is it true you and José came all this way to bring two little girls back to their folks?"

"Yes we did. José knew the way. We got them safely home. Where is Mr Dickenson taking the herd."

"Helena, Montana."

"If he needs help, do you think he'd hire us?"

"I think so. He hired everybody that was with Frankie B. and OK Bill. That is, Mrs. Sikorski, her daughter Antonina, Grace, the two Indian women, Mr. Coeburn, and Juan. He told them as long as they carry their weight and do some work for the betterment of the herd, they got a job with him."

"Well, that's nice of him."

"Mr. Dickenson is a good person. He treats everybody the same and he's fair."

"Tim, Grace is my daughter."

"Oh, ok. That's right. I heard someone say she was an Edwards."

"José, how you feeling?"

"I'm okay Señora."

"You want to get something else to eat?"

"Yes, I'm ready."

"How about you Tim?"

"Yep. I'm always hungry."

"Alright, shall we go back to the hotel?"

"That sounds good."

Out the back to the horses.

"I'm going to water my horse," José said.

"Good idea. Let's take them to the water down the street."

"Mrs. Edwards, I noticed your horse isn't shod."
"That's right, Tim. He's a Crow horse. My first horse was a Comanchero's horse whose owner was killed trying to keep me a slave. This horse's owner was killed by me before he killed me. One of the Crow killed my horse. The horse I ride and our pack horse are Crow. I hear you got a good cook that's also a good horseshoe man."

"That's right, Ma'am. Taters is a good cook and he does some horseshoeing for Mr. Dickenson when he can."

"Well, I thought I would wait till we catch up with the herd and see if he will do mine."

"I'm sure he will, for a price."

"Alright, shall we go eat? José, where is your walking stick?"

"On the horse, Señora. I thought I would try walking without it. Down the street they went, walking their horses to the water. A few of the townsfolk were watering their horses, so they waited their turn. They tried making small talk with people. Sheriff Wheeler tipped his hat as he walked by.

"Ma'am, José."

"Sheriff. Oh, Sheriff Wheeler, I'd like to introduce you to our new friend, Tim Shiloh. He came looking for José and me. Mr. Dickenson has been kind enough to send Tim to show us the way to the cattle drive. Tim, this is Sheriff Wheeler. Sheriff, Tim."

"Glad to meet you, Tim. Did you run into any Crow trouble on the way here?"

"No Sir, Sheriff. Why do you ask?"

"Well, because they're on the warpath, killing and burning! Killed a family and burned down all their buildings somewhere west of here."

"Sorry to hear that. That's the way we will be heading tomorrow."

"Well, that will give us something to watch out for," Margaret said. "I kinda expected some more trouble east of here since they were trying to kill José and I just a few days ago, not more than fifty miles east of here. Tim, you better sharpen up your shooting skills. We had to shoot to stay alive. Sheriff, thanks for the information."

"You folks have a good evening."

"Good meeting you, Sheriff Wheeler."

"Same here, Tim. Ma'am, José."

"Señor Sheriff." José tipped his sombrero and as they turned away, one of his spurs rang out in the dirt.

"Let's get to that eating we were talking about. Ready José?"

"Si, Mrs. Edwards."

"Yeah," Tim said, "I wouldn't be here if I would have run into the Crow. They would have killed me for sure. I'm damn scared just thinking about it now."

"Well, get it in your head right now, you're gonna do whatever it takes to stay alive. Clean your rifle and pistol and keep them fully loaded. Here we go, let's eat."

The three walked in the hotel and headed for the lunch room and sat down. A barmaid came to the table and took their orders.

"Would you like a beer with your food?"

"Yeah, that would be good," Tim said.

"How many?"

Margaret held up three fingers.

"Tim, do you have extra ammo?"

"Maybe a half a box."

"How about pistols, you got more than one?"

"Yes Ma'am, got two."

"Okay, clean them both, load them both, and buy more ammo before the store closes; and most of all, keep them both on you, not in your saddle bag. That'll give you the edge you might need."

"Okay, I'll do what you say."

"Good. Now let's eat."

The meal was being spread on the table with the beers and coffee.

"Let's eat. Um, smells good, just like home."

"Where's home, Tim?"

"Ogallala, Nebraska Territory. That's where I'm from. My pa works for the Indian agency. My mom is a teacher for Sioux kids. I got along with Sioux kids when I was growing up. Now I have to get ready to kill Indians!"

"Señor Tim, the Crow are not the Sioux! If you don't think you can kill, you best stay here in Stillwater. Because, if we get attacked like we did east of here and you can't kill to stay alive, we will be burying you!"

"José and I fully intend to shoot our way through any Indian attack— no matter what kind of Indians they are! But they will be Crow."

"We are friends with Shoshone, Comanche, and some Apache."

"We know what you mean. But you're lucky you weren't attacked on your way here to Stillwater. I'm surprised someone didn't tell you before you left

141

Fort Sill that you could run into some hostile Crow. Frankie B. should have said something. Oh well, now you know."

"That was a good meal. Tim, did you get enough?"

"Yeah, I'm fine. I wanna check in the store for bullets."

"Okay, we'll go with you."

They got the bullets and a few other things: more sugar, flour, coffee, and a bottle of whiskey (for medicinal purposes.) Well, you never know, and it wouldn't hurt to have a shot once in a while to settle the dust in the throat. They got their horses and rode them to the back of Doctor Clark's house. Evening was coming on.

"I'm ready to turn in for the night," Margaret said. "I'm getting my bed roll and laying down. You two can sit up all you want."

Horses were settled in for the night. A little washing up over a pan a water after a trip to the outhouse.

"See you two in the morning."

"Night Señora."

"Night Mrs. Edwards."

José and Tim sat down on a bench in the back of the house.

"It sure is a nice evening, José."

"Si. It is Tim."

"Are you healed up enough to ride all day for as many days as it takes?"

"Well, the doctor said no but I feel like I want to get Señora Edwards back to her daughter and our friends with Señor Dickenson. The sooner we get to the cattle drive, the better. If Señor Dickenson is shorthanded like you say, that makes his cattle herd an easy target for rustlers, Crow Indians, or

Comancheros. The sooner we hook up with him, the better. If the herd is slowly moving north, then we got a good chance of running into it by heading straight west and if not, then we can wait for them to catch up."

"You're right, José. Mr. Dickenson is short on wranglers. He was glad to have Frankie B. and OK Bill back with the extra people. I'm getting tired. I think I'll get my bed roll and turn in for the night."

"Mrs. Edwards had the right idea. I will too, Señor Tim, soon as I wash up little."

"Yeah, me too."

They both did a face wash in that water pan setting by the door and wiped with their bandanas, smacked their hats on their legs, grabbed their bed rolls, and headed in the back door. Mrs Edwards was fast asleep on the floor next to the doctor's operation table. They each picked their spot, rolled out the bed roll, and laid their rifle on the floor within reach. They took off their boots and stood them up for easy reach. Pistols, still in holsters, lay on the floor with their belts wrapped around them. Other pistols stayed where they were. Being used to sleeping that way out in the open on the ground, they could see no reason to change inside. Mrs. Edwards was sleeping the same way. Tired as they were, they slept good. Mrs Clark woke them up when she opened the door the next morning.

"Morning you all. Doc's come and gone already. You want gravy and biscuits and bacon and eggs?"

At hearing that, they all three just about jumped up.

"Yes Ma'am."

One at time, off to the outhouse they went to the wash pan. They were sitting at the table like birds in a nest.

"Yes Ma'am, coffee."

"José, there's the cream and sugar."

"Si. Gracias Señora."

"Just help yourselves."

"Ma'am, we would like to pay you more money if you just say how much."

"You never mind. I like doing this. Doc and I don't eat much. Sometimes people pay Doc with food, so we have plenty. I made up bag of food for you to take with you if you are leaving today."

"Yes Ma'am, we are as soon as we pick up our clothes from the seamstress."

Stomachs full, the three thanked Mrs. Clark and pushed themselves away from the table.

"Ma'am, can we help you clean up the table?"

"No you cannot. If any one of you pass this way again, I hope you will stop by."

"Ma'am, we don't know. We might. Now we will say our good-byes and leave. Tell the doctor thanks again for us. Bye."

Tim gave Mrs. Clark a hug. Mrs. Clark reached out for José and gave him a hug. José said something in Spanish, and turned to leave. The two women hugged. Out the door they went. Horses' saddles tightened up for hard riding. To the hotel for the clothes. Mrs. Horne was waiting, sitting in a rocking chair with the clothes on her lap.

"Here you are. You want to take a look at them. I sewed them up the only way I could."

She held up Margaret's, then José's.

"That's just fine." José paid her.

They each rolled up theirs and put them in their saddle bags, said good-bye, and headed out of town.

Chapter 6

The herd was north of Fort Sill, moving at a steady pace, maybe fifteen miles a day, sometimes more. Frankie and all the newcomers by now were settled in and used to punching cows. Mr. Dickenson said he was glad to have the help. Extra people meant extra money though. He said he'd give the newcomers each $50 when he got paid for the herd in Helena, Montana. That was agreed to by Carlyle Coeburn, Juan, Red Fox, Prairie Flower, Angelina, Mrs. Sikorski, the two young girls, Mrs. Sikorski's daughter Antonina, and Grace. Mr. Dickenson now had 20 people moving the cattle, 21 including himself. After a few days rest near the fort, they were now nearing Lone Wolf, Oklahoma, about 75 miles from Fort Sill. There's a big lake nearby, good to water the cattle and horses. They were still a long way from Helena, Montana, every bit of 2 months or more. If the weather got bad, they'll have to hold up somewhere or sell the cattle for a lot less money. Holding up for the winter is almost out of the question. Frankie and Angelina have gotten a lot closer in the last few days, spending their evenings together. OK Bill and Prairie Flower sit close to each other at evening meals around the fire. The rest of the crew are getting to know the newcomers. The foreman of the herd was Long John Lowther, a very tall man. There's a couple a gunslingers that are always threatening to shoot it out. One calls himself Dance Mead from Houston, Texas. The other one is Tommy Holbrooks from Virginia. They are good with cattle. A former slave named Harve kinda keeps to himself. He works well with everyone and the cattle.

"We need to pick up the pace if we are going to make 1300 miles before winter. Tomorrow we should make it to the river in Lone Wolf, Oklahoma. It is the nearest town and it's not close. The cattle and horses need water. Frankie, tomorrow when we get close to the river, you take one man with you and go into Lone Wolf and pick up some supplies."

"Okay, what we need?"

"Check with Taters and maybe you can take that wagon you brought with you."

"Okay, that's a good idea, but I'll have to unload it. It still has the guns and a couple of saddles and stuff on it."

"On second thought, Frankie, don't mess with it. Just take that other wagon. See if Taters will let you have it. It shouldn't have much left in it."

"Mr. Dickenson, I'd like to start picking up the pace. We still have around 1300 miles to Helena. I know it will be hard on the cattle. They'll lose some weight if we do more miles a day and our people will be more worn out at the end a day, but Im thinking about winter. We have a good chance. But we can't let up. What do you think?"

"I think you're right. I'll go along with what you're saying. Tomorrow we'll pick up the supplies we need to move on. Frankie, how are the women working out?"

"I think they're working out just fine. They are doing something all the time. If not with Taters, they drive a wagon or even ride herd, Sir, and never complain. I never told them to ride herd, but they just seem to know what needs doing and they do it. I won't let them ride herd at night by themselves. You know, we will probably run into hostile Indians or Comancheros before we reach Helena, Montana. Their intent will be to kill all the men and take the women and the herd. So I will start getting everyone prepared."

Frankie and his people already know how to fight. They've been through it with both the Crow and the Comancheros.

"One more thing, does that Mexican, Juan, seem like he'd go against the Comancheros if we were attacked by them?"

"I don't know, but he seems like he's glad to be with us. I been watching for outward signs and I don't see any. I have no complaints with him either. And Red Fox is as hard a worker as anyone," Frankie said. "We kept Juan and the other one that's with Mrs. Edwards because they really seemed sincere when they said they wanted to quit running with the Comancheros. Sir, Tim Shiloh should have made contact with Mrs. Edwards and José by now, I would think."

"Yeah, I would think so. We'll just keep a sharp watch out for them."

They kept driving steady till dark. Long John got a hold of Frankie and asked, "How many extra guns do you have in that wagon. And what about ammo?"

"I think we have about six rifles. Don't know about pistols."

"And you got about six extra horses fully saddled, right?"

"That's right."

"That was a smart thing to do keeping all that stuff."

"Well, at the time I could see a use for extra guns and horses and I was right. So, what ya thinking, Long John?"

"Well, if you don't mind, I'd like to give each man an extra rifle and the same with the pistols and extra ammo. While I'm thinking about it, get a case of ammo for the rifles and whatever you need for the pistols when you go into town tomorrow. After we leave the Red River after watering up, we are going on a tighter watch. Somewhere after the river, we are going to be hit by Indians, or bandits, and maybe even both before we reach Helena, Montana. You can be sure of that. And I want everybody prepared. Let's keep OK Bill and RedFox on point. Theres nobody better suited for the job. We'll be stopping for the night in about an hour. I'm gonna have a talk with everybody."

Night came up fast. The herd was stopped, and night duty was put in place. Everyone knows the routine by now. Taters got the wagon set up for dinner, couple fires started before night fell on them. Plenty fire wood gathered by the young girls. Everyone going to relieve themselves so they can be alert for anything. All the wagons and horses close and tied up.

"Keep as many horses saddled as you think you'll need," Long John said, overseeing everything.

Mr. Dickenson was helping out with the food and getting a big pot of coffee going. Mr. Dickenson never eats until he knows everyone has been taken care of and he never eats anything special.

Long John spoke up, "Attention. People, listen up. Starting tomorrow, we are going on a more secure drive. We have to sharpen up our watches and when we ride, I want you all to be more alert. We will be in more danger when we leave the river's edge. We still have a long way to go to Helena, Montana, and a lot of open territory. I don't mean to scare anyone, but the Crow are not too happy with us going through what they say is their land. And I believe the Comancheros will hit us sometime, too. And if you don't know what they want, I will spell it out for you. They will kill all the men, take the women to sell as slaves, and they will take the herd. All the people that came with Frankie and OK Bill already know all that. Mrs. Sikorski, Antonina, and the young girls were rescued from the Comancheros. Frankie, OK Bill, RedFox, Mr. Coeburn, Prairie Flower, and Angelina know firsthand what that fight will be like because they fought it already. They were prepared and that's what I want you to be— prepared. So, when we leave the river's edge, every man will have two rifles fully loaded. I think we have enough. Every man will have a holstered pistol fully loaded, and two pistols on them fully loaded. Frankie's people did all that and it gave them an edge. That's what we are going to do. You will have to shoot fast and shoot to kill. Because you won't have a second chance. Where's Harve at?"

"I'm here, Mr. Long John."

"Harve, can you shoot?"

"Yes Sir, I can."

"Can you shoot to kill?"

"I can, Sir, and I'm a good shot, Sir."

"Alright Harve, two rifles: one in a scabbard for a fast reach and one laying across your saddle. Holstered pistol and two on you cleaned and loaded. The women are already well-equipped. Since they already went through a couple of shootouts with Crow and Comancheros. So I would think you men could get some advice from the women, Frankie B., or Carlyle on how to stay alive. Since Dance and Tommy are gunslingers, I would expect them to be good shots. Am I right, boys?"

"Yeah Boss."

"If you two already have three pistols each, don't take any more. We might be running out."

"Okay Boss. We gotcha."

"So, tomorrow when we get to the river, arm yourselves and clean every gun. Frankie B. is going to the town tomorrow to get a few things along with a case a bullets. When he gets back, everybody grab some ammo. If anyone needs to do a little target shooting, go ahead, just don't use much ammo. Okay, if everybody understands, then stay alert day and night from now on. When Tim gets back with Mrs. Edwards and José Lopez, we'll have three more to help with everything and more eyes."

"Mr. Dickenson, do you want to add anything to what I said?"

"No, Long John, you said it just right. Tommy, you and Dance and John Davis can get back to the herd after you eat. Taters, I can smell your biscuits and stew. Let's eat."

Frankie B. looked for Angelina. She was taking her saddle off her horse. He walked over to where she was.

"How are you Frankie B.?"

"I'm fine. I was just thinking about you. You want to eat together?"

"Sure, I'd like that."

"Do you know where OK Bill is? My mother likes it when he comes to her. She hasn't said that, but I can see it makes her smile to herself."

"He's out with the herd. One of the boys will relieve him after he eats. Then OK Bill will come in and get his supper. If you're through, let's go get some supper."

"Okay, let's go. Frankie B., I'd like to wash my hands and face first."

"Okay. The girls set up a wash area over by the chuck wagon. You know I like it that we have women on this drive. You women do things different that is nice."

"What do you mean?"

"Well, like setting up a wash area before we eat. I think that's great. Ah, there's other things that men don't think to do. Let's get a plate and go over there where Prairie Flower is. Does she need help with her horse?"

"I don't think she does. She's got her saddle off. Mother, are you alright?"

"Yes, Im fine, just tired."

"Let me get you a plate and coffee."

"That would be okay, child."

"Mother, come sit by the fire and get warm. The sun is going down."

"It is my time of the moon to be spiritual."

"I know, Mother. If you want to be by yourself, we will leave you alone."

"No, I will be with you both."

"Here sit on this box. We will get your food. Here's your coffee."

Frankie understood but kept off the subject.

"You two both sit down and I'll get your plates," he said. He picked up two plates and filled them with stew, beans, and bread for both the women.

Mrs. Sikorski was sitting with the two girls and asked, "Is everything alright?"

"Yes, they're okay, just the monthly spirituality." OK Bill came in from his rounds, got off his horse, took off the saddle, put his horse in the rope corral, and nodded to John Davis who was keeping an eye on the horses tonight. He washed his hands in the water pan, shook his hands, and picked up a plate. Taters filled it with stew, beans, and a big hunk of bread. Grace poured him a cup of coffee. When he spotted Prairie Flower sitting with Angelina and Frankie B., he started in that direction. Mr Dickenson, and Long John were having their supper together.

Mr. Dickenson said, "How are you, OK Bill."

"I good, Sir. Cattle good, Sir. No afraid tonight."

Long John said, "Good, OK Bill. Rest up my friend. Tomorrow we will reach the river."

"I think so. I go to Prairie Flower and Frankie B. now."

"OK Bill, come over here. You okay?"

"I good."

Angelina, let's take a walk."

"Okay. Mother, you be ok?"

"I good."

Red Fox came in and headed for the corral, too. He took his saddle off and rubbed his horse with affection, and the horse responded with a nose butt

153

and a nicker. Red Fox headed for the chow table. A plate of hot stew and beans and bread was ready. He said, "I leave here. I wash face and hands first." Grace poured him a cup a coffee. He was back in a minute.

"How'd it go, Red Fox?"

"Good, Mr. Dickenson. I happy be here."

"Tomorrow we should make it to the Red River. We'll rest up and water the cattle and horses."

"Okay Long John."

Red Fox went over to the crew and sat down on a crate next to Juan. Mrs. Sikorski and Antonina were on his left side.

"How are you, Red Fox," Juan asked.

"I good. Horse need rest. I need rest. I like food; good food."

"I heard that. I'm glad somebody appreciates my cooking," Taters said. "I never hear that from any you others."

Somebody tossed a coffee cup at Taters and said, "You know we like your cooking, Taters. How about making an apple pie?"

"You get me some apples and I'll make an apple pie."

Tommy said, "Hey, isn't Frankie B. going into that town coming up tomorrow? Let's see if he can get some apples."

"That's a good idea. What other kind of fruit?"

"Hey Frankie B., come over here. If it's okay with Mr. Dickenson, could you get some apples in town tomorrow?"

"Heck yeah," he said. "I'll get whatever you want."

"We need some dessert. How about getting a bushel of apples? If they have tomatoes, get some."

"Anybody else? How about you women, you need anything?"

"No Sir."

Frankie B. asked, "Taters, you need flour?"

"Yeah, need some lard or butter, too. Lard's probably better; it'll keep better. Get a little butter. We can eat it right away, won't have to keep it."

Mrs Sikorski said, "I can help. I like makin' pies. Would that be okay?"

"Ma'am. That would be just great. Taters, you still gotta good supply of everything you need? I don't know how far to the next town after this one. Do you know, Long John?"

"No Sir, I don't know. Hey Carlyle, we got any towns after Lone Wolf?"

"I don't really know. I'm sure there are some but I don't know where. I'm trying to think. There should be a town on this side more up north. Maybe I'll think of it later."

"Harve, you want a go into town with me tomorrow when we get close to the river?"

"Sure, Mr. Frankie B."

"That'll be okay, won't it Long John?"

"Sure. You can take a wagon if Taters will let you."

"Yeah. Okay you all, Im turning in. Everybody knows who's on watch for the night. The cattle seem settled down. We shouldn't have any trouble, but don't let down your guard."

"Yeah, Long John."

"Okay. Keep 'em close together."

They all started turning in after Long John. In the morning, the rattling of the pans and smell of coffee got everyone to start to stir. Antonina and Grace were up early along with Taters setting things up.

155

Fresh water in the pan, soap, and a couple towels on the table. Coffee pots brewing, biscuits rising in an oven, some eggs, some bacon, and gravy! If that won't get you up, nothing will. Cattle bawling! Morning coming on.

"Okay people, let's get it before it's all gone!" Carlyle is always one of the first ones up for that first undefiled cup of coffee. Everyone else was coming to and heading into the brush for their talk with Mother nature. The morning ritual is always special. Eating with people that genuinely like each other and then getting to the work at hand. Today it's moving the herd to the river edge. A lot to do. The river is still about a hard day's ride away. Meal over with, cleaning, and putting things away for the day. Horses saddled, petted, and talked to. Horses seem to love the attention. Long John, on his horse, signaling to Red Fox and OK Bill.

"Start the herd moving."

No time to waste, catching up will be easy because of the slow pace of the herd at first. Juan was pulling out with the wagon and the five extra horses tied to the back. Mrs. Sikorski and Antonina were riding off to the left of the herd. Start-up was going well. Some mornings do not. Frankie B. and Carlyle were off to the right. OK Bill and Red Fox are in the lead, as usual. By now, the cattle have come to somewhat follow a leader. Dance and Tommy were already with the herd on the early morning watch. Harve and the two Johns were stowing their gear in their saddle bags, and riding off to the rear. Prairie Flower and Angelina will drive the other wagon today. Taters and Grace are in the chuck wagon. Mr. Dolphus Dickenson is the last one out of camp. The pace starts to pick up now that everyone is on the move . Long John spurs his horse to catch up with OK Bill. They ride together for a while.

"We will be going through Cheyenne and Arapaho Reservation land in a couple days after we leave the Red River area. OK Bill, you got any ideas how the Cheyenne and Arapaho will react?"

"They do not like we go through their land, but they will not attack. We should not look for trouble or start any trouble. Cheyenne no want trouble. Cheyenne always fight with Arapaho! Don't know if Arapaho there. If Crow there, we have fight. Crow want all land."

"Well, OK Bill, I wanted to get your opinion. That's why I want everybody to be alert. OK Bill, if you see or hear anything that don't look right, let me know as fast as you can. You and Red Fox are doing a good job. Don't get too far ahead by yourselves. That's when you're in the most danger. I think the Comancheros will try and take the herd at some place. OK Bill, I'll talk to you more about it later. You and Red Fox be safe. Oh, when we get close to the river, let me know."

Long John went back to Frankie B. who was chasing a cow that seemed to have a mind of its own.

"How's everything going?"

"Uh, okay. I haven't forgot about the supplies."

"Let's wait till morning with that, Frankie B. In the morning, you and Harve can head into Lone Wolf. I think we will be getting to the river too late in the day."

"Okay Boss, that sounds good to me. I'll let Harve know."

"Okay."

Carlyle and Constance Sikorski were riding together rounding up the cattle on the left flank. They each had their ropes loose, a few coils whirling them at the cattle to keep them moving. Constance was whistling at the cattle like an ole cow hand. Antonina was not far off. The women seemed to enjoy their jobs. Dolphus Dickenson thought to himself, *Everyone was pushing hard. I can really see it and these women are cowhands as good as they come. You can't take that away from them.*

The river was nowhere in sight yet. Red Fox motioned to Long John, so Long John pulled up to his side.

Red Fox said, "Town, we see now. Still long way off."

"Okay, Red Fox, you and OK Bill lead the cattle to a good spot at the river. I'll get more people in the front so they don't stampede if they smell the water. That could get a lot of them killed if they stampede. Hey Dance, get a couple of the boys around the front on both sides to kinda hold 'em back if you can, but don't get yourselves too far in front in case they run for it."

"Okay Boss."

Now that the river is in sight, we can be sure of the cattle and horses getting their fill and maybe clean up too. If the water looks clean and not freezing cold, would be a good chance for us to take a bath and wash some clothes. It's been a while."

"Hallelujah, some of you dirty cowboys can clean up and break in a few bars of soap," John Davis said.

"Yeah, I don't need a bath, but I'll just take one

anyway," Tommy said. "Don't know what smells worse, you or the cattle."

"Hey gunfighter, you don't smell like roses either you know?"

Dolphus Dickenson thought, *I can't wait. I feel so damn dirty.*

The women were more discreet about it, talking among themselves about a bath and washing clothes.

Long John said to Dolphus, "Mr. Dickenson, I'm gonna have the boys take the herd around all those trees. There's a lot more flat ground over there. I can see that from here. If our people are going to take baths, they need all the cover. Sir, especially our women. I want them to have more privacy. You know what I mean, Sir?"

"Yes I do and I'm glad to hear you say that because I will not tolerate any bad behavior from any of our men. You can tell them I said that!"

Long John rode hard to catch up with OK Bill before he made for the area. He got his attention and motioned with his hand and yelled, "Go around."

OK Bill knew what he meant but he pulled up to him anyway.

"We're going around the trees and bushes on the west side. Pretty much all our people want to take a bath, and I want them to have as much cover as we can get, especially our women. Mr Dickenson said he will not tolerate any bad behavior from the men to the women."

"I will tell Red Fox," OK Bill said.

"Okay good, anybody causing trouble will get themselves fired on the spot. The herd was started to the west side. OK Bill and Red Fox easily turned a bunch in the front. The cowboys close to the front followed without any problem. Looks like we will get to the river with day light to spare. Mrs Sikorski was getting the cattle to swing west along with Antonina. They both worked well with the cattle. Being from southern Illinois, they were used to a few head of stubborn cattle, but nothing like a whole herd. As she rode along, she thought about how her life has changed. *A short time ago, she was a house wife with two children on a small farm in southern Illinois when bandits, part of the Logan Belt gang that had been terrorizing southern Illinois and into Missouri, killed her husband, ran off her sixteen year old son, took her and her eighteen-year-old daughter hundreds of miles and turned them over to the Comancheros in Arkansas to sell as sex slaves. Thank God for Frankie Butler and OK Bill and the others for their rescue or no telling where her and her daughter would be now. Probably in Mexico. Constance wonders a lot where her son is. Hoping she can be reunited with him someday. Her and her dead husband have relatives in the area where they lived, so her son should have made it to one of them. She is so grateful to her new friends for all they have done for her and her daughter, Antonina. Working with cattle on a drive is a bit unusual for a woman and young girls, but she had learned to like it some. It's a small payment to make for what was done for her. I wonder how Margaret Edwards was getting along. She, too, was taken with her daughter, Grace, by bandits. It's been a while since she left with José to take the two girls, who were also taken, back to Arkansas to their parents. She should be working her way west to meet up with us somewhere on the cattle drive. Maybe any day now she will catch up with us. I miss having her around and her daughter, Grace, watches for her every day.* Things are starting to slow up. We are at the river. "Now maybe I can clean up. I feel so dirty."

Grace and Antonina came riding over to Constance. "Hope we stay at the river long enough to clean up."

"Yes, me too Grace. Let's get settled in for the night and get a supper started."

Everyone pushed the cattle together on the river edge. Taters was the first to roll in with the chuckwagon and next came the small wagon with more supplies. This was done so many times, everyone knows what to do. Mostly, get the cattle settled down for the night. They are all bawling for a spot to drink at the river edge. They will get their turn and quiet down. The cowboys and cowgirls will all take turns eating and watching the herd.

"Pretty close to the town, so should be no trouble with bandits— we hope," Carlyle was saying.

"Yeah, unless they are already in town drinking it up."

"Didn't think about that. Eew wee. One of us ought to go into town and check the saloons out."

"Good idea. I'll talk to Long John. See what he says."

Frankie B. caught up with Long John.

"Hey Boss, got an idea. We need to check out the town to see if any bandits are hanging around."

"I know you're going into town tomorrow for supplies. Get a good night's sleep and leave as early as you can before light. If it wasn't so far, I'd have you go in tonight. But rest up first. Take Harve and someone else with you. Do your buying and look around. That would give us an idea what's waiting for us. Don't take anybody that's a drinker. He'll be heading for the saloon."

"Tommy says he don't drink. I'd like to take him, if you don't care?"

Tommy was just coming in. Frankie B. walked over to him and said, "Boss said you and I and Harve are to go into Lone Wolf as early as we want. We take a wagon, buy our supplies, and look around. If there's bandits there waiting for the herd to arrive, we need to know. Are you okay with that?"

"Yeah, Frankie B. We are not looking for any trouble," Tommy said. "Think we should check with the sheriff?"

"Aah, maybe. Yeah. Good place to start."

Harve was just getting off his horse when Frankie B. motioned him over.

"Can you get up a little early tomorrow. You and Tommy and I are going in to Lone wolf and get our supplies. But also we are checking to see who's there. You know what I'm talking about?"

"Yes Sir, I sure do. I can be ready anytime you say Frankie B."

"Okay. We'll take our horses and the wagon team. Harve, make sure you take your weapons. You too Tommy, rifle and side arms. I'll get you two up, we can eat a bite and have some coffee, and pull out. Turn in early. I'll try to get a list of what we need.

"Taters, you got a list a what you need?"

"Yes Sir, here: flour, coffee, eggs, sugar, tobacco, salt. Got it all written down for you. If you can read my writing."

"Okay, I can. I'm gonna turn in, see you all tomorrow sometime."

Things settled down for the night. Cool breeze and some water birds squawking about something at the river. Fires burning for light to read by or for a little conversation before turning in. Frankie B. was already asleep when Angelina came over and moved her hand over him for peace and a blessing and a good night. The words were in Comanche, in a soft tone. OK Bill walked over to Prairie flower and touched his heart as they looked at each other. No words were spoken or needed. OK Bill and Red Fox would spend the night out on the edge of the herd, watching and listening for anything that would mean an attack was coming soon. The night turned out to be just another night, peaceful and quiet. Frankie B. got up early and helped Taters get the coffee going. The two young girls were getting up to help with the morning breakfast. As soon as Frankie B. got his cup of coffee, he woke up Harve and Tommy. They headed out to the edge of camp for the morning stretch and morning pee. With that out of the way, a face and hand wash up with cold water from the lake was in order before coffee, hot biscuits, and gravy. The girls had always set up next to the chuck wagon a big pan and made sure there was plenty of soap and towels for everyone. This cattle drive was a little different than most. It had a special touch that the women added to everything; a little touch of home life. Frankie B. was through eating, hitched up the wagon, and saddled his horse. Harve and Tommy need to get moving. The sun would be coming up soon and they wanted to be on their way before light. Their horses saddled and their weapons checked, they were ready and they moved out. Frankie B. was driving the wagon, his horse tied to the wagon. They headed out, moving along at a pretty good clip. It didn't take long to see a flickering fire off in the distance. The three stopped and Tommy said quietly, "What in the hell we got there? If it's what I think it is, we need to get back to camp and tell the others."

Frankie B. said. "Hold on. Tommy, can you sneak up to the fires and see who it is? We will wait here. Hurry as much as you can."

"Okay."

Tommy was back pretty fast. Frankie B., looks like Comancheros. I counted twelve. They are all sleeping except the one I killed with a knife. He saw me and was getting ready to fire a shot. I grabbed his rifle, looks like lever action. Let's get back to camp as quietly as we can."

Back at camp, they headed straight to Long John. and Mr. Dickenson at the coffee pot. Everybody started to gather around when they saw them coming back.

"We got trouble, Long John. Twelve, looks like Comancheros, sleeping. Be waking up soon. And coming after us. And you know what that means? Killing us, taking the women, and the herd."

"Listen up everybody. Juan, take off fast and tell OK Bill and Red Fox what's going on and tell them to scout a little west to see if there are any waiting to hit us at the same time as the others."

"Okay Señor, I will do as you say."

OK Bill heard Juan coming and grabbed him to keep him quiet. Juan told him what was happening.

"You go back tell Long John we are watching a fire, too. We will go out and see. We think someone is watching us. We will come in as soon as we know."

Juan hurried back and everyone was getting ready. Long John said, "Pass the word, weapons checked and loaded. Women, you know what is at stake. They kill all the men and take the women and the herd. There is no doubt about that. Let's keep three men on the west side of the herd rounding them off to the river. John Davis sings to the cattle; that might be just what they need if there's gunfire. Have him and Dance and Juan stay with the herd. Mr Dickenson, you got any ideas?"

"No, just do like you're doing. Get everybody prepared for a shootout."

Just then, OK Bill and Red Fox came in with two empty saddled horses and a Mexican tied to his saddle horn.

OK Bill said, "This one and two others were watching us with long glass and creeping in closer to us. No others but these three. We killed the other two."

"Get this guy off his horse and find out what he knows about the twelve. Tie him to that wagon wheel and get that fire going. Mrs Sikorski, will you put a branding iron in the fire, get it red hot. We don't have much time before we get attacked, so we need all the information we can get from this guy. Everybody, stay alert."

Prairie Flower came over to the fire and grabbed the iron. She went to the prisoner with the iron, put it close to his face, and said, "Who are you? Who you work for? What you going to do? Tell now or I cut out gut and tie to horse." She made herself look mean, and it worked. He told everything that they were going to do: kill all the men and take the women and the cattle.

"Taters, keep that coffee pot hot and people, eat on the run. Tommy, how about you get back out there and see what they're doing?"

"Okay Boss."

Tommy grabbed a biscuit and gulped down a cup of coffee and was off walking his horse.

"Red Fox, you and Carlyle go out past the herd and see if you can spot anybody else. Use your knives if you have to."

"Okay Boss."

"Oh, and if it looks all clear, get back. We might need you."

"Okay."

"Here comes Tommy in fast," said Frankie B.

Tommy said, "Long John, they're riding this way. The sun's coming up over their backs making it harder to see them clearly. But they will have to turn to the north to talk to us. Everybody stay alert."

Two rode ahead of the rest. They still had a ways to go.

"OK Bill and Tommy, get behind that tree with rifles on the two in front. If I yell fire, you shoot the two."

Just then, they all stopped. Then the two leaders came close. The rest stayed back. They were a mix of White, Mexican, and Indian. The two moved closer.

"Who is the gringo I need to talk to?"

"That would be me," Long John said.

"Gringo, give me the one that killed my man."

"I can't do that. He was only doing what I told him to do."

"Then give me your women and I might let you live."

"I can't do that either."

"Oh Señor, why not? You are making me mad. I will take them anyway."

"I don't think they want to go with you. Why don't you tell me your names so I can put them on your graves. If you don't go now and leave us in peace, you will be buried right were you're standing."

The one leader that was speaking spurred his horse in the direction of the women.

"How 'bout you come with us? We might let you live if you come with us."

Just then, Mrs Sikorski and Grace swung around and fired. The two fell, shot through the heart. OK Bill and Tommy fired and killed four others! The four that were left threw up their hands and yelled, "Don't shoot, Señor."

Long John yelled, "Hands high. Get off your horses, unbuckle your gun belts with your other hand. You feel lucky, go ahead and draw."

One did and Carlyle, who just got back with Red Fox from the west, saw him draw and fired the shot fast.

"Anybody else? Go ahead, then we won't have to put up with you. Someone take all the guns, knives, and ammo belts and put them in our wagon. Take their horses and put them in with ours. Off with your shirts and boots. Search them good. If you have to, have them drop their pants. Bring the other one here that's tied up. See if they know each other."

"Si, Señor, we know one another."

"So, you were going to take the herd, take the women, and kill all the men? You can start digging the graves for your friends."

"Si, but we were not friends. We just rode together. We were all working for the Big Boss across the border."

"Are there more groups working for the Big Boss?"

"We really don't know. Maybe, Señor. The Big Boss will really be mad and he might send more riders after you to kill you for sure. He has a lot of money so he can hire more."

"So, what do you do with the herds and women that you bring back to the Big Boss?"

"There are buyers for the cattle and the women from all over the world I'm told."

"What will happen if you go back without the cattle or the women?"

"I don't know for sure. He might let us go or he might have us killed. Señor, I think maybe we should not go back to where he is."

"I think you should look for a different kind a work."

"That is true, Señor, but what would that be. There is no jobs."

"Well, I don't know what to tell you. But if we let you go and you bring more bandits after us, we will fight you and kill you. Well, you can dig the graves now."

"Si, Señor, we will bury these. And then you will let us go?"

Long John turned to Mr Dickenson and some of the others. "Does anyone have any ideas what to do with these four? I wish we could lock them up somewhere till we get the herd to Montana."

"Yeah, that would be nice."

"Okay, here's what we'll do," Long John said. "After they get through digging graves, we can let them go: no guns or knives, no boots, one canteen. If they come after us again, we kill them. I can't see killing them now."

"I know," said Mr Dickenson. "It's just not our way."

"Okay you four. Listen to what I'm going to say."

"Si, Señor."

"We are going to let you go against our better judgement, but since we are not cold blooded killers like you might be. You can go but no guns, no knives, no boots, and one canteen. We will watch you with binoculars. You head straight south. If you turn and we see you turn, we will come after you."

"But Señor, we want to go away from the Big Boss. He is south. We want to maybe go away from him! We should go east. Maybe we will find some different work."

"Okay, then east. Frankie B. and Carlyle, empty out their saddle bags. Any money or anything of value give to Mr Dickenson. Give them their shirts back. Get on your horses and leave now before we change our minds and kill you. OK Bill, what you think?"

"I think you make a right decision for now. Might be wrong later if they come back with others."

"I know, but we are not killers."

On their horses, one full canteen, no turning back, they are let go.

Frankie B. said, "I'll watch them, Boss."

"Okay. Let's get back to work people, that's the best thing we can do now. Anybody want to start taking baths before it gets dark, go ahead. We won't let our guard down. If you go to the river to take a bath, let someone know where you are and keep your guns close. I would suggest the women go first and watch out for each other. Anything goes wrong, fire one shot and we'll come a running."

Mrs Sikorski said, "I'm going. I can't wait. I feel so dirty and my hair is like rope. Whoopee. Let's go ladies. Anyone coming with me grab your soap and towels."

Prairie Flower already had her towel and soap, so she was already heading for the river looking for a good place. They all took turns watching out. They washed some of their clothes.

"Mr. Dickenson, I'm going out to check the herd."

"Oh, and I want to make one thing clear, you men: leave the women alone! Anyone sneaking around the women and disobeying my order gets fired on the spot. You got it."

"Yes Sir, no second chance."

"You can dream all you want, but you stay away from them while they are at the river unless they scream or fire a shot. Hey Taters, when you get a chance, check out the new horses' shoes and do whatever you think."

"Okay, Boss. I'll do it a little bit at a time."

Long John hopped on his horse and rode all around the herd. The cattle seemed contented nibbling grass and staying close to the river. They'll fatten up with a couple days by the river. He caught up to Red Fox. He was so well hidden he almost didn't see him. Red Fox said, "I see you come long way. I hear you first, no see who so I hid."

Long John couldn't help but be impressed by the way an Indian can move and blend in to the land. He told him so.

Red Fox just said, "We can move like spirit."

"Where is OK Bill?"

"Him watch you all time. Him see you. You no see him."

"No, I don't see him."

Just then OK Bill moved his arm with a rifle in it and Long John saw him in the distance.

"I just want to say, the women are cleaning up, washing clothes, and taking baths in the river. I have to tell you two the same thing I told the men back in camp. Don't bother the women while they are bathing or you will get fired on the spot."

"No worry, we know what you say, good."

"Okay, then I'm moving on to the rest of the men."

"Okay, Long John."

He moved on and told the others, Juan and John Davis and John Johnson, the same thing. You can dream all you want, but stay away till they get back in camp. You guys need a break. Go in one at a time and ask someone to relieve you."

"Okay, Long John."

By the time Long John got around the cattle and the lake, it was getting pretty dark. The women were hanging clothes and brushing each other's hair. The smell of lavender was in the air. Not one man, complained about clotheslines and the smell. Some even breathed deeply. Not exactly what you expect on a cattle drive. Even Mr. Dickenson seemed to be enjoying the moment! He was laying back on his blanket against his saddle with his book opened on his chest breathing in the lavender. Frankie B. came over to Mr Dickenson.

"Sir, can I talk to you?"

"Yes, anytime!"

"Well, Sir, I been thinking. I should be going into Lone Wolf early in the morning for those supplies we need."

"Yes, what is the problem?"

"Well, I think we should get a box of dynamite along with two cases of ammo instead of one. Sir, I've heard a few times about how sticks of dynamite used by a few men can win a battle against a lot a men. And we probably will be attacked again before we get Helena, Montana. Sir, I hope I'm not stepping out a line?"

"No, Frankie B., that might be just what we need. Let's get Long John's opinion. I see him coming into camp now. Hey Long John, over here, we need a word with you."

"When I take care of my horse, I'll be right there."

"Go get your coffee. We'll meet you there."

"What's up?"

"Frankie B. has a good suggestion I think will interest you."

"Go ahead and talk. I'll eat and listen."

"Frankie B. thinks we should get a case a dynamite to use when we get attacked cause they probably will hit us with a lot more men. He says he heard where a few can kill off a lot with just a few sticks a dynamite."

"Yeah, I've heard. If you're prepared. I mean, you can place 'em in the ground and shoot 'em when riders go over them or you can light 'em and throw them and get a bunch. That's what you're talking about?"

"Yeah, that's it," Frankie B. said.

"Well Sir, if you're willing to buy a case, then Frankie B. and I will get our people ready. A box of cigars and matches come in handy when you're throwing sticks of dynamite. You know, you keep a lit cigar in your mouth to light 'em."

"Okay, we'll get a case."

"Sir, I still have that hundred you gave me for the supplies. You think we will need more?"

"I think we should use the money we got from the bandits' saddle bags to keep our people safe and secure since they are the ones that are causing all the trouble. What you think?"

"That's the best way to use it, Sir."

Mr. Dickenson opened the flap on his saddle bag and took out a few bills. Here's another hundred. What you don't use, I'll take back."

"Okay, Sir. I need to talk to Harve and Tommy before they go to sleep. I want to leave early, before light."

"Why don't you take another gun hand with you? Someone in town might get wind of what you're buying. Okay. How about Carlyle?"

"Good choice. Ask him."

"Okay. I'll ask him and check with Harve and Tommy to make sure they know we're going in the morning. Night Sir. Night Long John."

"Good night, Frankie B. See you when you get back."

"Night, Frankie B."

Carlyle was walking over for some coffee. Good chance to ask him about going with me.

"Carlyle, can you go with me and a couple of the boys early tomorrow to Lone Wolf for supplies? You can get your own bottle. We are picking up some extra supplies and need your eyes and guns. Long John okayed you going."

"Who's going?"

"Tommy and Harve."

"Okay."

"Let's leave before light. It's pretty far."

"Alright, I'll see you in the morning. I'll be right here having coffee and a biscuit, ready to go Frankie B. You know, there's a small town close by long before we ever get to Lone Wolf. We should check if they have a store."

"Good idea. We'll do that. I'm sure they at least have a saloon for you to get a bottle."

"Yeah, well, that's really not that important if we can get the supplies, right?"

"That's right. This small town, does it have a name?"

"No. Here's another idea you might consider. If we were to move the cattle up north along the west side of the river that we are already on, there is a small town close to the river. It's got a name like rock or something like that. OK Bill might know the name of it."

"I wish you would have told me about it a few days ago."

"Well, I just didn't think about it with all that's been going on."

"Okay. Hold off on going to Lone Wolf for now. I'll talk to Long John right now.

"Sorry to bother you, Long John, but something new has come to my attention. Carlyle just told me there is a small town close to the river north on this side which would cut a lot of time and miles off. I thought maybe we should at least consider moving the cattle in the morning along this side. We could all ride along together till we got close to the town.

Then, if it's early enough, I could cut off with my boys and head into Rock, or whatever it's called. Carlyle thought maybe OK Bill might know something about the town."

"Not bad. I never did like the idea of you having to go to Lone Wolf. It's way too far. Go ahead and plan on it. I'll ask Mr Dickenson, but I'm sure he will okay it. If it doesn't have a store with all our supplies, we will just have to wait for what we don't get there to go to Lone Wolf.

"Mr. Dickenson said sure. Anything is better than going all that way to Lone Wolf. Let's move the herd first thing tomorrow. It will be a surprise for our people, but we can all adjust."

"Long John, tell as many people tonight as you can. I know some are already asleep. I wouldn't wake them unless you think it's necessary."

Long John said, "I think I'll let OK Bill know what we are doing."

"Okay. Hey Frankie B., we are gonna do it first thing in the morning . There's something I want you to do. And I know it's dark, but how's about you and Carlyle riding out to OK Bill and Red Fox and telling them what we are doing."

"Now?"

"Yeah, now."

"Okay Boss. We'll get out there right away.

"Carlyle, you and I gotta get out to OK Bill now and tell him what's going on. And let's see what he knows about the little town."

Chapter 7

"Okay. Let's go."

Saddles on and off they go in the moonlit night. It only took a few minutes to find OK Bill and Red Fox.

"OK Bill, we are moving the herd along the river first thing in the morning. Do you know anything about a town on this side of the river up north?"

"Not much, small town, named Granite, for rock, I think. They have store with plenty supplies."

"Good, that's what we need. OK Bill, we gotta get back. We were told to let you and Red Fox know what we're doing so you can be ready to go in the morning. We'll see you and Red Fox tomorrow sometime."

Both Indians gave them a hand sign that was understood by both Carlyle and Frankie B. They swung their horses around and headed back to Long John, before he turned in, to let him know they carried out his orders. And that the town was called Granite. Next Frankie B. wanted to catch Harve and Tommy before they turn in for the night. They were opening up their bed rolls just as Frankie B. walked over. "Hey boys, you can sleep a little longer in the morning. We're not going to Lone Wolf after all. We're gonna move the herd up north along this side of the river in the morning. There's a little town called Granite a lot closer. We'll go there and get our supplies either tomorrow or the next day, however it works out. Just wanted to let you boys know. See you tomorrow."

"Okay."

"Carlyle, you turning in?"

"Yeah, thought I would."

"Me too. I still want to get up early. If it isn't too cold, I'm taking a bath in the river before we move out. I can't stand myself much more."

"You know, that's a damn good idea. I think I'll do that too."

So the night passed, warm air and a slight breeze from the south. Not much dew, just enough to make your nose cold if you didn't have it covered. Frankie B. was up and heading for the river after a morning cup of coffee. There at the fire with a cup in his hand was Carlyle enjoying his morning cup.

"You know, we could kinda look out for each other at the river you know."

"Yeah, that would probably be a good idea. Better bring your pistol. I got mine right here."

"Okay, let's go get this over with. You got a towel and soap.?"

"Yeah, I got mine. I'm gonna wash a shirt and pants while I'm in the water."

"Boy that feels good," you could hear them say as they rubbed and scrubbed.

Mr Dickenson and Long John joined them.

"Morning boys, how's the water?"

"Well Sir, it feels good to me."

"How about it, Carlyle?"

"Yes indeed. Nothing beats an early morning bath to get the blood pumping. I think Harve and Tommy will be next. I heard them talking about it at the coffee pot. Well, I'm ready to get out and hang this shirt and pants somewhere."

As Carlyle and Frankie B. were heading back, Harve and Tommy passed them.

"Morning boys. Water's fine, and oh, it's also wet."

"Well, thanks for telling us. We didn't know that."

Taters and the girls were busy getting the morning feed going. Long John and Mr. Dickenson were back in camp hanging up some clothes.

"Listen up everybody, we are moving the herd soon as everyone gets fed."

"Okay Boss."

"We're gonna try and make a few miles to that town close to where we're going to stop. We found out there's a little town just off the north tip of the river to the west. We're gonna try for that and hold the cattle there till we get some supplies. Everybody get your gear packed and ready to ride as soon as you get through with your breakfast. But stay alert."

"Mr. Dickenson, you want to try what we talked about with the horses?"

"Yes, it would be a good chance to see if they will stay with us, Long John."

"Okay Sir. We'll get everything moving in a little bit. Everyone, when you're ready, put out all the fires. Taters, you need any help packing up?"

"Not as long as you don't push me too much. We'll get picked up."

"How about when you can, get in front of the herd and find a good place to set up. OK Bill will let you know where."

"Okay."

"If you see trouble or feel trouble coming, let us know right away. I'm not sure how close that town is to the river. Hope it's not right on it. If it is, hold back a bit. The girls gonna saddle up and ride with ya?"

"Yeah, thought it would be okay."

"It is, but be careful and alert."

"Right Boss."

"Juan, can you drive the other wagon?"

"Sì Señor. Before you go get all the extra horses out, take their bridles off and see if they'll stay with the herd."

"I don't see why they wouldn't. But if they won't, we'll have to round them up. I don't want to lose them. You understand, Juan?"

"Sì Señor. I know Señor. Are we ready to move?"

"Go ahead, Long John. Get the cattle moving. I'll be the last one out a camp."

"Okay."

Everything was picked up and packed and they were on the move again. Clotheslines down; what is wet will stay wet for a while. Mr. Dickenson looks like a proper gentleman on his horse: all clean and neat after his early morning bath and clean clothes.

"Go ahead, Long John, I'll keep an eye on the horses."

"Okay Sir. Okay Juan, start letting them go, see where they head."

"Okay. There they go. Good, they think they're part of the herd. Don't lose any of the gear on that open wagon, Juan."

"Sì. I tie it down Señor. And put cover on it."

"Good. Watch those horses."

The cattle started to move along. With just a couple cracks of a few whips, John Johnson and John Davis got them going. Everybody followed and OK Bill and Red Fox were on the west side .

"We're off along the Red River. Whatever it is, it is," Long John said. "Everybody stay alert."

The extra horses from the bandits stayed with our horses. That's good.

"I guess I need to check with Taters to see if he had a chance to look over the extra horses," Long John was saying to himself.

Fires out, little smoke coming from a few ashes. Nothing left behind. Moving along.

"Prairie Flower, can you keep them away from the water's edge. They'll be breaking their legs in that mud and drowning?"

"Okay, Long John. Angelina, come over here and help. We got to get them up the hill."

"Okay Mother." Angelina turned her horse to nudge the cattle and cracked a whip. The cattle responded very well to the whip. Boy, did they move. She went tweet hey, tweet hey several times with her lips. In the little town of Granite, the talk was about a big herd of cattle coming up from Texas along the Red River that could be here tomorrow. The Mayor was saying at the Outpost Saloon, "We don't know what kind of riff-raff will be coming here and causing trouble. I think we'll go out and meet them and get an idea what's coming . They are still a ways off.

"Sheriff Malawy, how about sending someone out to get a look at them?"

"Okay, I can do that. First thing in the morning. Alright, let's have a beer."

The herd was moving north at a good clip.

"Yahoo. I'm gonna get me a beer. Maybe I'm gonna get me two beers to wash this dust down. Can't wait to get to that town, whatever the hell its name is."

Juan said, "Señor Dance, I will join you."

"Sure, Juan. That town can't be too far off. We'll see who else wants to join us."

Long John started to ride around the herd. Mr. Dickenson pulled up to Long John.

"I guess Granite's got a telegraph office, wouldn't you think? I'd like to send my wife and daughter a message and see how the place is holding up with most of us gone."

"Yes Sir, I would surely think so. I think most towns have one by now. That's a good idea. I'll send my sister a message. I need to know how she's getting along since her husband got himself killed. I' d say we'll be getting close to that town tomorrow afternoon, wouldn't you say, Sir?"

"Yeah, we should camp away from it. We don't want to scare the townsfolk. I'm sure they know we're coming. We been pushing pretty hard this afternoon. Let's call it a day in a couple hours. What do you think?"

"Yes Sir, fine with me. I was just gonna ride around the herd and see how everyone's doing. I'll go ahead and tell OK Bill and Red Fox to bed them down in a couple hours. And I'll get camp set up. I'll talk to you later, Sir."

"Okay, Long John. See you in camp."

Long John rode around and let everyone know what to do. "We did pretty good today."

Cattle all rested up. And their bellies fat. They seemed eager to keep moving. Juan was still keeping an eye on the horses. The horses were moving along just like the cattle, never once strayed from the herd. After today, they'll know what to do. Just follow the herd. OK Bill got the message and passed it on to Red Fox.

"We can stop the herd when we see sun going down."

Taters got out in front with the wagon. *In a couple hours, we can start another feed,* he was thinking to himself. Just another day. He was really glad the girls didn't mind helping out with the cooking and setting up the meals. They were a real blessing to Taters. If things change, he's gonna really miss them. For the two young girls, it's a good job. They understand that if they didn't do cooking and setting up chow lines, cleaning up cooking pots and pans, and even taking care of campfires, they would be punching cows all day when they're on the move. So they have never complained. Not once. Everyone on this drive has a job. It's the way it has to be. It was all agreed to when Mr. Dickenson took on an unusual crew with women and young girls. A few of the men have still to get a bath. They should be able to tonight when we settle in by the river. I guess they could wait till we get close to the town and then go in town and take a bath and pay for it. Na. I don't think so.

Long John. went looking for Mr. Dickenson to see if he might want to call it a day. He was riding herd just like anyone else. Long John swung his horse, Easy Rider, around and pulled up alongside.

"Sir, you ready to call it a day?"

"Yeah, I guess so, anytime you want to stop 'em."

"Okay Sir, I'll ride out to OK Bill and tell him to

take 'em to the water and we'll keep 'em there for the night."

"That will be fine, Long John."

OK Bill and Red Fox must have had the feeling cause that's what they were doing: slowing down and heading for the river's edge.

"Taters, you can start setting up by that tree there."

"Okay Boss."

Long John made the rounds just to say a few words to everyone. When he got to Juan, he said, "How the horses looking?"

"Señor, I watch them all day. They stayed with the herd."

"Good, one less thing to have to worry about."

"Si Señor."

Dance and the two Johns were close to the river's edge keeping the cattle from stopping for a drink.

"We're just about ready to hold up for the night."

"Yeah, you can let them start drinking water any time. I talked to OK Bill and Red Fox. They know we're stopping for the night. You guys had a bath yet?"

"No Sir."

"Well, this is your chance before it gets dark."

"Good idea."

OK Bill said to Red Fox, "I want jump in river, get dirt off tonight. You too?"

"Yeah, me too. I get someone to watch cattle."

"Where Frankie B., him watch cattle."

"There Frankie B. I catch him. Frankie B., we want jump in river, you watch cattle."

"Sure. You two go ahead. Keep your guns handy."

"We wash clothes, too."

"Okay."

"We wash before eat, not hungry till clean."

"I will get someone to help me keep the cattle from wandering off. Hold on OK Bill, I'll be right back." Frankie B. looked for Angelina. When he saw her, he rode over to her and asked if she would ride herd with him for a while, till supper was ready.

She said, "Yes. I'll tell my mother what we are doing. Be right back.

" Mother, I'm gonna ride herd with Frankie B. for a while. I think he wants to give OK Bill and Red Fox a chance to wash in the river before supper."

"Okay. Be careful."

The cattle seemed to enjoy the fresh grass along the edge. They weren't going anywhere. But it was important that someone be out there watching for anything or anybody running off a few head. When they rode up to OK Bill and RedFox, they knew they were relieved. They walked their horses slowly through the cattle without scaring them, straight to the river upstream from the cattle. Dance, John Davis, and John Johnson were just getting through with their baths and washing out some of their clothes. Red Fox gave a yell in Comanche and rode right into the river and jumped off his horse, all the while singing or chanting like it was a spiritual feeling getting clean. Maybe it was spiritual; after all, it was a long time since they had a chance to clean up. And it will probably be a while before they get a chance to do it again, too. OK Bill was a little quieter, but he rode into the river, also. He stripped off his top and took his head band off to let his hair down. And then jumped into the water. The horses just stood there enjoying the water just touching their bellies. It must have felt good. Not going anywhere till their masters needed them again. Frankie B. and Angelina rode along close enough that they were holding hands.

Angelina said, "Frankie B., let's pay attention to our job."

"Angelina, what? Oh, I just want to hold you."

"Oh yeah and then what?"

"Nothing, we got months to go yet before we get back to your Comanche camp."

"Okay then. So let's take it slow, Frankie B. You know what is expected of us and we are going to do it. The Chief, my mother, and my grandpa are trusting us."

"Okay, okay, let's get back to watching cows."

Everyone in camp was being fed a hot meal by now. Long John ate with OK Bill and Red Fox. Carlyle ate with Prairie Flower, Mrs. Sikorski, and the girls.

"Taters, did you have a chance to check the horses?"

"Yes Sir, I have checked some. The ones I checked are in good shape. Whoever shod them did a good job."

"Isn't one or two of them Crow horses?"

"Yeah, I think so."

"Okay, you better see how they're doing. If they need shoes, get them on when you have time."

"Okay Boss, that'll be something I'll enjoy doing. Haven't done it in a while."

"Long John?"

"Yes, OK Bill."

"I will go with Prairie Flower and watch cows so Frankie B. and Angelina can get warm meal. Okay with you?"

"Yes it is. I'll get someone to relieve you in a couple hours."

"That be fine, Long John."

With that said, the two walked away from the fire and saddled their horses and rode to where Frankie B. and Angelina were.

"You two go get warm supper. Prairie Flower and I will stay out here for a while."

"OK Bill, thanks, we could use some supper."

"Hi, Mother."

"Chananget, are you okay?"

"Yes Mother, I'm fine. We enjoyed being out here together. I will wait for you to return to camp."

"Okay Chananget. We won't stay long if someone relieves us."

"Mother, you got your rifle and pistols?"

"Yes."

"Okay then."

The smell of coffee was in the air and there were several pots brewing at the same time.

"Taters, you need coffee grounds?"

"Ah, we got 'em on the list. Frankie B. will get 'em at that store tomorrow along with a few other things. Granite is just up ahead. Long John, who's going in to that town?"

"So far, Frankie B., Harve, Tommy, and Carlyle. They're going for supplies. Don't forget, we are moving out this herd early next morning. We don't need a bunch of drunks that can't get up or a busted up town cause you couldn't stay out a trouble."

"Okay, we don't want that either, Long John. We'll see after Frankie B. gets back with the supplies whether we will want to go in."

Frankie B. and Angelina rode back into camp.

"Long John, can someone relieve OK Bill and Prairie Flower?"

"Sure. How about you two, John Johnson and Dance, for four hours? Then Harve and Tommy, the next four hours after that."

"Okay Boss, will do."

"Just keep them settled down for the night."

"Alright Boss."

"Okay, everybody get some sleep. Tomorrow we push these cattle as close to that town as we can so we can get our supplies, get out, and get back on the trail next morning."

"Alright, you heard the man. Get your coffee, hot beans, biscuits, and stew eaten, so we can clean up after you cowpokes. That means you ladies, too."

"Alright, Mr. Taters Barnett. Be nice or I won't make that apple pie, cherry pie, or whatever kind of pie I agreed to make. I guess it was apple, wasn't it?"

"Yeah. I guess it was Mrs. Sikorski. No offense meant."

"None taken, Taters."

"Anybody not eaten yet, get it. It won't be hot long. You know, Mrs. Sikorski, my wife used to make the best cherry pie years ago before she died. We were living near a little town in Illinois and they had cherry trees all over. They said some family from Germany planted the trees and they grew so well they spread all over. Must have been the soil. Anyway, those pies were the best. I don't think we can get cherries out here, do you?"

"No, but nowadays, they put fruit in cans. So let's have Frankie B. ask at the store. Is that alright, Mr Dickenson?"

"Yes, it sure is. If you can bake cherry pies, then I'm buying cherries."

"Thank you Sir. I'd be glad to. But if not cherry pies, then apple pies. That oven you got there, can it handle pies?"

"I think so."

"Then we'll have to give it a try. Might be hard on an open fire, don't you know? But I'm looking forward to pies. How about cakes?"

"Ah, yea I can make 'em."

Well, Frankie B. was listening to that conversation, and said, "I got pie mix on the list, some kind of fruit. I think I'm going to bed. The sooner we get going in the morning, the sooner we get to Granite."

Mr. Dickenson was already dozed off with an open book on his chest. All the fires burning good, nice and warm. Taters and the girls cleaning up after the meal.

Juan had been listening too and said, "I never knew how good things could be till I met you people. I sorry for any hurt I have caused. I don't know how I can ever repay you."

"Just keep working like you have been, that is all we ask. Right folks?"

"That's right, Long John."

"Well, I'm turning in to. See you in the morning."

"Good night Boss."

Frankie B. said good night to Angelina and turned in. OK Bill and Prairie Flower came into camp and said their good nights to everyone and went to where Prairie Flower had her bed roll. OK Bill took a blanket and put it over her shoulders. She was a little cold from the night air. She pulled it together and turned around to face OK Bill. As some Indian tradition says, if a brave puts a blanket around a woman he cares for and she opens up the blanket to let him in, they are kind of like what we would call engaged. She opened the blanket and OK Bill walked in, she pulled it tight around the both of them. They hugged for a while. When she opened it, he backed away and bowed his head, turned and headed for his bed roll. The boys tending the herd rode slowly around and sang and talked to the cattle. By now, after all this time, you could be sure the cattle knew their voices and it was also a way to keep themselves awake! Sometimes the night just won't get over with. Like when you're tired in the saddle. So morning finally came as it always does. Taters and the girls rustling around getting things going for another day of cow poking. Juan and Mrs. Sikorski and daughter Antonina relieved Harve and Tommy just before light. They looked like they were ready to fall out of the saddle.

"Thanks for relieving us," Harve said.

"Anything to tell us or has everything been okay."

"Naw, everything is fine. No coyotes or anything else. Not one coyote sneaking around or wild cat. We'll turn it over to you all."

"Okay, see you in camp."

Coffee is perking. Juan said, "I'm gonna ride from down river up around."

"Okay, then we'll ride from north down and meet you in the middle."

"Si Señora."

Cattle, some standing, some sitting, and some laying on the grass hardly paying attention to the changing of the riders that look out for them. Sun coming up fast.

"We better get a move on."

Mr. Dickenson and Long John were washing their faces with that cold water by the chuck wagon. Others getting their bed rolls shook and rolled up. Some were saddling up. Cattle were bawling.

In the town of Granite, Sheriff Stanley Malawy was having a discussion with the town elders.

"Is there really any reason to ride out to meet the herd. We pretty well know what they're doing. We know they'll come into town for supplies and do some drinking. You know my brothers and I can pretty well handle anything that they can throw at us. So what's the need to ride out and talk to them."

"Well, maybe we could set some rules. We have heard this man Dolphus Dickenson is a man of honor, that he upholds doing right, that he is a man of integrity. Let's give them a chance to see if they follow his rules. Now, Sheriff Malawy is also a man of integrity, so they say. His brother Tony is Marshall for the territory, and his brother Herman is Sheriff Stanley's deputy. The three of them have worked as miners, gamblers, security guards, and also Texas Rangers. The one thing they probably don't know is that Dolphus Dickenson and his foreman Long John F. Lowther are also old Texas Rangers. They have a reputation for not backing down when the going gets tough."

Sheriff Stanley just told the town elders, "If you all decide that you want me to ride out there and have a talk with them, I will. They should be getting close tomorrow. Tell you what, just to give you peace of mind, me and my deputy will talk to them before they ride into town."

"All right, Sheriff, that sounds good."

The camp picked up and fires out . The cattle are on the move. All hands working the drive. Taters and wagon rolling out. Long John swinging his horse, Easy Rider, around a couple times to see if everything was as should be. Being satisfied, he headed out. When he caught up to OK Bill and Red Fox, they rode along together for some time before Long John said, "Can you two get out in front in a couple of hours. I need to know when that town comes into view. I'd like to get there early even if we have to push a little harder."

"Boss Long John, you know they will know we are coming. And might come out to meet with us. I suspect they will."

"That's okay, we have nothing to hide OK Bill. If you talk to them before I do, just tell them all we want from their town is some supplies and maybe some cold drinks. If we can get our supplies today, we can be out of here tomorrow and leave them alone."

Moving on hour after hour, just after the sun was it highest, the town or something was spotted to the west, and coming over a little rise were a couple of men on horseback.

"That's okay, don't stop till I give the order."

"Okay Boss Long John," Red Fox said.

"Mr. Dickenson, with me, Sir. Let's ride out to meet them."

They were still a long way off. Nonetheless, the two rode slowly in their direction. Neither saying much. Just in case, their rifle was loaded as well as their pistols.

"Sir, remember when we used to Ranger, how we'd have a pistol between our legs when we weren't sure what was coming at us?"

"Yes I do!"

"Let's do it."

Seeming like it was taking a long time, they finally were getting close enough to see their faces. They were just as unsure about us as we were of them. They had their rifles out and laying across their saddles. When we rode up to them, they greeted us.

"Howdy, we're from Granite, the town you're getting close to. My name is Sheriff Stanley Malawy and this is my deputy Herman Malawy. We're brothers."

"Pleased to meet you, Sheriff. This is Dolphus Dickenson, the owner of a ranch in Texas and this is his herd, and I'm John Lowther, his foreman. What can we do for you, Sheriff?"

"Well, the people in town are a little nervous about your bunch. We have had a little trouble with cowboys before."

"Well Sheriff, we mean you no harm. All we want is some supplies and maybe a couple cold drinks. We operate under strict orders from Mr Dickenson. Ours is an unusual bunch. We have Whites, Indians, a Black, a Mexican, and five women. I will say this is a very disciplined bunch. As soon as we stop, I'd like to send in three of my men with a wagon to get our supplies. Is that okay, Sheriff?"

"Yes it is. Thanks for filling in a lot a details. Mr Dickenson, Mr Lowther, we will leave you now. We'll pass on what you said to the townsfolk."

"Before you go Sheriff, have you had any news about Comancheros in the area?"

"We've had a few run ins with them."

"We're heading for Helena, Montana, and wonder how soon we will be attacked, or what about cattle rustlers?"

"We haven't had any homesteads or ranches attacked in a long time. I think they usually stay more to the south of us, but with your big herd going north, you can be sure they gonna want to take it from you. And you said you had women riding with you. They will want them for selling. How about Crow Indians?"

"Some of our people had an attack from a bunch of Crow that didn't go well for the Crow. They didn't want us going through what they said was their territory. So they might be looking for us."

"We haven't seen or heard anything about the Crow either, Mr. Lowther."

"Okay then, Sheriff Malawy. We will be seeing you. Thank for the welcome."

"My pleasure." The sheriff tipped his hat and swung his horse around. He and Herman headed back to Granite, glad to have had a good conversation with Mr. Dickenson. The feeling was the same with Mr. Dickenson and Long John. Long John signaled to OK Bill to stop the herd in about an hour. That should get us close enough to the town. He then got Frankie B.'s attention. Both began heading towards each other. When they were sitting alongside each other, Long John said, "We'll be stopping in about an hour. Soon as we do, get your people together and head into town with the wagon. You got your list?"

"Yes Sir Boss."

"Do everything you can to prevent a fight or an argument from turning into a shootout. These people are nervous as hell for some reason! The sheriff didn't say why. Only that they are."

"I know that Carlyle and Harve can hold their powder and keep their mouth shut. But make sure Tommy knows what's at stake. If you run into trouble and need help, fire two shots fast together and we'll be right there. Okay. That's all. I got to talk to the rest of our people."

Making the rounds, he told everyone the situation and he swung back to where Mr. Dickenson was.

"Sir, what do you think?"

"I don't know. They must have had some bad experiences with a cattle drive."

"I guess so. Well, we'll do everything we can to make this one a good one for them."

"I know you will. We gotta keep these cattle moving. Still got a lot of miles to go."

"Yes Sir. I'd like to move out in the morning if we can get all our supplies today."

"That's good. Sir, I told some of the boys the other day they could go into town for a couple beers, but it would depend on what Frankie B. had to say about the way the people acted toward them around town. And I don't want any drunks the next morning. You going in with them would be a solution."

"Well, I hadn't thought about going in but it might be a good idea. You and I both should go in with them."

"Okay, when we get our supplies, we'll talk about it again."

Back in town, the big talk was all about the Malawy Brothers and what will happen when Bill and Felix Dunaman ride into town with their gang of green bandana boys. As the story goes, Bill was sweet on Margie Malawy, and her on him. But that Tony wouldn't stand for an outlaw like Bill Dunaman marrying his sister Margie. A call out in the street was expected at any time. The Dunaman's had a small ranch and some cattle, maybe five miles north west or so from Granite, and they like to come into town and raise hell every once in a while. Everyone expects them anytime, since they haven't been in town for a while.

Back with the Dickenson herd, OK Bill and Red Fox were beginning to turn the lead cattle towards the river. They might as well load up on water as long as they're near water. Might not have so much in the coming days. Frankie B. got together with Carlyle and told him what Mr. Dickenson and Long John said about getting in town for the supplies as soon as the herd stops.

"Let's stick together, and find Harve and Tommy, and get the wagon from Taters, if he can spare it this early and head for town."

"Hey, we lucked out. There they are over there."

"Before we head for town, I want to say something. Long John and Mr. Dickenson told me a little while ago that there's something making the townsfolks awful nervous. So we want to get in and get our supplies and get a sense of what's going on. I know what you want to do Tommy, but if you can wait till we get back and talk to Long John, then maybe we can go in together for a drink. Is that okay with you two?"

Harve said, "Yeah, I don't care."

Tommy said, "Ah, okay, let's see how it goes."

"Good. So now, let's get the wagon from Taters and ride in. Take your horse and fully loaded guns. If we run into trouble, we are to fire two quick shots and they'll come as fast as they can. Otherwise, no arguments with the townspeople and no gun play. Let's see if we can find out what the nervousness is all about. Who wants to drive the wagon?"

Harve said, "I will. I'll drive it in. Maybe someone else can drive out."

"Okay, let's go," said Carlyle. "Soon as we get in town, let's look for the sheriff's office and the saloon and the supply store."

Couple of miles and there was the town coming into view. Spread out, but not too big. And smoke was coming from something beyond the town. As we found out later, the smoke was from something to do with the mining of lead zinc. We just rode right in. People looked at us. We smiled and did a little waving. They waved back. That is, most waved back. Some gave us a slight nod. And out comes the law. Three tall guys. Looking at them, one could tell they were either brothers or they spent a lot of time together. All three had long black trench coats, big rimmed black hats, coats swung open, three badges, and plenty a hardware, plus a rifle. One started to talk. "My name is Tony Malawy. I'm the Marshall. These two would be the Sheriff and Deputy and they are also my brothers, Stanley and Herman."

"Marshall, we would like to buy some supplies and maybe have some of our people come into town and have a few beers. Would that be okay?"

"Let me tell you what is worrying the townsfolk. My brothers and I are expecting a visit from the Bill and Felix Dunaman gang any time about a family disagreement. I would suggest you do your business and stay clear of the goings on if they happen to ride in while you're still here. Do I make myself clear?"

"Yes Marshall, you do. The last thing we want is to get caught up in someone else's fight. Thank you, Marshall. We will get our supplies and leave."

The Marshall turned and walked back to his office with the other two after him.

Carlyle led the way to the general store that had a big sign above its door just down the street. They tied up their horses and the wagon and went inside.

"Can I help you? Are you all from that Dickenson cattle drive?"

"Yes Sir, we are. We have a list plus a few other things that I will add. Do you have dynamite?"

"Yes I do and cases of bullets, also."

"Okay, one case of dynamite sticks, one case 44-40's, case of 45's, and a box of cigars. My friends here will start carrying things out to the wagon.

Then I'll need the other stuff on the list. I have the cash here; in case your worrying about the money?"
"No sir!! I can see that you and your friends are honest! It's something that shows on a person right away."

Tommy and Harve were watching out the window, people walking the street normally. Carlyle was standing outside by the horses observing everything. Ole Carlyle has that keen sense of insight and quiet observation just like an Indian. They kinda pick up on everything. Carlyle has lived with the Comanche on and off most of his life. He is very much Comanche. The store keeper was moving things along. I guess he knew we didn't want to stick around any longer than we had to.

"Oh Sir, do you have any fruit in cans?"
"Yes I do. What are you looking for?"
"Maybe apples or cherry."
"I do have cherry and apple in a can."
"I'll take three cans of cherry and three cans of apple. We have a lady with the herd that said she will bake a cherry and apple pie if we bring back the fruit. She will need sugar, flour, and lard or butter. Well, I guess I have all that's on the list. We're ready to load. Harve and Tommy, can you think of anything that we are forgetting."
"Did you give us any soap and some towels?"
"Yes Sir, you had it on the list."
"Okay then, how much we owe?"
"Well, that comes to $150."
"Oh, do you have whiskey in bottles or is that something we can only get at the saloon?"
"Saloon, Sir."

"Okay, here's your money. Give me some kinda bill of sale if you don't mind."

"Okay, I don't mind at all."

"I'm not trying to be nosey but what is the family matter that the Marshall was talking about?"

"The three brothers have a sister Margie. And Bill Dunaman wants to marry her and they said no. Bill is supposed to be coming in to town to take her to his ranch. They intend to stop the marriage any way they have to."

"Well, we don't need to get involved in that. Ah, does Granite have a telegraph office?"

"Yes we do, right next to the sheriff's office. Ben. stays open late, sometimes till ten."

"And the saloon, does it have a lot of riffraff just looking for trouble?"

"Ah, sometimes that's all that's in there, but other times not. Today I don't know. I couldn't say. You just have to take your chances."

"Okay Sir, we're through here. Thank you so much."

"Well, thank you for your business. You boys have a safe journey."

"Thanks."

Carlyle and Harve got on their horses. Tommy drove the wagon. Frankie B. motioned for them to hold up. I think with all the supplies we got, we better head back to camp and not take the chance of getting robbed by hanging around here.

Tommy said, "Yeah, I think so."

"Harve and Carlyle, what you think?"

"Yeah," they both agreed.

Tommy snapped the reins and they were on their way out of town.

"Carlyle, what's your sense of the town?"

"Well, tense. Best thing we can do is stay as far away as we can."

The ride back didn't seem to take as long as going. They headed straight for Taters cook wagon. Long John and Mr. Dickenson walked over.

"Everything go alright?"

"Yes Sir. Got the cases like we talked. I got fifty dollars left. Here you are, Mr. Dickenson."

"Okay, thanks."

"And here is a bill of sale for what we bought."

"What's that town like?"

"Tense. They're waiting for something to happen between the Malawy Brothers, who are all of the law, and a gang that call themselves the green bandana gang. Their leader is a Bill Dunaman and his brother Felix. Seems that Bill wants to marry a Margie Malawy. And the brothers say it's not going to happen. No way to know how far each side is willing to go to get their way. Bill and Felix have a small ranch not too far from town. They are expected to ride in anytime. They do have a telegraph office that stays open late, Mr. Dickenson Sir, if you are going in to send a telegraph. Would it be alright if a few of us rode in with you and we stopped at the saloon for a couple of beers?"

"I think that would be alright. What you think, Long John?"

"Yeah. I'm going in to. I don't want to leave the herd unguarded, but I also want to be with our people if they get into trouble."

"Okay, get the supplies put away and ask who wants to go into town for two beers— no more and back! We will be leaving in a few minutes."

"Who's watching the herd now?"

"The Sikorski's and Red Fox."

"Anybody want to go into town to the saloon, saddle up! We're leaving right now."

Taters said, "I'm going. I need a drink."

Dance, Harve, Tommy, Frankie B., Carlyle, and Juan quickly got in the saddle and were heading out.

"That leaves OK Bill, Prairie Flower, Angelina, Grace, Red Fox, Constance, and Antonina to look after things. That should be fine for a couple hours."

OK Bill knows what to do here in camp.

"If anyone of you needs us, fire two shots fast and we will be on our way. We will leave now and be back as soon as we can."

Long John rode off with Mr. Dickenson and caught up to the others. The town quickly came into view. It looked peaceful enough.

"I'll go to the telegraph office and meet you at the saloon as soon as I'm through!"

"Sir, take Dance with you."

"Okay. We'll see you in a little bit."

The saloon was pretty empty, just the barkeep, a piano player, two saloon girls, five men: two at the bar and three at a table playing cards.

"Gentlemen, come right in. What's your pleasure?"

"Set us up with a cold beer," Long John said. "Sip your beer boys, at least wait till Mr. Dickenson gets here before you have your two beers."

With that, the piano player started to play. And in walked Mr. Dickenson and Dance.

"How's the beer boys?"

"Not too cold but tasted pretty damn good. Better get yours."

"Two more beers, Barkeep."

"Coming right up."

Carlyle asked the man for a bottle a whiskey.

"I'll just keep this for the cold nights on the trail."

"Here you go gent, that'll be three dollars."

"How we doing. Anybody ready for your second beer?"

"Set 'em up."

"Drink slow, let me catch up," Dance said.

"Any trouble at the telegraph office, Mr. Dickenson?"

"No. I told the man I'd be in the saloon for a while and to bring me any messages. He said he would so I'd like to wait awhile. I don't think it'll take too long. The three men playing cards at the table started to grumble about not having any beer. The bartender said, "I'll be right there."

One of the men got up and headed for the bar and pushed his way through and spilled Tommy's drink. Everyone moved away to make an opening. The man had on a green bandana. He was standing right in Tommy's face .

"You are in my way, cowboy."

"Well, you spilled my beer, you will have to buy me another one."

"I will have to what?"

"If you don't, we have a big problem."

"A problem like what?" and he backed up to draw on Tommy. Tommy drew so fast, it was like lightning. The man just couldn't believe the speed and it was aimed right at his heart and he knew he was a dead man if he moved a hair. After what seemed like an eternity, Tommy holstered his gun, and turned his back to him.

"Give this man a beer, Barkeep," the man said and walked to the end of the bar to get his beer and paid for his and Tommy's. Tommy was the fastest and coolest ever and no one there will ever forget that day.

Long John said, "Thanks for not escalating the situation!"

"Boss, I knew we couldn't afford to."

"Okay, who's had their second beer?"

Most had. Just then the doors swung open, the man from the telegraph office came bouncing in straight to Mr. Dickenson. "Here's your answer, Sir." He took his tip and left.

"Good news, Sir?"

"Yes. They're all fine and miss all of us. Okay boys, drink up and let's head back to camp."

They downed their last sip, some wiping their mouths on their sleeve and filed out the door. Mr. Dickenson paid the barkeeper and thanked him and went through the swinging doors and mounted up. Slowly they rode out a town. At the edge of town, they picked up the pace and in no time were back in camp.

Taters said, "Someone unsaddle my horse and I'll get to the meal. I suppose you all are hungry."

"Yeah, I guess we could eat a bite."

Tommy was the center of attention. Everyone was still amazed at the lightning speed of his draw. That guy barely touched his gun and Tommy's was aimed at his heart. I wonder if you might be looked for now as the man to beat by gun slingers trying to make a reputation for themselves."

"Sure, there's always that chance."

"Hey Dance, think you can beat this guy?"

"Nah, I don't know. He's my friend. We can try out sometime I guess. Just for fun."

"If you're like lightning, then you might."

"I know. I know. I saw him too, remember. If that guy had come at me like that, I hope I would have been as cool as my friend Tommy here."

"Uh, I think you would have."

"Shows over, let's eat something. Taters, what's on the menu?"

"Well, I got beans, fried potatoes, prairie chicken, thanks to my good friend Red Fox, the silent hunter, and we got rabbit, also thanks to my friend Red Fox."

"The Lord will provide. And Red Fox is his instrument. No pie yet?"

"I'm hoping in a couple days we can all enjoy Mrs. Sikorski's pies. How about it Mrs. Sikorski?"

"That's right, Taters. You give me a little time out of the saddle where I can wash my hands real good and I'll bake your pies!"

"Alright, Long John, you heard her."

"Sounds good, but early tomorrow we are out of here. From now on we are on twenty-four hour a day alert and extra security watches on the cattle and to keep ourselves alive! And I want eighteen to twenty miles a day. We have to start making up time. We still have a long way to go and winter comes early to Montana, folks. Mrs. Sikorski, you make those pies as long as we can keep moving in daylight."

"Yes I can. I have to use the eggs soon or they will go bad. Tomorrow, I will make two pies. As soon as we stop for the day, I'll get started. Antonina and Grace can help if Taters will let them."

"Sounds good," Mr. Dickenson said as he stood up. "I'm looking forward to those pies. My friends, I would like to thank you all for all the hard work you've done and are going to do. Long John is right. We don't have any time to waste. Thanks again. And we really do have to be more vigilant because we might be running into bandit country. Both Whites and Indians and also Comancheros. We, have to be on our guard. Long John will work with all of you to make sure you know that we can defeat any attack if we are prepared and we will be prepared. That's what that case of dynamite is for and a case a bullets. Anyone have any questions, feel free to ask. Thank you all again. It's been a very unusual day. But I did get a message from my wife saying everything is fine on the ranch and that everyone there is waiting for us to return and hope we get to Helena, Montana, before the bad weather hits. I told her we have the best people a cattle drive could have and if anyone could make it, my people could. She sent love and prayers to all of you. I think I will turn in for the day. I will see all of you tomorrow."

With that, Mr. Dickenson washed up a little and bedded down for the night with a book and a smoke by the flickering fire. Long John set all the watches and turned in for the night, too. Red Fox was sitting by the fire talking with Mrs. Sikorski and Juan. OK Bill was off to the side with Prairie Flower. Frankie and Dance were riding around the herd. The two young girls were helping Taters clean up for the night. Tommy and Angelina had the camp watch for the next four hours. Before the girls turned in, they will pile on more wood to keep the fires going and have some light for whoever wants to read or play cards or just sit by the warmth of the fire. Most chose to turn in early because the morning call for breakfast comes in the form of a banging pot or a come and get from the Taters man pretty early. Carlyle was leaning on his saddle by one of the fires having a last smoke for the day, about to pull up his blanket. Before he crushed out his smoke, he placed his rifle where he could reach it like everyone had done before they went to sleep. Harve just got through combing his horse and sweet talking to it. His horse, Jacko, keeps muscling against him as he talked like he understood every word.

"You sure are spoiling that horse, Harve. You better rest up, come here by the fire, and bed down, have a smoke."

"Yes Sir, I be right there. I just talking to Jacko. He likes to be petted, Mr. Carlyle. You know, Mr. Carlyle, I take that smoke now."

"Harve, how long you been with Mr Dickenson?"

"Don't rightly know. Few years I 'spect. Only free job I ever have. I got a good life now, and I wants to keep it. One thing I need to do that I haven't done yet is have a family. When we get back to Texas, I gonna talk to a young lady 'bout that. That is, if she will have me."

"Harve, good for you. How 'bout that tobacco?"

"Yes Sir, Mr. Carlyle, that's a good smoke I have to say. Mr. Carlyle, you and your people gonna stay with Mr. Dickenson when we get back to Texas?"

"I'm sure it would be very tempting if he'd have us, but we have to get back to the Comanche chief in Oklahoma. We promised the chief we would bring his two women members of his tribe back and if there's going to be any weddings, they would take place there in his camp with him. That was the conditions the chief set and we all agreed to it. You know, Angelina is my granddaughter! My son was married to Prairie Flower, her mother, when he got killed in a raid. So I have a connection to the tribe, you could say. Harve, I really enjoy talking with you but it's getting late and we all have to get up early and get these cattle moving."

"Yes Sir, but thank you for telling me all those things. I will lie down after I go look at the moon and wash my face. Good night."

"Good night, Harve. We will talk again."

By now, things have pretty well settled down. You could hear snores here and there. Fires crackling with a warm blue glow. All things are now in the hands of the night watch. Some said prayers to protect all of the cowhands and the cattle. Night will pass as always. And so it did.

Well, here we go, just before light: coffee is cooking, fresh water in the pan, and towels to get those sleepy eyes opened up, and cattle bawling. I guess even the cattle are ready to get moving. Mr. Dickenson was already having his coffee.

"Morning everybody. Let's wrap it up folks. The sooner we get going, the sooner we will get there. Breakfast is hot, but won't stay that way long. OK Bill and Red Fox, soon as you have your breakfast, you can get out in front and start them moving. Everybody remember what I said about extra vigilance. From now on, we are a target for bandits and hostiles. There's a lot of open country. Okay Long John, all men, two rifles and three pistols on you and fully loaded. Women, when you're away from the cook wagon, two rifles, one pistol in a holster, and two on you somewhere, loaded and ready for anything. Might seem like over doing it, but remember— shoot to kill or you won't stay alive. Okay people, we're moving out in fifteen minutes. Get those fires doused, pick up everything."

Frankie B. helped Prairie Flower and Angelina saddle their horses. Juan was driving the wagon with all the supplies, one rifle at his feet and another behind his back on the seat. Taters was on the cook wagon with Grace. They are well-armed, too. Carlyle kicked out a fire, looked all around, lit up a roll your own, and got in the saddle, checked his rifles, and pistols. Everything was on the move. OK Bill and Red Fox knew the routine: keep 'em, moving as fast as they can stand. The beef will lose some weight but they can gain it back fast when they get where they're going.

Long John was talking to Mr. Dickenson, "You think we should give each man two or three sticks of dynamite and a couple cigars with matches?"

"Yes, if they are not afraid to use them."

"Okay Sir, I will make the rounds and talk to everyone."

Frankie B. was the first to put three sticks in his saddle bags and cigar and matches in his shirt pocket. All the men agreed and took their share. Mrs. Sikorski said, "I'll take three and a cigar."

"Ma'am, you don't have to. We are already asking a lot of you just riding herd but don't expect you to throw dynamite."

"That's okay, Long John. I want to do all I can and you know no one would ever expect me to fight like that. Right?"

"You're right. I have to admit it, Ma'am."

Hours are passing. Everyone stops when they have to make a nature call or check a horse's shoe. Sometimes you stop just to rearrange your clothes." Mrs. Sikorski got her sticks and a cigar. The day was a full one pushing cattle, keeping them all moving in the same direction.

"The extra horses haven't been a problem, Long John, maybe we should ride them once in a while. I don't think that they will forget that they're tame, so to speak. But it might be good. And that'll give our horses a rest. I don't know if that makes any sense or not."

"Yeah, Taters, that could make a lot a sense. We can mention it to everybody. Those extra saddles, too. Anyone can use a different one anytime they want to as far as I'm concerned."

Mrs. Sikorski was starting to think about making pies. "Pretty soon I'll get started. As soon as I can stop and Taters stops, I can wash up a little, and start rolling out some dough, flour, and water, and crack a few eggs. Ah yeah, been awhile since I've done anything that could be called woman's work."

The herd is starting to slow down. That means Taters will be heading for a flat spot near a water hole if there is one. I can catch up with him. Antonina can help when she gets the horses settled in for the night.

Long John pulled up to Mr. Dickenson and yelled over to him, "We did good today. Now we can rest up and do it all over again tomorrow."

Chapter 8

Mrs. Edwards, José, and Tim Shiloh are nearing Arnett, Oklahoma. Making pretty good time for two injured people. Their injuries are healing up pretty well considering all the bouncing on horseback. Tim has to hold back for their sake. So far, no problem. Every time they pass someone or talk to someone at a water hole, they're warned to be alert for Comancheros. They are in the area. Many times they were told that they'd kill your asses and take the women.

"Yes Sir, we know that. That's why we can't let that happen."

José's wounds are pretty well healed up on his leg and his arm. Mrs. Edwards is a little slower with her side wound and all that bouncing. Anybody trying to take her captive is surely in for a big surprise, even with her side still hurting some.

José says, "Señora Margaret Edwards is the toughest mujer gringo alive!"

"And what I've heard about her, I damn well believe it! Ma'am, looks like we are coming into a town."

"I know, Tim, I been seeing it. How 'bout we have a doc take a look at my side?"

"Ma'am, I will find us a doctor."

Didn't take long for them to be riding right down the street to a doctor's shingle hanging above a door. They stopped and got off their horses. Margaret did need a little help. Tim was right there to lend a hand.

"Thanks, Tim."

"My pleasure, Ma'am."

"I can walk."

The door opened and an attractive woman who said, "Do you need any help?"

"No, I can walk myself."

Tim was thinking, *She must have been fooling me because I thought she was going pretty good, and now this.*

The doctor looked at her and said she has an infection. "I will need to lance it and hope we can get the infection under control or it will kill her. She will have to stay right here for a couple days. Can we get these dirty clothes off her?"

"Of course, Doctor, do what you have to."

"I'll have my wife get her cleaned up. You two can wait in the other room or outside."

"José, Tim," Margaret called them. She held their hands, one on each side. "You guys don't leave without me."

"We won't, Ma'am."

"Si, we are not going anywhere without you."

The doctor's wife took her clothes off her and gave her a sponge bath as much as she could. The doctor's wife's name was Ursula.

She asked, "Where are you from with all these guns, lady?"

"Well, if you only knew," and just left it at that.

"Ah, don't go too far without my guns. They have

saved my life a few times, and I'm kinda attached to them!"

"Yes Ma'am. But you should be safe here in Arnett."

"Don't bet on it, Ma'am."

José said, "Señor Tim, we better find a place to clean up and to sleep."

"Maybe if we clean up a bit, the doc will let up sleep on the floor in the room with Margaret."

"Si, maybe. Let's ask him now."

Tim knocked on the door to the other room. The doctor opened the door.

"Yes, ah, Doctor, where can we find a place to take a bath?"

"There's a bath house in back of the saloon down the street."

"Thanks, Doctor. Sir, if we cleaned up, will you let us sleep on the floor in Margaret's room? We don't want to leave her alone."

"I think that would be just fine. You two get something to eat and clean up. Then come back, put your horses around the back of this building. I hope to have Margaret sleeping and healing."

"Okay Doc, you don't know how much we appreciate it. We will be back as soon as we can." The door closed.

"Let's take a look at the back of the building, José . Oh, there's plenty of room back here. You wanna leave the horses back here now?"

"Maybe we should, seeing as how we have a lot of extra gear, rifles, and all."

"And Margaret's pack horse. Yeah, let's take what we need for a bath and walk. You got a change a clothes, don't ya?"

"Si."

"Since we got to go in the bar, you wanna have a beer?"

"Si, that would be good."

In the bar they got some hard looks. The bartender asked, "What'll it be?"

"Two beers, and how do we get to the bath house?"

"Right through that door."

A voice from somewhere said, "Looks like it's about time. All that grease from the greaser rub off on you, boy?"

They didn't answer back, just kept sipping their beers.

"Hey boy, I'm talking to you."

Tim turned and said, "You talking to us, boy." And spotted where the voice was coming from. It was a disheveled looking middle aged man just itching for a fight. Must have had too many beers 'cause he started to get up and his friends pushed him back down. One said, "Sorry Mister. He's had too much to drink."

José said, "Si, okay," and turned back to finish his beer.

Tim said, "Let's get to our baths."

"Si, Tim."

They paid and went through the big door and there it was, a big bath room with plenty of tubs.

"Boy, I tell you, I can't wait to soak my ass."

The proprietor was Chinese. He said, "You want bath?"

"Si. And can you have someone wash our clothes?"

"Yes. We do right away. You get in tub and soak."

"Bring that table over here by the tub. I need to put my things on it while I soak," Tim said.

"Okay, right away."

"And one for my friend here."

"Okay, right away."

Tim said, "Sure as hell we don't keep our guns close or that dumb son of a bitch will come through that door and get the drop on us. I intend to be ready. A smoke in the tub is, well, 'bout the best thing there is."

They managed to get through their baths without an interruption. Shaved, shook the dust off their hats, put on their clean clothes.

"How much do we owe you?"

"Two dollar each for everything."

"Here. José, you want to get something to eat now?"

"Si. I hope that drunk is sleeping it off somewhere. If he's not, then we might have a problem."

"You go out back door. You no have trouble."

"Let's go out the back José."

"Si."

Walking around the building in the street, they probably looked like different people all cleaned up. Except for José's sombrero. Tim has a large Vaquero style flat brimmed tan hat. Once they got the dust off, they looked like new. The Pink Cup Restaurant had good food to their liking. They ate up and headed for the doctor's place. They couldn't wait to see if Margaret had made any improvements, or whether the doctor had any new ideas.

"Let's check on the horses first."

"Okay."

They took the saddles off and put them on the railing, put the clothes in the saddlebags, took their rifles and saddlebags with them. José grabbed

Margaret's saddlebag also. They stepped up on the little porch and one of them knocked. The doctor's wife was quick to open the door. "Come in, come in, we have good news. Margaret is doing remarkably well."

"Thank God for that." José made the sign of the cross on himself and said something in Spanish. "Bring your things in and put them in the room where you will sleep."

"Okay Ma'am, thank you."

The doctor was with her. "I'm pretty sure I got the infection under control. I had to cauterize the wound and destroy some infected tissue around the wound. It has to be kept clean no matter what."

"Can she ride, Doc?"

"I wouldn't advise it."

"How 'bout a wagon, laying down?"

"Better. Let's let her sleep and see in the morning."

"Okay."

"Si, Doctor."

Margaret looked at the both of them and smiled. "I'll be okay. Boy, you guys look so clean and clean shaven, too."

"We had our clothes washed. We should get yours washed, too. Where are yours? I'll see if I can get them washed today."

"That pile over there."

"I'll go with you, Señor Tim."

"Okay, maybe you better go with me. I guess we have to walk, huh?"

"Si, unless we want to saddle two horses to go across town."

"Let's go before it gets too late. Margaret, you need anything or something to eat?"

"No, I'm fine. Ursula fed me. I'm good."

"Okay, we'll be right back."

The wash house wasn't too far. With every step, José's spurs made their sound and announced his coming on the board walk. Tim wears spurs sometimes but left them off after the bath. The walk didn't take too long. They could see that the saloon was filling up with all kinds of men. They really didn't want any trouble, so they went around the back to the bath house and knocked on the door. It opened and the same person said, "Come in. What we do for you, Sir?"

"Can you wash these clothes and dry them in about an hour?"

"Yes Sir, you come back in hour. We have ready. Two dollar, please."

"Okay, here you go. We'll be back in one hour." Back to the street walking along, the sheriff and a deputy came up to them.

"Can you tell me what you are doing in Arnett?"

"Sure, Sheriff." They explained everything they went through, and Margaret's condition at the doctor's office. And that they would like to leave town tomorrow. But they don't think that would be possible unless the doctor says she can travel.

"Okay, you are welcome to stay as long as you want but I will be keeping an eye on the both of you, so no trouble while you're here."

"Yes, Sheriff."

"Si, Señor Sheriff."

"The last thing we want is trouble."

They each tipped their hats at each other and moved on.

" I don't know why he thinks we are trouble."

"Si, it's probably because of me, Señor. A Mexican with guns is always a trouble maker."

"Yeah, you're probably right. We have to prove them wrong, José. I gotta look for a crapper."

"There's one back of the wash house. Let's go there and maybe Margaret's clothes will be ready by the time you're through."

"Okay."

The sheriff wasn't kidding about keeping an eye on us. See there, he's sitting outside his office watching every move we make. If we can, we should get outta this town tomorrow or that sheriff will surely pin something on us."

"Si."

After they both used the outhouse, the clothes were ready and they headed back to the doctor's office. A couple of cowboys came through the swinging doors at the saloon and trouble was written all over their faces. Nearly knocked them over.

"You know Mex's are not allowed on the streets after dark. You better get your asses off the street. Be dark soon. That goes for greaser lovers, too."

"Thank you, we'll keep that in mind."

"Will you look at that, a smart ass greaser lover." He pulled his pistol out but not fast enough. Tim was faster. No shots were fired. Tim took the pistol out of his hand and handed it to the sheriff, who was already coming across the street.

"Are we free to go, Sheriff?"

"Yeah, go ahead. I saw the whole thing. Damn good thing I did or I would have thought you started it."

"Thanks, Sheriff."

"Let's get out of here. It will be dark soon. Let's check our horses."

"Sure, Señor. Horses were fine."

"You know, I kinda have an idea. You think Margaret would be more comfortable in a wagon. Maybe we could buy one and use her extra horse to pull it. If it wouldn't cost too much."

"I don't know. Si, maybe."

"In the morning, let's check with the livery stable or blacksmith."

A knock on the door got them in the doctor's office and in the room with Margaret.

"How you boys doing?"

"Ah, we're okay. We came close to finding ourselves in jail."

"What?"

"Yeah. If the sheriff hadn't seen the whole thing, I'd say that's where we would be right now. I don't think we are very well respected here and some of the folks don't like Mexicans, they actually told us so. Let's get you well and get out of here before the sheriff frames us with something. And we get stuck in jail or worse. Margaret, can you ride without hurting yourself more. What does the doctor say?"

"I don't know. Is he in the other room. José, can you check?"

"Si, sure. Doctor, can you come in here?"

"Yeah. Gimme a minute. What can I help you with?"

"Doctor, can Margaret ride or would it be better if she rode in a wagon?"

"Ah, neither one is good if she wants to get better but if she sat in a wagon or even drove it, it might be better than riding if the seat had those springs to take some of the shock and she could lay down if she gets tired, and you could drive for a while. How about those Indian poles on the side of a horse? She could lay down?"

"Yeah, but where you gonna find any of those around here."

"Okay, we'll see about a wagon. We got an extra horse. If it will pull a wagon, I think we can get it. We'll check on it in the morning. Okay, Doctor?"

Tim said, "I'm gonna lay down here on my blanket and go to sleep. You two can talk all you want. You won't bother me."

"All right, Tim. José, if you want to sleep, you go right ahead."

"I will talk to you for a while, Señora."

José fixed his blanket and before he said a few words, he was sleeping. Margaret didn't waste much time either. Just as well. Maybe they could get an early start. They even forgot to tell her they had her clothes cleaned and dried. No matter, she can put them on in the morning. Ursula and Doc just left the room to let them sleep. Ursula and Doc were early risers, so they were already up before the three opened their eyes. Ursula did the cooking around there. The coffee, biscuits, and gravy were enough to wake them. As they thought this was a replay of the last town, Stillwater, that Doc Clark and his wife doctored them up and fed them in the morning.

Margaret said, "José, Tim, can you two help me? I've got to pee real bad and if I don't get off this bed, I'm gonna pee all over myself."

That got them to move. Ursula heard the voices and came in with a bucket.

"This is for Margaret. You two go to the outhouse in back and I'll help Margaret before she busts. Now git."

It was a warm, bright morning. One could hear a dog bark and a chicken crow. The smell of coffee was everywhere. After a wash in the pan near the door, they were back in the house.

Ursula said, "Don't you go anywhere. Sit right here."

Doc was at the table reading his town paper. Margaret was at the table with the biggest smile to greet the two. "I found my clothes. Thanks. They feel good and smell good, too. Did you sleep good?"

"Boy, did we."

José said, "Si, I sleep very good."

"Dig in you three. Don't be holding back. You must be hungry. We like having friends to eat with, right Irving?"

"Yes we do."

"José, here's the cream and sugar. We have friends from Mexico. We know how you like your coffee."

"Thank you, Señora. We are very grateful for all you are doing for us. We are thinking about buying a wagon, Margaret, and having your pack horse pull it with you on it. What do you think?"

"It will have to be one that doesn't bounce so hard. We don't want that side of yours breaking open any more. Do you think you could drive a wagon for a couple hours a day sitting on a soft seat?"

"Yeah, I can. But why all the pampering?"

"Don't you worry about us pampering you. We want to."

"Doc, Ma'am, do you know where we might find a wagon?"

"Yes. The blacksmith has a few wagons. You should be able to find what you're looking for, right Irving?"

"Right, and if not, then check the stable. He has horses and wagons, too. You know, I like that idea you had about the Indian poles, Tim."

"Yeah, but a wagon will have to do. Maybe we will run across some friendly Indians and they can show us how to make a sled. I guess that's what you call them."

"Okay Margaret, you stay here till we get a wagon. What do you think it'll cost, Doc?"

"Don't know, maybe twenty dollars."

"Hum, you know we still have one of those Indian rifles. You think we could trade it for a wagon?"

"Maybe, but I'm not sure we should. Might need it, Tim."

"Okay, how many rifles do we have?"

"Four, not counting the Crow rifle. Margaret one, you two, me one. I think we can trade it if they'll take it . What you two think?"

"I guess and maybe we can trade the wagon back for a rifle somewhere if we think we won't need the wagon later."

"Yeah maybe. That makes sense. Okay, and if they won't take the rifle, then we buy the wagon if we have enough money or we try to sell the rifle to someone in town. Okay, let's go José."

"Si."

"First, let's saddle up our horses and take the Crow horse with us. We can leave Margaret's here for now."

Riding through town, the blacksmith came up first. The Smithy was shaping a horseshoe.

"You got any buckboards?"

"Yeah, what you needing?"

"Let's see what you got."

"Right over there."

"What they cost?"

"That beat up one over there, I'll take twelve dollars. That little better one next to it, fifteen."

"We need something we can get across the open country with a wounded woman not bouncing as much as on a horse for a few hundred miles."

"Tell you what, I'll give you this better one for twelve if you got a hurt woman."

"You think this Indian pony will pull the wagon?"

"Yeah, they usually are used to pulling sleds as well as being ridden."

"We have a Crow rifle here. Would you be interested in buying it?"

"Maybe, let's see it. Pretty nice. Give you twenty bucks for it."

"José, what you think?"

"How 'bout twenty bucks and you shoe this horse Señor?"

"Okay. Then you buy the wagon for twelve? I'll get you the money. Here's two saw bucks (two ten dollar bills). Bring that horse in here and I'll shoe him now."

"When you get through, does he need any time to get used to the shoes?"

"Some do but most don't."

"Then let's hitch him up to that wagon. José, you got us a good deal. I wonder if Margaret would like to have her horse shod?"

"I suppose so but I don't know if we can afford to now. I guess she can switch horses if she wants to and ride the one with the shoes once she starts riding again."

"I guess so. Meanwhile, if she can drive the wagon and not end up with that infection all over again, that will be a blessing. It shouldn't be much farther to catch up with the cattle herd. Once we do, we can take better care of her. Let's get this pony hitched up and see what he thinks about his new shoes and the wagon he's going to pull for us. He's been eating the smithy's oats. He ought to be in a good mood, you think?"

Hitched up, the horse didn't seem to care one way or the other. José got on the seat and drove him around a little. He did just fine.

"If we are all squared up, Smithy, we will be on our way. Thanks for everything."

"My pleasure, gents. Maybe we can do some trading again sometime."

"Maybe."

Tim tied José's horse to the wagon and jumped on his horse. They rode over to the doctor's place. Margaret was getting ready. She walked pretty good, leaning forward a little. The boys came in the front door. Margaret and the doctor and Ursula were talking. Ursula was saying how she was amazed at the strength Margaret seemed to have.

"I'm not so strong, but I have been through a lot in the last month or two. It's hardened me up and I have learned to survive. Now I just want to catch up with all our friends and Mr. Dickenson's cattle drive. What will come after that, I don't know. But Ma'am, you and the doctor have been good to the three of us. Thank you so much. How much do we owe you?"

"If you have a few dollars, that would be enough."

"José, how much do we have?"

"We are okay, Señora. We have a few dollars."

"How about we give the doc five dollars?"

"Si, we do that. What he did for you is worth much more, I'm sure."

"No, no, that will be enough. You just keep your money. You might need it somewhere else. We will be happy with five dollars. And we are happy to have met the three of you. You know your next town will be Higgins, Texas. You probably should wait there till the herd comes through."

"That will give you more time to heal up. You all act like real gentlemen and lady. Not like some of the patients I see a lot of."

"Thank you. If we pass this way again, we will stop by to see you."

"That would be just fine."

After a few hugs and handshakes, they were on their way. Margaret said she would try driving. She had an extra blanket on the seat, a rifle at her feet, one behind the seat, and three pistols on her. And the horse did just fine. Margaret talked to it real soft and it loved it. Her other horse was tied on to the wagon. She was driving along with the two men alongside her keeping a close eye on her. They were making good time.

"I would say that was a good idea, the wagon with the spring seat, Señora. What you think?"

"It is a lot softer. I feel like I can do this for hours. Let's put on as many miles as we can before dark."

"Okay, Señora. We'll let you decide when to stop."

"Okay, José. You guys are spoiling me to no end. But I love you both. If we get to Higgins today or tomorrow, we should wait like the doctor said and ask around about the herd. Surely someone will have heard about the big herd coming up from Texas, I would think."

"You're right, Margaret. We still got some rough territory to cover but not for long. Maybe all day tomorrow. Then we should be there by night fall."

"I think we should stop for the night. I need one of you to change my bandage. It's turning red."

"Oh Margaret, you should have stopped sooner. Can you make it to that high spot where we can see all around?"

"Yes I can. Heya pony, let's go a little farther. Then you can stop for the night."

Over a few more rocks and holes they went. They helped Margaret to the back of the wagon.

"Lay back and let me see that bandage," José said. "Good thing we have plenty of extra bandages. I think I should wash my hands with a soap bar and water first."

"Okay, good idea, José."

José did. Then he took off the old bandage. It was a little red. He washed it softly and put on some salve the doc gave them and added a new bandage."

"That feels so good, José. Thanks."

"My pleasure, Señora."

"I can walk around a little."

Tim was getting a fire started in a low spot.

"I don't want this fire to show for miles in the dark. What we got for a meal?"

"Beans, bread, piece of meat we can heat up, and coffee."

"Sounds good."

"Margaret, don't do too much walking around. Sit here with your rifle and be our watch. Night is coming on fast."

Sun gone over the western mountains. Nice cool breeze keeping the bugs away. Saddles off the horses for a pillow.

"Do we still have that Crow bow and arrow?"

"Yeah. I'm gonna see if I can get a rabbit or grouse."

"Okay, Tim, you think you can hit one with it."

"I dunno. I'll try. Be back as soon as I can."

José got everything going for the meal that they had. "Señora, will you be alright for a little bit? I have to go."

"Yes José, go ahead. When you come back, I'll go, too."

"Okay, Señora."

Tim had a little luck. He got a grouse with the arrow and came back to camp.

"Where's José?"

"Ah, he had to go to the bathroom. Soon as he gets back, I 'm gonna go. Ah, what we using for wipes?"

"Whatever you can. We don't have anything special."

"I need to go too."

José came back and said, "Soon as I wash my hands, I'll help you up, Señora."

"Okay, José."

"José, if you want to get this grouse ready for cooking, I'll help Margaret. We both have to go."

By the time the two got back, the grouse was almost ready for the fire. They washed up as best as they could without using too much water.

"José, how's that bird coming?"

"I got it on a stick. There'll be a couple bites for the three of us."

"Okay, good. Margaret, keep a watch all around if you can."

"Okay, Tim, I will. If anybody has a fire going, we need to know. If you see its glow in the dark, it could mean someone is after us."

"Is that bird ready yet, José?"

"Si, here, have a bite and pass it on to Tim."

"Ah, that don't taste bad. A little salt and pepper helps a lot."

"We have some bread here."

"Okay, that'll have to do us till we get to the town. We'll be there early tomorrow, I figure, 'cause we're not too far away. Soon as you two want to go to sleep, just go ahead. I'll stay up and watch. José, you want to take over from me in about four hours?"

"Si."

"Margaret, you can relieve José in another four."

"That will be fine. We might be around Higgins for quite a while if that herd don't get there soon."

"I know. Hope somebody knows something about it. They will be looking out for us, too, so we can't miss them with a big herd like that. I figure they will probably want to stay a little west of Higgins either way."

"Yeah. Be good to get back with my good friends. And I guess you two'll be glad to see your friends."

"Si."

"Yes it will. We went through a lot with Frankie B. and OK Bill and the others. I miss my baby girl, Gracie." After a little more small talk, the two were off to sleep. Tim was very much awake. They didn't want to be careless now. The night was just another night. Nothing special. With morning coming, they were ready to move out after a couple cups of coffee and some left overs. The wagon was hitched up and on the move with all their belongings. Margaret was driving with two riding alongside.

"Now Margaret, if you would rather lay in the back, you just say."

"Tim, I think I will get in the back. I don't feel up to driving."

"Okay. José, you want to drive or you want me to drive?"

"You drive, Señor Tim. I would like to look around. I have a feeling we are being watched."

"Keep your guns close."

"You, too, Señora. I will look around and be back as soon as I can."

"Alright José, be safe my friend."

First thing José did was drop back and get off his horse. He didn't know if his horse would lay for him, but he tried it and he did. So they were both as low as could be and blended in with the sage brush. Both he and his horse were motionless for what seemed like a long time. And just as he thought, they are being followed or at least someone was going the same direction as they were. José could hear a noise. He couldn't tell what it was. He thought, *I'm gonna stay right here and let that noise pass me by since I'm off to the side, if my horse don't bolt and get me shot. Or whatever.* He started to talk to Rollo in Spanish. And Rollo responded almost with a muffled purr. The noise kept coming closer till finally José could see it was a man walking a horse with a young boy and girl seated on the horse. Looking all around, José could see there was no one else. He thought it was time to get up. But did not want to scare the life out of them. He just got up slowly. The man stopped in his tracks and froze.

José assured them he would not hurt them. They seemed to be relieved.

"What are you doing out here with those los jõvenes (young ones), Señor?"

"We are going to Higgins, Sir."

José must have been a sight. He probably looked like a bandit. He assured them he was not.

"But what are you doing out here all alone?"

"These are my grandchildren. I am taking them to their parents in Higgins."

"Okay, you can explain later. For now, get on that horse. Give me one young one and you one and we will catch up to my friends. The children can ride in a wagon with my friend! Let's hurry and catch up."

"We mustn't be far from Higgins."

"Yes sir, we are not far."

The boy got on with José.

"See my friends up ahead?"

"Yeah, we see them."

Catching up with Tim, he stopped with a surprised look on his face. And Margaret sat up, also wondering what was going on. José just shook his head.

"I don't know. Señora, maybe you can find out what these people are doing out here."

José said, "You children get in the wagon and we will go. Don't press up against Señora Edwards. She was injured."

The man was not sure what was happening with his grandchildren.

"Don't worry, Grandpa," the girl said. "The lady is nice. Grandpa, don't be sad. We are fine. José didn't hurt us. We need to go back to Higgins to Mama and Papa."

"What's your names?"

"I'm Agatha and this is Joseph. Grandpa is John Malawy. Grandpa was taking us to meet a stage coach."

"Out here?"

"That's what Grandpa said."

"I don't think there is one."

"It's supposed to come through here somewhere."

"Nah, I'd find it hard to believe a stage would go through this dangerous area. Why, they'd get everyone killed. They'd never out shoot the bandits or Crow. Something wrong with that."

"We were supposed to go to St. Louis."

"If all that's true, then somebody made a bad decision. And your parents let you go with your grandpa?"

"Yes."

"Your grandpa seems to be a little unsure about everything. Yes, Grandpa has been sick."

All the talking has been going on while they were riding. Tim was the first to see a town coming up over the hill.

"Grandpa look, Higgins."

"When we get in town, show us where your parents are."

"Okay. Phyllis Evens is our mama and she is married to Clem Wilson. He runs the Water Hole Saloon. Our papa died a few years ago."

"Is there a doctor in town?"

"Yes, Doctor Bill Dieterich. He's nice. Grandpa goes to him once in a while."

Two riders were coming out to meet them. Yeah, sure enough they stopped in front of us.

they have been caught and have to kill all of us to cover it up."

"I wish I knew just how far that herd is from us. I'd like to peel off to the south now and see if we could run into it and get some help from Mr. Dickenson and the cowhands. We gotta think fast. What are we to do? Whatever we do, we keep these kids and Grandpa with us. Do you both agree?"

"Yes."

"Before we get too close, let's stop and switch around a bit. How 'bout Grandpa drive the wagon or one of the kids drive the wagon. Margaret, can you get on horseback?"

"Sure I can. I'd be the best help on horseback if a shootout comes."

"Grandpa, can you shoot that rifle on your horse?"

"Yes, I used to be a pretty good shot at one time."

"Well, I hope you can now. You might have a chance to see if you still are. You kids listen up, can one of you drive that wagon?"

"I can, Sir. We both can."

"Okay. Joseph you drive. Agatha, you get in the back. We are going to turn left to the south when we get a little closer and get as far away from town as we can. Margaret, get on your horse now from the wagon. Nobody stop. Joseph, you get up here and take the reins. You got to hold tight, Joseph."

"Okay, I got 'em."

"José, you think we can turn left now? Let's go. Joseph, follow José. Agatha, you keep an eye on the sheriff. Has he stopped or is he still going into town?"

"Still going into town."

"Okay, let's get as far away as we can. Joseph, you're doing great."

"Señor Tim, let's keep going. If they come after us, we can stop and take a stand."

"Grandpa, do you have any family in town?"

"No. Wife's dead, son's dead."

"Agatha, that true?"

"Yes, our papa is dead. Our mama married again. Our step papa owns the saloon. He talks mama into things all the time."

"So Grandpa don't have any relatives?"

"As far as we know, he don't."

"Agatha, I'm asking because if you or Grandpa does, they could use them to get us to give you up as hostages. What you think they will do with your mama?"

"Grandpa says she won't help us. She don't care about us. She does what he says, Mr. Tim. It's getting harder to see what's going on in town."

"That's okay. We'll keep going. If they start coming after us, we'll see the dust."

José said, "They could fool us and say they will kill their mother if we don't come in and we won't know for sure."

"I know. How 'bout we stop and stay here for the night, and I'll sneak into town after dark, and have a look around. If their mama is being held against her will, I'll get her out."

"I don't know about that. How about you and I both go and get her, even if she isn't being held against her will. If she is involved in this act, she needs to be held accountable."

"I agree but just how do we pull this off. We should be able to find her somewhere around the saloon, I

234

would think. Between the two of us, we should be able to tie her up and carry her out of town."

"Okay, let's try. Margaret, you are going to have to stay here and keep a fire going so they think we are all here. If some of them try to sneak out here to us, then you have to do what you have to. Grandpa, Joseph, Agatha, come here. José and I are going into town to get the kids' mama. You have to stay here and help Margaret with whatever she needs you to do. And don't leave. Stay close together and keep a fire going and eat something and look after each other."

"Okay, we will."

"Where do you think we can find your mama?"

"Upstairs of the saloon. There's a stairway in the back. Her room is the first one on the left when you get upstairs. She might be drunk and asleep. If you take your horses into town, tie them up in the back. Hardly anyone uses those stairs. Mama goes out the back to get some air a lot. You could be there just as she is going out for some air."

"You think someone could be watching her, thinking she might sneak off?"

"I don't think we would know, Sir. Mama does what Clem tells her to. Mama said she is afraid of him. She told us he said he would kill Joseph and me if she didn't do what he says."

"Have you or Grandpa ever heard what he is doing that she is so afraid of him for?"

"She never did say. Only thing said is that sometimes she thinks he might have had something to do with my daddy's death."

"Oh kids, you have been a lot of help. Margaret, Grandpa, stay alert. We will be back as soon as we can. Pretty dark now. You ready, José?"

"Si."

"Let's ride as quietly as we can."

Chapter 9

They rode, not straight, but swung around just a little to kinda come in at the back side of town. The sod and dirt were soft coming in close to the edge of town. The horses hooves didn't make a sound. They both took off their hats and spurs and agreed that they didn't want to kill anyone if possible. But if they had to, no bullets. Only as a last resort. They both said they could use a knife very well. Coming up to the back of the saloon, they saw the steps and tied up their horses to a hitching post close to an outhouse. Looking all around and listening. Nothing but the piano in the saloon, that was good.

José said, "Before we go upstairs, I want to look up and down the street."

They both walked along the side of the building. Nobody in the street.

"I see the sheriff's office. Wonder where he is right now? I'm going around the front and look in the saloon and see what I can see."

"Si, Tim. Be careful."

Quite a few men inside and a couple of women walking around. There was one table that had men discussing something important. And most likely it was what to do about the kids and grandpa.

"Okay, we better get going with our plan before they get up from that table and start looking for us. Only thing is, I'd like to know which one is Wilson, I'd grab him to if I could!"

"Si. Maybe so, let's go."

A few horses were tied up in a few places down the street. Back around and upstairs, the door was unlocked. There is the room; no one in the hallway, now listen with an ear against the door.

Tim said, "All quiet in there. She must be asleep. I'll try the doorknob."

It turned and opened. There she was asleep on the bed.

"How do we keep her mouth shut?"

"Put a scarf in her mouth. If she wakes up, keep her quiet."

She didn't wake up.

"Okay, let's roll her in that blanket. What does she have on?"

"Her street clothes."

"Good. Let's roll her up and get outta here."

"Is there anything here we should take?"

"Grab that box. It looks like it might be some kinda medicine and grab those shoes."

Out the door and down the steps they went. Tim got on his horse and José pushed her up to him. The only way he could hold her was against himself with her head over his shoulder. She was out cold; if not drunk, then she had to be drugged up on something. She really didn't smell like alcohol. I would think she would if she was drunk. Looks like maybe someone was keeping her drugged up for a reason. So she stays out the way. *I think she will sleep all the way back*, he thought. He couldn't help but feel her body against his and smell her. There is something about the scent of a woman, even a drunk woman, that's making him breathe deeply. She smelled clean and like flowers. José got on his horse, and away they went back to their camp. A little ways away they could ride a little faster. Tim didn't want this ride to end. He was overwhelmed with this woman: the smell, the feeling of her soft body against his. When they got back to camp, Margaret heard them coming and was waiting.

"Have any trouble?"

"None. Any here?"

"No."

"Take this woman down and lay her in the wagon. She's out cold. Check her mouth. We stuck a scarf in her mouth. We didn't know if she would yell out and get us killed so we used the scarf."

"Okay, nah, she's breathing good. She don't smell of alcohol."

"I think she's drugged, not drunk."

"Tim, you could be right."

"How's everything here?"

"The kids are sleeping, Grandpa's standing guard with me."

"Grandpa, what you think? Is she drunk or drugged?"

"I don't know anything about drugs. She was a nice person before she fell in with Wilson. I don't know what he could have done to make her change."

"Maybe he's threatened her. I still feel like going back into town and grabbing him. José, you think we could grab him?"

"Maybe Señor, if we knew who he was. Right now, we don't."

"He was probably one of the ones sitting at that table in the saloon a few minutes ago."

"Yeah. If he had any intentions of coming up to her room for the night, he's probably there right now finding out that she's not there."

"Or will find out in the morning and then we can expect to have somebody come out here asking us a lot questions. Should we pretend like we don't know anything about her or should we say we got her."

José said, "I think we should say we will only talk to Wilson and don't even admit that we have her. Let's keep them guessing for a while. Keep her hidden here and get as much information out of him as we can."

"That's good, José. You think we can get any sleep tonight?"

"I sure don't know. They might be creeping around in the dark right now heading this way. So I don't know how we can sleep. I am going out, Señor, to see if we are being spied on! If anyone is out there, I will know. I was good at reconnaissance at one time. I think I can still do good, Señor."

"Oh, I'm sure you can."

Margaret was trying to revive Phyllis. She still wasn't coming around but she was mumbling something.

"I hope we don't lose her. She can tell us a lot about what is going on. And now she don't have to be afraid. José, you be careful."

"Si. I get back here in one hour, maybe two!"

Grandpa was already asleep, sitting up.

"We'll just leave him alone. Make sure Phyllis don't start yelling. That mumbling could turn into yelling and if anyone is close by, they'd hear her."

"Yeah, you're right Tim."

"Margaret, what do you think is wrong with her? She's not drunk, is she?"

"No, I don't believe she is. So she has to be drugged. It might be some kind of Indian plant. Or something like that someone used on her."

"I hope she pulls through, whatever it is. I really have a feeling for her that I can't explain. When I carried her here: that smell, that softness."

"Tim, you got bit."

"What you mean got bit?"

"They call that the love bug. Or you just might be over whelmed with smelling something other than a horse and a hard saddle. I don't know. If it lasts, it's the love bug."

"Well, Grandpa said she was a good person till she fell in with Wilson. So I'm sure she can be again. It sure is quiet. How long since José left?"

"I don't know. Maybe an hour. José is a good person, isn't he?"

"Yes he is. It took me a long time to trust him. But I do now. You know he was once a Comanchero. Living a terrible life. I truly believe he has changed for the better."

"God, I hope you're right."

"Well, he said he would go with me and take the two girls back to their parents and he did. And since then, he's been a great help, wouldn't you say?"

"Yes I would. As long as I have been with you both, José has been the best. Nothing out of the ordinary."

Phyllis seems to be waking up. But not yet opening her eyes.

"Thirsty, dry, where am I?"

"You're okay, don't be afraid. I'm Margaret. I'm here to help you."

"Where am I?"

"You're not in your room over the saloon. You're at our camp away from Higgins. We think you were being drugged and we took you away from Clem Wilson. Is that okay with you that we took you away from Clem Wilson?"

"Yes, I think so. Where are my kids?"

"They are here with us. They are sleeping in that wagon. You want to go see them?"

"Yes."

"Tim, will you help Phyllis? Is it okay if Tim helps you?"

"I think so."

Phyllis started to drop and Tim caught her just in time. Tim, carried her over to the wagon. With seeing her kids, she was satisfied. She had her arms around Tim's neck and he was loving it. There was that smell again and that soft fragile body that he would do anything for. If she only knew. Margaret was keeping a sharp look out for José. Tim put this blanket around Phyllis.

"Sit here on this wagon," Tim said, "and I'll get your shoes."

The case they brought with her shoes in it was a welcome sight to her.

"Do you have any socks?"

"Yes, in the case."

"Are these what you want?"

"Yes."

Tim knelt down and brushed off her feet and put her socks on and then her shoes.

"Tim, I think someone is coming. Grab your rifle."
Into the firelight came two images. One was a
stranger and the other was José.

José said, "Look what I found walking around in the
dark. Señor Tim, tie this one up. I am going back
out for another one. Be back as soon as I can."

"Okay José, be careful."

José was gone into the night.

"Over here, hands behind your back. Who are you?"

"I work for Clem Wilson. My name is Bates, Will
Bates. What in the world are you people doing?"

"We are helping a woman and her children and an
old man from being killed or taken by bandits. Does
Clem Wilson sell children and women?"

"I don't have to answer you."

"That's right, you don't have to. But after we knock
the shit out of you, you might wish you had."

Just then José came into view with two horses and
a body slung across the saddle of one of the horses.

"This is the other one."

"What happened?"

"He came at me with a knife and I was quicker."

"Okay Bates, who was he?"

"He worked for Clem Wilson."

"Who else is out there? José, make sure he knows
what happens if he don't tell the truth."

José came at him with the bloody knife.

"No, No, nobody else, the truth, I'm telling the
truth."

"When will they send someone else?"

"I don't know."

"Is the sheriff and deputy in on the selling of
people?"

"I don't think so. No one has ever said so. But the sheriff must know. I think he just looks the other way."

"In other words, we can't trust anyone in town for sure. How about the telegraph office worker?"

"He sends messages for Clem Wilson so he has to know about everything, I would think."

"Is there a mayor?"

"Yes."

"Does he know? Have the Comancheros ever came into town and talked to anyone?"

"Not that I know of. The mayor knows, but can't do anything about it. Clem has more pull."

"How many people work for Wilson?"

"Not sure, maybe a dozen."

"José, Margaret, we gotta do something about this. Here's what I'm thinking: we go back into town and get the drop on Wilson and as many others as we can, put them in the jail, telegraph the Texas Rangers, and get them here as fast as they can. Or we make contact with Mr. Dickenson and get them here as soon as possible and take over the town and wait till the Rangers get here. We don't know who we can trust. The telegraph operator may not cooperate with us. We wouldn't know what he was sending unless one of us knows telegraph dots and dashes. And I don't. Right now, we don't know who will cooperate with us. We'll need to find someone else in town that knows the telegraph codes. I'm sure someone else knows. José, what do you think? Margaret, what do you think? I'd like to move fast to catch them off guard!"

José said, "Let's go back into town and grab the telegraph operator before he sends off a message for help for Wilson. Maybe we can trick him into telling us who else can send messages in town."

"Okay, let's move now. Margaret, you got to stay here and make sure nothing goes wrong. Make sure this guy is tied up real good so he don't get loose and warn Wilson. In fact, put extra ropes on him. And I better make sure this other one is really dead. Don't need him attacking you. Just do what you have to. Looks like Phyllis and the kids are sleeping. Grandpa too. He could be waking up soon; you could use another gun. I'd like to put this guy in the jail, too, but I'll have to leave him here for now. When Grandpa wakes up, make sure he understands what's going on here and keep him away from this guy. Don't fire any shot unless you're being overrun or you need to save a life. Don't know when we will get back. Tell you what, if things go the way we want and we get the message sent to the Rangers and get the people locked up, we will fire two quick shots to let you know we're alright."

"Okay you two. Love you guys."

After they left, Margaret looked around just to see if there was anything she needed to do. The guy was pretty secure. A rope around his neck and around a high branch and arms tied behind his back and to the tree and to the wagon. He started in talking. "Ma'am, I won't hurt you. Just give me a drink a water."

Grandpa was waking up and looking all around. The kids and their mother were asleep. José and Tim, are making their way in the dark. A little light coming from the town was a help to keep them on target. By now it was probably about ten o'clock.

No one on the street. Although, someone was probably watching.

"So, let's go to the jail first and see what it looks like and if anyone is in there."

The back way was good, very dark around the side of the jail. José stayed against the building and came around the front and looked in a window. The Sheriff and two other guys were asleep in chairs. The cells were empty and wide open. One guy was dressed pretty neat, José told Tim. And they're ready to go inside .

"You think one of us should go for a back door?"

"Don't know. How 'bout we knock on the door and say it's Will Bates. Think they'd fall for that?"

"Yeah, they would."

"Okay then, here we go."

Tim knocked.

Someone said, "Who is it?"

"Will Bates."

"Coming."

The door opened. In went Tim and José, guns in hand.

"Make a sound and you're dead. Back to that cell and be quick about it. Give me your names."

The fancy one said, "Clem Wilson."

"Sheriff Jim Nations and my deputy."

"Okay, all three in the cell, gun holsters on the table with your left hand, on the floor with your hands behind your backs."

Hands and feet tied and separated, gags in their mouths, tied to bars so they can't move closer to each other and untie each other. José and Tim each stuck a pistol in their belts. Guess that would have given them each four pistols. They stopped at the door and Tim said quietly, "Now, we need to send that message."

"Si."

"I wonder who else we should be locking up. Let's get that message sent."

"Si."

Sneaking out the door, they looked for a sign that said telegraph. And there it was. A little light on in the back probably meant the operator was there. So a faint knock brought the man to the door.

"Yes, can I help you?"

"We need to send a message. It's an emergency." Inside they asked if there was anyone else in town that can send messages.

He said, "Yes. The mayor and the postmaster."

"Okay. Just wondering. We need you to lay down on the floor over by that stove and put your hands behind your back. We are gonna tie you up. If you open your mouth, you're dead."

Ties and belts worked good in place of ropes and they gagged his mouth.

"Next, we need the mayor in here sending our message. Outside, they looked for a house that might be the mayor's. Picking one, they walked over and knocked on the door. A man came to the door rubbing his eyes.

"Sir, are you the mayor," Tim asked.

"No, he lives next door."

"Do you work for or with Clem Wilson?"

"No, I do not. What's this all about?"

"We need your help. Can you come with us to the mayor's house right away? It's very important."

"I don't know who you are."

"It has to do with kidnapping of children and women. Do you know that's been going on?"

"I had my suspicions for a long time. Okay, I'll go to the mayor's with you."

He told his wife he was going next door to the mayor's with these gentlemen. The mayor came to the door.

"Sir, can we come in so we can explain ourselves?"

"Mayor, they have some information you will want to hear."

They explained everything from the beginning and what they thought was happening and that they wanted to get the Rangers here as fast as they can get here to take charge of the town. Also who else do they have to lock up."

"Mayor, can you use the telegraph key?"

"Yes I can. I used to be a telegraph operator."

"Then come with us and get that message sent as soon as you can. Do you know where to send it to get hold of the Rangers?"

"I think so. There are a few more men you have to lock up before we can feel safe, so they don't break out the sheriff and Wilson. They are probably in the saloon, if they don't know Wilson is locked up. Come on, I'll show you."

The saloon was quiet with the men the mayor was looking for. They were drinking and playing cards. José and Tim walked up to the table and Tim said, "You four men are under arrest. Stand up and take your gun belts off with your left hand. And do it slow. If you flinch, you're dead."

The mayor said, "Do what he says."

José collected the gun belts and they marched them out the door to the jail. The three were still tied up like they left them. They put the four in the other cell and then untied the first three. They were full of questions.

"You're all under arrest for kidnapping and drugging a person. Mayor, we are taking over the town as the law with your permission until the Rangers arrive. Swear us in. And we will bring our camp people in. Who else do we have to be looking for? Mayor, we have to work close together on this. Feed these people and don't break the law in any way with regards to them. José and I will secure the town. Mayor, let's get that message sent out now please . You know you will be stuck with us till the Texas Rangers get here. José, can you stay here till we get back?"

"Si. I will stay."

"And Mayor, can you get a couple other men in here and deputize them: somebody you know for sure you can trust."

"Yes."

"Be really sure you can trust them. Or they will let them out and we are dead."

Back at the telegraph office, the man we tied up was still there.

"Can we trust this guy?"

"No. He's been sending messages for Wilson for a long time. So no, you can't trust him."

Tim grabbed him by the neck and said, "Who have you been sending messages to the last few days for Wilson?"

"Don't hit me . . I'll tell you. To someone across the border."

"What were the messages?"

"I might still have them here. Let me look."

"Mayor, get that message sent. Make it fast before I break this son of a bitch's neck. I'm mad as hell. When was the last message from Wilson to whoever?"

"Yesterday. Wilson said that there was a problem. Someone had interfered with the plans."

"And what were the plans?"

"Pick up two kids and come in for the women later."

"Tim, I got a message back from a Captain Stephen Fuller. I said it's urgent. He said he could be here in about two days with a detachment of ten men. He has been trying to break this kidnapping ring for some time. Just keep everyone in the jail and be careful. Someone might try to break them out."

"Okay, Mayor, this town has to stay on lock down. I mean, tight control. I'd like to bring my people into town. I need to go out and get them now but I can't. Mayor, can you and this gentleman get a few people up and arm them to watch the town so I can go out and get my people. And take this guy to the jail. Is there anyone else that can send telegraphs?"

"Yes, the postmaster."

"You better get him up and sit here while you're doing something else. Mayor, we got a crisis here and you better make the doctor aware of the goings on. We might need him."

The mayor took the telegraph operator to the jail. José let them in and put the guy in a cell.

"How is it going, José?"

"Okay, Señor Mayor, they got tired of yelling at me and quieted down. Señor Mayor, I need to be out there with Tim. Can someone else watch the jail?"

"Yes, I'll get someone."

"I got the keys. I will keep them on me for now."

"Okay, good idea, José."

Two of the townspeople came in the jail.

"Mayor, what we supposed to do?"

"Watch the prisoners, nothing else. Stay away from the cells. If they need water, leave your guns on the table and don't get too close. Same with food. Have food brought in from the hotel. It's important that you don't screw this up. We have to hold on to the prisoners till the Texas Rangers get here and that might not be for a couple days. Listen to me, if you can't handle this job, I'll get someone else."

One said, "I can do it ."

The other said he didn't want to.

"Okay, go, I'll get someone else. Leave that rifle here."

He set it on the table and walked out the door.

"Okay, keep that door closed to the cell room. Stay out here, no talking to the prisoners. You got it? You're Chuck Hayes, right?"

"Yes Mayor. I'm Chuck."

"I'll get another person to sit with you but for now, do what I say. And you don't have the keys, so don't worry about them. Keep your rifle in your hand. But don't shoot me if I come through the door."

José and Tim got together and said if the mayor can run things for a while here, we should go out and bring in our people.

"I know I said I would fire a few shots if we got control, but I don't want to alert any of Wilson's friends if they're out there waiting. José, how 'bout I go and you stay here and keep a grip on things?"

"Okay, go now and I'll tell the mayor."

Tim hated to leave but he knew he had to get to Margaret and the others and hoped he wasn't too late already. The ride to the camp was a cautious one in the dark. Margaret heard him coming.

"Tim?"

"Yeah, it's me. We got the town under control. I didn't want to fire any shots and alert the wrong people. We need to get back in town as quick as we can. Grandpa, get in the wagon and as soon as we move out, you follow. Where's Phyllis?"

"She's sleeping, kinda groggy."

"The kids?"

"Sleeping. Put everything in the wagon and let's go. Bates in the wagon. The dead one in the wagon. Put out the fire. Make sure Bates is tied up good. Let's move."

Driving wagons in the dark is not good, but they didn't have a choice. They had a little light coming from the town to go by. That was good. Didn't take long to get back into town. Four men with rifles met them. Tim thought, *I hope the hell these are our people.* They were. That was a relief. They pulled up in front of the jail. José and a couple others took Bates and put him in a cell with the rest.

"Now we need the undertaker to take this body off our hands."

The mayor said, "Try to get some sleep, and eat something. Phyllis can go back to her room if she wants to and the kids, too. Anyone know what the time is?"

"I'd guess it's about 1 a.m. I'm tired as can be. I need a little sleep. I'm going to the saloon and find a corner to lay down in. And tell the bartender the bar is closed until further notice. Margaret, move everyone into the saloon. If we are to keep control, the bar has to be closed."

"I agree."

"No strangers in town either. I wish our people with the Dickenson herd would get here."

"I know."

"Mayor, are you okay with what we are doing?"

"Son, you are doing just fine. Someone has to be in charge. José and you can be the law till the Rangers get here."

"I'll be sleeping for a bit. Check with José if you need anything or wake me."

Margaret had moved Grandpa and the two kids and Phyllis in the saloon. The bartender didn't like it but didn't argue about it.

"Who's upstairs in the rooms?"

"No one right now," he said.

"Who owns the saloon and hotel?"

"Mr. Clem Wilson, as far as I know."

"Do you know what Wilson is up to?"

"Not really, only what I pick up on once in a while."

"Okay, I'll talk to you again later. For now, get all the doors locked. No whiskey sold till I or José okay it! You understand?"

"Yes Sir."

"A little beer, maybe. When I say a little beer, I mean one or maybe two glasses, no more. I don't want any drunks in town while this lock down is going on. We need the cooperation of the whole town to get this done. Now, I'm going to lay down for a couple hours. You know where I'm at if you need me."

José was heading to the saloon with the mayor. Margaret was seated at a table facing towards the door. Rifle on the table, her hand not an inch from the trigger. Their gear and supplies on the floor by her feet. Grandpa, seated at another table with the children sleeping on a blanket on two tables put together. Phyllis was sleeping sitting in a chair next to the children. José and the mayor came in the swinging doors. Margaret mentioned right away that the upstairs needed to be checked for doors and windows. José asked the mayor if he could send a message to the next town south of Higgins to find out if the Dickenson herd was through there yet."

"Yeah, good idea. We sure could use their help."

"Just them being here would be enough. I'm going upstairs to check around. Señora, can you get the bar man to make some coffee and something to eat for us?"

"Yes, José, I will."

The only room that looked like it had anybody in it was Phyllis' room. José jammed a chair against the door knob of the door going down the outside stairs in back. All windows were locked and too high to come in anyway. The bartender had the coffee going and some food on the table.

"Señor Mayor, can we get that message sent now?"

"Yes, José, let's go."

"Señora Margaret, will you be okay for a while till we get back?"

"Yes, I'll be fine. Go ahead."

They sent the message and got a reply right away. The best news they could have gotten—yes, the herd was passing their little town. So it should be showing up here tomorrow or the next day. Whoever was on the other end said if it's important, they could send someone out to tell them you need

254

help as soon as possible, because they're not far away.

"Okay, tell them we need their help."

José crossed himself with his little crucifix he carried in his pocket.

"Señor Mayor, with the Dickenson people, and hopefully the Texas Rangers getting here tomorrow or the next day, we might survive this thing."

"If we don't get hit tonight. I know we are a sitting duck."

"Señor Mayor, I have really got to get some sleep. I am ready to drop. Let's go by the sheriff's office and see how things are and then go to the saloon. We can see if Tim is up."

At the sheriff office, things were quiet. They must be sleeping or pretending to be asleep. At least it's quiet. Their two guys were playing cards and well-armed.

"Don't let anyone in here unless you're sure who they are. Look through this window. In fact, don't let anyone in here except Tim, José, or me until I change it. When the Dickenson herd gets here and the Texas Rangers get here, then that will change. You understand what I'm saying?"

"Yes Sir, Mayor."

"In a couple of hours when it gets light, I'll try to get someone to relieve you." José, we have people well-armed walking the streets. They're not as good as Rangers but they can shoot."

"Si, that is a good thing."

"In the morning, we need to tell everyone what's going on. The telegraph operator from Reydon, Oklahoma, sent someone out to the Dickenson herd to give the message. Didn't take long to catch up.

They were bedded down for the night. OK Bill heard him coming in the dark. He took him straight to Long John. He gave Long John the message. And he quickly left going back to Reydon. Long John woke Mr. Dickenson and explained everything. Long John said, "I'm gonna send OK Bill and Frankie B. ahead. They should get there in a couple of hours. They can find out what is going on. And we will be there later on in the day, I would hope. Is that okay with you, Sir?"

"Yes it is. Get them going right away."

Frankie B. was sleeping. And OK Bill just came on the watch. They both should be rested up.

"Get them something to eat and get them going. They both know Tim Shiloh. And if he says he needs help with defending a town, then we gotta send help."

"Yes Sir, I'd like to go along but I might need to stay with the herd."

"Long John, you just go ahead. I'll get the cattle moving soon as everybody's up. We'll get there a few hours after you. We shouldn't have any trouble. So go ahead."

"Okay, Sir."

They woke up Frankie B. and explained everything to him. He was getting ready as they spoke. OK Bill was already aware of what was going on. He was having a cup a coffee and checking his rifles and hand guns. They ate a little and had their coffee.

"We will see you in a couple hours, Mr. Dickenson."

"Okay. Don't worry about us, we'll be fine. I'll have Red Fox lead the herd; shouldn't be any trouble.

We'll hold the herd on the edge of town when we get there."

Long John, OK Bill, and Frankie B. took off. The moon was all the light they had to go by. And that was not much. Long John rode behind OK Bill. He knew OK Bill's senses were almost like an animal. If anyone could get them there without breaking a horse's leg or falling in a hole in the dark, OK Bill could. As they went, they could see light coming up slowly in the east. Must be about 5:00 or 5:30 a.m. on a clear sky night. Frankie B. wanted to hurry up but he knew there's no hurrying. OK Bill was doing his best. Before too long, they knew they would start seeing flickering lights from the town of Higgins. Just had to be patient. Something is going on there that they knew nothing about, only that Tim Shiloh needed help. Long John stopped. He needed to tighten up his saddle straps. He felt that they were not as tight as they should be. Frankie B. just stopped and waited. OK Bill got off his horse and motioned for them to be quiet—no talk. They all three put their hands over their horses' mouth and stood still. With a hand sign, OK Bill let them know someone or something was out there in front of them. Long John held OK Bill's horse and rubbed its nose. Time passed slow. All of a sudden, two Apache's appeared. The other one had a badge on his chest.

OK Bill said, "This one Ranger, him name is Tracker Jack. Him work with Ranger Captain Stephen Fuller. They camped not far."

"Have him to tell the captain it's Captain Long John Lowther. We're coming over to him."

"Okay, Long John, you follow."

Frankie B. thought he was about to meet the other great captain in the Rangers—Captain Stephen Fuller. Captain Long John F. Lowther and Fuller were legends. When they were young, they fought the renegade Indians and Mexican bandits under their Captain, Dolphus A. Dickenson. They never brag about it, but someone should. You can see their pictures in courthouses and in saloons. Even though they knew each other, they would move with caution, fingers ready at any moment in case it's an ambush and not the Captain. Creeping through the darkness, being led by two Apache. One trusted the other, knowing nothing about them. OK Bill believed Tracker Jack, so he must be alright. They finely reached the Rangers' camp and it was the captain. There were handshakes and hugs and introductions.

"We need to move into the town as soon as we are all ready."

"Okay, let's go in as soon as we can see better. Do you know what the problem is?"

"No, only that our friends, Tim Shiloh and José Lopez and a Margaret Edwards are holding the town. That's all."

"Lt., get the men ready, we're going in. Rifles in hand."

"Right Captain."

Captain Lowther on my right.

"Have your people draw their rifles?"

"Yes Sir."

"All right, let's go. Be sharp men."

"Yes Sir."

A slow ride down a hill into the town, ready for anything. Just like so many times before. For Long

John, it felt like old times. The streets were empty. They stopped in the middle of town at the Sheriff's office. José, Tim, and Margaret came out. Rifles in hand but over their heads. Just to make sure.

Captain Fuller asked "Captain Lowther, these your people?"

"Yes sir, they are."

"Okay then, put your rifles down."

The Mayor came running out with a whole lot a townspeople.

"Thank you, Captain, for coming so soon."

"Well, Sir, I've been on to this Wilson guy with his selling people for some time, just never knew where he was. Looks like he was under my nose all the time and we didn't know it."

"Well, Sir, Tim and José here got Wilson and a lot of others locked up for you to do something with. We were afraid some of the bandits would break them out. We knew we couldn't defend the town without help."

"Okay, Mr. Mayor, we'll take it from here."

The sun was just coming up. Couldn't be a better sun rise.

"Captain, will you be having breakfast with us?"

"Mayor, that would be fine. One of my men is a cook. He can help. Lt., get the men on their posts. Mayor, while we are here in Higgins, we will enact Marshall law. Bring me any one you think would be a suitable sheriff and deputy and I will interview them."

"Yes Sir, I'll do that."

Captain Fuller had fifteen men with him. Even better than expected.

"Mayor, can you have someone show these men where they can rest their horses and camp for the night? And let's get a look at the prisoners."

The two captains went into the jail.

Long John said, "Tim, you and José did one hell of a good job locking up these sons a bitches."

"Well, Boss, it sorta just came our way and we did what we had to. Boss, I could not have done any of this without José. Sir, I think he did more than I did to control the situation. And a lot of thanks to Margaret. She did a lot even thou she is wounded."

"Well, alright, you can relax a little now.

" Captain, the herd that we're with will be here in a few hours. I'm sure you will be glad to see an old friend."

"Who might that be?"

"Captain Dickenson. He owns the herd coming up and has a ranch in Texas. I believe you will see him very soon. One thing I have to insist on is these prisoners. They have to be treated well. If you don't, they might walk out of court free. And we don't want that. Tomorrow or the next day, I'll get them to the nearest court house and we'll get them tried. Some of the townspeople might have to testify in a court. Will they do that?"

"I don't know. I suppose so."

"Because if they don't, there might not be much of a case."

"Tim, José, and Margaret could help build a case against them. That woman and her children and the grandpa are victims. Wouldn't that be enough?"

"Maybe. Are there others?"

"There must be others because the telegraph operator sent messages to the bandits for Wilson, I am told. You would have ask around town and get all the information you can get before you leave, Captain."

"On second thought, I need to send for a judge and have a trial here where everyone is at. Check with the mayor. He should know more about the people in town than anybody."

"Captain, I closed the bar to whiskey and allowed only two glasses of beer. You want to change that ruling or leave it the same for now."

"Ah, Tim, that was a good idea. Let's leave it that way for now. We don't need drunks taking shots at us."

The cook came out of the saloon and said, "There's a big spread of food set out on the tables in the saloon, Captain. You want the men to eat?"

"Yes. Tell the Lt. He will handle it."

The two men walked over to the saloon.

"There's no room for error in this case. I can't express it enough, Captain. Let's see what they've cooked up. I haven't had much to eat the last few days. We tried to hurry here as fast as we could. We just kinda ate on the move. Every one of my boys agreed getting here fast was important and it could save lives. So now the Rangers can eat a proper meal."

The mayor was busy talking to men about the sheriff's job. So far, nobody had much interest. Margaret had the town doctor take a look at her side. He said no infection had come back. It should heal on its own, just don't bump it.

The herd was nearing the town; they could see buildings in the distance. Mr. Dickenson was saying to the men, "We need water for the cattle. It might be a problem. I don't know of any water holes around. If the town has a few deep wells, we might be able to rest a day. Otherwise, we have to keep going till we find water."

OK Bill and the other Apache, Tracker Jack, were sitting at a table in the saloon eating and talking. "When the herd gets here, good Comanche with Him, Red Fox, good friend."

Long John asked the mayor about water or any water holes around.

"Don't know of any. Our two water wells have been all we've needed. Never did look for any more."

"Is it okay with you if I tell Mr. Dickenson to water the cattle at each well for a bit?"

"Yes, certainly. That's the least we can do, Captain Lowther."

"If we can let the cattle drink a little each at your two wells, we should be okay for a while. Have the people stock up on water, just in case we run them a little low. I'll ride out and meet the herd and tell them to go to the two wells. The cattle can drink at the troughs a while."

"That would be fine."

Both wells are at the edge of town, one on each end. Red Fox saw Long John coming and hurried to meet him.

"It good see you."

"Yes, Red Fox, we didn't have any trouble."

"That good, my friend."

"Lead the cattle to the well you see coming up. I'll tell Mr. Dickenson and the rest."

"Okay, Long John."

He got the best welcome from everyone. They were glad to see him with a smile on his face; that meant no trouble ahead.

"Taters, you can park your wagon on the other end a town where there's another well. We'll water the cattle at each well."

Mrs. Sikorski was all smiles at seeing him.

"The Rangers got there when we did, so everything is fine."

"Well, good to hear, Long John. I guess we were all worried some."

Mr. Dickenson pulled up alongside Long John, "Good to see you. How'd it go?"

"Very well, Sir. The Rangers got there at the same time we did. They secured the town. There's someone waiting to see you."

"To see me?"

"Yes Sir, Captain Fuller."

"Well I'll be, so he's still Rangering?"

"Yes Sir, he's got fifteen men with him. Before I forget, Sir, there's two wells, one on each end of town. We can water the cattle a bit at each one. Not like we'd like to, but if we go easy with the water, there should be enough for all of us. When we get the herd settled down, we can talk more."

The cattle were headed around the town and not through it. Once they'd drunk a little at the first well, they'd push them around to the other well. It was working pretty good. Settling down a little ways from the town, it was a lot of cattle. Right around a thousand head. If they can all get a little drink, the wells should be able to hold their level. If these two wells are separate and deep, they should be able to come back up to their levels fast. If not, then we might have to be digging another well for the town.

"Long John, maybe we should dig a well anyway. If anyone has experience with wells, let's talk to them. Give us the shovels and we'll start digging."

"That's a great idea. I'll go back to town and talk to the mayor and see what he comes up with. I'll do it right away."

"We might just need that water, Long John."

Long John caught the mayor coming out of his office.

"Mayor, can we talk, Sir?"

"Yes, by all means."

"Do you know anyone that has well digging experience?"

"Ah, the survey office manager. What do you have in mind?"

"Let's go see him. Sir, if we can dig another well, we would all be better off."

The man listened and said there was a place he'd always thought would be a good place to sink a well. It stays wet almost all the time, but never comes up to the surface."

"Where is it?"

"Not far, about a thousand feet from where the Rangers are camped. You got time to go take a look at it now?"

"Sure do, let's go. Bring some men and we'll see."

Picking up a few shovels, they headed out to the spot with a couple of townspeople and a couple Rangers with the Lt.

"You're right. It does look moist, like water is close to the surface. If we could get another well going, that would be great for the town and for us too while we're here. Let's dig and see."

Long John grabbed a shovel and started digging. The rest of the men saw what they needed to do and got right to it. Before too long, they had a hole going down over their heads and still no water, just wet sand.

"Well, that was a good idea," someone said.

"You men can go if you want, I'm digging a well."

"Okay, Long John, I'll help you."

A few more feet and there's water. I know it, I can smell it.

The mayor said, "He's right. I can smell it, too. Can't you smell it?"

The Lt. jumped in with a shovel. "I can sure as hell smell it, too. I know what water smells like. We got ourselves another well."

They musta dug down ten feet and there it was bubbling to the surface.

"Throw down that rope and get us outta here."

The Lt. and Long John were standing in water. They shook hands and congratulated each other.

"We better get outta here."

"Let me get a taste. Mmm. It's good water. Let's see if it comes up to the top."

The man from the survey office said, "I don't know much about water levels but I think when it fills up a hole, it's from a water aquifer. That's a good thing. It will almost never stop filling up."

"Men, we did good here today. People looking for water should be as lucky as we were today. This water well belongs to the town of Higgins. But while we're here, we will use it. Mayor, you need to do something to fence it and secure it somehow or build something over it. Hopefully, it will be a water source for the town for a long time."

"Yes and I know I can speak for the town when I say thank you all so much."

Back in town, the mayor was telling everyone about the well. Captain Fuller was having a reunion with Captain Dickenson. They had a lot to talk about. Captain Dickenson was one of the early leaders. He got his training and commission while under the command of Captain Morris and Daniel Parker. They created a body of Rangers to protect the Mexican border. And so, the two young men, Stephen C. Fuller and John F. Lowther were signed up when they were probably no older than eighteen or nineteen and they were a perfect fit into that kind a life. They did so well that they were promoted often because of their bravery and coolness under fire. Hardly anyone matched their ability to remain calm and make rational decisions under pressure. It wasn't long before they both were promoted to captain, under Captain Dolphus Dickenson. So he is almost like a father to them. Their respect for him is total. Captain Dickenson retired after a number of years in the Rangers and settled down on his ranch. He had bought it years earlier with the wife and daughter. He didn't get to spend much time with them while in the Rangers. John F. Lowther followed his captain and retired after a few years. He went to work for Captain Dolphus Dickenson as his ranch foreman. Now, Captain Stephen C. Fuller, who is still in the Rangers, comes back into the lives of his two most endeared friends.

Chapter 10

Margaret got hugs from her daughter, Grace.

"Mama, it's so good to have you back. I was worried about you. I thought I might never see you again."

"I didn't want that to happen but I knew you would be well taken care off if it did. You will be glad to know that José and I got the girls to their parents. Those girls are tough. And José worked out just fine. He did just what he said he would. I trust him now as well as anyone. He and I went through a lot. We fought side by side and saved each other's lives several times. We were both wounded and could have bled to death. We did what we had to do."

When Antonina saw Margaret, she ran over to her and cried as she hugged her and squeezed her.

"I am so glad you are back."

"Antonina honey, I love you. I remembered your sweet smile when we were many miles away from each other. You and Grace are like sisters and two daughters to me."

José came over to Margaret to see how she was doing.

"Señora Margaret, can I get you something or do something for you?"

"No José. Come here." She grabbed him by the hand and pulled him to her. I just told the girls how you and I have learned to trust each other. I could not have made the trip without you. They hugged. José, in an embarrassed sorta way, tipped his sombrero, turned, and walked away.

Angelina and Prairie Flower were still out with the herd. Harve just got in, and with his coffee, he walked over to Margaret.

"Mrs. Edwards, I'm so pleased to meet you, Ma'am. I hear you been injured, Ma'am."

"Yes I have. But I think I will be alright. José pulled me through."

"Ma'am, I'm Harve. I been with Mr. Dickenson some time. If there's anything I can do to help you, it would be my pleasure."

"Thank you, Harve, for your kind words. I'm glad to meet you." She gave his hand a squeeze.

Harve bowed and tipped his hat three times to the three ladies. He turned and his spurs gave off that distinct sound as he walked away. You knew you had just been in the presence of a cowboy. The cattle were moving along, stopping briefly at the two water wells, then standing around at the new well till they got pushed out of the way by the newcomers wanting their turn. The new well is working just fine. The mayor had a few carpenters take a look at what will be needed to fence in the well after the herd moves on. José sat down with Juan and Harve. Dance poured his coffee and looked around. Seeing the three captains sitting together, he walked over to the table and motioned if he could sit down.

"Of course, Dance," Mr. Dickenson said. "Sit."
"Captain Fuller, this is Dance Mead, one of our top hands. Dance, the three of us used to Ranger together some years ago."

"Mr. Dickenson, that's what I heard."

Long John finished off his coffee and stood up. Looking at Mr. Dickenson, he said, "I think I'll make the rounds, Sir. You think we might pull out of here tomorrow?"

"I suppose we should. We still got a long way to go."

"Sir, is there anything we need to pick up from the store while we're here?"

"I don't know of anything. We stocked up pretty good at the last store. You can ask around."

"I will."

"Mr. Dickenson," said Captain Lowther, "we will be going through open country. We expect to get attacked by either bandits, or Crow, or rustlers before we get to Montana. But I reckon we can handle anything that comes along. Be nice if we were all riding in the same direction. We could ride with you up to Lipscomb, probably a day's ride from here. They have a courthouse and a judge there. I need to get this Wilson case taken care of and get back to Austin. I'm thinking about putting in for my retirement. I'm getting a little old for all this chasing here and chasing there. I like what you've done, Captain, since you left the Rangers. Have a ranch and some cattle. Camilla and I talk about marrying. She has her one son, and I have my daughter that are pretty well grown up and on their own."

"Yeah. Well, it might be that time for you. If you decide to ranch, I could cut out some cattle and help get you started. Just let me know when we get back from this drive."

"Okay, Captain, I'll keep that in mind. For now, I guess we need to get outside and see what needs our attention."

"Okay. We'll talk later. Dance, good to meet you."

"Yes Sir, Captain."

Captain Fuller told his Lt., "Let's get a meeting set up in one hour in the saloon. I want you and the two sergeants there. We need a plan."

"Okay, Captain."

At the meeting, they used a back room where they could talk in private.

"Here's what we got: a town without a sheriff, people scared, two jail cells full. We have to set someone up as sheriff or stay here and run the town, ourselves."

"Captain, how about that Tim Shiloh and José Lopez? They stepped up and took charge when someone needed to."

"Well, they might be okay but they are Captain Dickenson's men and needed for the herd, I would suppose. Lt., can you write some of this down so when we get through, we know what the hell we decided on?"

"Yes Sir, Captain. Sir, how 'bout we ask Captain Dickenson and the two men in question if they would stay as sheriff and deputy, temporarily of course. Maybe till they come back from Montana which would probably be four to six months."

"Good, Sergeant Ross."

270

"I heard that José Lopez and that woman, Margaret Edwards, are not yet part of Captain Dickenson's crew. Maybe the two of them could stay for whatever time it took for the captain to get back from Montana with his people. I heard the woman is wounded and needs a little doctoring. But also that she fought and killed quite a few Crow and killed some Comancheros, too without blinking an eye after she was rescued from captivity. Sir, I'd say she is tough as nails. Her and José could run this town, or any town. And we know José is a law and order person, and tough."

"Sergeant Ross, I like that idea. Okay. We will take that up with Captain Dickenson and the Mayor. Next subject is what to do with the Wilson people. They all belong in jail for a long time. If they were selling women and kids, we need to get them to a bigger jail and a trial before some of their friends try to break them out. The town of Lipscomb is just up north about a day's ride from here. What I understand, it's a bigger town and has a courthouse and a judge. Oh, you know what I should do is telegraph the sheriff up there and tell him I would like to bring these prisoners up there for trial while Tim Shiloh and the others are here. They are witnesses to some crimes, and others in town would be witnesses, too. Lt., make a note to do that right away. If we get those two things planned out, we can probably get back to Austin. Is there anything else I'm forgetting? Lt., Sergeants?"

"No Sir, I don't think so."

"How 'bout it Sergeant Ross?"

"No Sir, I don't think so."

"Okay Lt., let's get these questions asked. Lt., you go talk to the mayor. How would he feel if we set up José and Mrs. Edwards as the law. And Tim Shiloh, if need be. I say need be because he could be a vital witness. Then we gotta know if they're willing to serve. I'm going to send a message. I hope the postmaster is in the telegraph office."

He was. The captain got the message sent to Lipscomb. The sheriff there quickly talked to the judge and he said bring them up. The judge is aware of the crimes being committed against women and children. There are women and children in the Lipscomb area missing and the town is the county seat. The mayor was open to whatever suggestion the captain made about the law in town. Captain Dickenson said if José and Margaret wanted to stay a while as Sheriff and Deputy, that would be alright with him. And even if Tim wanted to stay, he could, too, if it would help the case against Wilson and his men. José and Mrs. Edwards said they would do whatever it took to get those people behind bars or hung. José made the comment about him being Mexican? How would the people feel 'bout that, and a woman?

"Well, I'd guess people would like some law and order so that might not matter much."

The people didn't seem to mind the last two days who the sheriff was. OK Bill and Frankie B. gave José and Margaret their support. Tim said that if the town needed him, he would stay also for a few months or however long it would take. Meanwhile, they need to look for somebody permanent.

Juan said, "José, I, amigo am proud of you. Your family would be, too."

OK Bill and Red Fox gave José the peace sign.

Red Fox said, "You good brave. You fight to help this woman, then you fight to save other woman and young ones. I will help you be law man if you need!"

José said, "Thank you, my Amigos Red Fox and OK Bill."

The mayor called a special meeting of the three town councilmen. They will have to decide who they want to pin a badge on. We need to get this decided. The Rangers are leaving in the morning and so are the Dickenson people. We have to have someone we can trust. It was unanimous.

"Give José the sheriff's badge and fifteen dollars a week and Mrs. Edwards the deputy's badge and ten dollars a week. We'll add expenses for travel and plus a percent of licenses issued and fines levied. Let's give Mrs. Edwards doctor fees on her injury."

That was unanimous, also. That was accepted on condition that when Captain Dickenson and his people came back on their way back to Texas, the town would have someone else lined up for both jobs unless other arrangements were made ahead of time. By now, Margaret was getting around pretty good with the help of a cane. But like the mayor said, "She is nobody to mess with."

Margaret said she wanted to go back to being a homebody sometime soon, but looks like that will have to wait .

"What's Grace going to do?"

"I'd like to have her stay with me but there's nothing here for her. I don't know. It could be six months here. If Grace stays here with me, I'll have to get a place for her and me to live."

Margaret asked Grace, "Do you want to stay here with me till Mr. Dickenson comes back this way?"

"Yes, Mama. I missed you. Now you're back. I want to stay with you. I can help. Your side, you know it's not fully healed up yet. And I can help you in other ways, too."

"Well, if you want to stay, I'll have to get us a room or a place. If they have a school here, would you like to go to it?"

"Yes, Mama. I know I will be nineteen in a few months. But I missed out on school the last two years and I'd like to catch up on more."

"Well, okay then, let's ask the mayor about a place and the school."

They went over to the mayor's office and he motioned them in.

"Come in , come in, I'll only be a minute…

What can I help you with?"

"Mayor, I need a place to stay, Sir. This is my daughter, Grace. She will be staying with me while I work here."

"Sure, I know of a place on the edge of town. It might be a mess now, nobody lived in it for a few years. If you don't mind cleaning it up, you can stay there."

"How much?"

"Nothing."

"Nothing?"

"Sure, I don't know if anybody owns it. We'd rather have someone living in it than not."

"Okay. Let's go look at it."

A short walk from the mayor's office, and there it was.

"Margaret, it's not much, but it's dry when it rains. Let's go inside, I'm not sure what to expect any more than you are."

The inside didn't look the best. A broken table, a couple chairs, small fire place, and even a cook stove. The floor seemed sound. Three small rooms. "If you and Grace can clean it up, it's yours."

"Sir, we will take it. However, I have one request. You can tell me no if you want. I will understand. José and I have been together for about six months now, not as man and wife but as a man and a woman eating, sleeping, riding, and fighting to stay alive together. He has saved my life several times. I would like for him to have a place in here with Grace and me. I would feel safer. And I know he will need a place more than just sleeping in a jail cell. I would like him to have a place to go to eat and rest. Is that ok with you, Mayor? I'm not saying something more won't come of us, but for right now, that's how it is. I have come to care dearly for him. So if that's okay with you, I will tell him he has a place with Grace and I?"

"That is okay with me. I really do understand what you're saying."

"If people talk and make something more out of it than really is, I can't help it."

"I tell you what, you just go ahead and tell José he has a place to live and we'll see how it goes."

"Thank you, Mayor. Grace, let's find José and tell him what we've done."

"Okay, Mama. I hope you know what you are doing."

José was working out all the details with the Rangers on how to transfer the prisoners to

Lipscomb: a covered wagon with each man chained to the other was decided on. They found José with the Ranger Lt.

Margaret said, "I know you're busy, but I just want to tell you we found a place to live while we're here in Higgins."

José was set back and said, "Señora, what are you talking about." In a low voice saying, "We can't live together. Señora, what makes you even say that?"

"José, when you get through with what you are doing, I want to show you something."

"I'm through here, Señora."

"If you are, then come with me. Do you remember Grace?"

"Si, Señorita Grace. He touched his two right hand fingers to his sombrero and said, "How are you, Señorita?"

"I'm fine, José. Thank you so much for helping my mother. She has told me some of what you and her had to do to stay alive. Thank you so much."

"Señorita Grace, we only did what we had to do. I'm grateful to Señora Margaret. She saved my life." Looking at Margaret, José said, "Where are we going?"

A short ride in a buckboard and they were in front of the little three room house.

"Grace and I are going to stay here and I want you to have a room. The mayor said we could live here free. I want you to have one of the rooms."

"Señora Margaret. No. I think it would make my job harder. There are people who don't like me being sheriff already. What do you think they will say if we live together?"

"I explained it to the Mayor, and he said he'd be okay with the arrangement."

"That all sounds good but I don't think it's that simple, Señora. Let's just see how things go for a while. I will help you fix the place up and I will eat here. But I will sleep somewhere else, at least for now. Is that okay with you, Señora Margaret?"

"Okay. Well Grace, let's clean it up. Around the back, I saw a big copper tub. I want that inside to take a bath in. José, can you help us bring that tub inside?"

"Si. I have something I need to do first. I'll go and get back as soon as I can. Oh Señora, the mayor wants to swear you in first thing in the morning. He already did me."

"Why don't we go do it right now so people can know that they have law and order."

"Si, good. I will feel better."

"Grace, you want to come with us or stay here?"

"I'll stay here and start cleaning things up."

"Okay, be right back."

They caught the mayor just coming out the door. "Mayor, how 'bout swearing me in now and I'll start being a deputy. I see José already has his badge."

"Fine, Deputy, I'm glad you are ready." One, two, three and she was sworn in with badge pinned on all legal-like.

"Thank you, Mayor. I will try not to disappoint you and the people of this town."

"I'm sure you won't."

They headed over to the jail for a look around. It is still being looked after by two men from the town. Tomorrow, that will change.

"Señora Margaret, do you want to get something to eat."

"Let's get something and take it to the house and eat with Grace."

"Sì. I would like that. Is there a place behind the house for the horses and buggy?"

"Yes there is."

"Okay, good."

"That's where I saw that tub. We'll get it inside?"

"Sì."

Grace had cleared out the cobwebs, swept the floor, and even mopped. The place looked better and smelled better, too.

"See Mama, it didn't take too much."

"Why Grace, you're right. It's gonna be a home. We are lucky the well is close by too. First thing in the morning, I want that tub inside. I am gonna soak in hot water."

The cowhands with the herd were starting to come in for the evening meal. Everyone was slowing down for the day. Taters had the meal laid out with the help of Antonina. Frankie B. and OK Bill were eating together with Prairie Flower and Angelina. Mr. Dickenson and Long John were in line with their plates and cups. You could smell the apple pies. Mrs. Sikorski is spoiling this bunch with those pies. "Better get a piece before they're all gone," Tommy said. "Hey Harve, want a piece a pie?"

"Sure do. That smell reminds me of being back in west Texas. My mama sure could bake them apple and cherry pies and them fried pies, too. A young lady I admire a lot made them fried pies at a church doings back in Texas and got me in the marrying mood. Tommy, you ever eat a fried pie?"

"Sure did, Harve. In southwest Virginia, they make them fried pies at the country churches a lot of times, mostly apple when the apples come in."

"Yeah, they're mostly apple in west Texas, too. Ah, Mrs. Sikorski, Ma'am, have you ever made them fried pies?"

"Yes I have, Harve. My husband and son would race each other to see who would get through eating faster so they could get the last fried pie. If my husband got through faster, he'd still give my son half."

"Ma'am, sorry for your loss. I didn't mean to bring up those memories for you."

"That's okay, Harve. I am fine."

Long John and Captain Fuller talked about leaving at the same time tomorrow on the way to Lipscomb. The herd and cowhands might just be a deterrent, in case anybody was thinking about breaking out the Clem Wilson bunch.

"I'm wondering now if we will have to stay in Lipscomb till after the trial if that town don't have much of a law force. I hope there's a marshall stationed there with about a dozen men. If not, it'll fall to us to protect the citizens."

"Yeah, Stephen, you just might not get to put in for that retirement you were talking about yet."

"Yeah, I know John. I'll get to it whenever we get back. I told Camilla this shouldn't take too long. It always takes longer than we like, I know. She's tired of waiting for me to put in my papers. I don't blame her one bit."

Well Stephen, you better get going with it before she dumps you for the other guy."

"What other guy?"

"I don't know. I just made that up. But you better think about that and get those papers in. Stephen, I'm going back to the herd. I'll see you in the morning."

"Okay John, I'm gonna keep some of our boys in town camped right in front of the jail. We'll be ready to move out early. See you then."

Margaret and Grace slept in their house. José slept on the porch on his blanket and saddle. When morning came around, the whole town started to bustle with activity. A lot of coffee and plates of biscuits and gravy were being dished out in the saloon and at the Rangers' camps both in town and out by the new well. The Rangers had split up into two groups last night. Captain Fuller had the covered wagon brought up in front of the jail and had the prisoners brought out and secured in it. They had a good meal just like the other townsfolk. They wouldn't be seeing Higgins any time soon. The question came up from several people about the businesses and building that Clem Wilson owned in the area and town. Who would own them now and run them? The mayor, acting as his own legal adviser, looked up the very question in his law books. He had the qualifications to be a lawyer; after all, he had gone to law school back east. He just never went on for his law license. He said, "The property will be in receivership, meaning the town will manage and run all businesses and property of any of the accused till either they sell or the judgement of the court declares there be a sale. As far as managing businesses," the mayor read, "he alone can appoint who he wants to run them." Phyllis and her two children were also waking from a good night's sleep. Something they haven't had much of lately. Phyllis was finely completely clear headed after what seemed like days of going in and out of a drugged state. It seemed like Clem Wilson kept her in a drugged state so she wouldn't know or care what happened to her children. And when the time came for her to be handed over to the Comancheros, she wouldn't put up a fight. Now with all that behind her, Phyllis needed to get her strength back. The town doctor will take a look at her today sometime when everything settles down. Tim Shiloh made it a point to look in on her every once in a while. Tim asked Long John if it would be alright if he looked in on her one more time this morning before they pulled out?

"Sure, you can catch up easily Tim."

"Long John, I have to tell her how I am feeling."

"That's okay, Tim, you won't be satisfied until you do. Sometimes a thing will get stuck in your craw, and you won't be satisfied till you get it out."

The cattle were already moving slowly. OK Bill and Red Fox had an early start.

Mr. Dickenson said, "That's okay, Long John, let them go. They'll be moving so slow at first it won't matter. Anyway, Taters is 'bout packed up so he'll be moving the two wagons. It's gonna be a hot one today. Did our people pack up extra water like I said?"

"Yes Sir, we got every available barrel, canteens, and a few water skins full."

"Good. We should get pretty close to Lipscomb by late afternoon, I would say. After that, it will be three days or more before we reach liberal Kansas, and we don't know about water. From now on for a while, it will be water where we find it. I asked Carlyle if he knew of any water holes going north. Said he didn't know. OK Bill said he didn't know of any either. Frankie B. headed back in town to say a few words to José and Margaret. He found them together at the house.

"José, I just want to say that I wish you and Margaret well and God bless you both. When we come back this way, I expect to see you two keeping the peace here in Higgins! You both and Grace have been the best fighters and friends I've ever run into. I hate to leave you behind. If we run into bandits, I'll be wishing you three were with us. I can't stay long. The herd is already moving, I gotta go, my friends."

"Amigo, you have been a good friend, also. Señora Margaret, do you not think so?"

"Yes I do. If we didn't have a job to do right here, we'd be riding right along with you."

Grace said, "Frankie B., thank you again. You have showed Mama and me how to survive. We don't have to give up thanks to you. We know how to fight."

He hugged the three of them. "I'll be thinking 'bout you, wondering how you're doing. Ah, we'll see each other in 'bout six months, I suppose."

"Hasta la vista, Compadre."

"Bye José!" Frankie B. got up on his horse, touched his hat with his right hand fingers, swung around several times, and was off to catch the herd. By now, the wagon with the prisoners and the last of the Texas Rangers had pulled out and things got almost too quiet. Tim was still on the other side of town at the hotel trying to get the up the nerve to tell Phyllis how he felt.

"Phyllis, you said you don't remember me from the other night taking you out of this room."

"That's right, Tim Shiloh. Thank you for getting me outta here. I don't know what Wilson had in mind for me. I can only imagine."

"If you don't remember me, that's gonna have to do for now. But I want you to know that holding you close to me, feeling you, and smelling you was the greatest feeling I have ever had. I wonder if you might allow me to hold you again before I go?"

"Yes Tim, come here." Phyllis grabbed him and they hugged. Tim hung on for the longest time. "You know I'm broken and I have been abused. Why would you want me?"

"Phyllis, I don't know, I just do. If you will allow me to see you when we come back this way, I would be honored."

"Yes you can."

"Okay, till then. I will look forward to seeing you again. Bye. Bye, Joseph and Agatha."

"Bye Tim, we will remember you."

Tim went down the outside stairs. Phyllis could hear every step he took from the jingle of his spurs. One last look at the door upstairs, then a slow ride out of town. Things unclear in his head. Catching up to the herd was no problem, they hadn't gone too far. Tim caught up to Long John to see where he wanted him. "How 'bout you fill in that spot behind Frankie B. and Angelina?"

"Okay Boss. I want to talk to you later, okay?"

"Sure, anytime."

The Rangers were out in front. One of the young Rangers was driving the prisoner wagon. The wagon was surrounded front and back by other Rangers. A quick stop was made every once in a while for a drink of water or to relieve water. No wonder with all the bouncing and shaking in that wagon. Mr. Dickenson was right out there moving around the herd. Talking to everyone as he went. When he got to Mrs. Sikorski, he couldn't resist saying something about the pies.

"I like how good the pies are and make sure you have enough to keep making more."

"I will, Sir. I'm happy to keep making them."

"Ma'am, would you like to help Taters and Antonina more with the meals or are you okay with riding herd?"

"Ah, I don't know. Maybe I could change off once in a while, Sir. I know how important the meal is for everybody after a work day. I was used to cooking for my husband, two sons, and daughter."

"I'm sorry for that, Ma'am."

"I don't know what happened. My husband and a son were killed and one of my boys run off. He's sixteen. And as you know, Antonina is with me. They didn't bother with him. All they wanted was me and my daughter. If it wasn't for Frankie B., OK Bill, Carlyle, Red Fox, Prairie Flower, and Angelina coming on, the Comancheros when they did, Antonina and I would be… well ,Sir, you know what we would be. If we would even be alive by now."

"Yes, Ma'am, and I am sorry. What was your husband like?"

"He was kind and gentle. They killed him and my older son right away. They didn't take any chances. When my son Hansie ran out the back door, they didn't even chase him. I think he is being taken care of by my husband Jacob's people. He had a lot a relatives living close to where we lived in southern Illinois."

"I didn't think the Comancheros raided into Illinois!"

"The bandits that took us, I don't know what you would call them. They were a mix of White and Mexican, and very mean. They took us and a few other women to Arkansas and traded or sold us to other bandits that called themselves Comancheros. I know cause I heard them use the word."

"Ma'am. We fought them all around Texas in my younger days and no matter how many we killed, there was always more. And there are still plenty of them. I hope we can be ready if they attack us. Don't forget, we are in more danger from bandits, hostile Indians, and Comancheros now than we were. Everybody must watch each other's back, and keep your powder dry, as the saying goes. Ma'am, do you have a few sticks of dynamite?"

"Yes."

"Do you know how to handle it?"

"Never have but just let someone threaten us and I'll soon learn how."

"I'll have Frankie B. give you and Antonina a few tips. Would that be alright?"

"Yes Sir."

"Okay then. When we get the herd to Montana, if you want to stay with my regular hands and go back to Texas with us, I will see that you have a job and a home."

"Thank you, Sir."

"Ma'am." Mr. Dickenson tipped his hat and moved on around the herd.

OK Bill and Red Fox had a good lead on the cattle and that made the cattle in front pick up the speed. That's what they wanted, get to Lipscomb, Texas, early before night fall. With things going the way they are, they will make it easy.

Carlyle and Dance are chasing the ones that don't want to keep up. Sometimes that's a really tough job. The cattle wander into a gully or quicksand where you gotta rope them and drag them out and they are too dumb to help get themselves free. Prairie Flower and Angelina kept them moving from left to right in the back. Red Fox motioned to OK Bill he was going off to the west. OK Bill gave him the go ahead. They each understand sign language, even from different tribes. Within a short time, Red Fox was back from over a hill with a deer draped over his saddle. He went past OK Bill straight to Taters' wagon. Taters saw him coming and stopped. They put the deer in the wagon. Red Fox jumped back on his horse without even touching his stirrups. Taters walked over to Red Fox's horse and held its head with his left hand and rubbed its forehead then signed to Red Fox, *Thank you, my friend.* Red Fox signed back, *Friend.* He swung his horse around and went back to the herd. Juan, pulled up with the other wagon and said, "Deer meat is good, Señor."

"That's right, something different, I think they will all appreciate it. As soon as we stop, let's get it cut up and on the fire."

"Si Señor. We need to hurry in this heat."

"Yeah. Let's you and I go on ahead and find a spot and gut and clean it before we make camp."

"Si Señor, that's a good idea."

They hung the deer on a tree branch and did all the cleaning and cut it into manageable pieces ready for the cooking fire. Took a while. Everyone was past them, except Carlyle. He stayed behind to keep a sharp eye out for trouble. Once they got the meat in the wagon and covered up, they were finished there. There was no sense covering up the remains. The buzzards and scavengers would only have to dig it up, so they left it in the open, cut down from the tree. They could still see the tail end of the herd and a couple riders, not sure who they were.

Carlyle, all of a sudden, said, "We got company. Get out of the wagons, grab a rifle, and stand on the back side by your other rifle. They look like Indians." Carlyle sat on his horse, one rifle already in his hand. Taters fired two quick shots. "Then both of you cover me while I talk to them. They might not have seen the herd passing if they just come on us from the east. Long John will have heard those two shots. How many do you make?"

"Ah, I see five. All have rifles in hand. I make them out to be Crow, looking for a fight."

Long John and the others did hear the shots.

"Could be an ambush to take the herd or to take the prisoners. Frankie B., you and me, let's go."

He yelled to fire two shots for the Rangers. Mr. Dickenson quickly fired, the Rangers stopped and took up defensive positions and sent a rider to find out what was happening.

"We don't know yet. Get some binoculars on Long John."

Mr. Dickenson stopped the herd and said, "Tighten up, everybody, tighten up where you are. Do a 360° look around. Make sure no one is coming at us from all sides."

Dance said, "Sir, I got an eye on Long John and Frankie B. They're at the wagons. Looks like they have about five Crow coming at them from the east with rifles in hand. Taters and Juan are out of their wagons covering Carlyle on horseback, waiting to have a talk and see what they want."

"Good to see you boys."

Frankie B. said, "Well, we heard the shots and come a running. Taters, you still know how to fire that rifle?"

"You bet your ass I do. Staying alive is one habit I'll never forget."

The Crow pulled up and one yelled, "You not belong here. This Crow land."

Carlyle responded, "This is Shoshone land. Not your land, not my land. Shoshone chief say we can cross to Montana."

"You lie, this Crow land. You give us deer to cross."

"No, I not lie, we will give you some deer meat if you leave in peace. Otherwise, we will fight. And you will die," Carlyle said. "We have many more riders over there. They heard our shots. Where are your riders? Take this meat and leave us. If you were Shoshone, you would say to us, 'Go in peace.' What do Crow say?"

Crow say, "This our land. We have much fight in us."

Carlyle asked, "Which one chief?"

"No chief, much warrior. Chief Long Horse over hill, very brave."

Carlyle turned and said to Long John, "I hope I'm not putting you in danger. But did you hear the brave say his chief is Long Horse. I'd like to tell him my chief is Long John, and see what he says about that. Maybe that will get us out of killing them."

"Go ahead, Carlyle!"

He swung his horse back toward the Crow and said, "My chief name Long John, very brave Ranger, kill many enemy."

"We know Rangers, very brave Whites," the Indian said. "Chief Long John? That make him big medicine. My chief big medicine."

Long John came around the wagon, and took out a big piece a deer meat, wrapped it with a piece of deer hide, and walked over next to Carlyle and said, "I'm Long John. Take this meat and give it to Long Horse, a gift from me, Long John. Tell him, I know war and killing. I want only peace with the Crow!"

The Indian took the piece of meat.

Long John walked right out to the Crow sitting on horseback without a fear in the world and handed it to the one doing all the talking. And said, "Peace. Tell Long Horse I will meet with him if he wants to talk peace."

The Indian said, "Peace, Chief Long John." They turned their horses and rode off slow like they had to figure out what just happened.

"Well, Long John, one less war to fight."

"That's right, Carlyle. I think maybe we got to them. They can't keep fighting all the time. I bet they don't even have enough to eat half the time. Maybe we'll get to see how they live, if we get an invite from their chief."

"Okay, let's get back."

"Taters, Juan, Frankie B., Carlyle, good job. We don't want to start a war out here. Maybe we headed one off . How close are we to that town, I wonder"

"I'd like to not get too far from here in case we or I get invited. This could be a real breakthrough on peace with the Crow that we and the Crow need. Mostly the Crow need."

"Long John, I have to say, if anyone is a peacemaker, it's you."

"Yeah, well, Carlyle, I been fighting and killing for so long it feels good to talk about peace. The Crow have no reason to fight for land that has been Shoshone home land anyway."

Back with the herd, everybody wanted to know what was going on. Carlyle did a lot of explaining. Mr. Dickenson said, "Let's keep these cattle moving. We want to make Lipscomb as soon as we can. We can talk as we go. We only have a few miles. And I'm hoping for water. The cattle are getting agitated."

"Yes Sir." There were a few other yes Sirs. "Captain Long John, I believe you are right on calling for peace with the Crow. If only they take you up on it."

"I hope their chief wants to talk peace. Sir, even if they don't want peace with us, maybe they will think about it when the next whites come through. You know it would have been so easy to just kill them; easy if they would have pushed us. I just didn't want to. There could have been a lot more of them just over that hill waiting for us to make a wrong move."

Captain Fuller came riding through the herd to see what was going on. "Captain Lowther, what's happening?"

"Well, I kinda talked them into peace, at least for now. I don't know how long it will last. I gave their chief, Long horse, a gift of a fresh piece of deer meat. I've yet to hear back from them. I told his braves I would talk peace as Chief Long John to Chief Long Horse. Somehow his braves think I'm on the same level as their chief because I'm Long John. I didn't discourage it since it kept us from killing the five of them."

"Yeah, I see what you did. It can't hurt."

"If they come to get me for a talk with the chief, I'll see what he's willing to agree to."

"Okay, John, see what you can do. You know we been through these powwow's before over the years. Sometimes they're productive and other times, a waste a time."

"Okay, we'll see."

"You be careful, John, if you go back out there. I'll see you later. I gotta get back to my boys. We're almost at Lipscomb."

"I'll try, Stephen. I think you should take your cattle around the town. I hear there's a creek on the other side of town. Plenty of water."

Captain Fuller rode up to Mr. Dickenson and touched his hat and said, "Captain Dickenson, see you in town, Sir."

"Okay Captain."

By the time Captain Fuller got back to his men, they were already at the edge of town.

"Lt., let's see what kind of law they have here and get these prisoners locked up in the jail."

"Yes Sir, Captain."

"Sergeant, keep the men close to this wagon till we turn over the prisoners. We need to see what we got here."

Three men walked out of the sheriff's office with badges on.

"Are there any Rangers here?"

"Not right now. I'm Marshall McCoy, Bill McCoy. This is Sheriff Ray Jones and Deputy Randy Smith. Are you Captain Fuller?"

"Yes I am. Before I turn over these prisoners, I will need some kinda proof of who you are. You got any proof?"

"All I have is a letter from Marshall Powers, my boss in Austin, Texas. The judge here, and the mayor in Lipscomb knows me as the sheriff."

"Okay, let's go over to the courthouse now and clear this up."

"Let's go, Captain."

"Lieutenant, keep these men in place till we get back."

"Yes Sir, Captain."

The courthouse was just a short walk from the sheriff's office.

"Sheriff, you lead the way. I've never been here before."

Once inside, the Mayor stepped into the hallway.

"Can I help you, Captain? I'm Mayor Dick Haverman."

"Yes, come with us to the judge's office."

"Sure, be there in one minute."

A secretary stopped them. "The judge is busy. Can I help you?"

"We need to speak to the judge. It is very urgent."

"Wait here and I will tell Judge McIntosh."

They could hear, "By all means, show them in." The judge was cordial.

"Come in, come in. What seems to be the problem?"

"Judge Macintosh, I'm Captain Stephen Fuller of the Texas Rangers."

"Yes, I have heard of you. Good to finally meet you," the judge said with a hand shake and a how do you do.

"Can you tell me who these two men are?"

"Sheriff Ray Jones and Deputy Randy Smith."

"Do you or the judge know if they have any connection to Clem Wilson or any of his men?"

"No Captain, I do not have any knowledge of that."

"Judge, do you, Sir, have any knowledge of that?"

"No Captain."

"Then will you both accept responsibility of the prisoners?"

"Sir, you might want to take a look out at the prisoners."

"Yes, I suppose we should."

"Judge, you will need to start the proceedings for a fast trial. And get more marshalls in Lipscomb. You will need them for yours and the town's protection."

"I will do what I can, Captain Fuller."

293

"Okay Judge, then I will put these men in the custody of Marshall McCoy and Sheriff Jones. I will have to stay here in Lipscomb with my men for a few days till more Marshalls get here. Judge, can you get things moving, Sir?"

"Captain, a trial takes time to put together."

"Judge, that's why you need extra security. A lot can happen before a trial ever starts."

"Okay, Captain, I understand your concern. The marshalls should be back in a couple of days."

"Well Sir, I'd get a message to them right away, if I were you. I don't know what kind of connection this Clem Wilson has with the Comancheros but if they lost money on this deal for the woman and her young kids, they might just try and break him out. They would destroy this town and kill a lot of people in the process. And without backup, the sheriff and the marshall wouldn't have much of a chance."

"Okay, Captain. I know I'm a little slow, but you've made yourself pretty clear. The mayor and I will work together on backing up the sheriff and the marshall. Sheriff and Deputy, if you will come with me, we'll get the prisoners in the cells."

"I hope you got more than one cell, Sheriff."

"Yeah, we have three in the sheriff's office and three in the basement of this building."

"Good."

"Where you want them?"

"Which one is the more secure?"

"Probably this building."

"Okay then, let's get 'em in here. I will talk to you later Mayor Barnett and Judge Macintosh."

"Captain, thank you for staying with us for a few

days. You will want to set up camp. I would suggest the way you came in, just out of town."

"Thanks Mayor. That will be fine."

They left the court house to the gathering of a lot of townspeople outside asking what was going on. The mayor stayed back to explained. Captain Fuller motioned the Lt. to bring the wagon around the building. He went back in for a look see down the stairs and through a door to get down to the basement floor. Everything looked pretty secure. The cells were spread out from each other, which was good to keep the men apart. The whole basement was built from stone, bricks, and quarried blocks. No windows to the outside. About as secure as you can get.

The Lieutenant yelled, "Sergeant Reading, get the prisoners out and down these steps. Keep them chained together till I tell you otherwise."

They marched them down the long stairs and split them up into the three cells. Then they took the leg irons off .

The lieutenant said, "Sheriff, get some men down here that you know for sure you can trust. Sergeant, put two men down here till the sheriff gets his men here. And have them stay out of the cell rooms."

"Okay, Lt."

The captain was busy talking to the mayor about supplies.

"Mayor, do you have a supply train or wagon coming this way anytime soon? There's a lot more people here now than you had this morning. Can you feed everybody? My rangers have some supplies but not enough for a couple weeks. I hope to God we won't have to stay that long! But Mayor, we might. I'd suggest you get on your telegraph and get as much supplies as you can. And I wouldn't wait too long to get your marshalls and supplies before some bandits or Comancheros cut the wire. That cattle herd out there wants to pull out tomorrow. So don't count on them fighting for this town, unless we get attacked tonight. Then they would be the best fighters you could have, except for my Rangers."

"Captain, I guess you could say I don't have the experience you and your people have. So thank you for the advice. I'll get to the telegraph office right now and take care of the supplies and marshalls."

"By the way, Mayor, can you trust the operator to send your message, word for word?"

"I guess so, Captain. I never thought about it before."

"Well, you better be sure because we have the telegraph operator from Higgins here locked up in the jail with the rest of the Clem Wilson people. So I would suggest if you know anybody else that can send and receive messages, you better grab them and take them with you when you're sending messages from now on. It could be a matter of life and death."

"Yes Captain, I understand what you're saying. I do know someone. I'll get them right now."

Chapter 11

Long John and Mr. Dickenson were sitting around having their evening meal. The deer was cleaned and all of it roasted on an open fire with Taters' special home recipe. Taters said you needed to brush on his mix while it roasts. Plenty of the hands volunteered and spent a few minutes brushing on the gravy mix. Everybody will have a chance to try it and finish off with a piece of Mrs. Sikorski's homemade pies. Frankie B. and OK Bill finished off their meal of deer roast with gravy and biscuits and, of course, apple pie. They were heading out to relieve Red Fox and Tommy when a gun shot went off.

Long John yelled out, "Anybody hit?"

A lot of no answers came back.

"Well then, we better find out who fired that shot. Is everybody here that's supposed to be here or is anyone missing?"

Dance took a quick check. "Nobody missing Boss."

Just then, Carlyle came into the middle of the camp with a young boy by the neck. "Here's your shooter," he said. "He was hunting for a deer, shot and missed."

"Okay Carlyle, is he telling the truth?"

"As far as I can tell he is. He said his mama and brother and him are hungry. They live in a cabin not far from here."

"Tell him to cut off a piece of meat for himself and his mama and brother. And grab some biscuits." The boy did and said a quick thanks and was gone with his sack of grub.

Frankie B. and OK Bill went off and relieved Red Fox and Tommy so they could have their evening meal.

The Rangers were having their meal, too, when they heard that shot. And they, too, did the roll call on names. Everyone had his pistol in hand looking for the shooter. One of the Rangers rode into the Dickenson camp to see what they knew. Satisfied that they were not being attacked, he headed back to the Rangers—after a good cup of coffee and a piece of apple pie .

When he left, Dance said with a laugh, "Now I suppose they'll all be coming around for piece a pie and coffee."

Harve quipped, "Yeah, and I wouldn't blame them, would you, Dance?"

"I guess not. The Rangers will probably kidnap Mrs. Sikorski so she can make apple pies for them." Long John was listening to the B.S. about the pies and said, "Okay, cow punchers, if we don't have to rescue Mrs. Sikorski from the Rangers, we move out early tomorrow morning. So I'm turning in early. It looks like we are not going to get a visit from the Crow chief or at least not till morning. So as soon as I walk out to the edge of camp and get a look at the stars, I'll be turning in."

"Yeah, I guess we should, too. We all need our beauty sleep," one of the guys said.

Mr. Dickenson was already asleep with his book open on his chest. Antonina was busy putting more wood on the fires. Gotta keep that coffee warm, and have a little light for a while yet. Not everybody turns in early. And when the watchers and riders change, they head for the hot coffee pot.

The Rangers, a short distance away, were doing the same. A few were staying up to guard the courthouse where the prisoners were kept. The mayor sent his telegraph for more marshalls to hurry back and to get more supplies of every kind brought in. The townsfolk were turning down their lamps and going to sleep for another night. The marshall was doing some last minute paper work, while the sheriff and deputy were outside getting a sense of what was going on in the saloon. No rowdy bunch in there tonight, so it should stay peaceful. Nobody from the Dickenson people or the Rangers were in the saloon. Just a handful of locals. Captain Fuller, the Lt., and Sergeant Reading were sitting around a fire sipping on a cup a coffee.

"Captain, we ever gonna get back to Austin?"

"Well, Sergeant, I'd like to leave in the morning, but we can't do it. We'd be leaving this town to the mercy of whoever wants to break these guys out. We don't know for sure if there is anybody. But we can't take that chance. Hopefully it won't be more than a couple of days till the marshalls get back, then we can leave. You know, Captain Dickenson and his people are leaving in the morning. They gotta get that herd to Helena, Montana, before the winter hits. So we will do whatever it takes to keep this town safe. I got plans I have to put on hold till we get back. So we won't stay any longer than we have to."

"Okay Captain, that's all I needed to know."

"Ah, Sergeant, tell the men to sleep with one eye open. And don't get to far away from their rifles. Oh, and keep a couple sentries on duty on each end of town. If we're gonna get attacked in the middle of the night, I want to be ready. You know how we did things before when we were fighting those sons a bitches down close to the border. We sleep with our boots on and our horses saddled. It could be the same kind of bandits we're up against. And if not, then we got the upper hand."

"Yes Sir, Captain."

"Ah, Lt., I'm going over to the telegraph office and send out my own wire to the marshalls. Maybe I can get them moving a little faster. First, I got to find out who the other person is the mayor was talking about to send a wire."

"You want me to go with you?"

"You know, maybe you should."

They headed straight to the mayor's home. The mayor was sitting on his porch with his wife when they saw the two coming, walking briskly along. They both tipped their hats with their fingers and said, "Ma'am, Mayor. Nice evening."

"Yes it is, Captain."

"Ma'am, this will only take a minute. We need to ask the mayor who is the other telegraph operator. I need to send a message."

"It's Jim Moore. He works in the post office. He's probably home now. He lives outside of town about a mile out this direction."

"Okay, Mayor. thanks. Ma'am," they did their finger to hat salutes and left.

It was a nice evening for a ride, so they got on their horses. Going by the post office, seeing the door open, they stopped. Jim Moore was in there doing some last minute work.

"Jim?"

"Yes Sir, what can I do for you?"

"Well, I understand you know telegraph code."

"Yes, Captain, I do."

"I would like you to accompany us to the telegraph office and make sure we are sending and receiving the accurate message. I don't know who I can trust. The mayor seemed to trust you. The man doing the sending, what about him?"

"Captain, he hasn't been here too long so no one knows him. Captain, you write down your message here before we go and I will send and receive for you. So if you want, he won't know your message. Keep it as short as possible."

"Okay, good idea."

Message put on paper and the three of them walked over to the telegraph office. The man didn't like the idea but the captain told him it was top secret for the government. And he said he understood. With the answer in his hand, out the door they went back to the post office.

Jim said, "Have a seat. I'll get us some coffee. Captain, I'll tell you a secret. I'm actually with the government. The U.S. government sent me here. I won't say why, but I will say it has nothing to do with the post office. Captain, I have to insist that neither of you tell anyone. The mayor and the postmaster knows. No one else in town knows."

"Okay, Jim. Lt., you got that?"

"Yes Sir, Captain."

Captain Fuller got the answer he was hoping for. "We will get there day after tomorrow," signed Marshall Powers.

"Okay, that takes care of that. Jim, how do you communicate with your officials. I hope you have another way in case the wires get cut."

"The mail, but it's a lot slower."

"You know if anyone attacks this town, the first thing they will do is cut the wires."

"Yes, I'm aware of that."

"Mail isn't too good either. They would stop a rider."

"But it's all I have."

"Okay, Jim, we gotta go. We may be talking to you again."

"See you, Captain, Lieutenant. Remember what I said, I need the cover."

"You got it. Lt., let's turn in. Make sure the boys are on their toes. Just in case."

"Alright." The night was coming down, already pretty dark. Everything at the Dickenson camp was quiet: fire crackling, some bugs were the only sound, even the cattle were quiet. The eyes of the night watch and herd riders were very much alert for anything. So far nothing. As the morning started to come around, both camps began to stir. The cooks and helpers have the responsibility to get the day started off on the right foot with how the morning feed goes. That's what Taters says. If your coffee is not too hot or not too cold or not too weak or not too strong, and if your biscuits aren't burnt, then you will most likely have a pretty good day. Mr.

Dickenson was up washing his face when Carlyle was already sipping his coffee and Mrs. Sikorski was just heading to the creek for a bath. Her daughter Antonina was still Taters' helper. Getting the wash pans full a water, towels, and soap on the tables, plates, coffee cups, and whatever was needed for morning meal. Long John, still sleeping for a while. Frankie B. was waking up, close to Angelina, each with their heads on their saddles. OK Bill and Red Fox will get the herd moving in about an hour. Mr. Dickenson and Long John filled everyone in yesterday. We are moving out, heading for the high country as soon as everyone gets fed. By now, Long John was waking himself up, splashing cold water in his face. Dance and Tommy and Juan just came in for their hot meal. Mr. Dickenson sat down with his plate of biscuits and gravy with a piece a deer meat and a steaming cup of coffee. He looked around to see how everyone was doing. And spotted Mrs. Sikorski combing out her hair and thought to himself, *As soon as she gets through eating, we are moving out.* Long John told everyone what he wanted them to do this morning to get started with the herd and he'd catch up. He wanted to say a few words to Captain Fuller before they left. The captain saved him a trip.

"Can you spare a cup of coffee, Sergeant Taters?"

"You damn well betcha, Captain. Just get down off of that old nag of a horse and I'll pour you one myself. Have you had your breakfast yet?"

"Yeah, I've eat. Just wanted to say good luck with your days ahead to all of you. And may the good Lord ride with all of you. I hope to see you all back in Texas when you get back." He shook Captain

Dickenson's and Captain Long John's hands. And got a hug and a hand shake from Sergeant Taters. Looked all around and said, "Goodbye, you all. Thanks for the coffee." He got on his horse and rode off a short distance, stopped, swung his horse around, and with two fingers touched the wide brim of his hat. He then went back to his men.

Mrs. Sikorski just finished her breakfast. Mr. Dickenson got up, threw the last bit of coffee in the fire, and said, "Okay, Long John, let's ride."

"You heard the man, OK Bill, move 'em out."

Red Fox walked over to his pinto, straightened the eagle feather on the horse's bridle, rubbed his nose, and said something soft to the horse. It must have liked what he said 'cause it answered him with a loud nicker and pushed against Red Fox. He tightened up his saddle and jumped on, Comanche style, and caught up to OK Bill. They said a few words to each other and went to work. As soon as OK Bill rode out in front, the cattle followed. Red Fox stayed on the west side till Prairie Flower and Angelina showed up, then he fell back for a while. Carlyle came up the back. Red Fox and Carlyle had a short conversation, then they parted. Red Fox went ahead to look for water. Typical day: Juan, driving one of the wagons, Long John rode along with Mr. Dickenson at the tail end.

"I sure hope we can have a few weeks or even a month without any surprises or shootouts. Just boring pushing cattle every day. I don't mind helping out when we're needed or meeting up with old friends. But you know what I'm trying to say, Long John?"

"Yes, I do Sir. We're running out of good weather. And we still got a long way to go. Let's go till dark for a few days and see if we can pick up more miles. I asked Red Fox to scout out ahead and look for water. So if you don't see him, that's why. I don't know of any rivers or lakes along the way, till we get to the Yellowstone, so we're gonna have to depend on water holes and wells and uncharted creeks. If they're out there, Red Fox or OK Bill will find them."

"Okay, Long John, you know what you're doing." This day and the next couple of weeks were just ordinary days: up in the morning, push cows all day, night time relaxing, and good food coming out of the chuck wagon, Red Fox shooting a deer or rabbit quietly with bow and arrow, and Mrs. Sikorski and Antonina making those delicious apple pies and once in a while cherry pies and smaller fried pies if they were able to buy canned cherries at some local general store. Things were going pretty well. By now, they were close to Denver, Colorado, when trouble hit. A gang of rustlers tried to take the herd away. They were no match for the Dickenson people. After about a half hour of fighting, five rustlers were dead, six were tied up, and on their way to the Denver jail after they dug the graves for their accomplices. The dynamite really did come in handy. But they only used two sticks and two bullets and the whole thing was over.

"Before the day is over, we should be in Denver. We can turn these six over to the sheriff." Long John praised everyone for a great effort and how well we all worked together. Prairie Flower surprised the heck out of them when she killed two with a stick of dynamite. Unfortunately, it killed their horses, too. Juan killed one with a stick of dynamite. Mr. Dickenson killed one with a rifle and Tommy beat one to the draw. The six were ready to quit after that and gave up. They are tied to their horses' saddle horn. And followed behind by Mrs. Sikorski and Prairie Flower. They kinda got the message, with both rifles aimed at them. Five more horses tied to the wagon Juan's driving. More guns and saddles.

"That's alright, we didn't ask for 'em. We'll add them to our surplus of guns, knives, and ammo," Long John told Juan. "Keep these horses tied to the wagon for a couple days, then turn them loose with the others, and see if they stay with us."

"Si, Señor. The others are doing just fine. I watch them every day."

The herd was getting to Denver early so they went on past. Frankie B. and Long John took the rustlers in to the sheriff and explained what happened.

"Can you be here for a trial?"

"How soon is the trial?"

"Don't know. Could be soon or could be couple weeks. All depends on the judge."

"We gotta keep pushing these cattle to Helena, Montana."

"Tell you what, these rustlers are wanted for other cattle rustling and a few murders so we should have enough for a trial, plenty of witnesses to put them away for a while. Tell you what, you telegraph me here in a couple days and I'll tell you if you will be needed for evidences against them."

"Okay, Sheriff. If that's all you need from us, we'll be on our way. Oh, what do you want to do with their horses? They're tied up out front. We got their guns and holsters, too."

"Leave them here. And I'll take their guns, too."

"I kinda thought they would be considered trophies of war, so to speak, Sheriff. They should never be able to use these weapons on another human being."

The sheriff put his hand up to his chin and thought for a second.

"You know what, Mr. Lowther, take the weapons, leave the horses. These guys are going to prison. It's almost a sure bet. I might need their horses to ride them out of town, but I don't need their weapons."

"Thanks Sheriff, we can use the rifles and pistols, and whatever ammo they have along with knives. Our herd has a long way to go. We can use them. Frankie B., get everything tied on to our horses and we'll be on our way. Bye Sheriff, we might see you on our way back unless you need us sooner. I'll telegraph you as soon as we hit a town. Hopefully we won't be too far away. I'd hate to have to ride back a long way."

"Bye, boys, see ya."

They rode through Denver and caught up with the herd.

"Here you go, Juan, more guns for our people. Put them in the wagon. How's everything going?"

"Good, Señor."

"Okay then, let's keep 'em going as long as we got light."

Mr. Dickenson saw long John way off and motioned him to come over.

"How'd it go, Long John?"

"We got them locked up. I guess it's up to the court now. The sheriff there said they are wanted for murder and rustling, so they probably will end up in prison. I need to send him a telegraph when we get to a town in a couple days in case they need me and Frankie B. for witnesses. I hope not. We'll see, Sir."

"Yeah, that would be bad if you had to go back." Frankie B. went over to Angelina and squeezed her hand, and tipped his hat to Prairie Flower.

"Is your mother having any problems since she killed those two rustlers?"

"I don't think so. She seems pretty normal to me."

"Okay. It is a big thing, you know. I just wondered."

"I know, but she knows that they had to be stopped or one of us or more might have been killed and the cattle taken. So I don't think she has a problem with it. I believe that is the Comanche way. I, Angelina, see it that way too."

"You know, Angelina, I understand what you're saying. I feel the same way. The men I killed would have killed me or any of our friends, so I don't lose any sleep over them. I don't like killing, but it becomes necessary living out here. Let's talk about something else. Can we cuddle up when the air gets cold?"

"Frankie B., I do believe you want what you can't have. But I will show you how we show our love for each other."

"Okay, I will freshen up and see you later when we stop."

"Okay."

Mr. Dickenson called out to Long John. "Let's keep going for a while yet. Have Taters go on ahead and get set up and we'll stop when we catch up with him."

"Yes Sir, that's sounds good to me."

Red Fox shot a rabbit and a quail the usual way, with a bow and arrow. Soon as he gets a chance, he will take them to Taters and the night meal will have some of the best cooked rabbit and quail in the country. Taters really knows how to roast and season them, some kind of secret recipe he says. Don't matter, everybody loves his cooking. The sky is starting to dim. In the west, the sun is going over the mountains. Taters pulled up his wagon in a flat spot quite a ways ahead of the herd and started set up. Antonina broke away from the herd and rode up to Taters. She tied up her horse to the wagon and checked the water.

"We still have enough for everybody," she said to Taters. "And some for washing and cooking. But it is going down. We better ask OK Bill and Red Fox to start scouting for water."

"Well, I'm sure they know 'cause the cattle need water. They can't be without water for too long. Anyway, we can have our coffee."

Just then, Red Fox rode up with the rabbit and quail. He got down off his horse and handed them to Taters.

"Well, good, everybody will like the extra meat. Thanks my friend."

Red Fox nodded and got back on his horse and left. As soon as the meat was ready, it went on the fire. The riders started to come in. Harve asked if he could help out with anything?

"Harve, if you don't mind, help Antonina with whatever she needs."

"Okay." They worked together and everything was done. The meal was served when the riders got their turn. The coffee was kept hot with Harve piling on wood to the fire. Mrs. Sikorski didn't bake any pies for a few days. And they missed them. Angelina and Prairie Flower stayed with the herd till it stopped. Then they came in for a piece of that rabbit or quail, and beans. Taters tried to give everyone a piece that wanted it. Long John got with OK Bill and Red Fox. And while they ate, they talked about water.

"How 'bout one of you scout ahead for water tomorrow. We're getting pretty desperate. Even if we have to go off the straight line. We don't find water soon, a lot of the cattle will start dying."

Mr. Dickenson went around the whole herd to see how they were holding up. And so far so good. Not one of the cattle were bawling. They're not starving for water yet. But they will be tomorrow night if we don't find water. And as the night come on, everybody rested up their way: some sang along with a guitar, others played cards, and Frankie B. found his way to Angelina. He remembered her promise: to show him love the Comanche way. When he got to her, it was dark, almost fully dark. He could see she was wrapped in a blanket with her back turned to him. When he got up to her, she said, "Take off your gun belt and your hat. I hope you washed your hands and face?"

"I did. I don't want to smell like cows or horses." Angelina turned and opened the blanket wide. She had on something, but not much. He moved instinctively inside the blanket, and she closed the blanket around both of them. He knew he couldn't stay there very long. His loins were starting to tighten up, along with something else tightening up.

Angelina said, "I will marry you, if you want me. This means we are each other's forever."

"Yes, I want you. I mean, I will marry you. You know what I mean."

"Yes I do, Frankie Butler."

He held on to her and could smell her and could almost taste her. Her skin was fresh and smelled like lilacs. They both held onto each other, and he kissed her. She responded with a kiss he will never forget. Now he did what he thought he was supposed to do, he pulled away. She closed the blanket and turned around. Frankie B., you should leave me now. I will dream of our wedding when we get back to the camp of my father and my mother."

Without a word, he put on his gun belt and hat and walked away, pondering what had just happened. He thought, *I'm gonna marry this girl if we ever get back to the Comanche camp. Probably not gonna be for another six months or more. That's like an engagement. That's what it is.* Frankie B. spread out his blanket and laid down with his head on the saddle. I think I need a cup of coffee. Up he came. I feel my heart is racing like a horse. In the morning, everything started out in the usual way. Off they went with the herd. Today we need water.

OK Bill said, "We find water."

After the herd got going pretty good, OK Bill motioned to Red Fox.

"I look for water. You stay with herd."

Mr. Dickenson rode along with Mrs. Sikorski for a while.

"When we get to East Boulder, we will get some supplies and you can get your pie filling, if that's alright with you, Ma'am."

"Yes Sir, it is."

As they rode on, everything was just fine.

Then OK Bill came around to Long John and said, "There is wagon at water hole. Three women and dog. We get there soon. Maybe they gone. Long John, what we do?"

"We keep going. We need water."

Mr. Dickenson came over to see what OK Bill said. "Three women in dresses and a dog at water hole not far ahead on a wagon; two horses, three rifles. Don't know about pistols."

So they kept up the pace to get to the water hole. Getting to the water, they could see the women just sitting there like they were waiting.

Mr Dickenson was the first one to talk to the women. "Hi Ladies. What are you doing out here by yourselves?"

One said, "We left Boulder and are heading for Montana. We have our guardian angel here— referring to the dog. His name is Gabriel, like the archangel."

Mr. Dickenson said, "Oh, I see. You think he'll be enough to fight off a bunch of bad guys?"

"I don't know. I would hope so."

"My name is Dolphus Dickenson. My people are coming up soon with the cattle."

"Well, Sir, we are Orlies, Clarius, and Glada. Two of us are teachers and our sister, Orlies, is a newspaper editor. We heard there is need for our professions in Montana."

"Well, Ma'am, there probably is, but you have a long way to go and it is not safe by yourselves. You would be wise to reconsider. It just so happens we are heading for Helena, Montana. It's going to take us a while to get there, but if you are not in a big hurry, you would be better off going along with us. We can offer you some protection."

"Well, we need to talk it over among ourselves."

"Yes, by all means. Here come my people. I do already have some women with our hands. You make up your minds and let one of my people know."

"Okay, Mr. Dickenson. Can we stay in your camp tonight, Mr. Dickenson?"

"Yes, you sure can."

The three young women were glad to be in a safe camp. They talked to Mrs. Sikorski, her daughter Antonina, Prairie Flower, and her daughter Angelina. They told them of the many dangers that could befall them. And that they would probably never make the trip. They would most likely be taken by the Comancheros and if they lived, would end up in Mexico.

Clarius said to the other two, "This would be a better way for us to get to Montana. Even if we have to work as cowhands. What do you two think?"

"Yes, I listened close to what those women said about being killed or worse. I'm for staying with these people. We will never get to Montana on our own. So if they will let us tag along or work as cowhands, I'm for doing it. How 'bout you Orlies? What you think?"

"I think it's our only choice."

"Okay, then let's talk to that Mr. Dickenson."

They didn't see him so they made their way to the cook wagon.

"Sir, can we help out with something?"

"Well, yes Ma'am. But who might you be?"

"Well Sir," Clarius spoke up, "we were at the water hole when Mr. Dickenson came up and he said we could stay in the camp tonight. We are Clarius, Glada, and Orlies. We are traveling to Montana."

"Pleased to meet you, Ladies. I'm called Taters. I'm the cook. If you really want to help, we would be grateful. The young lady coming up is my helper. She is Antonina. She's the daughter of Mrs. Sikorski."

"Yes, we've meet her and her mother."

"Okay then, ask her what she needs. We need to get things moving along. Supper for this crew has got to be coming up. How about pies? Can either of you bake pies?"

"Oh sure, we all can. What do you want?"

"I got a couple cans of cherry. Make us some cherry pies and they won't let you go anywhere. Mrs Sikorski bakes apple pies when she gets in early from riding herd all day. She's tired, but does it anyway cause she knows they love it."

"Well heck," said Clarius, "we'll make your pies. Where's the stuff? You got any apples? We'll make them, too."

"I got a few. They're not looking too good, but maybe you can save 'em."

They got busy and created three great looking pies. The hands could smell 'em as they were coming in. Long John saw the women with white flour on their hands and dresses. *Boy, they didn't waste any time.* Mr. Dickenson sure has a soft heart. He takes in anyone. And now they're baking pies already. Supper was served with apple or cherry pies tonight. The crew will never forget. Red Fox didn't bring in any rabbits or quail today. But the pies more than made up for just having beans and stew. The women were introduced to everyone as they came in and washed up for the meal. Tommy asked if he could take care of their horses and wagon.

"That would be great," Orlies said.

"Ma'am, I'm pleased to meet you. I'm Harve. I hear you all have a dog. I heard he is your angel Gabriel."

"Yes he is. He is our protecter. And he needs to be fed. He is on our wagon. Here he comes now walking with Tommy. Tommy made friends with him.

"Mr. Taters, can I have some scraps for our dog?"

"Yes Ma'am, Miss Glada, here you go."

Mr. Dickenson talked to the women.

"If you are interested, you can ride along with us on your wagon. Or you can switch off once in a while and ride a horse. We have plenty of horses and saddles. If you want to change clothes, we have some. If you would like to ride herd like the rest of us, you can do that, too."

"Thank you, Sir. We have some clothes to change. I think I would like to ride a horse."

"Ma'am, and which one are you?"

"I'm Orlies. My sisters can do what they want . I'd like to ride a horse for a couple days."

"That's fine. In the morning, have Juan show you the horses and you can pick one out. They're all broke in, but haven't been ridden for probably a month. Juan can show you our saddles, too. Ma'am, can you handle a rifle and pistol?"

"I sure can."

"Well then, you will get a rifle and pistol, too. Everyone riding with us needs to have a rifle and a couple pistols. And not be afraid to use them. I mean, really not afraid to use them. All of our women have shot and killed bandits. And before we get to Helena, Montana, if you go that far with us, I'm certain you three women will have to make that decision. You should talk to the other women on how to get good at handling a rifle and pistols. And practice up when you get the chance. Ma'am, I don't mean to scare you. But you need to know what you're up against. They will come after us. And most of the time, they intend to kill the men and take the women captive to sell to the highest bidder. Along with the herd. So, can you shoot to kill? Think about that. Frankie B. and OK Bill have been through a few shoot outs along with Mrs. Sikorski, her daughter Antonina, Angelina, and her mother Prairie Flower before they caught up to us. They all have fired their weapons to either save their own lives or to save one of us. And just the other day, we had a run in with rustlers. Five of them got killed and we took six to the Denver jail. None of us got hurt. Because we worked together. If you're thinking you can't do all that, Mrs. Sikorski can tell you how she felt. And how she feels now. Might be a good idea to talk to her about her and her daughter's captivity. And what she is willing to do to make sure it doesn't happen again."

"Okay, Mr. Dickenson, I will."

Everyone settled in for the night. Watches were set to go around the clock. Morning came and another day.

"Looks like rain," Frankie B. was saying to Long John.

"Yeah," he replied, sipping on his coffee. "How about those new women. Mr. Dickenson was telling

316

me we will escort them to Montana somewhere. We are to make gun hands out of them and fit them to a horse if they want one."

"Sounds good to me."

"So Frankie B., get Juan to take Miss Orlies out to the horses now before we get moving. Let her pick a horse, saddle, rifle, two hand guns, and a holster for one pistol if she wants a holster. If not, then she can hide the pistols on her. Tell her all that, Frankie B. I'd do it myself if I had time."

"Okay, Long John, I'll do it. No problem."

Juan just got the word so him and Miss Orlies picked out her horse and got her a saddle. They got the saddle on the horse together.

"Now, Señora Orlies, you have to put a rifle in that scabbard. Here, you take this one. I will empty it of bullets for now so you can get used to it. And here are two pistols. They have bullets in them. Be careful, Señora. Would you like a holster, Señora?"

"Yes I would."

"Okay, you pick one, Señora. You should have your sisters do as you have done. Maybe not today, but soon."

"Okay, I will talk to them about it, Juan, and thank you for all the help. And we need to get out of these dresses and into something more suitable for riding, with a cattle herd. She changed into a riding skirt and blouse that she had in a suitcase on the wagon. She put on her holster after making a few adjustments to it . Her hat was just fine. By now, the herd was moving. Clarius and Glada were driving their wagon. Miss Orlies rode up alongside them and tipped her hat.

"Morning, Ladies."

"Orlies, is that what you were talking about?"

"Yes."

Even Gabriel wasn't quite sure it was Miss Orlies. "Yes, this is what they want you to do in the next couple days."

"Okay, fine with us," Clarius said. "I'll do mine tomorrow. Is that alright?"

"I'm sure it is."

The herd moved pretty fast once it got away from the creek. Miss Orlies didn't have any trouble with her horse. It seemed to actually like being around people. I guess its previous owner must have taken good care of it.

Frankie B. rode up to Miss Orlies, tipped his hat and said, "Morning, Ma'am, I'd like to talk to you."

"Okay. What about?"

"Well Ma'am, we had to have the same talk with all the women in our crew about staying alive if we get attacked by either rustlers or Comancheros. So far, so good, our people have worked well together. One advantage you women have is the bad guys don't expect you to fight back. That's where the edge is. Keep your rifle fully loaded and ready to pull out at a moment's notice. Practice holding it in a firing position. Keep your pistols fully loaded, also. Hide one on you someplace where you can get to it fast and not drop it. Keep the other one in your holster ready to pull it out and fire as fast as you can and don't forget to pull back the hammer for the first shot. You can practice while you ride. Just don't shoot anybody. If we are attacked, pull your rifle out and lay it across your saddle horn, and listen closely to Long John or Mr Dickenson or myself. Ma'am, I hope I have not scared you. But that is the way it is out here. And it is starting to rain. Don't get too far away from the herd. You could get lost in a heavy rain storm, Ma'am. I will talk to you more about all of us pulling together."

"Oh, Frankie B., how are we going to pay for the horses, saddles, rifles, pistols, and food all the way to Montana?"

"Don't know, Ma'am. You will have to take that up with Mr Dickenson."

"Alright, Frankie B. Thank you for telling me what to expect. I will try to get myself and my sisters ready."

It did rain pretty hard for a time, not causing any delays. By the time the day was ending, it stopped and everyone was drying out. A water run off through a gully was very welcome for the herd and the hands. Sitting around the evening meal, the three newcomers walked over to Mr. Dickenson with the question of how to repay him for everything.

"Well Ladies, how about you work some while you're with us and you each get to keep your horses, your saddle, your rifle, your pistols, holsters, and anything else you may get from us. And when we get to where you are going in Montana, I will give you twenty-five each. But you have to work some. We will get you to a place in Montana of your choosing. How does that sound?"

"I say yes. Oh, I'm Clarius, Mr. Dickenson."

"Okay, then, how about you other two?"

"It's very fair, Mr. Dickenson. If we were out there by ourselves, I can see we would not make it. So I say, let's stay with the herd. I kind of like it anyway. Mr. Dickenson, I'm Glada."

"Miss Orlies, you are pretty quiet."

"Yes Sir, I was just thinking about all the things Frankie B. was telling me as we rode along this afternoon. It's just a matter of time before we are fighting for our lives. Is that right Mr. Dickenson?"

"Yes, it could be. But probably not that bad. And here's another thing, we are pretty used to protecting our women. But you have to be ready if you are the target. If we are set upon by rustlers, it will be different than by the Comancheros. Do you know what I'm talking about?"

"Yes Sir, I do. Okay sir, I will do my best to get my sisters and myself ready. If you want to, I'll drive our wagon tomorrow and Clarius and Glada can get their horses and gear. Is that alright with you, Sir?"

"Yes indeed. That's what I was hoping to do soon. Do they have riding clothes like you have ?"

"Ah, yes, something similar."

"Then ladies, you should start wearing them. You will be more comfortable getting on and off a horse, and doing the chores around camp."

"Yes Sir. And we will try to fit in with the rest of your people."

"Here's another thing. I think you will find that our people keep themselves clean and wash their clothes regularly. In the morning, you will find several pans of water with soap and towels by the cook wagon to freshen up. If you handle any food while helping Taters, I will expect you to at least wash your hands. Is that a problem?"

"No Sir, we will get along just fine. We are on the same page as you, Sir. Thank you for clearing that up. We are, if nothing else, in favor of much soap and water."

"Okay, then, I will see you in the morning, Ladies."

"Good night, Mr. Dickenson."

OK Bill and Red Fox were coming in for the night. They both passed by Glada, Clarius, and Orlies.

OK Bill looked straight at them, nodded, "I Apache! You know Apache people?"

"No. But I am pleased to meet you. I'm Orlies. What is your name?"

"I OK Bill."

"No, I mean what is your Apache name."

"Ahatahkakood is my name in Apache. No one ask what your name before you for long time! White lady, this Red Fox, he Comanche."

"Red Fox, I'm pleased to meet you. I'm Orlies. What'

s your name?"

"I, Cu la al ke, that my Comanche name, it mean fox. These other two, they have same mother, same father like you?"

"Yes they do, Red Fox. This one is Clarius and this one is Glada. They are my sisters."

"Yes. They don't speak much like you, Miss Orlies."

"That's not true. They just don't know what to say to you."

"Don't be afraid, we mean you no harm. We talk later, we eat now with Prairie Flower and others."

Prairie Flower and Angelina sat patiently watching OK Bill and Red Fox talk to the newcomers, not showing any emotions. They joined together with OK Bill and Red Fox and walked through the line for their meal and coffee. Clarius, Glada, and Orlies got behind them in line. The meal was great and that coffee was 'bout as good as it gets. In the morning,

Orlies drove the wagon like she said. The other two got their horses and gear. They rode the rest of the day. Orlies had her horse saddled and tied up to the wagon. The two girls rode alongside the wagon. If you'd rather drive the wagon, tie up your horse and get in.

"Nah, we're kind of enjoying ourselves. Been a while. Whoever had these horses before sure had them trained well. They are the easiest to ride."

"I know. And these saddles are not the cheap ones either. All this gear is top price, I bet. Makes me wonder. I know these people didn't steal this stuff. They're not that kind. But what are they doing with this stuff and all the horses of previous owners."

"Orlies, you're the one who always has things figured out. So what you think. Look in your saddle bags and see if you find anything."

We did. Nothing.

"Let's just be glad Mr. Dickenson took us in or we'd probably be dead by now, or headed for a Mexican brothel."

"Yeah. Let's work at whatever they need. If you two want to help Mr. Taters with the food, I'm sure he can use the help baking and such. I'm gonna herd cattle. You two do what you want. Here comes the one they call Long John. Let's see what he wants."

Long John did the usual fingers to the hat. "Ladies, good day to you all. We will be coming to a town called Rawlings, Montana, in the Medicine Bow area probably tomorrow. If you need anything from a store—soap, towels, anything for your hair, clothes—let me know. We will be stopping for some of our supplies. You can go in with one of our people. And if you need any money, let me know that, too."

"Uh, Mr. Long John, I gotta ask, why are you people being so kind to us? You don't know us from Eve. I'm Orlies."

"Well, okay, Miss Orlies, we would help anyone that needs help so you can accept our help or not, it's up to you all."

"Okay. It just seems strange. Thank you very kindly, Sir. I have one last question, Mr. Long John. Where did all these fine horses and expensive saddles and guns come from?"

"If you really must know, we kept the horses and their saddles, rifles, and such from the bandits we've either killed or put in jail. What were we supposed to do with their belongings once we've buried them or put them in jail? Is there a problem with that?"

"No Sir, Mr. Long John. I'm Clarius."

"Okay then, Miss Clarius, is there anything else? Some of us here are former Texas Rangers, including myself. So we were trained to help, but not to back down from a fight. By the way, there should be plenty of water to clean up tomorrow. Ma'am, it has been a pleasure talking to you all. Any more questions? I'll do my best to answer them."

"Thank you, Sir."

Daylight was slipping away. Taters was starting to scan the horizon ahead for a good place to make camp for the night. OK Bill and Frankie B. were just riding together. Red Fox got a couple quail with bow and arrow. He handed them over to Antonina. She smiled and nodded.

"You haitse," she said, meaning friend.

Red Fox smiled back. and went back to work. He still had about an hour to go before he was ready to quit for the day. He wondered where Antonina learned the Comanche word for friend. But it was welcome, nonetheless. Long John got up to OK Bill and asked about any water ahead?

"Little creek coming up, Long John."

"How far?"

"No far."

"Okay, good, that's where we stop."

Frankie B. and OK Bill were riding along talking casually, and yet OK Bill sensed there was water ahead. An Indian seems to have a connection with the earth that white man doesn't have. Sure enough, there it was: a water stream coming up from the ground and filling a small rock basin formation. The cattle might drink it dry, but for now we have water. And anyone that wants to clean up a bit has to compete with the cattle. Might not sound to appealing, but water is where you find it. All the women grabbed their soap and towels. As well as some of the men.

"Don't forget the rules." Long John passed on the word about the women: any of the men bothering the women while bathing is fired, no second chance. The water seemed to keep coming up no matter how much was used up by the cattle. Looks like everyone will have a chance to bathe either tonight or in the early morning. The Evens girls already decided they'd bathe in the morning and fill up their water barrel that they got hanging on the side of their wagon after everyone has filled up.

"The water clears up fast, but we'll wait a little while after everyone is through," Glada said. "We don't need any soap in our drinking water."

Meanwhile, everybody got fed and now was settling in for the night or heading for the water with their towel and soap. The night came and went without any problems. The cattle were pretty well filled up. Most walked away leaving the small pond to the bathers and anyone that wanted to fill up their barrel, or other container, and canteen. Soon as daylight came, the herd was started on the move by OK Bill and Red Fox. Everybody caught up as they could. Mr. Dickenson was last to leave. The Evens girls got their barrel filled up last with nice clean fresh water. They got going and then Mr. Dickenson mounted up, looked all around, one of his rifles in his hand, just in case. The herd began moving at the normal pace. Long John has his mind set on going around the Yellowstone area to stay on more flat ground and not be a target for rustlers or bandits quite so much. The other way, of course, would be to go straight through the Yellowstone and Rocky Mountain area risking more dead cattle and colder weather from the higher elevation. Mr. Dickenson still isn't convinced.

"Well Sir, you're right, we can go straight through the Yellowstone and maybe save a few days. But how about the cold weather and maybe snow. It could block us in. And lose a lot of cattle from frostbite or broken legs falling on slippery ground. I suppose our people should have a vote on which way to go."

"Good idea, Long John. We'll wait till we stop and ask everyone at the evening meal."

Everyone was asked what they thought. Most liked the longer way to stay warmer and might be safer. Although going around meant going through Crow homeland in part of the Big Horn, Montana territory.

"And for sure we will be trespassing, as far as the Crow are concerned. Maybe giving them a couple cattle might satisfy them."

"You're right, Long John. I heard they are having a food problem. Okay, that settles it. Long John, we go around."   Mr. Dickenson thought it over and said, "We have a better chance than going through the foothills."

OK Bill and Red Fox agreed.

"If we have to fight the Crow, it will be up to them. We'll not shoot first."

"That's right," Frankie B. added ."I sure hope it don't come to that."

Mrs. Sikorski changed the mood around the camp with her very delicious pies. Taters and Antonina set up the meal of smoked deer meat with a gravy mixture of potatoes and carrots and those good ole biscuits. Can't beat that. The Evens girls even bragged on how good it was.

"And those pies, almost as good as ours," Clarius said with a laugh. "And coffee fit for a king. Now to rest up and do it all over again tomorrow."

In the morning, the cool air and dew made that first cup a coffee taste extra good. Glada and Clarius both agreed they'd make some pies this evening as soon as Taters set up camp.

"Guess I better ask him if we got the makings. Might have to make something else.

"Mr. Taters, Sir, do we have apples or cherries to make a pie or two?"

"Ah, let me see just what we got, Miss Glada! Looks like we got one can of cherries, no apples." "Okay. We'll make a cherry pie and how about a pie with some of that stew with carrots in it? Ever have one a those?"

"Sure, if it's made right, it's the best tasting thing a cowboy, or cowgirl, can ever eat out here."

"Well Sir, I can make beef stew pies. I guess I can make a couple with deer meat. As long as we got flour and lard and salt for the pie crust, I can make it."

"Yes Ma'am, we got it."

"As soon as you stop this evening, Mr. Taters, I'll get with you and get started. Is that okay?"

"Yes indeed, Miss Glada. I'll be looking forward to your pies."

When evening came, Glada and Clarius were right there pitching in with Antonina and Taters and getting those pies put together. They did turn out to be a welcome treat for everybody. The talk of the camp.

Mr. Dickenson said, "You better make those stew pies again. I can't have you two washing dishes when you can make meals like that."

"Well, thank you, Sir. By the way, Mr. Dickenson, we were thinking Glada and I are very good teachers and we thought maybe we could do a little teaching if anyone was interested after the evening meal. We can cover most subjects."

"Well, that is something you will have to take up with the hands. I have no problem, as long as it don't interfere with driving the herd during the day. I wouldn't do more than an hour after the evening meal, Miss Clarius."

"Sir, that is what we were thinking. So we have your permission to ask everyone if they would be interested?"

"Yes you do."

So they asked around and did get a few interested maybes. Not anything else, so they didn't pursue it. If anyone gets interested after thinking about it, they will have to ask us. Day after day the herd was kept moving along. Water was not always available. Some days were much more of a challenge than others. But they were nearing their goal, and good thing since the water was starting to get colder. Forty degrees is downright cold when you're riding against the northern wind all day and nights get a lot colder. Bozeman, Montana, is coming up and then about another hundred miles to Helena, and the army is supposed to meet us there to buy up the cattle.

Chapter 12

Some supplies were picked up in Bozeman. Plenty of pie makings for one thing. When in Bozeman, Frankie B. was in a gunfight with a gun hand from a local ranch. Frankie B. outdrew him by a mile. He didn't kill him, just shot him in the arm. The local sheriff let him go. Plenty of people saw the whole thing. Frankie B. was pushed into the whole thing. So they picked up their supplies and left. Next day out in the open, OK Bill in the lead and Red Fox on the west side, Red Fox spotted about ten riders far west on the horizon riding about the same pace as they were. That spells trouble.

Long John said, "My guess is they will try to take the herd before we get to Helena. So we do all the work and they get paid for it. We are not going to let that happen. Everybody on high alert. If your saddle don't have a rifle scabbard, get one out of the wagon and put it in front if you can. Get your second rifle and all the ammo you want. Anyone wants to handle dynamite, take two or three sticks and make sure you got a cigar with matches. They might not hit us for a couple days, but then, it might be tomorrow. Tonight we are going to reconnaissance them. We need to know where they are at all times from now on. For now, we act like we don't know they're out there. Frankie B., how 'bout you and OK Bill get as close to their camp as you can. Red Fox, you go, too, but stay back and cover them. Wait till it gets dark. Get back safe. If you need to kill any, do it with a knife or bow and arrow. Don't leave any weapons behind for them to use on us. Got it?"

"Got it, Boss."

"Harve and John Johnson, stay in the dark around the herd beside the regular riders and make sure nobody penetrates our camp like we are doing to them. Got it?"

"Got it, Boss."

"It's possible they intend to come in all sides, so everybody in camp watch all around us till this is over. If there are any Comancheros with them, we'll know tonight."

Camp was setup. The smell of food was in the air. A few pies were made to go with the meal of deer stew and beans.

Orlies asked, "Mrs. Sikorski, how do you handle the tension?"

"Just let it go. There is nothing you can do about it, Miss Orlies. These men are experienced. They have been through this kind a battle many times before. And they know how to handle bandits. Listen to what they tell you at all times. I have confidence they will get us through. If you have to shoot, then don't hesitate. Check your rifles and pistols, make sure they're loaded. Do you have two rifles and two pistols each, you and your two sisters?"

"Yes we do."

"Sleep close to them and keep your dog quiet unless he's telling you something important. We will know something tonight when Frankie B. and OK Bill get back."

Mr. Dickenson walked around and talked to everyone.

"We are a team and we need to stay calm. As soon as it gets dark, Frankie B. and OK Bill and Red Fox will get us the information we need so we know how to prepare. Meanwhile, have your meals and a piece of pie and a good cup of coffee."

The cool night air kept everyone close to a fire and bundled up with extra clothes. The cattle were calm. That was a good thing. I guess the cool air had an effect on the cattle, too. Long John was watching with binoculars for any movement and light from the riders. Frankie B. and OK Bill were having another cup of coffee with their pie. Red Fox joined them. It was dark enough now that they were ready to go. Long John gave them some last minute instructions. They led their horses out of camp into the dark. They knew approximately where the riders' camp was.

Long John told them, "If you kill any of them, don't leave any body behind if you're able to bring them back here. That will confuse them. They won't know what happened to them."

"Let's ride as close as we can get and walk the rest," Frankie B. said. All three agreed. They saw a flicker of light so they headed for it. Didn't take long before the light got bigger. They tied up their horses and all three started the walk. Wasn't long before they spotted a rider, rifle in hand, wearing a sombrero, riding very slow. They let him go—for now anyway. Red Fox touched Frankie B. and OK Bill to let them know he was staying back to cover them.

They nodded, no words were spoken. The two got close enough to see there were three more sombreros. That could only mean one thing— Comancheros. They heard a few words, but not much. A Mexican lifted up a toast to the words, "Arroyo Episcopal," which in English means Episcopal Creek. They don't look overly armed: just a rifle and pistol each. No bandolier or bullet belts across their chests. That probably means they are confident.

We go now, OK Bill motioned. Getting back, they made their way to Red Fox. He had a body tied to a horse with an arrow stuck in him.

"Him come too close, him see me."

"That's good, one less to worry about. Was he the one we saw?"

"Yes, him one."

OK Bill motioned go, I brush ground so they can't tell anything happened here. Very quietly they made their way back to camp . OK Bill did a bird call ,just before entering the camp. Mr. Dickenson and Long John knew it was OK Bill. They have used it many times in the past. Once in the camp, there was a relieved feeling by everyone that they made it back safely. And brought back a dead bandit.

"Let's get this guy checked out and buried. Juan, get this guy's saddle off and put it in the wagon with his guns and check his saddle bags for anything that might tell us who he is."

"Si, Señor Long John."

"Carlyle, can you get someone to dig a grave and wrap him in a blanket. If you find a name, make a small marker. Put whatever could be useful for us in the wagon. Any spare clothes, if they're not too dirty to keep and that sombrero. I can see using that sombrero sometime. Tie up his horse to the wagon for a few days. We don't want it wandering back to the bandits. Any money and documents to Mr. Dickenson. Red Fox, get something to eat and then head back out to cover your trail and see if anyone is coming our way."

"Right, Long John."

OK Bill say, "I go, too."

"Alright, you two go. And Frankie B., you cover them this time."

"Right, Boss. I'm on my way."

They headed back out and moved quietly. Frankie B. moves like an Indian. He's been around OK Bill so long, he's picked up some of the Indian traits. Definitely a good thing. They didn't get too far when a voice said, "Don't move. I have a clear shot at you in the moonlight!"

And about the same time, a falling noise. Red Fox shot him off his horse with an arrow.

OK Bill said, "I go ahead, see if more."

"Good idea, OK Bill. We will be here getting things ready to go back to camp. You be safe my friend."

OK Bill moved on ahead. He would stop and listen to all the night sounds. If anyone is moving around in the cover of night, he would hear it or smell a different odor. *There was no one,* he thought to himself. When he got close to their camp, he could see they didn't seem to be on extra alert. Throwing caution to the wind, you could say. That being in our favor. Not having anything new to report to Long John, OK Bill headed back to Frankie B. and Red Fox. They were ready to go when he got to them. It was a short trip back walking the horse with the dead bandit. The bird call came from OK Bill and they were in camp with their second kill for the night. Long John welcomed them back with a pat on the back. "Where did you find this one?"

"Not too far out, Boss. He got the drop on us. And Red Fox took him out with another arrow."

"Okay Carlyle, get this one ready for burial. Juan, take care of this horse."

"Si Señor."

"Mr. Dickenson, I don't think they will wait. I think they will hit us tomorrow. What you think, Sir?"

"I think you're right. Tighten up the watches and in the morning, we'll be ready for them."

The night was tense. Nobody got much sleep. Orlies was cat napping on and off when Gabriel, her dog, woke her. He was clearly not happy about something. She quickly got up and shook Long John.

"Somebody must be outside the camp. Gabriel, my dog, is growling. Something is bothering him, Sir."

"Okay, I'll take care of it."

He woke Frankie B. and said, "See if you can find out what is out there. You take the right side and catch up with John Johnson. He should be close by and see what he knows. I'll get someone to check the left side." He got OK Bill and Red Fox to check all around from the west side of camp down to the south. If anybody was out there, they disappeared into thin air. Kinda sounded like an animal was being chased by a cat or a bear. OK Bill and Red Fox didn't have a sighting or smell of man or animal, so things settled back to blankets being pulled up or finishing their coffee and back to sleep. The rest of the night was uneventful. Morning came as usual. Not much sleep. No one complained about the false alarm. It's better than not knowing an attack was coming. Gabriel got a few pats on the head and 'Good dog, keep it up.' Gabriel liked the attention. Now to the matter of the bandits. By now, they should know their two compadres are gone for good and probably were killed by the Dickenson people stalking them at night. If they don't act soon and try to take the women and the herd, they won't be able to. The Dickenson people plan to go out again tonight and maybe take out a couple more bad guys. Meanwhile, everyone helped get things ready to move out. Juan had the two extra horses to make sure they were watered and grass fed, tied to the wagon, and ready to move out when Long John gave the word. Gabriel will ride in the wagon till he gets bored and then he runs with the riders.

Mr. Dickenson is passing the word, "Everyone be extra vigilant. Get your dynamite sticks if you're going to use them and everyone be ready. Rifles at the ready. Clarius and Glada were in their wagon, their horses tied to the wagon in case they wanted them. The graves were made of the two bandits with a cross, no name. The only information in their saddle bags listed the name of someone across the border in Mexico. Mr. Dickenson said he would look them up when he got back to his ranch.

Long John, with a loud voice said, "Get 'em moving. A few more days, we'll be in Helena. That's what we came here for. If we got to fight bandits, bring 'em on. We'll have 'em for breakfast."

We could see the bandits on the ridge following us and getting closer by and by.

"Alright, everybody, get ready. They're coming in close. How many you make out to be, Tommy?"

"Dance, I see ten."

"Yeah, that's what I see. They must think we're a push over."

 Long John rode over to where OK Bill and Red Fox were riding alongside Frankie B. You three drop into the back without them seeing you and come up behind them. Can you do that?"

"Yeah Boss, it'd be a pleasure."

"If they come over to us, you can come up behind them at a distance. Find some cover and keep your eye on them and me. If we need you, I will take off my hat and put it back on. If I do that, kill about five of them. Then play it by ear."

"Got it, Boss."

OK Bill added, "We will cover you, Long John." The bandits were so close we could see five sombreros, three whites that looked like hide skinners, and two Indians that were not recognizable from a tribe.

Mr. Dickenson said, "It's time to stop the herd and see what they have to say."

Long John whistled and threw up his hand. Everybody had an eye on Long John, so it did not take long to stop the herd.

Three came forward and the rest stayed back: two sombreros and one white.

"Buenos Dias, Señor, Señora."

Long John said, "What can we do for you?"

"Señor, we have come to relieve you of the cattle and maybe your Señoritas and Señoras, Señor Ganado Forman. How do you like that?"

"Well, I don't like that very much, Señor. What is your name and the name of your compadres because when we bury you, we want to put a name on a cross? Would you like a cross with your name on it?"

"My name is General Rodrigo Zapata. I might bury you, Señor. So what is your name?"

"My name is Long John to you General."

"Long John. That is a funny name, Señor, ha ha."

"Well, not as funny as General because you are not a real general."

"What you know?"

"I know because a real general does not go round relieving people of their cattle and women. I will sell these cattle to you and the women can go with you if you can talk them into going. Why don't you ask them? They'll probably blow your damn head off. Before you do, you better kiss that rosary hanging round your neck. It might be the last thing you ever do, General."

"Señor Long John, they don't look so tough to me. And you don't look so tough to me, Señor Long John."

"Well, I don't claim to be tough."

Orlies had her arm around Gabriel's neck so he wouldn't jump off the wagon. She held on tight and muzzled him, too. General spurred his horse over to where Miss Clarius and Miss Glada were seated on their wagon. They each had a rifle in their hands.

"I will take these two, Señor Granado Forman." he reached out his hand to grab Miss Glada by the arm as Miss Clarius pointed her Henry lever action rifle at his heart and said, "If you touch her, I will shoot you off that horse." He pulled back his hand.

"Can you really shoot me, Señorita?"
He then grabbed the rifle as she pulled the trigger. He was dead the second he hit the ground. Quickly, Long John took off his hat and put it back on his head. Five shots rang out and five more dead. The ones left tried to shoot it out with OK Bill, Red Fox, and Frankie B. They were quickly shot off their horses. The two that came into camp with the general quickly threw down their rifles and put up their hands and yelled, "Don't shoot, don't shoot." Carlyle said, "Off your horse, on the ground." Tommy and the two Johns tied them up on the ground.

Long John said a few words to settle everyone down. "Let's get all the horses and weapons gathered up. The fight is over folks. They died for nothing. That's the worst part of the whole thing. If they had their way, we men would all be the ones laying on the ground and you women would be their slaves. As terrible as the whole thing is, it could be worse. Miss Clarius, are you going to be alright?
"Yes sir, I think I will be okay."

"Get these two bandits digging. They got a lot of graves to dig. Mr Dickenson, what do you want to do with these two?"

"We'll see. Juan, get some help and tie up the horses to the wagons, split them up. All weapons in the wagons. Carlyle, check all saddle bags. Papers and money go to me. Let's find out from these two who they're working for. It's too bad we can't drive cattle where we want without having to kill every rustler in the country. I wish I could tell them before they attack us that they are no match for us. And the biggest mistake they all seem to make is to underestimate women. As soon as we get all these guys buried, we move on. We still got some daylight left."

Long John looked around and said, "Give me one of those shovels. It's gonna take too long if these two dig alone. Somebody get the dead ones' pockets emptied and roll them up in a blanket. Anybody want to help dig, grab a shovel. I'd like to move on as soon as possible."

Miss Clarius walked over and picked up a shovel and started digging.

Mr. Dickenson said, "Ma'am, you surely don't have to dig graves."

"I know but it will make me feel better, Sir. And I want to help us get moving."

"Okay then."

Everybody went back to their jobs. Taters got a pot of coffee going and that was very much welcome, after what everyone had been through. The digging went on till all the dead were in a proper grave and a marker with a name, if the two live ones knew their names. The cattle were moved towards a water hole about ten miles north. They got there just at dusk. Taters got things going for a meal. Juan left the saddles on the horses just for the night. He said he would get them off in the morning and free a few of the horses to join the other horses and see how they stay with the others. Long John told him he didn't care as long as he keeps an eye on them and don't let them stray. Mr. Dickenson, as he ate, talked to Long John about freeing the two rustlers in the morning.

"I guess I could hang them as guilty as they are. But I just don't have the stomach for it. Or do you want to give them to the nearest sheriff?"

"Sir, I'd like to give them to a sheriff. If he wants to try them and hang them, be fine with me. Like you said, they are guilty. They could be wanted in the area for other crimes, too."

"Okay then, that's what we'll do. We got a town coming up tomorrow. Episcopal Creek and then Bedford along the Missouri river. We can let them off at one of them towns. Meanwhile, keep them tied up to a wagon wheel and keep a guard on them. "Carlyle, can you watch these two and get someone to relieve you through the night. Tie them up real tight."

"Okay, Boss. I will take care of it."

The night was uneventful. Morning came, not like other mornings. Everyone was ready to move on. With what had taken place here yesterday, too many graves reminded them of what had happened. After a quick morning meal, they were on the move. Miss Clarius was on her horse out with the herd having a chat with OK Bill. He reassured her that she did the right thing. He wasn't there, but he knows that one thing the bandits do is push all your feelings and emotions and try to scare you.

OK Bill said, "We have been through this kind of fight many times before. I hope the Great Spirit gives you peace with your thoughts. These bandits came looking for trouble and to kill us. We did not let that happen."

"Thank you, OK Bill, I feel better."

Miss Clarius rode on with her feelings greatly improved. She patted her horse and talked to it. It responded with a head jerk and a low whinny.

"I think I will call you Peaceful because that is what you are and you make me feel at peace."

The others were all dealing with their emotions in their own way.

Mr. Dickenson and Long John rode together talking about getting into Helena probably tomorrow and maybe sending a couple riders in ahead to let the army know we're here ready to sell these cattle.

"Okay, let's send Frankie B. and Carlyle. You think they will be enough?"

"Sure. They are pretty cautious. They both know how to deal with people. The railroad comes through Helena because of all the mining going on in the area and Butte as well, so the cattle will be loaded on cattle cars for the army."

The Evens sisters have mixed feelings about getting to a big town in Montana. After all, that's what they set out to do but now they have become like family with the Dickenson people. Miss Glada said she had never met people as kind and caring as these people. "I'm not sure I want to leave them."

"Well, I suppose we don't have to. You know Mr Dickenson said we are welcome to ride down to Del Rio, Texas, with them and look for a job. I know we don't have much time to decide. They'll probably only be here a couple days. Let's see what's here first."

"Okay, that's what I was thinking. I wonder how Clarius feels about it." Miss Clarius agreed.

"Let's check around here and see."

Long John made the rounds talking to everyone. He was mostly concerned with their feelings about the cattle drive coming to an end.

"Tomorrow, we will be in Helena."

Tim Shiloh said, "I'm heading back to Texas with you all. I have to check on a lady in Higgins, Texas."

Mrs. Sikorski and her daughter said, "We are Texas bound. After all, we gotta pick up Mrs. Edwards, her daughter, and José in Higgins, Texas, too. I suppose it's a long way from Del Rio. I heard Texas is a big state."

"Yes Ma'am, it is a long way back to Del Rio. How about you, John Johnson?"

"I need a job. I go where you go, if you need a cowhand. Me and John Davis and Tommy Holbrooks and Dance Mead talked about it. We ain't never worked for anybody as fair as Mr. Dickenson and you, Long John. We're staying, if you'll have us."

"Yeah, you got a job. How 'bout you, Harve?"

"Boss, you know I'm staying. I gots me a woman on the ranch down in Del Rio. I want to marry if she will have me."

"Harve, you are a good man. She'd be smart to grab you up while she can before some other woman grabs you."

"Boss, I thank you for the kind words."

"That's okay, Harve. I'll talk to you later. I gotta talk to the others.

"Red Fox, would you like to stay with Mr. Dickenson and go back to Del Rio and work on the ranch?"

"Don't know. Have to go back to Comanche chief in Oklahoma with others first. Maybe come back if okay with you, Boss Long John?"

"Yes it is, Red Fox.

"Okay everybody, let's call it a day. Tomorrow we will be in Helena. Soon as we get paid, you get paid. Let's rest up here tonight and head in tomorrow."

Taters, as always, with his helpers, had the meal ready: coffee brewing, deer meat stew, beans, biscuits, and everybody had favorite pies made by the Evens girls. Mr. Dickenson went around thanking everyone for getting the herd here to Helena.

"Anyone here that wants to stay with me and go back to Del Rio and work on the ranch or look for a job there, we should be heading back in a couple days after we get paid and rest up. Tomorrow morning, we will send Frankie B. and Carlyle ahead to make arrangements to hand over the cattle to the army and we should get paid."

Frankie B. had a talk with OK Bill, Carlyle, and Red Fox about going back to the Comanche camp in Oklahoma. How do you think we should do it?"

Carlyle said, "I think we should go all the way to Higgins, Texas, with the Dickenson people and then turn east and head for the Comanche camp in Oklahoma. The weather will be turning cold and snowing before too long. Let's get these women back home as soon as we can. Chief Bengalese will be glad to see we've kept our word. OK Bill, Red Fox, that sound good to you?"

"Good. That good way."

"Any chance the chief has moved the camp?"

"Maybe. Don't know. Or they could have been

raided by Crow on the rampage. They can fight Crow very well. Done before. Kill many Crow."

Prairie Flower and Angelina joined the conversation.

"We want to tell you what we feel."

"Okay, let's hear what you feel!"

Prairie Flower spoke, "In my heart, these people are family and like tribe." She touched her heart with her hand flat against her chest. "These are our people now. We do not want to leave them. No one has ever treated us as good as Mr. Dickenson and his people— Indian or White. But we must go back to the camp of our Fathers and our Mothers, if only for a while. I have spoken from my heart."

Angelina said, "Mother speaks for me, also."

OK Bill added his voice to the conversation. "I have long time feel these are my family, too, and I'm Apache. And you are my family, Comanche and White. Let us go back to Comanche Chief for a while."

Red Fox said, "We go back for a time. Spirit tell us what to do."

"You're right, Red Fox."

Frankie B. added, "We said we would go back to the Comanche camp and that's what we will do. I think OK Bill and I will keep our jobs with Mr. Dickenson. Right, OK Bill?"

"Yes, Frankie B. We are happy to do the work Mr. Dickenson gives us. I go back to Apache camp later. Now I go with Prairie Flower back to Comanche camp. Chief Bengalese, maybe him say to me Ahatahkakood, you strong warrior. You can marry this woman Toh-Tsee-Ah."

"What you thinking, Carlyle?"

"Yeah, I think you got your mind made up to marry Prairie Flower. Chief Bengalese is a reasonable man. He won't object. And Frankie B., I guess you're thinking on the same lines about Angelina."

"Yes Sir, I sure am."

"For now, we better get some sleep. Tomorrow is the big day."

"Carlyle, you and I are supposed to go in to Helena and meet with the army people about the cattle."

"Yeah, I know Frankie B. Soon as I have that last cup of coffee, I'll be bedding down. Night everybody."

"Night you all."

The fires were burning down, everyone was either sleeping or close to it .

Frankie B. said, "Before I turn in, I think I'll load up the fires. It's getting pretty cold."

"Yeah, I'll help you," Carlyle said.

"Okay, thanks."

The herd is in good hands. Mr. Dickenson is sleeping with his book open across his chest. Long John is walking around with his rifle in his hands, trying to stay awake.

Carlyle said to him, "Better get some sleep, Boss. Tomorrow you'll have to be awake. Tonight you should sleep."

"Yeah, I know, Carlyle. Guess I will. Wake me if you need me."

"Okay Boss."

Long John was so sleepy he went off to sleep as soon as he hit the blanket. Carlyle walked over to him, covered him up, and took his hat off his head. The chin strap was hung up on his nose but he didn't even feel it. The warm fires were bright and inviting to anyone looking to take the herd even this close to Helena. Bandits never give up. Seems like they work harder than if they had regular jobs. The herd was settled down. The boys were singing to the cattle. They were used to hearing Harve, Dance, the two Johns, and Tommy's voices for months now singing or just talking to them. They had them all tonight. OK Bill and Red Fox were both uneasy, just like Long John. OK Bill told Frankie B. he felt like he should check one more time around the herd. So he went out into the dark night. When he got close to one of the riders, he would let them know he was coming up on them with his one and only bird whistle that everybody in camp knew very well. The riders would acknowledge with a whistle of their own. No talking, no lights. They knew OK Bill very well. When OK Bill was satisfied around the herd, he came back into camp and bedded down. The morning came as usual. Coffee was brewing, gravy even smelled pretty good, and Lord, how about those biscuits with honey and jelly. And if you want it, there was a pan full of deer meat frying up. Mr. Dickenson and Long John were already sipping their coffee. Carlyle wasn't far behind, splashing water in his face. Frankie B. woke up suddenly and grabbed for his rifle. Once he touched it, he felt safe. It was still pretty dark. The air was cold. Fires were rekindled for some heat and some light.

"Alright folks, the sooner we get to Helena, the sooner we get paid and get a load off our shoulders. Rise and shine."

Mrs. Sikorski woke and thought, *What do I do? Stay in a place like Helena, Montana? And do what? Or stay with Mr. Dickenson and his people and go to*

Texas. I'll go into Helena and see what's there. But I don't think I'll stay here.

The Evens girls are even having second thoughts about staying here. And this was their aim in the first place.   Everyone was up and fed, horses saddled up, cattle moving. OK Bill and Red Fox in the lead. Last fire put out. Mr. Dickenson on his horse, rifle in hand looking all around in every direction, nothing moving, except north to Helena.

"We mustn't be far from Helena, 'cause there's kinda dust in the air looking north."

Carlyle and Frankie B. already on their way to meet someone in town about what to do with the cattle. A lone rider was headed our way.

Long John got in front, moved his arm forward, "Keep 'em moving. I'll talk to the person."

Closer he got, he could tell it was a young woman. He tipped his hat with, "Morning Ma'am. Can I help you?"

"Morning Sir, yes you can. I'm Diane Binks. I carry the mail in these parts. I have a special delivery letter for a Mr. Dickenson. I thought I wouldn't wait for you all to get into town. Is there a Mr. Dickenson with the herd ?"

"Yes Ma'am, there is. He's the owner. That's him coming up here now. You can hand it to him yourself."

Mr. Dickenson gave her the same hat tip courtesy with, "Ma'am, can I help you?"

"Yes Sir, I'm with the postal service. I have a special delivery for you, Sir. I didn't want to wait, since it was special."

"Well, thank you."

She turned and kept riding along with them. He opened the envelope. It was from the army department of procurement. It said, ***"In case we are late driving in Helena, Montana, hold cattle till we arrive. Pen them if pen big enough, if not use own discretion. Major General Kaczmarek."***

"Miss?"

"Yes Sir?"

"Is the army in Helena."

"No sir, but they got the word ahead that they would be getting in sometime today. By the way, I'm Diane Binks. I deliver the mail for the U.S. postal service in Helena."

"Yes Ma'am. Thank you, Ma'am, for bringing the letter out to me. Can you show us were the cattle pen is at?"

"Yes, I'd be glad to. You don't have much of a ride."

"Ma'am, do you think the cattle pen is big enough for all the cattle?

"Ah, um. maybe, can't say for sure. Sir, you got a lot a cattle. We have some women with us that might be interested in staying in Helena if they can find the right job."

"I'd be happy to show them around."

Sheriff Steve Bullock of Helena was waiting at the edge of town, just to show his authority.

"I hope you people are here to rest up and head out in a couple days."

Mr. Dickenson said, "We will be the most peace-loving cattle drive you've ever seen. We don't cause trouble. We stop trouble, Sheriff. A lot of my people are former Texas Rangers and all the rest have been around us so long, I'd say they're Rangers, too.

348

They have the Rangers discipline. But we don't mind spending a little money and cutting loose, if you will allow us that privilege. By the way, I'm Dolphus Dickenson, the owner. This is Long John Lowther, the man in charge. We are both Captains in the Texas Rangers. I might add, if you need any help with law enforcement while we are here, we would be glad to assist you."

"Captains, it's a pleasure meeting you both. I don't think we will be needing any help. Thanks anyway."

"Good day, Sheriff, we will be putting our cattle in that pen over there. We will talk to you later. Sheriff, we have a few women with us and some Indians and a colored man and a Mexican. We want them to be treated with the utmost respect by all of your citizens. They have been through some bad times. We won't take any disrespect of them."

"I fully agree, Captain. Later then." The sheriff swung has horse around and rode off.

"Miss Binks, are you friends with the sheriff?"

"Not really, but he's honest and I would vote for him if he runs again."

"Thanks, that's good to know."

OK Bill and Red Fox started to run the cattle in the pen. They were being watched by a hand full of the saloon patrons as they just came through the swinging doors.

One a them yelled, "What you think you're doing, Injuns?"

OK Bill and Red Fox ignored them and went on with their job. Now Carlyle and Frankie B. came up, looked at the hecklers, but never said a word. As it turned out, the cattle pen held most of the cattle.

"It's a big a one, biggest I ever saw," Long John said.

Soon all the Dickenson people pulled up to the pen. When Harve and Juan came up, the insults continued on them. Long John rode over to where the insults were coming from, got off his horse, tied it to the rail, took a bag of tobacco out of his shirt pocket and rolled a cig, then asked one a them for a light. They were all watching him so they forgot to keep up the insults and two of them tried to give Long John a light at the same time. He got his light and kept talking to them. They offered to buy him a drink in the Central Saloon. That ended the heckles. Long John untied his horse, walked it to the pen, and they got on with penning the cattle, as many as they could.

"We'll just have to watch the rest till the Army gets here. Hope it will be today like they said." Mr. Dickenson expressed his gratitude to Long John for defusing the situation with the hecklers.

"I know. I had to do something before it got out of hand."

"Well, you did a great job."

"Well Sir, it might not be over just yet. I want to see all our people walk into a saloon for dinner if they want to while we're here without being insulted or pulled into a gunfight. Sir, I would tell our people to come and go as they please, but be careful. The dumb asses are still here. The Evens girls need to have a talk with Miss Diane Binks. She will most likely know if the school system is in need of teachers or the newspaper looking for help."

A young boy came running up to Mr. Dickenson. "Sir, Sir, the army is coming into town."

It's true, the army was coming into town from the east side.

"Well good, looks like about fifty men."

Major General Kaczmarek was not with the men. He sent Captain James Styles to receive the cattle. They are from Fort William Henry Harrison located about four miles northwest of Helena. But because they were out putting down an uprising by hostiles, they were coming in from the east on their way back to the fort.

"Captain, are you authorized to receive the cattle?"

"I am, if you are Mr. Dolphus Dickenson."

"Yes Sir, I am."

"We put as many as we could get in the cattle pen. The rest, as you can see, are outside the pen. Can your men handle them all."

"Yes, they can. We have been through this a few times. Mr. Dickenson, I am authorized to pay you for one thousand head, give or take fifty. Is that to your satisfaction."

"Yes Captain, it is."

"Then you can pick up your money at the bank this afternoon."

"The horses you see, Captain, belong to me."

"I'll have my men cut them out right now," said Long John.

"I will ride over to the bank with you, Mr. Dickenson."

"Thank you, Captain, that will be just fine.

"Long John, will you tell OK Bill and Frankie B. to join you and me at the bank to witness the transaction."

"Captain Styles, can you have two or three join you?"

"Yes Sir, we will be happy to."

At the bank, the transaction went smoothly. Mr. Dickenson asked for cash in the amount of fifty thousand dollars. He brought two saddle bags. He put all the money in one saddle bag. He had something in the other saddle bag so they both looked the same. He put them both on his shoulders. Everyone was thanked for their participation. And out the door they went. As soon as Mr. Dickenson and his hands were alone, he gave the bag with the money to OK Bill and the other he carried. They went straight to the camp where Taters was set up.

"Long John, can we set up a table for everyone to get their pay? You don't have to rush but we should get it done sooner than later. You know where the ledger book is?"

"Yes Sir, I'll get it."

"Okay people, listen up. After you get paid, you are free to go anywhere you want. But I need to caution you, there's a few people in town that would push you into a fight, so be careful and use common sense."

The table was set with both saddle bags on the table and the ledger book. A few entries were made and they began. Everyone got their pay and was asked to stay on. If you want to work with me and the double DD ranch down in Texas, we will be leaving probably in two days. Talk to Long John as soon as you can so he knows who to look for when we leave. If you blow all your money in the saloon, that's your problem. Don't expect any sympathy from me. There will be no advance money handed out. I will be fair but not foolish." Everyone kinda knew Mr. Dickenson was a fair man. The Evens girls got in line for their pay and they got exactly what Mr. Dickenson promised when they signed on and he reminded them they could have the horses, the saddles, the rifles, and the pistols. And that if they decided that they didn't want to stay here in Helena, that they would be welcome at his ranch in Del Rio either as an employee on the ranch or till they find the job they want. They all three said thank you and said they would think about it and look around Helena while they are here. Gabriel, their dog, got a pat on the head. They went straight to the post office to ask Miss Diane if she knew if the school was needing any teachers.

"As a matter of fact, I believe they do," she said. "And the newspaper office is on the way. If you would like, I can take you there now. You can leave your horses here at the post office and we'll take my wagon. Quite a few soldiers in town. That should be a good thing."

The school office was glad to talk to Glada and Clarius. They have quite a few children with the population growing every day.

"What can you ladies teach?"

"We can both teach the 3Rs."

"Is that correct?"

"Yes Sir, it is. With a few other things like history and being proficient in the English language. Sir, we are sisters and trained at the same time and constantly strive to improve ourselves. We do have papers to authenticate what we are saying if you would like to see them."

"Yes Ma'am, I would. Ah, I see, yes indeed. It says here you both taught in Denver in lower grades and in the high school level."

"Yes Sir."

"Why did you leave your previous jobs in Denver?"

"Because we heard that there were opportunities for us to do more teaching in Montana. And since we came in to Helena with Mr. Dickenson and the cattle herd, we feel we don't have much time to check around. Like I said, we came in with the Dickenson herd and will leave when Mr. Dickenson and his people leave in a few days if we don't get jobs. And we also have a sister sitting outside your door that would like a job with a newspaper in a professional capacity. So we can all three be together. Sir, if I may be so bold, can you decide by tomorrow about this time? Surely you can see why we need to know."

"Yes Ma'am, I do. And I will take it up with my assistant this afternoon when she gets through with a meeting."

"We would appreciate it very much. Now, if you will excuse us, we need to go to a newspaper to see if our sister can get a job. Miss Diane Binks is willing to show us around. A newspaper office is our next stop. Thank you, Sir. We will check back with you tomorrow at this time if it is alright with you."

"Yes Ma'am, that will be just fine."

A newspaper office was a short wagon ride from the school office. The four went in because there seemed to be plenty of chairs in a waiting room. And Miss Diane knew the manager, Tom Miller.

"Tom, I'd like you to meet Miss Orlies Evens, Miss Clarius Evens, and Miss Glada Evens. They are sisters. Miss Orlies is looking for a newspaper job. Her two sisters are trying to get a job as teachers."

"I do have some openings. What is it that you are looking for?"

"Sir, I can do most anything around a newspaper. I can set type, I can go out and get a story, I can print, I can edit, I can do ads, and I can even deliver if I have to. I did all these jobs in Denver with small newspapers. Sir, I have a Letter of Recommendation if you would like to see it."

"Indeed I would. I see you come highly recommended by the Denver Post. That's a pretty good-sized paper, isn't it?"

"Yes Sir, it is. I know, since I'm a woman, I would probably have to work for a man. I would take the job anyway. Unless you are willing to take a chance and hire me as my own boss answering only to you. There is one thing I must tell you, we came in today with the Dickenson herd and they will be leaving in two days. If my sisters don't get a teaching position, then I will not take a job. In other words, if one of us does not get a job, then the other two will not take a job. Did I make myself clear?"

"Yes, I understand."

"Can I expect an answer by tomorrow at this time?"

"Yes, of course, I will talk it over with my Associate."

"Thank you, Sir. Until tomorrow.

"Miss Diane, what kind of living quarters could we expect to find if we stay here?"

"I think you wouldn't have any trouble finding accommodations. There are plenty of one room or two room flats around town."

"We would need a place with a bath of course."

"If you would like, you can stay at my place tonight and have a hot bath and a change of clothes in the

355

morning to impress your prospective employers."

"That would be about the best thing you could do for us. We will be glad to pay you."

"I'm sure you would, but that will not be necessary. Let's get your belongings."

"Clarius and Glada, what do you think?"

"This is great."

"Yeah, this is what we left Denver for. We'll see what tomorrow will bring."

"I don't know about you two but I can't wait to get a bath."

"I know, Clarius."

They headed out to the camp and said hi to whoever was there. Taters was there setting up a small meal for whoever wanted it.

"Taters, we are going to stay the night at this lady's place. She's Miss Diane Binks."

"Pleased to meet you, Ma'am."

"Please to meet you, Mr. Taters."

"Ma'am, while you're here, why don't you grab a bite to eat? Biscuits are just coming out of the cooker oven and here's some butter and jelly and the coffee is hot."

"Looks like most of the hands were gone, probably in the saloon. If that's your dog, he can come with you if you want him to."

"Sure, he'd like that." Glada untied him and he whimpered and whined like he was so happy to see us, and jumped up on her horse in back of the saddle. Didn't bother her horse a bit. Soon as they got their change of clothes and a quick bite and coffee, they were off headed back to town. Glada, suggested that they stop at the saloon and see how the Dickenson people were doing.

"Miss Diane, do you ever stop in at the saloon?"
"Sure, I don't make a habit of doing that but I do once in a while."
"Then would you mind if we did now. We have so many friends that we rode in with. I'd really like to see how they're doing."
"Sure, I'd like a cold beer, or not so cold, whatever they got. Do you mind girls?"
"Not at all. Let's stop in. You know there are other saloons in town but this one is the closest to your camp so there's a good chance most of your friends are in there."
They were still dressed like cowhands. Miss Diane was dressed in a riding outfit, so they shouldn't look too much out a place. Or draw too much attention. In they went. Gabriel went right with them. First one they saw was Mr. Dickenson sitting at a table. He motioned them over and stood up. "Ladies, please have a seat."
"Thank you, Sir."
He helped each with their chair and then sat down himself. A true gentleman. You can order something to eat in this place if you like."
"Do you know where the others are at, Mr. Dickenson?"
"Some are in here. The rest, I don't know."
"Have you seen Mrs. Sikorski or her daughter?"
"No, Ma'am, I have not. I did over hear some of them say they wanted to explore the town. She could be with them."
Miss Diane said, "There are more saloons in town. Some with trouble just waiting to happen."
"Well, we hope they don't get into trouble."

357

The girls thought they would just have a beer and then go get cleaned up for tomorrow's job interview. Mr. Dickenson ordered for them. "Bartender, can you bring three beers?"

"Yes Sir, right away."

"Sir, may we buy you one?"

"No Ma'am, I think I've had my fill. But I will have something to eat. Would you like something to eat?"

"Actually, I would," Orlies said. "Let's see what they have." A sip of their beer and they were asking the bartender what was on the dinner list.

"Ma'am, we have a menu and a very good cook."

"Well, that's good to know. Can you bring us a menu?"

"Yes Ma'am, I will be right back."

Steak cooked the way you like it was at the top of the menu with biscuits loaded with gravy. Chicken with potatoes and gravy. And that's what they all had. The chicken was good. Something they haven't had for a long time. They told Mr. Dickenson they had a good chance of getting a job here in Helena. They said bye to him and each gave him a hug and headed to Miss Diane's place for the night. Soaking in the tub and washing their hair was great. Laying out their clothes for the morning and having a good night's sleep was welcome. Miss Diane was off to the post office early. Left the three of them getting themselves ready with plenty a time to spare. Coffee and toasted bread for breakfast. They had time to iron out the wrinkles on their dresses. Miss Diane was back at noon, offering to drive them to their appointments. They accepted so they wouldn't have to get on a horse with their dresses. First stop was the school office. All four went in. A woman asked them what they wanted.

"Ma'am, we are here to see Mr. Caldwell."

"Alright, he will be with you in a few minutes. Please have a seat."

Mr. Caldwell came out to greet them with his assistant. "Ladies, this is my assistant Mrs. Evers."

"Pleased to meet you, Ma'am."

"These two ladies are the Evens sisters that applied for a teaching position in our school. If you don't mind me saying so, you look a lot different than you did yesterday."

"Yes Sir. Yesterday we came right off the trail. We have had time to clean up a bit, thanks to Miss Binks."

He looked at Miss Binks and said, "Ma'am."

She nodded and said, "Sir."

"Miss Clarius, Miss Glada, we need teachers that have your back ground so we are going to hire you both. We can talk about your pay now or later, whichever you want. But I can tell you, we intend to pay very well for your services. Let's see, this is Wednesday. How about you start Monday of next week?"

"That will be fine. It will give us time to get settled in."

"You meet with us Friday and we can discuss your pay and schedule."

"Thank you, Sir and Ma'am. We'll have to go now and see if our sister Orlies will be hired as well."

"I understand, Ma'am. We will talk later. The newspaper office was locked so they sat on chairs outside the door. It wasn't long. Mr. Miller pulled up in a buggy.

"Sorry I wasn't here to greet you ladies. Come on in. Have a seat. I was out getting a condemned man's account of the crime for a story line. Right now, I have to do several different jobs. Our other reporter is getting a story from our governor. Ma'am, could you handle an interview with a governor or a condemned man?"

"I have and I can."

"When can you go to work?"

"How does tomorrow sound?"

"Miss Evens, you are hired. I'll pay you whatever you were paid in Denver and a little more. How does that sound?"

"I was paid pretty well in Denver."

"Okay, come in my office and we will discuss the terms."

Miss Orlies got up from her chair and stood there for a second in her white blouse and dark green floor length skirt looking very professional and turned to her sisters. She got the approval she was looking for from her sisters. She went in the office with Mr. Miller and did get the pay she asked for. The three now had the jobs they had come to Helena, Montana, for. Now they had to find a place to live. Miss Diane offered to help with that too.

Chapter 13

At the camp, the hands were starting to make their way back after a few hours of drinking and looking the town over. OK Bill and Red Fox stayed at the camp with Prairie Flower and Angelina and kind of looked after things. They didn't have any real interest in going into a town anyway. Frankie B. and Harve went into town for a bath and couple drinks but were back by now. Mrs. Sikorski and Antonina were back also after a bath and some new clothes. They still had a day or so before the Dickenson people would pull out and head for Texas. But Mrs Sikorski, had said several times how she missed being a whole woman. She also spent a little time in a library reading and looking for subjects that her and Antonina were interested in. Books were always part of her upbringing and life as a married woman. A library offered her the first opportunity to see any pictures, paintings, or art since that day last year back in southern Illinois when her husband and son were killed, her other son run off, and her and Antonina were taken by the bandits and passed on to the Comancheros. It has been very traumatic for the girl. She hasn't talked about it very much but sometimes she can hear her daughter crying at night. Maybe going back to Illinois and looking for her other son would be good for her. Probably good for both of them. Constance has yet to bring up the subject with her but she is thinking more about it. It would be a good opportunity to go with OK Bill, Frankie B., and the others as far as they go through Oklahoma. Juan, Carlyle, Dance, Tommy, the two Johns, and Tim were making their way back after a little drinking. Carlyle went along with them as a father figure. They seemed to like it. Carlyle bought himself a bottle and kept sipping on it while watching over the boys. It didn't bother him. Most of them were really plastered, not being used to drinking. Long John headed straight to the telegraph office to send out a telegram to his sister Kate back in Del Rio. She had some hard times since her husband got killed on the wrong side of the law. Long John doesn't have any family other than his sister. A woman named April, that is a good friend of his sister Kate, is someone he would like to see when they get back to Del Rio. Soon as he got the telegraph sent, he headed for one of the saloons to have a few beers. He sat at a table with his back against a wall. An old habit of not making his back a target after years of being a Texas Ranger, making a few enemies along the way. Someone will usually recognize him and push him into a fight. *Being up north and away from Texas*, he thought, *I should be okay.* Mr. Dickenson happened to be going by and spotted Long John's horse outside the saloon. He stopped in to see if he wanted some company.

"Hi, Long John, mind if I join you?"

"Why heck, yeah, Sir, have a seat. I stopped in for a couple drinks after telegraphing my sister. The fellow said he would bring me a message if there is one."

"Oh, okay, I was just on my way back to the camp when I spotted your horse. I'm in no hurry. If you don't care, I'll sit with you for a while."

"Absolutely. Can I order you anything?"

"I'll take a beer."

In the swinging doors walks the telegraph operator with a message for Long John.

"Okay, good. I was hoping for a reply from Kate. She says she's fine. She misses all of us. She's working with kids for now. Hurry home."

"That's good, Long John."

"Thank you, Sir."

"Let's talk about supplies early tomorrow, okay with you?"

"Sure, that's right, we want to get going day after tomorrow. Well Sir, I'm ready to head back to camp if you're ready."

"I'm gonna get a bottle of Helena's best sipping whiskey before we go. You want one, too?"

"You know, I think I will."

They both bought a bottle. People bragging about how good it was and it's made right here in Helena. Something to sip on cold nights. Off to the camp they went.

Long John said, "You know, Sir, it's pretty nice here."

"Yeah, but wait till winter hits, you'd wish you were somewhere else."

"Yeah, I guess."

"They say it gets down to six below zero. It's hard to stay warm at that kinda temperature."

"Yes Sir, I think I'll stick with Texas."

Back at camp, they joined in with the hands sitting around having their coffee and a bit to eat and talking about any ole thing. Juan was strumming a guitar and singing low in Spanish. It sounded so good. Some started to join in as best they knew the words. With the fires warming and the coffee hot, you couldn't ask for more. Mr. Dickenson was already lying down close to a fire, head on his saddle. Didn't take long for some of the others to do the same. Taters let it be known he was taking the day off tomorrow.

"Anybody wants to cook tomorrow, be my guest. I'm going into town early, get a bath and a shave, play a little poker, and do a little drinking. That shouldn't be a problem. One thing we have is folks that can cook. Who wants to get up early and make some biscuits and gravy?"

Mrs Sikorski said, "I will if I get some helpers."

Prairie Flower volunteered. "I will be glad to help."

"I can help, too," Harve said.

"Mother, I will get the pans of water set up with the tables since I do it all the time anyway."

It was pretty well known that we would be pulling out the next day. Long John told everybody to do whatever you want tomorrow but be ready to ride the next morning, so we don't have to look for you. And I guess you know the Evens girls all three got jobs so they won't be going to Texas with us.

"I hope we can all see them before we leave."

"Yeah, that's right."

In the morning, Mrs. Sikorski and her help got the breakfast going without any problems. Taters was already gone. Coffee was brewing with biscuits and gravy or jelly if you wanted it. Then people went on their way back to town to browse around.

OK Bill, Red Fox, and Frankie B. sat around and talked. Mrs. Sikorski, Antonina, Prairie Flower, and Angelina joined in the conversation.

Constance asked, "If we decide to go back to Illinois, could we travel as far as you go to Oklahoma? How close do you get to southern Illinois?"

"Ma'am, it's still a long way. I guess it's about four hundred miles or so more. That would take a lot of traveling with us though."

"Antonina and I would like to look for my other son. He's about seventeen now. I'm sure he's okay. He's probably living with his uncles. But we'd like to see him."

"Yes, Ma'am, of course you do."

Frankie B. comforted her with a hug. She cried a little.

"If you folks wouldn't mind us tagging along as far as you're going, we'd be grateful."

"Ma'am, I don't think we'd mind at all. Would we?"

"You come with us. I look after you. I help you."

"Thank you, Red Fox."

"Some of us might be able to go with you beyond the Fort Smith area. Will you be staying in Illinois or would you come back with us to the Comanche camp?"

"I don't know, Frankie B. I have mixed feelings about the whole thing. I almost feel like there is nothing there for me anymore. Are you and OK Bill staying in Oklahoma?"

"No. Not as far as I'm concerned. What about it OK Bill?"

"We still work for Mr. Dickenson. We go to Texas. Maybe we get Chief Bengalese, the Comanche, to come to Texas. Plenty Comanche in Texas. Winter warmer in Texas."

Carlyle just got through checking the extra horses. He got another cup of coffee and sat down next to Angelina.

"Hi, my dear."

"Hi, Grandpa. Grandpa, do you think Chief Bengalese has ever been to Texas?"

"Now that, I don't know. He might have. You know Comanche and Apache don't always get along in Texas."

"I know, that's what I've heard. Well Frankie B., you and OK Bill might just be the ones to get Chief Bengalese to move camp. After all, Comanche are not that popular in Oklahoma either."

"You got Osage, Pawnee, Kiowa, Cheyenne, Arapaho, and our camp of Comanche. They're all stealing each other's horses and sometime women, and whatever they can get. That's how my son and Prairie Flower's husband got killed in a raid." Carlyle dropped his head for moment. Then gained his composure. "Angelina never had a father. She was born after his death."

"Carlyle, would you move to Texas?"

"I don't know. Probably, if the whole camp picked up and moved. Sure, I would go right along with them."

After that, the conversation switched.

"It sure will be nice to be on our way to Texas. Are we all ready?"

"I'd say we are."

Juan grabbed a coffee and sat down with them. Just then, riding into camp, were the three Evens girls. "Hi, everybody. We wanted to see you all before you leave in the morning."

Long John came walking over and helped them off their horses. "Good to see you. We heard you all got jobs and are staying in Helena."

"Yes, at least for now. The jobs seem to be just what we wanted," Orlies said. "Matter of fact, I'm working today at the Independent Record Newspaper. You want to give me a story?"

"No, but you can put in a few good words about Mr. Dickenson's people not being a rowdy bunch and you can include yourselves."

"Now see, Long John, you did give me a story. I will write about our experience and how kind you all were to us."

Glada asked Long John, "If our jobs don't work out for us, can we join you in Del Rio and maybe look for jobs there?"

Long John looked over to Mr. Dickenson.

"Yes Ma'am, you don't like it here, you come down to Del Rio and we will help you all we can. I don't know if we will be coming back this way or not. If you decide you don't like it here and you want to come to Texas, let us know and we will help you get there somehow."

"Thank you, Sir. We appreciate everything that you have done for us."

"That's quite alright. God bless you and keep you safe."

"Thank you, Sir. We need to get going. Everybody, give us a hug."

They got their hugs and got back on their horses and left. It was a sad parting. Everyone seemed to like the three of them. They fit in very well, worked hard at whatever job was given to them, and never complained.

"Well, we got to see them. I was hoping they'd come by. Did everybody get there supplies till the next town? Mrs Sikorski, did you stock up on cans of cherries and apples and anything else for those delicious pies?"

"Yes, Long John, I didn't forget."

"Looks like everybody is back from town? Juan, how many extra horses do we have?"

"Ah, Señor, ten and much more saddles and guns and other things."

"That's okay, Juan. We earned every damn one of them."

"Si, Señor Long John."

"You think we can herd them back to Texas or we gotta keep them tied up."

"Señor, maybe so. We can try to herd them. If they won't stay together, then we tie them to our wagons."

Night was starting to cover the whole land, fires burning low, two on guard with Carlyle and Tommy taking the first watch. Antonina got the two fires going good, then said she was going to turn in for the night. We might as well rest up and get an early start in the morning.

Long John was already stretching out his blanket. "See you folks in the morning."

Frankie B. and OK Bill were both quiet, looking into the fire, no doubt wondering what lay ahead. The night was a peaceful one. Soon as morning came, everyone was up. Taters was his usual self-serving the best breakfast anywhere. Antonina and Harve got the water pans and towels and tables set up. Mr. Dickenson and Long John were first to wash up for breakfast. The coffee was ready. Antonina had two pots brewing up the coffee.

"Soon as everyone's ready, we're moving out," Long John said. "What do ya think, Harve?"

"I think I'm ready, Boss."

"Juan, you and Harve tend to the horses for a couple hours. The rest of you pick up your stuff and put out the fires and let's head for Del Rio. I'm gonna call out your name. Everybody give me a 'here' or an 'okay:' Mr. Dickenson, Mrs. Sikorski, Antonina, Prairie Flower, Angelina, Juan, Tommy Holbrooks, Red Fox, John Davis, John Johnson, Harve, Carlyle, Tim Shiloh, Dance Mead, OK Bill, Frankie B., Taters. After each here or okay was heard. "Did I miss anybody?"

"No Boss, you got us all. We count eighteen."

"That's what I got. Let's ride. I would like us to all look after each other as much as possible. It's a long way to Del Rio and we made some enemies that might try to catch us off guard. Let's not let that happen. Rifles fully loaded, two for every man and woman. Two or more pistols."

Mr. Dickenson added, "Don't get separated from us unless we know about it. If someone looks like they're falling asleep riding, don't let them wander off. Keep in mind, we are in unforgiving country. As soon as we let down our guard, we are on the losing side. We will ride close together sometimes and spread out sometimes. Keep our two wagons in sight. Taters or a helper will be driving the chuck wagon. Juan or any volunteer will be driving the other wagon. We need them both. When you need to stop, let someone know. Don't stop alone. Have someone stop with you and let the rest of us know so we always know where you are. We'll get back to Texas, if we work together.

Riding all day without cattle seemed a little strange. Now they can all concentrate on the small band of horses. Sooner or later, the peace will be broken, you can depend on it. Days turn into weeks. Riding about twenty to twenty-five miles a day will take us about fifty days to get to Higgins, Texas, where some of our good friends will leave us to head for the Indian nations around Fort Smith, Arkansas. And Mrs. Sikorski and Antonina will go on even further to southern Illinois. That will leave Mr. Dickenson, Long John, Harve, Dance, John, John, Tommy, Taters, and Juan. Tim Shiloh, maybe. He has to check on a certain young lady in Higgins. And then there's Mrs. Edwards and her daughter Grace and José. We don't know if they will be going on to Del Rio with us or staying in Higgins as the law. So we got every bit of fifty days ahead till things change. Pitching camp every night, sitting around taking it easy after the meal, and finishing off a piece of pie with a cup of coffee. Mrs Sikorski said she didn't mind making pies. She always made plenty of pies for her family back in southern Illinois. "You're all like my family now."

Four days later they were picking up a few things in Bozeman, Montana. The talk around Bozeman was about the Crow Indians, how they stepped up their attacks on other Indians, as well as Whites.

"I remember the talk I had with some Crow braves that we gave some deer meat to about their Chief Long Horse and I having a peace pow wow a few months ago. Where was it? Somewhere around Higgins, Texas, wasn't it?"

"Yeah, it was."

"We need to have that talk and stop the killing."

"If you have another chance to pow wow with them, you better do it."

"Yeah, I know Carlyle. If I get another chance, you should come with me . I don't know about OK Bill, and Red Fox. Would the Crow have any respect for them or not."

"I don't know. Probably not."

Day after day things were going okay. No sighting of the hostiles. Then about a week out of Bozeman, Red Fox spotted a dust cloud going the same direction they were, only on an angle from east to southwest. Our paths could eventually cross. Long John sent Tommy and Harve on ahead to check on what was making all that dust. Whatever it was, it was moving fast. Didn't take long. Tommy and Harve were back riding alongside Mr. Dickenson and Long John.

"There's ten men riding fast like they're chasing something or someone. We stopped and looked at them with binoculars. They look like buffalo hunters. But I'd say they're not. They got something black hanging from the saddles. And we all know what that is. The sons a bitches are scalp hunters. Going around killing Indians just for scalps and keeping the Indian wars going. We never will have any peace with them on the loose."

Mr. Dickenson was listening. He has always had a strong dislike for scalp hunters.

"Back in Texas, we didn't tolerate them. We just keep riding. Up ahead is a little town coming up. We need to stock up on a few things and we're all needing water. If that's where the scalp hunters are heading, then we will get a look at them."

Sure enough, there's a lot of horses tied up outside the saloon. We rode in minding our own business heading for the general store. Couldn't help notice a lot a scalps hanging on their saddles. They must have made a recent killing.

Long John asked Mr. Dickenson, "Do you want to do anything about these sons a bitches?"

"I can't abide what they do. I'm gonna have a talk with the sheriff. Then I'll let you know. We do have the ability to put them down you know?"

"Yes Sir, I was thinking the same thing."

A couple of them were sitting around outside the saloon and saw us go by. Watching us, especially our Indian friends. Mr. Dickenson tied up outside the sheriff's office and went in. The sheriff said he didn't like scalp hunters but he wasn't able to do anything about them and as long as they don't cause any trouble in town, they can drink all they want. Mr. Dickenson asked the sheriff if he would mind if we put them out of business.

"Well, I don't know exactly what you have in mind but I can almost guess. Just don't shoot up the whole town. Little Dubois has a small population and we don't want to lose any of them."

"Okay Sheriff, I just don't want any more scalps taken. And there is really only one way to deal with these sons a bitches."

Mr. Dickenson left the sheriff's office and caught up with Long John and the rest.

"We kinda got the go ahead from the sheriff. How you wanna play it? If we were in Texas, I'd say we could do things within the law as Rangers. How about we get this sheriff to deputize some of us?"

"Did you tell him we were Texas Rangers?"

"No, I didn't. I don't know if he would care. We just about got all the supplies loaded in the wagons. Hold on. Long John, how about you, Frankie B., Carlyle, and I go have a beer. I want to see for myself what these scalp hunters are like and what they're bragging about."

"Good idea, Sir."

"Make sure Frankie B. and Carlyle know what we are up to. Anybody else that wants a beer, tell them to come on."

When Long John said, "Anybody want a beer, come on," most of them jumped up and said they were going. All the men headed for the saloon including Juan, Harve, OK Bill, and Red Fox.

OK Bill turned back and said to the women, "You need help, fire two shots, we come help."

They nodded and said, "We will. You be careful."

Mr. Dickenson, Long John, Frankie B., and Carlyle went by the sheriff's office.

"Sheriff, give me four badges and swear us in now or we will put on our Rangers' badges. If we arrest some of these sons a bitches, you got anybody to lock 'em up and keep 'em locked up till the marshall gets here?"

"Captain Dickenson, this is a small town. I don't have any help but one deputy."

373

"That's what I thought. Okay Sheriff, get that drunk out of the cell. We might be needing it."

The sheriff swore them in and they put their badges on, under a coat or vest for now. They caught up to the rest and they all went through the swinging doors together. All eyes turned and set on OK Bill and Red Fox. The scalpers were mostly sitting at tables.

One of them said, "Hey, send those two redskins over here. We will take good care of them and that black one, too. We know how to take care of them, too." Nobody answered. He stood up and said it again. This time a lot louder.

Long John turned and said, "They're with us. We just came in here for a drink and some answers."

"What answers?"

By then the Dickenson boys had the door, bar, and upstairs covered.

"Who do all those horses out front belong to?"

"They belong to us: me and my boys, if it's any of your business. Don't be a worrying about those horses. I said, send those redskins and that black over here."

"Well, I just thought you might care about your horses loose heading out of town."

"What?"

"If you don't believe me, see for yourself. But before you do, unbuckle those gun belts real slow and put them on that table."

"I don't think we will. Are you the law or you just don't like us very much. Which is it?"

"I'll tell you what, four of us are the law." They showed their badges.

Long John said, "I'm gonna send everybody out of here but us four and then I'm gonna tell you again to unbuckle your gun belts, and if you don't, the four of us are gonna send as many of you to hell as we can. We don't like scalpers and it's illegal in this territory."

"No it isn't, Mister Law Man."

"It is. I just made it so. All right, everybody out but the four of us."

They all went out and left behind Frankie B., Carlyle, Mr. Dickenson, and Long John. With each one, the swinging door made a faint sound. Carlyle stood there with a rifle lowered, a holstered navy colt, and a shiny pistol in his belt. Frankie B. reached down slow like and threw back his coat tail on his right side, the leather strap was already off the hammer of his colt. The other one stuck in his belt looked like it was ready for business. Long John and Mr. Dickenson both brushed back their coats at about the same time. With the light coming in the doors, it was easy to see the shiny colts in their holsters and the ones in their belts.

Long John spoke up again, "Now Mister Scalp Hunter, I'm gonna say it again to all eight of you. Put your holsters on the table. Easy does it. Nice and slow. You are under arrest!"

The scalpers started to unbuckle their belts and pulled their guns instead and fired. That was their mistake. The four lawmen outdrew them, killing three. The other five dropped to their knees! A squeak in the steps, Carlyle swung around and got one more with a gun in his hand. Long John got a second one coming out of a room aiming his gun still in a holster. The two of them came crashing down over the railing onto the floor, full of broken glass and blood. Mr. Dickenson and the three were hit, either with bullets or flying glass. Glass was still in the air falling when the sheriff came through the door. A huge chandelier that hung in the middle of the ceiling was ripped off by one of the half-naked men coming off the second floor from the railing. The five were stripped of their guns and knives and marched off to the jail. Doc Grzeszkiewicz came in and checked on the wounds of the lawmen and the dead bandits. By then, all the Dickenson people were coming in to see if they could help in any way. Mr. Dickenson had a bullet wound through his left arm above the elbow. Long John was hit in the right leg, above the knee. Frankie B. had a bullet graze on his neck. Carlyle just got showered with broken glass and had blood all over.

Long John asked, "Is everybody alright? And how's the women? OK Bill, get somebody to catch all the scalper horses. We are going to claim some of them. Tommy and Dance, gather up all the weapons from the dead and get them in our wagon. Doc, do I have a bullet in my leg or did it go through?"

"Just lay back, I don't know yet."

"How's Mr. Dickenson?"

"His bullet went through."

Mrs. Sikorski came in, her boots crunching glass as she walked around the upset tables and chairs, to where Long John was sitting, pulled off her glove, and rubbed Long John on the forehead.

"My dear, relax, our people are doing what needs to be done. You need to get that leg taken care of. Doc, Grzeszkiewicz will be right back. He's looking after

Mr. Dickenson and Frankie B. over there. I'd say you got a bullet in there, no exit wound."

As soon as the doctor came back, he said, "Couple you guys come over here and hold this gentleman down."

Tommy and Harve came over.

"Grab that bottle on the bar and pour as much whiskey down him as you can and get him on that table. This is gonna hurt like hell."

"I know, Doc, I've had a few bullets dug out of me before."

"That's okay, take a big slug outta that bottle anyway. That leg area is a very tender spot."

Mrs Sikorski put a wet towel on his forehead and rolled up her glove and had him bite down on it. He was sweating a lot and the leg was bleeding out.

"Okay Boys, hold him down. Here goes. He's out. Good, he won't be jerking that leg. I need to go deep next to the bone. It's all the way in there. Hang onto him in case he comes to and jerks. Ma'am, can you heat up a knife."

Mrs. Sikorski called the barkeeper who was standing by the door. "Do you have a hot stove in the back ?"

"Yes Ma'am."

"Heat up a big knife. Make it as hot as you can. We need to cauterize this wound."

"Yes Ma'am, right away."

Doc got the bullet out and cauterized it . "He won't be walking on this leg for a while. I need to check on those other two. And see to the dead. Then I'll be back. I'd keep him laying down, for now."

"Okay Doctor. Thank you so much."

"Yes Ma'am."

Mr. Dickenson and Carlyle came over to see how Long John was doing.

"Looks like Long John is out to the world."

"Yes Sir, he's still out. He'll be fine. He's been through this before."

Frankie B. was met at the door by Angelina and Prairie Flower. They sat down with him on a bench outside the saloon, and brushed glass out of his hair and wiped sweat off his forehead. His wound on his neck was all bandaged up by the doc, so they couldn't see how bad it was.

Frankie B. said, "It's alright, it didn't hurt much. Probably will tomorrow."

OK Bill came walking back in town with five of the scalpers horses. Mr. Dickenson was sitting on a bench near Frankie B. OK Bill stopped at Frankie B., looked straight at him, and said something in Apache. Sometime later he would tell him it was an Apache prayer to heal his friend. Frankie B. said he did recall a feeling of peace coming over him at that moment.

Mr. Dickenson motioned to OK Bill and said, "Tie the horses up with our extra horses for now. We'll decide what we want to do with them. And get those rifles off the horses and in our wagon. We might be staying here a few days. We gotta get Long John back on his feet."

After a tense night, the morning finally came around. The talk over coffee might be considered a little different with Long John laid up and Mr. Dickenson with his left arm bandaged and held up with a sling of some kind so he can't use it . Frankie B. was walking around with his neck wrapped and somewhat stiff. Long John was carried out of the doctor's office by John Johnson and John Davis, and put in the back of a wagon. They brought him out to the camp. When everyone saw him sitting up with his legs hanging down at the back of the wagon, they whistled and cheered. That pleased him a lot. Harve even made him a crutch.

"Boss, you shouldn't be getting on a horse I heard the doctor say. You can use this crutch, or you just call me, I'll help you get around."

"Thanks, Harve. Tomorrow you can help me get on my horse. Day after, we will be heading south if Mr. Dickenson and Frankie B. feel up to it."

"Are you sure, Boss? The doc might have other ideas about you riding."

"I know he will but we need to get to Higgins, Texas. Then we can rest up some more."

Mr. Dickenson and Frankie B. were discussing the very thing about leaving as soon as Long John felt good enough to ride. Mr. Dickenson telegraphed the army at Fort Washakie, Wyoming. The general there said a detachment of fifteen men was at Crowheart. It's about half way between Fort Washakie and Dubois. They should get to Dubois sometime tomorrow to take charge of the prisoners.

"We should be able to leave after we give them a full report. Juan, looks like we got a few more horses, saddles, and belongings."

"Señor Dickenson, I will take care of them. We almost need another wagon to carry all the saddles and guns, Señor."

"Okay Juan, see if you can make do for now."

"I will, Señor."

Taters poured himself a cup a coffee and sat down by Mr. Dickenson and Frankie B. He clearly had something on his mind, but didn't say a word, just sipped on his coffee. After a bit, he spoke.

"Do you know, well hell, sure you know, Mr. Dickenson, scalping Indians for bounty isn't against the law all over! If it's legal here, you might have a problem, Sir."

"I know, Taters, I did give that some thought."

"Unless they weren't wanted for other crimes, you might be held for murder and other charges. You and Frankie B., Carlyle, and Long John."

"I know. So far, I couldn't find out anything about the scalping law in this territory. When the army gets here, we'll know more."

The army got there around noon the next day. Captain George Pinter was the commanding officer. First thing he did was look for Mr. Dickenson.

"Are you Captain Dickenson from the Texas Rangers?"

"Yes Sir, I am. And I'm retired."

"That's all well and good, Sir, but once a Captain in the Texas Rangers, always a Captain in the Texas Rangers."

"Well Captain, I agree with you on that. But I don't expect other people to think that way."

"Well I do, Captain Dickenson. What happened here?"

"Well, Captain Pinter, I have to be honest with you and say I don't like scalp hunters for any scalps, White or Indian. We hunted them down in Texas, and shot it out with many of them. And that's sorta what we did here."

"Well, Captain Dickenson, some say it's not illegal anywhere. As far as I'm concerned, you are free to go. But I need more to hold those five in the jail. Have you or any of your men questioned them?"

"No Sir, we have not."

"I guess I better do it then. Would you like to come along? You might have some questions you'd like to ask them?"

"Yes Sir, I would like to. How soon?"

"Soon as I find my legal officer, Lt. Isaac. You go ahead. I'll get a couple of my men and meet you at the jail in about a half hour."

Mr. Dickenson got a hold of Long John, Frankie B., and Carlyle. They put Long John on a wagon and the four drove over to the jail. Captain Pinter was just arriving so they went in the jail together. The sheriff agreed to the questioning . The scalpers answered all their questions. They said they had taken part in a lot a killings of Indians for their scalps and a few whites that tried to stop them. Mostly in the Dakota territory, some in Montana.

"Sheriff, I will take these five back to the fort, and keep them locked up till I get some answers from the law in the Dakotas and Montana if they are wanted. Is that alright with you?"

"Yes Sir, Captain Pinter."

"Then I will leave with them in the morning. I will need their horses if they are still here."

"They will have to pick out their horses."

"That's fine, Sheriff. Then I will see you in the morning."

"Yes sir."

Mr. Dickenson and the three were finished here. They talked it over and thought they might leave tomorrow or at least the next day. Long John was anxious to get moving.

He said, "I can sit on a horse or a wagon as well as sit around here and not be moving. We need to get to Higgins."

Everyone was in favor of getting outta Dubois. So they said their goodbyes, turned over the horses to Captain Pinter for the five scalpers, got some supplies, and left. Long John got some help from Harve getting on his horse.

He said, "I have been shot up worse than this and still rode a horse."

They rode well into the day as long as they could see and camped for the night. Mrs. Sikorski made a couple pies. After the meal of beans, roasted rabbit and quail which Red Fox supplied with his bow and arrow, the pies were cut up and passed around. In the morning, they were all up early so they got an early start. Five days of riding daylight to dusk put them in Jeffrey City, Wyoming. By now, Long John was getting on and off his horse pretty much by himself. Although Harve offered to help him, he would never wait. Long John offered to buy Harve a beer at the saloon in Jeffrey City.

"Yes Sir, Boss, I can use a beer."

After we eat, I'm going into town for a beer. Anyone coming?"

Just about everyone said they wanted to go. Frankie B. asked Angelina if she wanted to drink a beer?

"I don't know. I never have one. I want to go where you go, Frankie B. I will try it."

Mrs. Sikorski and Antonina, Tommy, Dance, John Johnson, John Davis, Tim Shiloh, Juan, and Carlyle ate as fast as they could and took turns at the wash pan.

"Okay Boss, you going or not?"

"Just hold them horses. I'm going. Taters you going?"

"Na, I ain't going, I still got my bottle."

"Mr. Dickenson?"

"No, you folks go ahead, and don't get into trouble."

"We'll try not to."

OK Bill, Prairie Flower, Red Fox, two shots if you need us . We'll come a running. I don't know about the rest of them, but I'm not staying long, just a couple beers and I'm ready to head back."

"Okay, Long John."

A short ride and they were in Jeffery City, a small town not much more than a saloon and a couple stores. Quite a few horses tied up at the Split Rock Saloon. When Long John limped in with the rest, all eyes turned to see who was coming through the swinging doors, and then they went back to their own business. Except for a bunch at the bar. They didn't want to make room at the bar. So Long John and the bunch headed for a couple of tables, slid them together, and moved the chairs. A ring leader at the bar commented on the noise coming from the strangers. It was obvious he had too much to drink and was looking for trouble. The barkeep came over and took their order and looked at Angelina and Juan and Harve extra hard but didn't say anything. The loud mouth at the bar kept spouting off. Finally he said, "We don't like Indians, Mex's, or Niggers in these parts," and looked straight at them when he said it.

Long John had enough. "Cowboy, tend to your beer and leave us alone," he said.

The barkeep said, "Cowboy, that's Captain Long John Lowther, Texas Rangers, and a couple of other Rangers. You might want to leave them alone."

"I don't care who they are," and turned around and started to walk toward the table when Frankie B. got up.

"What is your problem, Mister? You better go someplace and sober up before you get yourself killed."

"I don't need you telling me what to do, you young Indian lover."

With that, Frankie B. calmly walked over to him and knocked him cold, dragged him out by the collar, threw him into a watering trough for horses, turned around, and walked back in and finished his beer.

He asked, "Angelina, how do you like beer?"

By now, she had a few sips.

"Not anything special," she said. "Frankie B., does this always happen when you go to a beer place?"

"Uh, it does happen a lot. Beer makes some people crazy."

Mrs. Sikorski calmly finished her glass of beer and added that some people will drink too much and don't know when to stop. When all had finished theirs, they all walked out, mounted up, and headed back to camp. The drunk was still trying to get out of the water trough when they rode out of town. Frankie B. rode over to where he was, looked down at him, and said, "You don't know how lucky you are. I might have shut you up just in time. You were pissing off a lot a people at that table. He spurred his horse and they all left.

Back at the camp, it was just another day. Something more to think about in this unforgiving land. In the morning, they pulled out and headed for the next town. Without anything unusual happening, nine days later, they were coming up to Fort Collins, Colorado, wagons loaded and extra horses staying together like a band.

Juan said, "Good Señor Boss, soon we be in Texas."

"Not so fast, Juan, we still have a long way to go."

"Ah, really, Señor Boss?"

"Yep. I bet we still have a thousand miles to Del Rio." "I'd say you're right, Long John."

Mr. Dickenson asked around. "Any of you need anything from town? Taters, you need anything in Fort Collins?"

"I do. And I'm going in for a drink. Anyone coming. As soon as we get through with the meal, I'm going in."

Mrs. Sikorski and Carlyle said they needed a few things, too, so will be ready when you are.

"Long John, are you going?"

"I don't think so. I might have to bust some drunk's head. I'll just sit around here and keep warm by the fire."

Frankie B. and OK Bill stayed close to the fire. It was getting downright cold. Angelina and her mother were cleaning up after the evening meal. Antonina talked about going into town just for a look and something different.

"That would be fine, just stick close to your mother. All of you stay armed like we've been doing all year. Taters, Constance, Antonina, Carlyle, and Harve left the small camp at the edge of Fort Collins. The general store was the first stop. Harve asked if it would be alright if he went to the telegraph office?

"Sure Harve, but be careful."

"Okay then, I'll meet you all in the saloon."

"There's a couple saloons."

"That's okay, I'll find you."

"Harve, I don't know if that's a good idea."

"What's that, Mr. Taters?"

"You going off by yourself."

"I try to keep myself out of trouble."

"When you get through, stop by here first. We might still be here."

"Yes sir, I do just that."

They went on to the general store to each get what they had come for. Carlyle asked if anybody saw the telegraph office when we rode into town. No one had. Taters asked the store owner.

"Out the door and to the right, walk a bit, and cross the street. You'll see the sign."

Carlyle told the rest, "I got my stuff. I'm going looking for Harve."

"Okay, good idea. Looks like we'll all be through here in a minute. We'll be in the saloon we passed riding in."

"Okay Taters, see you all in a bit."

Harve was having a hard time with the telegraph operator. The man keep saying, "You can't send a message, you don't know what that is, boy."

Harve was about to walk out when Carlyle came through the door, a big strong looking mountain man in buckskins and a lever action Winchester 44-40 in his right hand.

"Having trouble, Harve?"

"Yes Sir. I just want to send a message to my lady friend in Del Rio at the Dickenson ranch. I know what that is. The man keeps saying I don't know what that is."

Carlyle walked up to the counter and said, "Can you write down this man's message and send it to the Del Rio, Texas, town?"

"We don't do messages for his kind."

Carlyle calmly set his rifle down on the counter and said, "Will you send this man's message?"

"Hell no."

At that, Carlyle grabbed him by the top of his hair and smashed his head down on the counter. The man raised himself up with a bloody face and said, "You broke my nose you old son of a bitch."

Carlyle put his pistol against the side of his head and said, "You start writing now or I'll break it again."

"I can't see."

"Start writing."

He grabbed the tablet covered with his blood and said, "What you want to say, boy?"

"Miss Shirley Chung, can we sit by the creek when I get back? I miss seeing you."

"If answer to Denver, Colorado, where does this go?"

"Dolphus Dickenson ranch in Del Rio, Texas. How much that cost ?"

"That will be four dollars. You got four dollars, boy?"

"Yes sir. Here you are. Now can you send it."

"Okay. I'll send it."

Carlyle told the man, "Send it, every word. If you don't, we'll know when we get to Denver and I will be back if you didn't. You understand?"

"Okay, okay. Who's gonna pay for my nose?"
"Here's five bucks, go see a doctor." Carlyle slapped the five down on the counter and they stood there and listened as the man tapped on the telegraph machine. Then walked out the door, got on their horses, and rode through town to the Split Rock Saloon where Taters and the others were waiting.

"Took you a while."
"Yeah, I know. We had to convince the man to send the message for Harve."
"Oh, really. Is that his blood on your sleeve?"
"Afraid so."
"Mr. Carlyle, I thank you for helping but you might get arrested."
"Harve, it was worth it."

No sooner had he said that when the sheriff walked in and came straight to were Carlyle was sitting.
"Mister, I need to have a talk with you. You are the only one with buckskins on so I'd say it's you that roughed up the telegraph operator."
"That's right, Sheriff. He wouldn't send this man's message because he's black. I changed his mind."
"By breaking his nose and busting up his face. Isn't that a little extreme."
"Well, Sheriff, I gave him five dollars to go see a doctor."

At that everybody laughed a little.
"If you're gonna be outta this town and the area by morning, I'm not going to hold you."
"Sheriff, I'm gonna be outta here in about ten minutes, as soon as I finish my beer."

The sheriff tipped his hat as he looked at everyone at the tables and said, "Ma'am," to Mrs Sikorski and Antonina.

On leaving, they rode slow to the camp.

Taters was the first to say, "We better leave early before the telegraph operator decides to press charges and we get stuck here for don't know how long. Not to say that I wouldn't have done the same thing."

Mr. Dickenson added, "Thanks, Carlyle, for helping out Harve."

"Yes Sir. I just couldn't stand there and let that man talk down to Harve like he was dirt. I just hope he sent the message. I told him we will find out when we get to Denver. Cause that's where the reply will come to if there is one from Harve's friend. And we'd be back if it didn't go, right Harve?"

Harve laughed a little.

Long John asked, "What's so funny, Harve?"

"Well Sir, the man had so much blood on his face and eyes, he might not have been able to see the right words on the paper."

With that, they all laughed.

"Carlyle, you must have done a good job on him."

"Yes sir, I reckon I did."

Taters poured coffee for anyone that held out their cup, and then held up his cup and said, "Here's to Carlyle."

Everyone raised their cup and said, "Here's to you, Carlyle."

"If we are going to get an early start tomorrow, we better be turning in."

"Yes Sir, Long John."

Mr. Dickenson was already sacked out with his book and a smoke. OK Bill and Prairie Flower were cuddled up in a large Indian blanket. Frankie B. and Angelina were just getting their second cup of coffee, settling down. Soon everyone would be asleep except for the two men on watch, John Johnson and Tommy Holbrooks. The four hours went fast for the boys on watch, then John Davis and Dance Mead took the watch till Mrs. Sikorski and Tim Shiloh came on to watch till dawn and everyone started getting up. Coffee was hot, biscuits and gravy were on the camp stove. Antonina did the water pan, soap, and towels and helped with whatever was needed. And it didn't take long before they were all up. They kinda wanted to get going before the town woke up. OK Bill and Red Fox were first to get their saddles on. Frankie B. saddled up Alice for Angelina. OK Bill saddled up My Friend for Prairie Flower. The four mounted up and rode together. Carlyle and Mr. Dickenson made the rounds making sure the fires were out and swung their horses south and they were off to another day's adventure. Three days went by and they were in Denver. Harve went straight to the telegraph office. "Nothing here for you, boy," the operator said. "You might want to check the other office across town."

"Thank you, Sir."

There was a message in the other office. It read, *Yes Harve, miss you, be safe.* He couldn't wait to tell Carlyle. Carlyle patted him on the back and said, "You're a lucky man, Harve."

Soon as they had picked up a few things at the general store, they were out of town heading south.

They had not ridden far when Long John suddenly realized John Davis was missing.

"Mr. Dickenson, you want to wait here or we all want to go back into Denver."

"I think we should all go back in case there's trouble."

"Okay, let's go. He passed the word and they all turned back, checked the saloons, but no sign of him. At the sheriff's office, he was in a jail cell with a bloody head.

"Sheriff, this is my man," Mr. Dickenson said.

"What's he done?"

"Disorderly conduct."

"I'd like to talk to him."

"Okay."

"Davis, what happened?"

"Don't really know, Sir. I went to a room with a girl and got hit on the head and robbed."

"What all they get?"

"I had about fifty bucks, three pistols, two rifles, my boots, my horse, and my hat."

"Sheriff, I can vouch for this man."

"Who might you be?"

"I am Captain Dolphus Dickenson, Texas Ranger, and this is Captain John Lowther, Texas Ranger. We know this man. He is one of my hands on my ranch in Del Rio, Texas. We just came through on our way back to Texas after driving a herd to Helena, Montana. We are both retired from the Rangers but still hold the rank of Captain. If you would like, you can check with the governor's office in Austin."

"No sir, that won't be necessary."

"Sheriff, I would like you to let this man out so we can go after the ones who robbed him. Do you know all the girls that work at the saloon?"

"Pretty much, let's go over there and see."

"Davis, let's go to the wagon and get you some boots and a couple guns and a horse."

"Yes Sir, right away. Sir, somebody beat the hell outta me."

"Sheriff, where can we find a doctor?"

They helped Davis out the door and sat him on the back of the wagon.

"How 'bout somebody find a doctor. Juan, saddle up one of the horses and get two rifles and two pistols and plenty of bullets."

Mrs. Sikorski went through the clothes on the wagon and came up with a pair a boots, hat, and coat that looked his size. Tommy came back with a doctor.

"Just sit still, Son. I'll check you on that wagon." Antonina had already got a wet towel from the water pump a few feet away next to the building. She was wiping John's face and cleaning him up a bit.

"It seems like the sheriff didn't do a thing to check his injuries. I'd sure hate to be in your jail."

"Well Ma'am, I thought he was drunk and fell down those steps where we found him."

"Well, I just think you could have took better care of an injured man."

"Yes Ma'am. I can see that I should have. Thank you, Ma'am, for pointing that out to me."

By now, he was looking better . Doc said he took a bad hit to the head and left eye. He could use two stitches on the side of his head.

"If you hold still, I'll do it now."

"If you can hurry a little, Doc. I'd like to get going after a horse thief or two."

"I'll go as fast as I can, Son. I'll need to put a bandage over the stitches to keep it clean and dry."

"Thanks, Doctor. What we owe you?"

"Two dollars will be fine. Bring him around my office in the morning if you want."

Mr. Dickenson paid him and said, "Thanks again. Let's go over to the saloon and see if we can find the girl John was with. John, can you walk?"

"I can, Sir."

The boots were a pretty good fit along with the hat and coat. Juan had his new horse ready. He was stuffing a rifle in a scabbard on the saddle, a gun belt was hanging over the saddle horn.

"Sheriff, you mind coming along?"

"No, I don't mind, let's go. I can help."

John gave the horse a hug and rubbed it on the face. He said something soft to the horse and it responded with a whinny nicker. He adjusted the gun belt, pulled the pistol out and spun the cylinder as he looked over. It was loaded but he needed to see it for himself and did a double backwards spin putting it quickly in the holster. I'm ready."

"You need any help getting on your horse?"

"No, I think I can make it. He mounted up with no hesitation. A short ride and they were at the My Brothers Bar. All went in plus the sheriff just leaving those watching the horses and the wagons. They made quite an impression. That many coming in at one time. And the loose horses were standing outside with the wagons. Juan stayed close to the door and keep an eye on the horses. He'd talk to them once in a while and whistle. They knew him and wouldn't hardly go any place without him, so it was unlikely they'd run off unless someone chased them out of town. The barkeeper was kept busy serving the whole crew while answering the questions about the girl they were looking for.

"Sure, I remember the boy there with the bandaged head. He went upstairs with Rose. She is sitting over there at that table."

She saw them come in the door. She was sitting with a man. John Davis walked over to the table and picked her up by the hair. The man protested.

John said, "Sit down and don't go anywhere. I might want to talk to you."

"Who the hell are you?"

"I'm the one she set up for a robbery and a beating. If you are part of it, I'll be talking to you next. If not, you can go. Rose, is that your name?"

"Yes Sir."

"Do you remember me?"

"Yes Sir."

"Who busted my head and robbed me besides you?"

"They will kill me if I say."

"I might kill you if you don't say. Do they live here in town?"

"Oh no, they came into town and left right after."

"After what?"

"After they robbed you and two others."

The sheriff caught that. "Who are the other two?"

"I don't know. I just heard them talk about two others."

"What's their names and where did they go?"

"They talked about going to the gambling halls in Cripple Creek near Colorado Springs. They didn't say but I think they owed some money to someone

there. One kept saying they had to get back."
"What's their names?"
"They never did call each other by a name. I don't know. They were in my room when we went in. They hit this man and dragged him out the door and down the steps. That's all I know. They said they'd kill me if I told anybody."
"Sheriff, did you catch all that?"
"Yes I did. How you want to handle this?"
"Well, I know I'm going after those two and get my stuff back. Sheriff, if she is telling the truth, then I wouldn't charge her with anything. When I catch those two, I'll find out about her, if she was telling the truth. You want me to bring them back here or bury them there?"
"Well, you don't have to go that far unless you have to shoot it out with them, then you can bury them wherever you are."
Mr. Dickenson said, "Sheriff, we can telegraph you what we find out. Would that be okay?"
"Yes Sir, that would be fine."
"I wouldn't hold this woman, she has it hard enough."
"I won't."
"Well, Sheriff, nice meeting you. We'll be on our way."
"Finish your drinks. We're heading for Cripple Creek. That's about a three days ride."
"John Davis, John Davis, take me with you. I can help you since I got you into this mess. I'd like to help you get your things back."
"Ma'am, I don't know. Mr Dickenson? She knows what they look like. She could make this thing go faster."

"Yes Sir, then what?"

"Then you bring her back here if that's what she wants."

"Who's your boss here?"

"Nobody. I just started here a month ago. I lost my family in a fire and have no one. If I'm going to eat, I had to do something."

Mrs. Sikorski said, "Get your things, girl."

"Rose, my name is Rose."

"Rose, get your things."

Mr. Dickenson motioned for her to come with him.

"You got a horse?"

"No Sir. Got a few things in a room upstairs, that's all."

Mrs. Sikorski went with her to get what she had and to make sure nobody stopped her.

"Juan, saddle another horse for the lady."

"Si, Señor."

"Does anybody owe you any money?"

"No Sir."

"Can you ride?"

"Some, Sir."

John Davis said, "I'll help her."

As they headed out the door, Juan called her. "Señorita Rose, here. Here is your horse and your hat. The sun it is hot."

Juan, helped her on the horse.

"Thank you, Sir."

"I'm Juan, Señorita."

"Thank you, Juan."

Chapter 14

They were all riding slow out of the town. Rose looked for John Davis and rode up alongside him. "John Davis, I'm Rose Caldwell."

"Yes, I know."

"I know you don't like me but I didn't have anything to do with those men robbing you."

"Okay, how did they know where I was going?"

"I don't know. Maybe just a good guess."

"You really think so?"

"I don't know."

Rose stuck close to John Davis all day. When they set up camp, she was the hardest worker, pitching in wherever she could. She watched John Davis. When he needed coffee, she got it for him. She checked his stitches, rolled out his bed roll, anything she could to help. At night, she stayed as close as she could to him. She knew she didn't want to go back to that kind a life in a saloon. She was no whore and didn't want to become one. Antonina gave her a pair of pants and boots and Angelina gave her a shirt.

"Thank you all. I don't have any money."

"Don't worry about it. We all needed help one time or another."

Mrs. Sikorski gave her some advice. "Learn how to saddle a horse and take care of it. Can you cook?"

"Yes Ma'am. I'm a good cook."

"Okay then, help Taters with the meals but slow down, don't overdo it. And keep babying John Davis. But again, don't overdo it. Slow down, and you'll fit in just like we all did. Mr. Dickenson and Long John are good people. They have helped a lot of people but they are deadly in a fight. We all learned a lot from them, how to fight when we have to, and we have killed when we had to. If you want to stay with us, watch and listen."

"Thank you, Mrs. Sikorski."

"That's okay Rose."

Long John rode alongside John Davis. "How you feeling?"

"Pretty good, Boss."

"We been going for two days now. Getting close to Cripple Creek. I think you should check Rose out on some fire arms tonight. Tomorrow or the next, we will be going into Cripple Creek and I want her to point out the two and then stay back where she can't get hurt. But she needs to be armed and know a little about pulling a pistol if she has to."

"Okay, Boss. I'll take care of that."

OK Bill and Red Fox were watching the horizon for anything different like they always did. All of a sudden, what looked like a dust storm came up far and to the southeast.

"Better tell Long John. Red Fox, you go."

Long John and Frankie B. were both sitting on their horses looking at the dust with binoculars.

"Long John, you see?"

"Yeah. Thanks, Red Fox."

"What does it look like to you, Boss?"

"Don't know. Got a couple ideas. Can't be buffalo, they been pretty well wiped out. Could be a cattle drive. If it's Crow Indians, it's a lot of them making that much dust."

"How 'bout sheep?"

"Yeah, I was thinking the same thing. Let's keep moving ahead. Pass the word. Everybody on the alert. You all know what that means. Everybody check your weapons."

John Davis told Rose, "Stick by me. You ever use a gun?"

"Yes I have, and I'm a pretty good shot, too."

"Okay, let's catch up with Juan."

"Hey Juan. Can you pull out two pistols and a rifle and a small holster?"

"Si Señor, John. For the Señorita?"

"Yes, she said she can shoot. We might just need another gun."

They stopped long enough to get her holster on and check the weapons. Her saddle already had a scabbard, so Juan loaded the lever action rifle and handed it to her. She handled it like she had some experience, checked the sight, and slipped it into the scabbard. The small holster fit without much adjusting. Two pistols loaded, one in her belt and the other in the holster, and they were back with the others. That dust is still moving towards us. Mr Dickenson sent OK Bill and Frankie B. on ahead to see what it was.

Long John gave everyone a pep talk as they rode, "Be ready for anything. We don't know what's making all that dust but we'll be finding out as soon as Frankie B. and OK Bill get back."

The men were back with bad news: a severe dust storm.

"There is a small herd of cattle, maybe a hundred head, but they're not the problem. A dust storm is coming our way. Don't think we can get out of its way. We can try. Everybody high tail it west. Try to find a gully or a sharp hill to get against. Put something over your head and the horses and when you stop, turn the horses around so they don't have to breathe all that dust. Okay everybody, now move it."

They did go as fast as they could. The two wagons were a little slower with the extra horses in tow. But luckily, there was a high wall ravine that they banked up against and waited out the storm. When it finally stopped, they were pretty well covered deep in it. Everybody worked together to dig out.

"Let's keep going and see if we can find that cattle herd."

They were dug in not more than a half mile from them.

Long John hollered at them, "Hello there, you okay, you need any help? We mean you no harm."

There was only four of them. Mr. Dickenson kept a sharp eye on them.

"Where's your cattle?"

"They scattered."

"If you need any help, let us know." Long John, was communicating with them back and forth. Meanwhile, they kept riding, shaking off the dust. Mr. Dickenson pulled up to Long John, "How bad was it? Did we lose any horses?"

"No Sir, and everybody is okay. You know though, I'd bet those four stole those cattle. I just have a feeling."

"Well Sir, you might be right. You want to go back and talk to them some more?"

"Only if we run into the owners."

"Okay. Looks like a ranch coming up on our right. Let's stop there and see if we can water the horses." They were spotted coming up to the ranch house. Five men stepped out with rifles leveled at them. "State your business."

"Yes Sir, we were hoping we could water our horses over there in that branch of water."

"You can. Who are you?"

"My apologies, Sir. I'm Captain Dolphus Dickenson, Texas Rangers. This is Captain John Lowther, also with the Rangers. We are on our way back to Texas from taking a cattle herd to Helena, Montana. We are retired Rangers, but still hold the rank."

"Okay, Captain Dickenson. This is the Beckwith ranch. I am Eli Beckwith."

"Yes Sir, pleased to meet you. I believe four men just stole about a hundred head of your cattle. We passed them a while back. Does that sound possible?"

"Yes it does. We were wondering what happened to them."

"If you'd like, we'll help you get them back."

"That probably won't be necessary, we've got plenty of men."

"Okay, then we'll just water our horses and be on our way."

"Thanks, have a good day."

"Same to you."

"It's just as well, we don't need to be getting involved in their problem. We got to get to Higgins, Texas, anyway."

"Well, you're right, Sir."

OK Bill and Frankie B. took off and everyone moved out. Juan was driving the wagon and leading the horses. Angelina rode up to Frankie B.

"Will you hold my hand for a while? I just feel, I don't know, sad I guess."

"Sure, come closer." He held her hand and kissed it tenderly. "Well sweetheart, what is bothering you?"

"I don't know. I just get sad sometimes."

They rode along together. The horses got into step with each other moving along at a steady clip.

Red Fox bagged three quail for the evening meal, rode up to Antonina and said, "You take?"

She smiled and said, "Sure, hand them here!"

They were tied together. She hung them over her saddle horn till she would have a chance to clean them. Wouldn't be too long. The days were shorter now.

OK Bill and Prairie Flower rode alongside each other for a long while without saying anything. OK Bill was constantly scanning the horizon as he rode and Prairie Flower knew it. She would let him concentrate. He had a good handle on what was coming and going. All you could hear was the steady hoof beats of the horses and an occasional whinny. Prairie Flower broke the silence when she had to stop to pee. Then they would both stop. OK Bill made it a point not to stare at her but he did continually move his eyes around the area. When she was through, she poured out a little water on her hands, rubbed them together, and shook them dry .

Then they mounted up and caught up to the others. Mr. Dickenson rode out ahead of the party and found a suitable place for the night. Taters pulled up the wagon and started to set up. Juan also pulled up the other wagon and the horses right with him. Mrs. Sikorski and Antonina tied their horses to the wagon so they could get started. Constance had in mind to make a couple of apple pies for everybody. Juan took care of their horses. Tonight he felt that he should hobble them, meaning two front legs tied close together so they can't wander off or be chased off. Before OK Bill and Prairie Flower got close to the camp sight, OK Bill spotted two movements in the rolling grass. His instinct told him it was trouble. He thought Prairie Flower had seen it to. She said in a very low voice, "I see."

Neither changed their stride. Call Frankie B., low. Frankie B. and Angelina were not too far off. Prairie Flower knew what to do. She held her right hand down and shook it. The bracelet on her wrist made just enough noise to get Frankie B. to look over. He didn't see at first.

Angelina said, "Look, Frankie B."

OK Bill held down two fingers and pointed in and hoped he would understand.

OK Bill said, "When I say go, you turn your horse and get Angelina over to Long John."

Frankie B. slowly moved closer. When OK Bill thought the time was right, he said go.

She turned her horse and yelled to Frankie B., "Two in grass, maybe more."

OK Bill and Frankie B. charged and jumped off their horses with rifles in hand, crouching back to back. Just then, the ground opened up. There were more than two. Back to back they put up a tough fight. They were killing them as they came out of the ground: five or six, some Indians, some Mexican— Comancheros for sure. They killed all but one and he wasn't gonna live long. He died right after saying Cuerno Verde would be coming after them. They wanted their money, horses, and their women they paid for. Cuerno Verde was known in the southwest meaning dangerous man. Both OK Bill and Frankie B. were hit in the arms. Bullets went right through. Mr. Dickenson and the others came to help. Long John made sure all were dead.

"Pull these dead out of the holes, pick up all weapons, look for papers or anything that might say who they are, then bury them."

Frankie B. and OK Bill's arms were bleeding pretty badly. Long John just got over his shot up leg and now we got two more wounded.

OK Bill shook his head, "You bandage up, we ride." He looked at Frankie B. and got a smile and, "You damn right. And here we are in 1888, and we still have to fight and kill to get from one end of this country to the other, from the north to the south. What's wrong with people?"

"You're right, Frankie B. It's a kill or be killed world out here. Not just here; it's still pretty much that way all over. Anyway, if you can, head for the camp. We'll get you both a good cup of coffee. Everybody stay alert. They'll be coming after us. Could be at any time day or night. They will be even more determined to kill us now and get the women. We gotta make sure that doesn't happen. I need a couple of men to do reconnaissance for us. If we can find out where they are and how many there are, I want to hit them before they hit us. Does that make sense"

"It sure does, Long John."

"How 'bout you Red Fox. You're a pretty good tracker?"

"I go, Long John."

"Okay, that's one. I need another."

Carlyle said," Boss, I can do it. I'm pretty good at tracking."

"Okay. Start out at where these dead ones hid in the grass and back track them and get back here as soon as you can. If you have to kill any, do it with a knife or if you have to shoot, then kill as many as you can. Got it?"

"Got it, Boss."

"Can you do anything now that it's getting dark?"

"We can. Give me a cup of coffee and I'm ready to go. How 'bout you, Red Fox?"

Red Fox said, "Ready."

Off they went leading their horses and looking for any signs. There was still enough light to see tracks moving around the grassy area where they hid, and leading away from the sight over a little incline. Looks like they had waited a while, moving around and eating and drinking. It was fairly easy to see which direction they came from: boot and moccasin tracks leading off to the west. No evidence of horses, so their gang can't be far off.

"How come they didn't come when they heard gun shots?"

"I know, that's what I was thinking. Maybe they're farther away than we thought."

It didn't take long to find out. Moving slowly in the dark, they heard something unusual— horses. But not walking or running, just moving in one place. Slowly, they crept up on them. Five horses tied up to a rope between two trees. It had to be the dead bandits' horses. Did they act on their own when they attacked us or what the hell was going on?

"I think we should go on a little farther. Let's follow the horse tracks a ways."

"Okay, we go."

The back tracks went on towards the town of Saddle Mountain, which was still a ways off.

"Hold it, Red Fox, let's get these horses back to the camp and see what Long John wants to do."

They came riding in with five horses in tow, to everybody's surprise.

"This is all we found, Boss. Tracks lead off to that town of Saddle Mountain. If there are any more, that's probably where they're at."

Long John seemed to think if we didn't hit the rest of the bandits, they'd be coming after us. Mr. Dickenson agreed.

"Okay then, how we gonna handle it. Let's all ride toward that town and see what turns up. We should be good till early morning, then we go west. Juan, you got more horses. What does that make, about fifteen?"

"Señor, twelve. These five more make twelve."

"Get those saddles in the wagon and all their gear. Anything important, let us know. Money to Mr Dickenson."

"Si, Señor."

"I'd like us to all stay together. We're like a small army and we fight well together. Do you agree?"

"Yes Sir, I do. But what about OK Bill and Frankie B.? They can't use their arms very much."

"I know, but they are better off with us anyway."

"Yes Sir."

"As long as they can ride."

"Don't worry, we can ride." Frankie B. and OK Bill are still recuperating from arm injuries, each had several bullets in each arm, in that shootout with the ones that they killed.

Prairie Flower and Angelina are helping out all they can. Anything the two can't do, the women are right there doing it for them and tending to their wounds. Their fingers weren't hit, so they still got good finger movement; no broken bones, just flesh wounds.

OK Bill said, "We both Apache. We heal good. We fight now if have to. Frankie B. like blood Apache."

Frankie B. was pleased with OK Bill. He grabbed him with his hand and hugged him, no matter the pain.

After the meal, they all turned in early except the ones on watch, four men tonight. Everyone gathered in close to keep warm by the fires. Before the sun started coming over the eastern]mountains, they were up and getting ready to move out. Mr. Dickenson and Carlyle were sipping their coffee and talking about a plan of action that can overpower the enemy. Long John joined in.

"How 'bout we get to that town as soon as we can and two of us go in and find out how many there are and what their plans are?"

"You think we can do that?"

"And if they're coming this way, we hit them and wipe them out."

"That sounds good, Long John, if we can make it happen."

"Okay, let's get going and work on the details as we go. Anybody know how far that town is from here?"

"I would guess no more than a day's ride from here."

"So, let's move out."

The morning meal was over faster than usual. This time, Prairie Flower and Angelina helped with Frankie B. and OK Bill's saddle after they checked their bandages. Long John laid his second rifle across his saddle and told all the men to do the same and women if they wanted to.

"Anybody want a couple sticks of dynamite, get them now and a cigar to light them with. These bandits want us dead, so let's make sure that doesn't happen. Any questions?

"OK Bill and Frankie B., how's your arms? Can you hold a rifle? Maybe you shouldn't try. Just see how a pistol feels. If not, just stay outta the fight. I don't want you two getting hurt any more or killed because you're not able to handle a gun."

"Okay, Boss."

Mr. Dickenson brought up the rear. "Red Fox, how 'bout you scout out ahead but don't take any chances with those bandits. Tommy, you and Tim Shiloh can stay up front and relay anything from Red Fox."

"Gotcha, Boss."

A lot of riding and so far nothing on the bandits. Late in the afternoon, close to the town, and still nothing. Long John pulled up to Mr. Dickenson.

"You know what I think, Sir. I think they circled around and are coming up behind us."

"You may be right. Okay, John Johnson, you and John Davis scout the rear but be extra careful. We are going to stay right here till we know something. If you need help, fire two shots."

"Okay, Boss."

"Juan, you okay?"

"Si Señor, I'm fine."

"Carlyle, you keep an eye on everything here. I'm going north a ways to see if they're there."

No sooner than that being said, bullets started to fly.

"Everybody down and hold onto your horses."

Juan had just tied up all the extra horses so they won't be running off.

"See anything?"

All of a sudden, a voice rang out.

"Señor, we let you live. You give up your women and the horses, we let you live. We got you now."

"Where the hell is that coming from?"

"We got you surrounded. Do you give up?"

All of a sudden, more shots from the north and east. And the sound of a horse running. Sounds like running away. Then all quiet. After what seemed like a long time, the silence was broken from the east.

"Hold your fire. We're coming in. It's Johnson and Davis."

They came walking their horses and bringing in another horse with a body across the saddle.

"This one almost busted my head when he threw his rifle at me." John Johnson had blood all over his head and face. "I shot him off his horse. A lucky shot in the dark. We don't know if any others are out there." John Davis wasn't hurt. Rose ran over to him and stood in front of him.

"Thank God you're all right."

"I'm okay, Rose. Get someone to clean up Johnson's head. He got a pretty good whack from that rifle."

Long John came in.

"Hold your fire. It's Long John."

He was in the saddle with another horse in tow, body across the saddle. I snuck up on this one and another one, the other one's horse bolted when I fired a shot and took off running with him stuck in one stirrup. Anybody hurt here from the stray bullets?"

"No, Boss, we're good, except Johnson here. He was hit with a thrown rifle. We're patching him up now."

"Mr. Dickenson, how 'bout we hurry into that town?"

"Okay, let's go. Everybody start moving. Bring these bodies. We'll look for a sheriff in town."

It didn't take long until they're in the town, not making much noise.

"If any of the bandits are in the saloon, they might not know we're here. Stay sharp people. We don't want to get any of us hurt. Carlyle, check the saloon while we hold up here at the sheriff's office."

Carlyle went up to the window of the saloon and looked inside, and to his surprise, there were about a dozen men together: sombreros, westerns hats, and Indian feathers. They were most definitely Comancheros having a good ole time, not knowing their friends were killed. The sheriff wasn't too concerned about the dead. Mr. Dickenson told the Sheriff about being attacked and killing a few of the bandits, including the two outside.

The sheriff just said, "Take them over to the barber. He's also the undertaker."

"Okay, we'll do that. But here's the thing, Cuerno Verde might be in your town. You know who that is, Sheriff?"

"Sure, I know he's the dangerous man."

"Okay then, you should arrest him and his gang. He's wanted for murder and kidnapping women and a whole string of other crimes."

"How am I going to do that with only myself and one deputy?"

"We'll do it for you if you deputize us and we'll hang the whole bunch."

"I don't know about that. I mean, I don't know if that would be legal."

"Well, you want to let them ride out of here and kill more people, kidnap women, young girls, and men to sell into slavery?"

"Come on now. They have been doing that for years and getting away with it."

"No more. This is where it stops. Either in this town or out of town in the open," said Long John, standing alongside Mr. Dickenson, rifle in his hand. "Sheriff, we are Texas Rangers. We spent a good part of our lives hunting down murderers and bandits."

"I know and that's good but you have no jurisdiction here."

"We would if you'd deputize us."

"I know but I'm not gonna do that."

"Let's go, Long John. You want to stop in the saloon for a drink?"

411

"You know what, I do. All of you stay out here and wait for us. Carlyle, you want to come with us? Long John and I are going in for a drink."

"Sure, I'll go for drink."

"Okay, pistols loaded, take a rifle with you, fully loaded. We stay close together."

In they went, right up to the bar, laid their rifles on the bar. And right away they heard,

"Señors, what are you doing in my town with those rifles?"

"Your town," Mr. Dickenson said.

"Yes, my town. You know who I am?"

"No and I don't give a damn."

The bandit started to walk over to Mr. Dickenson with his pistol in his hand and when he cocked it, the three turned. Mr. Dickenson shot Cuerno Verde. The other bandits all reached for their pistols. Carlyle and Long John fired so fast they got most of the bandits. Five were left standing and threw down their guns. Mr Dickenson was hit in the shoulder, Long John was grazed on the arm, Carlyle wasn't hit. The sheriff and his deputy walked in.

Mr. Dickenson said, "Sheriff, take these five and put them in your jail. I'll come by in a little bit."

The Dickenson people came in just like they have before after a shootout. Long John walked through the mess and looked at the dead just to make sure they were dead.

"Get all these guys' guns away from them."

The barber walked around and reckoned he had some work to do, he also being the undertaker.

"Does anybody know if this one is Cuerno Verde?"

Several people including the barkeeper said, "Yeah, that's him."

"Okay, good. Get a doctor in here and dig this bullet out a me. Juan, OK Bill, Frankie B., those horses and their guns belong to us, gather them up."

"Si Señor."

"Frankie B., I think we better buy another wagon; see if you can find one, we'll supply the horses. Long John, Carlyle, soon as the doctor gets this bullet outta me, I'd like to go over to the jail and talk to the five we have locked up. I'm ready to hang them. What you think? Not much law here, wouldn't you say?"

"Ah, you're right about that, Sir."

The doctor went to work digging the bullet out and patching up Mr. Dickenson. "You'll be alright, just a little sore for a few days."

"I understand, Doc. How's your arm, Long John?"

"It's fine, just a scratch."

It was dark outside and not expected but shots started coming from the roof of the hotel and somewhere else. Some of our people are outside. "Anybody hit?"

"No, Sir." Frankie B. yelled to stay put till we get 'em."

A flash of fire from a rifle pin pointed out the one on the roof. Frankie B. fired rapidly with his Henry lever action, poured five shots into the area and got 'em. He came tumbling down through one roof over the second floor, then another roof over the ground floor; no doubt one of the Comancheros. Frankie B.'s arm was getting a workout. OK Bill made it across the street and was looking for the other shooter. Mrs Sikorski threw a lit lantern out into the street and the shooter fired giving himself away. OK Bill saw where he was and emptied his Henry into the area, rolling him out and bouncing him off a tin roof to the ground. OK Bill reloaded and was cautiously going over to him when another one fired from behind a stairway. Lucky his shot missed. Mrs Sikorski got him with one shot. Tim Shiloh and Tommy headed upstairs to search the rooms in the saloon and hotel for more. They didn't find any more.

"We might as well stretch out in the saloon for the night, everybody. We'll keep Mr. Dickenson in here and make him comfortable. He's sleeping now, had a lot of pain and passed out."

"Alright, Long John."

"Taters, can you rustle up some food for our people?"

"I'll get right on it, Boss."

Long John looked all around and asked, "Who's the boss of this saloon? Anybody?"

Some people were still cowering in place around the saloon.

" Come on people, get up and get on with your lives. You're not hurt, get up, and get moving. Somebody tell me who's the boss of this saloon?"

A weak voice came from a corner table. "I am, Sir. I own the place."

"What's your name?"

"Helvety, Joe Helvety. I own this place."

"Well, get up and get your people moving, clean it up, and bring me a damage report. Don't wait too long. We'll be leaving in the morning if my boss can travel. If not, then as soon as he can."

After a meal, everyone helped straighten up the place and looked for a place to lay down for the night.

"I'm going over to the sheriff's office before I turn in. How 'bout you, Frankie B. and OK Bill, going along with me. Mr. Dickenson wanted to talk to the sheriff about the ones he has locked up. Since he can't do it now, I'm going for him and you two go with me as witnesses."

"Sure, Boss."

They walked over and the sheriff met them at the door.

"Mr. Dickenson can't make it tonight. He's sleeping after getting a bullet dug outta his shoulder. He wanted to talk to you about hanging these five tomorrow."

"I don't know about that. How 'bout we let a judge decide. I sent a telegraph to Judge Phillips over in Guffey, not too far from here. He thinks he can be here about noon tomorrow."

"Okay, as long as somebody does something about killers like these. And I don't mean with a fine and a slap on the wrist. Do you know if all of this gang was here or are there other's we need to know about?"

"Long John, I'm not sure about that. They didn't come here very often and when they did, I left them alone as long as they behaved. So I never knew exactly how many there were."

"Can we talk to them?"

"Sure."

Let's talk to them now. "Any of you guys have anything to say?"

"Sure, we've had a good run," one of them said.

"Oh, like what?"

"Like we did what we wanted when we wanted and had enough men to back it up."

"You mean like kidnaping women and young girls and selling them to the highest bidder?"

"Yeah, and doing what we wanted to the ones we wanted."

One of the other ones said to the one doing all the talking, "Shut your damn mouth. Can't you see what they're trying to do, you dumb bastard?"

And they started fighting in the cell.

"I've heard enough, Sheriff. You see why we want to hang them."

"Sure, and I can almost hang them myself. And I might, if that judge don't get here at noon tomorrow." "Can you let one of my people know when he gets in?"

"Yes Sir, I'll surely do that, Long John."

"Thanks, Sheriff. We'll be in the saloon all night. If anything comes up, let me know."

Frankie B. just shook his head as they started to leave. "These sons a bitches need to be at the end of a rope."

"I know, but let's see what the judge says."

"I guess you're right, Sheriff. See you in the morning."

In the saloon, it was pretty quiet except for a few playing cards. Long John assigned a couple watches just in case.

"We don't need to be caught off guard, so stay sharp. Don't let anybody through that door or the backdoor unless you know what their business is. Got it?"

"Yeah, Boss."

Well, we got through the night without any interruptions.

Carlyle was saying to Harve sitting there drinking their coffee, "I hope we can get the hell out of here today or at least tomorrow."

Taters was working with the saloon cook to get a meal going. The crew was starting to come alive. Juan had put all the horses in a corral south of town and was up early checking on them. They were fine, so he headed back to the saloon for some breakfast. As he walked along, he heard, "Psst, psst." When he looked over, there was a gun pointed right at his head and two men, one Mexican and one gringo, motioning him in the alley.

"What do you want, Señor?"

"Now, you are going to walk real slow to the jail." They had to walk past the saloon to get to the jail, and that's when they were spotted by Tommy standing by the door.

"Hey, come look, who are the guys walking with Juan? That don't look right. I think they got a gun on Juan."

Long John came to the door. "Sure enough, they must be trying to get the five outta the jail." He stepped outside the door and said, "Hold it right there."

They stopped and put a gun to Juan's head and said, "I'll kill him if you come any closer."

"Now, you know if you kill Juan, you both die. You need to talk to me."

"There is nothing to talk about."

"Are you sure about that?"

The sheriff was standing in the doorway listening to the whole thing.

"What is it you want?"

"We want you to let our compadres out of the jail, Señor."

"That's not going to happen. Lay down your guns and you will live. Otherwise, you will die right where you stand. You want that?"

Just then, Juan grabbed one of the guns and went down and fired, hitting one. The sheriff shot the other one. Both dead, for nothing.

"Juan, are you okay?"

"Si, I'm not hurt."

The undertaker didn't waste any time. He came with a helper to pick up the bodies.

"Looks like there were two more that we didn't know about."

"Yeah, and how many more?"

"Well, there's a good chance that this is all of them. I hope."

Mr. Dickenson had a good night's sleep and was feeling better. He was up and walking around.

"I need a good cup of coffee."

"How's your shoulder, Sir?"

"Much better, Mrs. Sikorski, sleep is a good medicine."

"Yes Sir, it sure is. I can get you a plate of biscuits and gravy if you like."

"Ma'am, that would be great. I'd appreciate it."

"You sit down at this table and I'll be right back."

"Thank you, Ma'am."

Long John filled in Mr. Dickenson on the judge coming today and the three that we killed last night along with the two a few minutes ago.

"Sir, I talked to the sheriff about hanging the five we got locked up, but he insisted on waiting for the judge. I talked to the five. They don't have any remorse. The one that did all the talking bragged about what they did. That's the kind you don't mind hanging."

Meanwhile, the judge got into town and was at the sheriff's office.

"I'd like to get over there and hear what he has to say."

"Yeah, I would, too. I'm through eating. We can go if you're ready."

"Don't worry about me. I can walk okay."

Frankie B. and OK Bill went along. The judge was not a softie by the way he sounded. He had heard about the gang and was glad to see them come to an end, one way or another. He seemed to have the utmost respect for the Texas Rangers and he had heard of Captain Dolphus Dickenson and his men cleaning up the bandits of the Panhandle all the way to the border.

"Judge Phillips, this is my foreman, Captain John Lowther. He's known as Long John."

"Oh, I've heard of Long John just like you, Captain Dickenson."

"And this is Frankie Butler and OK Bill. They are more than hands, they're like family. My ranch would be nothing without men like them. And I have to say, my people are all the best. Judge Phillips, what would you like to see happen with these men?"

"I'm gonna look at some law books on cases like this one and sleep on it . We all know these men are guilty as anyone can be. I will at least give them a hearing tomorrow."

"That's fair, Judge. We'll be going now, see you in the morning."

"Yes Sir, that will be fine."

"Mr. Dickenson, you know we got a lot of miles to make up before we get to Higgins, Texas. "

"Yes, I know Long John. As soon as we hear from the judge in the morning, I'm ready to go. How's Juan doing?"

"I don't know. I guess he's alright. I think he's been in shootouts before. I'll check on him."

Back in the saloon, Long John asked if anybody had seen Juan.

"Yeah Boss, he's sitting over there with Harve and Mrs. Sikorski."

"Juan?"

"Si, Señor."

"I'm just checking on you. Mr. Dickenson wanted me to check and see how you are doing."

"I'm okay, Señor. Sometimes we must kill. I'm glad I got out of that kind of life or that could be me laying there dead."

"You're right, Juan. By the way, if any of you need anything, you should get it today. We are hoping to leave in the morning. We can't stay around here too long. We have a lot of miles to cover."

"Okay, Boss. Yeah, we can use a few things."

"Juan, do you know if Frankie B. got us another wagon to put some of our gear in?"

"Si."

"Can you pick out a couple horses that you think would be good to pull the wagon or if you like, you can change them off to give them all a turn."

"That I would like, so they don't forget who's boss."

"Okay, Juan. Harve, walk with me over to the jail."

"Sure thing, Boss."

"Keep an eye on Juan. You know he shot and killed one of the bandits and I'm wondering if he's okay with it."

"Ah, Boss, he's okay, he's just like all of us with Mr. Dickenson. We do what has to be done."

The judge hasn't shown up yet at the sheriff's office. Mr. Dickenson was there waiting for the judge, too. Then the judge walked in and said, "Good morning everyone."

"Morning Judge."

"Okay, getting right to it. I will give these men a fair hearing and unless they can clear their names of the charges I have against them, you can rest assured they will hang. Now Sheriff, you will be responsible for the hanging. How would you carry it out?"

"Don't know judge. I guess I can take them outside of town to that lone big oak tree and hang them there."

"Mr. Dickenson, do you have any objections?"

Mr. Dickenson looked at Long John and then looked at Harve and then back at the judge. "No Judge, I have no objections. When is all this going to take place?" "Right now. Let's get this over with."

"Okay, prisoners, listen up. We are going to have a legal hearing with Judge Phillips, so spread out in the cell and sit down. The judge wants to ask you some questions."

"Sheriff, swear them in using their names."

"Each one of you state your name and raise your right hand and swear that you will tell the truth so help you God. That formality over with, the judge asked if they had taken part in kidnaping women and young girls and killing their husbands and or family members in the process. They all admitted that they did. The judge asked if any of them had raped and killed any women or girls over the years. They all admitted that they did. They all said that they had robbed and killed many over the years. Two were repentant and sorry; the other three said they didn't give a damn, just get it over with. The judge pronounced sentence. "I sentence you to hang by the neck until you are dead. God help you. Sheriff, you may carry out the sentence."

"Okay, Your Honor. Let's get 'em out."

The deputy tied their hands behind their backs and took them out and sat them down on a long wagon. The undertaker was already out front anticipating the hanging.

"Sheriff, I'll get five ropes from the store. Be right back."

"Okay, Jim."

"Mr. Dickenson, how about you and your two men witness the hanging?"

"Sure. Harve, you okay with that?"

"Yes Sir, I've seen hangings before."

"Alright, let's head out to that big tree and give the undertaker more work."

Townspeople were lining up in the street. It's hard not to have some pity on anyone being hanged. But if anybody deserved hanging, these five men did. They raped and killed for years with a very bad bunch. When they got to the spot of the hanging, they stood the men up and put the ropes around their necks.

"Any last words?"

Only one asked to be forgiven, the other four cursed everyone. Frankie B. and OK Bill were standing close enough to hear the cursing.

Long John said, "It's a real pleasure to hang these four that don't even know when to quit. They'd go right on killing if we hadn't stopped them."

"Yeah, Boss."

"Last few days, we didn't set out to do it, but we rid the world of some very bad people. The five were hung and turned over to the undertaker. Now, we can move on."

"Yes Sir, Mr. Dickenson, I go along with that."

Chapter 15

Back at camp, everyone was packed and ready to move. John Davis and Rose were thinking about heading for Cripple Creek to get his belongings back and make the ones that beat him pay.

"Go ahead, everybody. We'll catch up. Rose and I are going to Cripple Creek."

Long John thought they would want to do that. "How 'bout a couple of the boys go with you. I'd feel better that way."

"Well, I guess so. Who wants to go with me?" Dance and Tommy said they'd go.

"Okay then, let's go. I'd like to head out now. Can you boys go now or you wanna wait? I figure if they're there, they might not stay too long. And my things might be all over the place if they sold 'em."

"Okay, let's go."

"We'll get our stuff and catch up."

"That's what I thought. Rose, you ready? Shouldn't take long to get to Cripple Creek. It's not too far."

"Okay John, let's go. We should be able to catch up with you folks tomorrow, if we're lucky."

Mr. Dickenson and Long John said they'd also catch up after they talked to the saloon owner.

"I told the owner to let me know about the damages. Can we give him a little money to help out?"

"Yes, I must have heard you saying that when I was passing out or I dreamed it. So let's go see him."
In the saloon, they asked for Joe.
"Check his office over there."
They knocked on the door.
"Come in."
"Joe, I see you got the place all cleaned up."
"Yeah, wasn't bad."
"We thought we might help you with some of the cost."
"Na, no cost, wasn't bad. Thanks anyway. Can I buy you both a drink?"
"Sure, we'll take a drink."
They stepped back out to the bar. Joe walked around to the back of the bar and reached down for one his better whiskeys. The brand was Deerhammer 100 proof, Colorado sipping whiskey. He poured three shots. They all three clicked the classes together and downed them. Mr. Dickenson and Long John both said, "I'll take a bottle. Matter of fact, give me two bottles. I'll take one for Carlyle. How much?"
"On the house," Joe said. "It's worth it for you to rid the territory of some really bad ones and I'm grateful to you."
"Well, we thank you. Be glad to pay."
"No pay. Thanks again."
"Thank you."
A hand shake and they were off catching up to the bunch. They both rode up on opposite sides of Carlyle and Mr. Dickenson pulled out a bottle and handed it to Carlyle.
"This is a free gift from the owner of the saloon. He gave us three bottles."
"Really?"

"Yes indeed."

"I bet Taters will be jealous."

"No doubt. Where we gonna be by nightfall?"

"We ought to make it to Witcher Mountain today."

Carlyle, you think we can go over this mountain or do we have to go around?"

"I would almost think we'd have to go around it looking at the size of it."

"How 'bout OK Bill and I check it out. There might be a narrow slip somewhere."

"Okay, but you better hurry. Tomorrow, we should be outta the more mountainous area and make better time. I'd say we should make it to, ah, hold on a second, looking at the map, Cañon City." Everybody was glad to be away from Saddle Mountain. Too much violence at one time. At least this time, they knew that the world would be a better place without Cuerno Verde, (the dangerous man), and his gang.

OK Bill and Carlyle were back pretty quickly. "Follow us, there's a trail that must be unknown to most. Might be a little rough but shouldn't be a problem for the horses. Juan, keep the loose horses together, don't let them stray."

"Si, Señor Boss."

Long John caught up with Carlyle and OK Bill.

"OK Bill, you think there's any hostile Crow in these mountains."

"I no see anything looks like Crow."

It turned out to be a wise decision, except for the colder air. It was pleasant and quiet. It must have cut off miles and nobody minded that. Wasn't long until they could see the little town of Witcher Mountain coming up.

"Uh, we'll ride in and pick up a few supplies. And we'll make camp out of town."

"Okay, Boss."

"Juan, how the new horses doing?"

"They're with the rest, Señor. The thing is, when I take the saddle and the bridle off them, they go right over to the others and don't stray."

"That's good, Juan."

"Si, Señor."

The little town of Witcher mountain was quiet. Townsfolk came out to see our bunch as we rode in and then went about their business. We picked up what we needed and all of us went in the Horse Head Saloon. We could smell the cooking as we went through the doors. Since they didn't have but one cook, they were glad to have Taters volunteer to help and Antonina helped with the dishes. The owner, Buck Rose, was full of smiles with the extra money coming in. Taters asked if they carried that Deerhammer Whiskey.

"We sure do."

"Okay, when we get through eating, I'll talk about it some more."

They cooked up a few chickens and the fixings to go with them. When they got through and things got cleaned up and put away, the owner, Buck Rose, came over to the tables with the bill and Mr. Dickenson paid it readily.

"I'd like to pay your cook and his helpers," Mr. Rose said.

"Okay. You talk to them about that."

Taters said all he wanted was a couple bottles of that Deerhammer Whiskey.

"Okay Sir, you got 'em. Young lady, what do I owe you?"

"I want a bath and my hair shampooed."

"You got it," he said.

He called his woman assistant over and gave her instructions. She took Antonina by the hand to the back room. Mrs./ Sikorski went, too. "I got to see this. I'm gonna get one, too."

"Well, this is a day not like the last few we've had."

"You're right,. Sir," Frankie B. added.

"Okay everybody, if we're ready, let's head out and make camp."

Out the door they went to their horses. The loose horses were standing close as they could get to Juan's horse and were even glad to see him and let him know with their whinnying, neighing, and nickering when he came out the door. Juan couldn't help but laugh at the sight.

"Juan, you sure must be babying them."

"Si, they are like my babies, these horses."

They set up camp at the edge of town. First thing was to get that fire going and going good to get the cold air off. Mr. Dickenson was still favoring his left shoulder, rubbing it and stretching out his arm.

"Ah, it's coming around. Well, we better get some coffee going."

"I'll have it going in a few minutes, Captain."

"Thanks Taters."

Mrs. Sikorski and Antonina both had their baths and hair shampooed. Mrs. Sikorski had to pay for hers, but she didn't mind a bit.

"Ah, you wouldn't believe how good it feels. Now we can feel like women for a few days."

Angelina and Prairie Flower were listening and hanging on every word. They wanted a bath really bad.

Angelina asked, "Could we get a bath or is it too late?"

"Now that I don't know."

Frankie B. said, "How 'bout OK Bill and I go with you and we'll see if you can."

"Now, you know they might give you trouble cause you're Indian."

"Mother, you want to go?"

"Okay, we go, I so dirty I try anything."

They got their baths and hair washed. The Chinese were working the baths and clothes' washing and they didn't care about them being Indian. So they helped out at the baths and washed their clothes and dried them as much as they could. Frankie B. and OK Bill got their baths, too, while the women combed out their hair. The four of them came back to camp making everybody envious.

Everyone turned in, except the watch. Morning came quickly. They ate and got moving. The day was just another day. By late afternoon, they were coming up on Cañon City. They better have several places doing baths cause 'bout half of us are going in for one. There were several places doing baths. That worked out well.

Meanwhile, back in Cripple Creek, John Davis, Rose, Tommy, and Dance looked at all the horses tied up as they rode in and sure enough, there was

John Davis' horse with his saddle and rifle tied up in front of a saloon. They pulled up next to it and John checked the saddle bags. His spare pistol and a few other things were still in it.

Tommy said, "How you want to handle this?"

"I go in with Rose just behind me. If you spot one or both, you tell me. Can you do that Rose?"

"Yes."

"You two cover me but watch your backs."

In the swinging doors they went. No one seemed to pay any attention right away.

Rose said, "There's one of them."

"I know, that's my hat and my vest. You see the other one?"

"Yes, he's at the other table."

They were both playing cards. Tommy and Dance covered the other one while John walked over to the table and stood for a second in front of the table. As the man looked up, he knew he had been caught red handed.

John said, "Stand up, you son of a bitch, and take off my hat, set it on the table, take off my gun holster, slow like, and set it on the table, too. Now, take off my vest, put it on the table. Empty your pockets on the table. Where's my boots?"

"I don't have them."

John walked around the table and said again, "Where are my boots?"

"I don't have them."

John picked up the holster off the table and checked the pistol, spun the cylinder, and smacked the man across the face with it as the cylinder was still spinning.

He quickly said, "He's got your boots," and pointed across the room. Tommy and Dance looked at the man and he stood up. He started to take off his boots.

Tommy said, "Come around the table and take them off and put them on the table. Empty your pockets on the table. Gun belt on the table.

"John, are these your boots?"

"Yeah, they're mine."

"How 'bout this other stuff?"

"Fifty bucks and that knife is mine.

"Where's all my clothes, my big coat, and my bed roll?"

Dance picked up the boots and came close to the man.

"He said they sold them."

The sheriff came in and looked around the place. "What seems to be the problem?"

"Well, Sheriff, these two beat me, stole my horse and everything I had, and left me for dead."

"Where was it?"

"Ah, Denver."

"That's a long way from here."

"Not really. I just want my things back. Looks like they sold all my clothes. Here's what it is, Sheriff: my horse, saddle, rifle, three pistols, boots, hat, and clothes. Oh, and a bed roll, a knife, and box of ammo."

"Alright, take what's yours. You gonna press charges, boy?"

"I would, but I don't want to stick around, Sheriff. I'll just settle for my stuff."

"How much money you figure they owe you?"
"Well, I had fifty bucks that they got plus my clothes."
"Sounds like maybe another fifty might do it."
"I'll settle for that, Sheriff."
John, picked up his hat, his vest, holster, and fifty off the table and then, with one punch, knocked the guy over the table. He walked over to the other table where his boots and knife were with some other stuff. He picked up another fifty bucks, his knife, and boots and knocked this guy over the chairs.
"Thanks, Sheriff. Be seeing you, Sheriff."
Rose was already out the door. Dance and Tommy followed. They left the town with John's horse in tow and as much of his things as they could find.
"Thanks for the backing, boys."
"No problem, John, we're glad to help."
"Rose, you okay?"
"I guess so. Though I'm kind of worried that those two will kill me."
"What makes you think they'll look for you?"
"I don't know. Just something inside me."
"Rose, do you think they saw you?"
"I don't know. I never looked like this when I was in Denver, so if they did see me standing by the door, they might not have known it was me."
"Let's ride and put on a few miles before dark. Let's see if we can catch up to the Dickenson people before dark."
"Okay John, let's try."
"We only got 'bout twenty miles to Cañon City. They can't be too far ahead of us. If we keep going, we'll catch 'em. You know another thing?"
"What's that Dance?"

"Those two we humiliated back in town could be dogging us if they get enough courage."

"You think the sheriff let them go right away without questioning them?"

"Now that, I don't know. Could be. They might have nothing to lose if they owe a lot a money to someone in that town that's getting tired of waiting for their money. Let's watch our rear."

It got dark before they knew it, and they felt like they were just stumbling around in the dark.

"Let's make camp, John. What you think?"

"Yeah. We can get an early start in the morning."

"Rose, you okay?"

"Sure John, whatever you think. Right now, getting a good hot fire going and some coffee would suit me and how 'bout a can of those beans with pork and bread. Don't sound too bad with coffee."

All the while, not letting their guard down, the men will take turns at watch.

"Rose, come sit with me by the fire under this blanket."

"Okay, John, soon as I get this can open and get us something to eat it with."

Dance said, "Hey Tommy, you want to sit with me under this blanket?"

"Ha, ha. You know what we need? We need us a couple of women."

"You're right. Tommy, I think I'm gonna work on that."

Rose laughed. "There's plenty of women just waitin' for handsome cowboys like you two to come along."

"That right, Rose?"

"Yes, most of the women working in the saloons would rather not but some don't have a choice. Most men think they're all whores. But they're not all. And a lot of those would give it up if a man would have them."

Noise in the brush got their attention.

"Anybody there, come out with your hands up." Tommy pulled out his pistol, and leveled it on the brush. An old Red Bone hound and an Indian girl came out.

"No shoot. Old chief sick," she kept saying. A girl was no more than sixteen. She turned and with her hands open pointed to the ground where the old Indian lay. "Can you help Chief?"

Rose jumped up and said, "Let's get him by the fire. You both must be cold."

"Cold, yes cold."

"What's wrong with the chief?"

"No, no, sick. Water sick."

"Sounds like he drank some bad water."

"Is he your grandfather?"

"Hum," she pointed to him and then herself.

"I'd say he's her grandfather. Let's get some coffee in him.

"Where's your people?"

"No people. Him, me. No people."

"What tribe are you?"

"We Apsáalooke. White's call us Crow."

"Okay, you're Crow. We will help as much as we can. Where's your horses?"

"Mex take both horses."

"Okay, you need some food."

All the while, the hound was sitting by the old chief and wagging its tail.

"Tommy, we got more of those bean cans?"

"Sure, we got two more."

"Let's open them up and warm them a little. We can get more tomorrow in Cañon City."

"Okay John."

"Dance, can you keep up a close watch? Somebody might have been following them."

"No follow. Mex hit chief, hit me."

"How come they didn't take you?"

"Say me no good Mierda (fuck). Too small."

"Oh boy, that's a slap in the face. Tomorrow we'll take you and the Chief in to Cañon City and see a Doctor."

"That's where they go— The Mex, the Mex's men."

"Okay, maybe we'll get your horses back. Our people should be in Cañon City. Let's all get some sleep and go to Cañon City and get those horses. What is your name? What are you called?

"Akhamenn, like a deer."

"Okay Like a Deer, you and Chief stay by fire tonight. We will take you to Cañon City in the morning."

The chief must have had nightmares. He would cry out like someone was after him, all through the night. He must still be sick. He can't sit or stand. "We will have to make a drag sled to pull and get him to a doctor."

Rose was up first and spotted a rabbit when she was doing a nature call. The thing just sat there. A rock and a fast cleaning and the thing was roasting on a stick. Coffee brewing filled the air. Like a Deer woke and looked all around like she wasn't sure where she was. John woke and reached around for Rose. She watched him and smiled to herself.

435

Tommy was already up being the last on watch. Dance jumped up and grabbed his rifle.

"Okay Dance, we're ok. Go take a walk and then we'll divide up this rabbit with our coffee."

"Sounds good. I feel like I could eat the whole thing myself."

"Yeah, I know."

"Who got the rabbit?"

"Rose."

As soon as they got through eating, Dance and John built a sled and roped it to one of the horses. They got the old chief on it and away they went with the young Indian girl riding the sled horse. Wasn't long till they could see a town coming up. They made their way in town slowly, and checked every horse. The two Indian horses they were looking for were tied up alongside horses with Mexican saddles. Tommy stopped and untied them and took them along with them. When they found a doctor's office, they were all tied up in front.

Someone was sweeping the porch and said, "Looking for a doctor, are ye?"

"Yes Sir. Doctor in?"

"Yep, he is."

"We got a sick Indian here we'd like him to take look at."

"Okay, I'll help you bring him in."

Tommy and Dance sat down on the porch and kept an eye on the saloon to see if anybody would come out and look for the horses. John, Rose, and Like a Deer went in with the old chief.

"What seems to be the matter?"

"We don't know. We found them last night. The girl here kept saying water, like he drank some bad water. That's all we know. By the way, I'm John Davis, this is Rose Caldwell, the girl is Like a Deer, and the Chief we don't know his name."

"I'm Doctor Louis Vertie. Pleased to meet you."

"Our two friends outside took the Indian horses away from the Mexicans in the saloon. But the Mexicans don't know it yet. The horses belong to the two here. We mean to have it out with them if that's what it takes. The girl kinda said they beat the old chief and slapped her around, took their horses, and left them for dead in the cold till we came along. So we aim to get their horses back."

"How come they didn't take her?"

"You will have to ask her yourself, Doc."

"Like a Deer, did they hurt you?"

"They hit me . They said I dirty Indian. No Mierda (fuck). They kick me and they take our horses and go. I hear one say Cañon City."

"Doc, you do what you can for both of them. We will settle with the bandits and be back."

"Okay, you be careful. Those bandits are like snakes."

The old hound dog stayed by the Chief.

Tommy and Dance got what they were waiting for. Two Mexicans came out of the swinging doors and looked around. It took them a while to notice the two Indian horses were gone. Then one of them spotted them up the street by the doctor's office, and they started to walk to where the horses were. Seeing Dance and Tommy sitting on the porch, one of them yelled, "Hey Gringo, what are you doing with our horses, you Hijos de puta (son of bitches)?"

Tommy answered back. "They're not your horses. You took them from an Indian Chief and his

437

granddaughter and I just took them back, you sons a bitches. You know horse stealing is a hanging offense?"

"Gringo, can you back up those words?"

"I think I can." With that, Tommy and Dance got up from their chairs and stepped out into the street. Dance said, "I think you better turn around and get on those two old horses tied up by the saloon over there and ride out of here before you bite off more than you can chew."

"You cachorros jõvenes (young pups), I think we will have to kill you."

The town's sheriff came out of his office and was listening. He turned and struck a match on the door jamb and lit up a cigar. John and Rose came out about the same time and sat on the porch. Just then, the gun fire began and the two bandits just barely cleared their holsters when two well-placed bullets from Tommy and Dance ended their lives. The guns fell from their hand as they fell to the dirt street. Two big sombreros rolled a few feet away. The sheriff walked out into the street, looked down at the two, stepped over them and asked Tommy and Dance what that was all about."

"Sheriff, they beat an old Indian Chief and his granddaughter last night, took their horses, and left them for dead. We came along and found them shivering in the cold a few miles from here. We brought them to the doctor. That's where they're at now. The two on the porch, John Davis and Rose Caldwell are with us. I'm Tommy Holbrooks and this is Dance Mead."

"Well, it was a fair fight as far as I could see, but don't go anywhere while I talk to the two in the Doc's office."

"Okay, Sheriff, we'll be here. You got anybody to bury these two?"

"Yeah, don't worry about it. I'll take care of them. If you want, you can have their guns but leave their horses here. I'll sell them to pay the undertaker for burying them in a box."

"Okay, Sheriff, we'll collect their guns and knives. We also want the two Indian horses that they took."

"Okay, you got 'em."

The Dickenson bunch heard the shots and picked up their pace. Frankie B. got out in front and was coming into town just as the undertaker was picking up the bodies from the street. He rode slowly down the street past the undertaker up to were Tommy and Dance were walking up on the porch of the doctor's office. That's when he spotted John Davis and Rose sitting there.

"What the...? Was there a shootout?"

"Yeah, there was. Tommy and Dance were the winners. Those two laying in the street were the losers. It's a long story, Frankie B. We got two Indians in the Doc's office here that the two Mexicans laying out there beat, stole their horses, and left them for dead. We come across them last night. One's an old chief, the other is his granddaughter."

The town sheriff went in to talk to them about it.

"I see the rest of the Dickenson people coming in town. I, for one, am glad to see all you guys."

OK Bill and Red Fox pulled up to where Frankie B. was.

"You need us help?"

"As a matter of fact, you can. Both of you go in and see if you can help the old chief and the girl. Maybe translate for them. The sheriff went in to talk to them."

"Okay, we go. Frankie B., you come with."

"Good idea."

Good thing they did. The sheriff was not getting anywhere with the chief and the Doctor was getting annoyed with his questioning. The Indian girl was trying to understand as well as she could but just didn't understand. OK Bill and Red Fox brought a calming effect to the two Indians. But not to the sheriff. He looked up and said, "What the hell do you two want?"

They probably did scare the sheriff: two Indians and a white man walking in fully armed to the teeth. Covered with dust.

"Hold on, Sheriff, we're here to help." Frankie B. was doing the talking. "My two friends here will help translate for you. Red Fox, you know Crow?"

"Maybe some."

"OK Bill, you?"

"Know some."

"Okay, Sheriff, tell them what you want to know. And they will get you an answer. By the way, I'm Frankie Butler and this is OK Bill and Red Fox."

"I'm Sheriff Beaufort Powers. The doc here is Louis Vertie."

Frankie B. touched his hat with his fingers. OK Bill and Red Fox nodded and OK Bill went over to the old chief and touched his arm and the chief opened his eyes and smiled. The girl wasn't quite sure, not being used to Indians from other tribes. Red Fox took out a charm from a leather bag around his waist and offered it to the girl. It was a small rock with a bird carved on it. She took it and held it in her hand moving her fingers over it. It seemed to put her at ease. She began to talk and went on and on using a lot of hand signs that only another Indian would have a chance of understanding.

The sheriff said he had heard enough. "Okay, I got the picture. Her story is the same as John Davis and the other two. There won't be any charges."

"Glad we could help out, Sheriff."

"I'm going outside. You three coming?"

"We'll be out in a little bit."

The doc could only come up with what everybody already knew: the old chief has some kinda stomach problem. "You want to take him outside. I gave him a glass of quinine water. I'm hoping it will clear up whatever is making him sick. Now, you might have to get him in a privy. If this works, he'll be needing one soon. See how he's moving around already. I'd say he needs one now. There's an outhouse out this back door."

"Let's get him out there before he makes a mess in here."

OK Bill and Red Fox carried him out and sat him on one of the holes. They left the door open so the granddaughter could keep an eye on him. Meanwhile, John Davis, Dance, and Tommy were sitting down at the Handlebar Saloon with Mr. Dickenson and Long John to have a talk about what had lead up to the shootout. The explanation was satisfactory, so they didn't dwell on the details more than was needed. John Davis motioned to the barkeeper, "Bring us something that will knock your socks off for me and my friends here."

"Yes Sir, coming right up."

Frankie B. asked Angelina and Prairie Flower to look in on the young Crow girl and the Chief. behind the doctor's office, then headed for the saloon. Right up to the bar. "Give me a good stiff shot of your best. Or wait a second, you got any of that Deerhammer Whiskey?"

"Yes Sir, I do."

"Okay then, I'll take a couple shots of that." Downing two shots, he spotted Long John and the others and headed for the table. The doors swung open and the sheriff walked in, looked around, and headed for the same table.

"Who is the boss of this bunch?"

"I guess that would be me, Sheriff. I'm Dolphus Dickenson. These men are in my employment along with all the rest of the folks you might have seen us with. We have a spread in Texas. We're heading back from a cattle drive."

"So then, you won't be staying long."

"That's right, Sheriff. We should be out of here tomorrow as soon as we get a few things from the store."

"That's what I wanted to know."

"Uh, Sheriff, what about the old chief and the girl?"

"What about them? They're on their own."

"Really. You know they can't fend for themselves."

"This town isn't taking in old Indians."

"Sheriff, we'll see to them. We don't mind helping them out. I guess we'll talk to you later, Sheriff."

"Okay, Mr. Dickenson. Maybe I'll see you before you leave."

"Frankie B., see if OK Bill and Red Fox can find out where the chief and the girl where heading or where they want to go."

"Okay Sir."

The old chief started to feel better after the quinine water worked its way through him, although he still was weak and probably couldn't ride a horse yet. Frankie B. asked OK Bill if he knew where they were going or where they wanted to go.

"Young one say don't know. Chief leave tribe to die. She won't leave him."

"Then we will take them with us till we find a place for them."

"Maybe not good to do Frankie B. Old Chief ready to die."

"Can you tell Mr Dickenson what you just told me?"

"Come, I tell him."

They walked in the saloon and sat down. OK Bill leaned his rifle against the table. Frankie B. laid his on his lap.

OK Bill said, "Old Chief ready to die. Young one, no leave him till he die."

"Really?"

"Hum, he will die soon, Mr.. Dickenson."

"Then we will take them with us till he does. Is that alright to do OK Bill?"

"That be good. Can't leave them here."

"Okay. Let's get some sleep and leave in the morning."

When daylight came, they were all up eating, cleaning up, getting their supplies, and tightening up their saddle cinches for the day's ride.

Prairie Flower came over to OK Bill and had some bad news. "The old Chief had died. We tell Boss." Long John said, "Let's take him out of this town and bury him in the hills we see in the distance, if it's alright with Like a Deer." She said he lived his whole life close to Mother Earth and would want to sleep in her arms. The mountain would be fine." "Okay everybody, let's ride. We got a burying to do in those mountains."

The chief was wrapped in a blanket and laid in the wagon. Like a Deer rode her own horse close behind. The sheriff and the townspeople came out to see them off. John Davis commented on how Like a Deer rode saying she and her horse were like one. "I'm sure glad we rescued her horse. It prances like an Arabian like it's floating with its finely chiseled head. And Like a Deer sits it like a princess."

When we got to the foot hills, we all stopped. The foot hills crossed the Arkansas River and went into the Phantom Canyon. Like a Deer led the way.

Red Fox passed the word, "There is a burial grounds the Crow have used for many seasons. That is what Like a Deer said."

A ride up and around rocks and shrubs and bushes and there it was—the burial grounds.

Long John asked, "How do we do it?"

Carlyle knew a little about their custom. Among the Crow, the dead was wrapped in a robe and placed on the bier with the feet facing to the east. The bones are collected later and placed in a rock gap.

"We need to build a bier with poles. Let's get to it."

"Hold on, we got company."

444

A band of Indians came, Crow we all supposed. Six with shields, war clubs, headdress, and painted faces on horseback. Mr. Dickenson and Long John got back on their horses and rode the short distance to talk. Like a Deer went, too, but she didn't act as if she was glad to see them. At least she was able to communicate with them. Once they understood what we were doing there, they eased up. They knew the dead Chief and the young woman. They said they would give the chief a proper burial. For us to leave.

"What about the granddaughter of the Chief?"

The Crow doing the talking said, "She can stay with them and they would take her back to their camp or she can go with us. She has no family to look after her."

Frankie B. said, "Looks like it's up to her. Ask her OK Bill what she wants to do: go back to the Crow camp or stay with us?"

"She say already she no like living with the tribe since her mother died. They expect her to be a slave to whoever takes her in."

"Ask her if she wants to go with us. She will be free to choose what she wants to do."

"She say she want to go with Prairie Flower and Angelina if they will have her. They say they will be as family to her."

"Tell her we will wait for her down the mountain after she says goodbye to her grandfather."

OK Bill told the young woman what was said. About an hour passed and Like a Deer came riding down. She went straight to Prairie Flower and swung her horse around and said something in her native tongue. Red Fox thought it was a Crow prayer to bless her new family and her journey.

"We should go now," Angelina said and gave her horse, Alice, a little kick.

Everyone started to move. Long John and Mr. Dickenson looked at each other and spurred their horses with that look of (what do I know) expression on both of their faces. Tater's chuck wagon and the other two wagons with Juan driving one and Antonina driving the other moved out. The horses followed behind Juan like they were his babies. Both Mr. Dickenson and Long John stayed back for a long time. Frankie B. and OK Bill, followed close behind but did not lead. The new member of the crew fit right in and stayed up front with Prairie Flower and Angelina. Every once in a while, one of the men would ride up to Long John and pass the time a day. Mrs. Sikorski eased up to the front and got alongside Prairie Flower. They rode together for a long time talking. When the sun went down, the women picked out a campsite and signaled to Taters to set up by a little stream. Everyone had a full day riding and was ready for a meal and sleep. Antonina ate with Angelina and the other women and one of them said, "Like a Deer needs to get checked out for two pistols and a rifle." Prairie Flower asked her if she ever handled a rifle or a pistol.

"Rifle, yes. Pistol, no," she said.

"Okay, we need you to practice and carry a rifle on your horse that you can grab quick and two pistols or more."

"Okay, I do what you say. I look at you and see only one gun on your side. Do you have two pistols, Angelina?"

"Three, and they are fully loaded at all times. You never know when you will come up on something and we don't want our weapons to be seen. We want to be seen as weak so we will have the advantage. It has worked for us many times. Like a Deer, do you understand?"

"Yes I do."

Prairie Flower did the best she could to interpret. "Would you like a better, more comfortable saddle? We have plenty?"

"I have never rode on one."

"Okay, let's have Juan find you a saddle. You look with him. He'll fix you up with a saddle and the guns you need. If you would like some clothes, we have them, too. Like a Deer, you will be just fine."

She got a change of clothes, a saddle, the guns she needed, and a lot of encouragement from all the hands. Like a Deer started to pick up English. It seemed to come easy for her. As the days went by, Like a Deer helped with just about everything. Taters didn't mind a bit if she wanted to help with the meals. Juan got help with the horses. She made a good scout, too, helping OK Bill and Red Fox and even practicing shooting rabbits and quail getting the meat for the evening meal. Even cleaning the rabbits and quail with Antonina. Going through the little towns helping with the supplies. Always finding time to comb her horse and talk to it in the evening. She seems to have even lost some of her shyness. Day after day, riding with OK Bill and Red Fox seemed to be what she liked a lot . No one gave her orders, and she adjusted well to her new way of life. She was little with long black hair. Mr. Dickenson liked to talk to her and help her along with learning English.

"A few more days and we'll be in Higgins, Texas, and we'll see how Mrs. Edwards and José are getting along. Been quite a while since we've seen them. We'll be leaving Colorado, riding a while in Oklahoma, then we'll be in Texas. Another day's ride and we'll be in Higgins, Texas. First, we have to find a flat spot to rest up for the night."

Taters picked a nice place near a creek. The crew pulled in around him. Mrs. Sikorski had it in her mind to make a few pies. After cleaning up a bit, she got started with the last couple cans of cherries. Antonina and Like A Deer cleaned the quail and rabbits and got them ready for the fire. Harve helped set up. John Johnson and John Davis got the fires going. Everybody had something to do. Carlyle worked on two big pots of coffee. The meal today will be biscuits and gravy with quail and rabbit, beans, and pies that are out of this world. As the sun set, the smell of coffee and biscuits was enough to make anyone hungry. Tommy and Dance took the first watch. Long John walked all around the camp with his rifle in his hand. Once he was satisfied with everything, he laid it down next to his saddle and bed roll and sat down and waited for the coffee to boil. Juan was having a conversation with the horses. They seemed to love every word as he walked among them patting them on the head or backs. Everyone got in line for the evening meal and when it was all over and things cleaned up, it was a time to rest up. Mr. Dickenson, with his head laying across his saddle, was smoking a pipe and reading poems. Reading glasses were resting on his nose close by the fire. Long John was checking the watches before he turned in. Like a Deer was curling up on her blanket with her dog, Henna (meaning red), laying close to her feet. The dog was missing the Chief. Frankie B. was sitting on a blanket with Angelina, sipping on a cup a coffee. OK Bill and Red Fox went out into the dark. They say to do that, you get one with the earth and if anyone is out there following us, they will know it, they will feel their presence. After a while, they come back in camp from the other side and let Long John know that it was all quiet. That's what he wanted to hear. Fires dying down to a blue flame still heating the area. People falling asleep. The night watches changed as usual. And didn't disturb anyone. Another peaceful night . No one slept late. Antonina and Like a Deer were up early with Taters getting things going. Breakfast was served and they were off: wagons, horses, and everyone to get into Higgins early.

Chapter 16

Riding into Higgins, Texas, they were met at the edge of town by their friends, José and Margaret. Mrs. Sikorski and Antonina jumped off their horses, as did Margaret, like family getting together after a long separation. A lot of hugs and handshakes. José looked like a lawman. No more sombrero. Instead, a black, big-rimmed, large Stetson hat and all black lawman suit. Margaret was also dressed in a black big-rimmed hat and black riding pants with a suit coat. Both were well armed. Their badges had a shine to them.

José said, "We are so happy to see all of you. We have talked about this day when we would finally be together."

"How have you been, José? You both look so good. It must be going well for you two."

"Si, it has been good."

Antonina asked, "Where is Grace?"

"She will be here. Come into town you all. Do you want to stay in the hotel?"

"I don't know, maybe so. Mr. Dickenson, what you think?"

Mrs. Sikorski said, "I want a bath."

"We got plenty of bathtubs in town."

Grace came running down the street and hugged Antonina. They hugged and jumped and screamed.

"There's too many of us for a hotel. Margaret, we

should just stay outside town tonight. Tomorrow, we can get our baths and supplies. Are you and José staying here in Higgins or are you coming with us?"

"Mr. Dickenson, José and I are really struggling with deciding."

"If you left with us, is there anybody ready to step up and replace you both?"

"We have told the town council that we might be leaving. Quite frankly, they don't believe us. We have worked with two men that would be glad to take over. They can handle things if we leave."

"You know, Margaret, not all of us will be going on to Del Rio, at least not at this time."

"Okay, yeah, Constance. I remember now. Frankie B., OK Bill, Prairie Flower, Angelina, Carlyle, and Red Fox will be heading back to Eastern Oklahoma."

"That's almost right. Antonina and I are going with them as far as we can, and then going up into southern Illinois. Margaret, I really would like to see if we can find my son. If he's alive and how he's doing, and hold him. Antonina dreams of seeing him. So we really need to try."

"Well, Constance, I kinda feel like going with you."

Everyone had gone into town by now. Juan settled the horses at the edge of town at the camp. And Long John was already sipping a whiskey at the saloon and ordering a meal. Frankie B. and OK Bill talked a good bit about pulling out tomorrow if the rest are willing. The sooner the better. Angelina and Carlyle agreed. Red Fox and Prairie Flower said it would be fine. Like a Deer asked if she could go with them. Prairie Flower said it would probably be

451

okay, but we need to ask the others. Constance asked about the bath house.

"You can use my tub, if you want. I have one at my house."

"Okay, I need that more than anything."

"Let's go to my house. I'll let you in and then I got some rounds to make."

"How does José feel about leaving?"

"He never did feel like a lawman so I think he would leave if I did. He is a good and honest man and he is fair and just with people. But he really don't care about being a lawman, even thou anybody you ask will tell you he's a good lawman."

"Are you and him living together?"

"We are now. It took us a while to get together. I wanted to right away, but not him. So, we do care for each other, a lot. We really have it good here but you know, we could get killed in a shootout any day. But it's probably not any more unsafe than fighting Indians or Comancheros. At least here, we wear a badge and someone might think twice before shooting at us— maybe— that is."

"Have you had any big shootouts since you put on the badges?"

"Yeah, a couple."

"How'd you do?"

"Well, we buried a few bad guys. Here's my place. Let's go inside. You can make yourselves at home."

"Come on Antonina, let's take a bath. I'll go first, then you."

"You have to warm up some water on the stove. There's a well around the corner."

"You just go ahead if you have to be somewhere to be. We'll be alright."

"Okay, I'll be back in a little while."

The Dickenson people set up camp outside of town where Juan had the horses. A few of them headed for the saloon to wet their throats. Frankie B. caught up with Mr. Dickenson and told him of his plans to leave tomorrow if we can get all our supplies lined up and we'd like to take an extra horse along loaded with the supplies if he didn't mind.

"Not at all, take two if you want."

"No Sir, I think one will be enough."

"Whatever you need."

OK Bill and Red Fox walked up just then with Prairie Flower, Angelina, and Like a Deer.

"You know Sir, we'll probably make our way down to Del Rio when we get everything worked out with the Comanche chief."

"I know Frankie B., I hope you will. You will have a job waiting for you. In fact, you all have a job if you want it. You should talk to the chief about moving his people down to Del Rio. You know there are other Comanche around."

"Now, that I wouldn't know about, Sir."

Red Fox said, "Chief not happy in Oklahoma. Winter too cold. Sometime no deer or buffalo for people to hunt. Maybe want go to Del Rio if plenty food."

"We can talk to him about it."

"I don't know about the food. I do know there's plenty of cattle."

"Sir, we'll keep that in mind."

Mrs. Sikorski and Antonina were all cleaned up and combing out their hair when Mrs. Edwards and Grace came back.

"Oh good, you're finished. You ready for some supper?"

"Well yeah, but we have imposed enough. We need to get back to the camp. Why don't you come back with us and spend a little time with everybody?"

"Okay, that's a good idea. Soon as José gets here, we'll go. Let's get this tub emptied out while we wait."

"How do you empty it?"

"Here, I'll show you. Just pull this plug out and it runs through the floor."

"Really?"

"Yeah, that's it. It runs away from the house."

José did his rounds checking the town and then headed to the house where they were waiting for him.

"Do you have supper ready?"

"No. We thought we would go out to the camp and visit with everyone and maybe get a bite of something out there."

"Oh, okay Señorita. I need to wash my face first, then we go."

Constance was saying how nice a place they have here. "Wouldn't you miss it if you gave it all up?"

"Yeah, probably would."

"José, do you want to give this up?"

"I would if you did. Otherwise we stay. This is the most, how you say, respected thing I have ever done."

"Respectable?"

"Si. I think we can stay a while longer. Then maybe when we get tired of this place, we go to Texas. Let's go see our friends now and eat something and see what they think."

The hands at camp were glad to see their good friends. José hugged and shook hands with everybody. Margaret wiped the tears from her cheek over and over again as she was so happy to see everybody. Grace and Antonina had some catching up to do. After all, they hadn't seen each other for over six months.

Mr. Dickenson said, "Before I bed down, I want to say that you three are welcome at my ranch if you decide to leave Higgins. Anytime. If you decide to go tomorrow, you're more than welcome. We hope to leave sometime tomorrow heading for Del Rio. Some of our friends are leaving us and heading for the Comanche camp and also Mrs. Sikorski and Antonina are even going farther. They're going up into Illinois to find some family. I hope they will consider coming down to Del Rio, too, when they get their business taken care of. I will see you all tomorrow. Good night everybody."

Everyone said good night back.

José looked at Margaret. "We should go Señora."

"Yeah, I know. We'll see you all before you leave. Good night everyone."

"Goodnight José, Margaret, Grace."

They headed back to town. When they got settled down in their house, the three of them began to talk about leaving or staying in Higgins.

"Momma, I really like it here but I also would like to stay with our friends. They are like family."

"I know, Grace, I feel that way too."

"I, too, Señorita. So, what do we do? Here's what I think we should do. Stay here for now. We can always leave later."

"I think you're right, José. Grace, is that okay with you."

"I think that will be okay for now. But I sure hope we can see them all again."

"Okay, so we stay here for now. We can talk about it again."

Everybody in camp turned in shortly after José and them left. And were getting up early before the sun came up. Long John sipped his coffee while he and Carlyle talked about going different ways today.

"Long John, I will miss this bunch and you. We all worked well together a few times when things got tough."

"That's right Carlyle, we did. I hope to see you again, Carlyle."

"I hope to see you again, too. We might just come down to Texas, you never know."

Frankie B. and OK Bill were just getting up. Angelina laid there thinking, *This is where we leave our good friends and things will change starting today.* Prairie flower got up and started packing things up.

"Do you think we will need more than one horse for supplies?"

"I not think so, Frankie B."

"Alright, I'll cut out a big male horse and we can start loading him up. Anything else we need from in town, let's get it and as far as I'm concerned, we can start going east. I'll get our people together and have a talk.

"Mrs. Sikorski, Antonina, Carlyle, Prairie Flower, Angelina, Like a Deer, Red Fox, OK Bill, I just want to get a head count and have a little talk. Let's choose a leader now before we get going. I'm perfectly willing to let anyone take the job. Now is the time to say."

Carlyle said, "I like the way things were when we left the Comanche camp and headed west Frankie B. You did a good job making hard decisions and staying calm when we needed it. So I choose you Frankie B."

"Frankie B. will do just fine," Mrs. Sikorski said.

"I know you weren't with us when we left the Comanche camp and don't really know what we went through, but I'm telling you, we were attacked a few times and we got through just fine with Frankie B. staying calm and making the right decisions."

"That's good enough for me."

"I'm ready to go if the rest of you are."

"Yeah, no reason to waste time."

Long John raised a cup a coffee and said, "Hope you all have a safe trip and we will be seeing you in Texas soon."

Carlyle raised his cup and said, "Hope your trip will be safe, too."

They said their goodbyes and after stopping at the general store, were on their way. OK Bill took the lead. Antonina took hold of the pack horse.

"I'll lead it for a while. Would that be alright?"

"Sure, we can change off. Nice day, not too windy. We should be able to make good time and put on some miles."

Carlyle rode around and made sure everyone had their weapons fully loaded and at the ready. Like a Deer needs to practice her shooting some.

"How 'bout she gets the rabbits and quail for the evening meal unless we decide to move without making noise."

"Today should be alright."

Red Fox rode alongside Like a Deer and asked her if she would like to shoot his bow and arrow since that is how he gets the rabbits and quail for the evening meal.

"We can do it as we ride, if you would like."

"I can use the bow and arrow some. Grandfather show me how."

"We can see tomorrow if you can hit anything. Today we just ride."

Frankie B. passed the word that the little town of Vici will be coming up and we better get a few supplies and load up on water.

"After this town, there won't be any for a few days. The sooner we get through this unforgiving territory, the better. We can't be sure what the Indians will do with us going through their land the second time. The Crow and the Arapaho claim it. I only hope our Indian companions will be enough to get us through without the locals trying to kill us. Everybody stay alert and keep your guns loaded at all times. Let's stay as quiet as we can. Maybe we can get through without a shootout. The town of Vici, Oklahoma, is coming up. We need to get a few supplies and rest up tonight and maybe we can get a good meal in town this evening. Tomorrow, we start going southeast and head for the Chickasaw nation and the Comanche camp. There won't be any towns for probably a week or more before the Comanche camp. So let's go into the town and get a few things and see about a meal.

"Mrs. Sikorski and Antonina, I suppose this is where you start going a little north, northeast to Illinois. I really don't like the idea of you two going by yourselves."

Carlyle took his hat off and smacked it on his knee and said, "They aren't going by themselves. By God, I can't let them go alone. I'm going with them. The rest of you just go on to the Comanche camp and I'll get there when I get there. After all, I'm not the one that has to ask the Chief if I can marry someone."

That brought a laugh out of just about everybody. Frankie B. thought for a second and said, "Good, I was thinking about something like that. I didn't want them going alone. Mrs. Sikorski, are you okay with Carlyle going with you and Antonina?"

"Yes, thanks Carlyle."

All nine rode into the little town. People came out and watched them, wondering if they were bringing trouble to their town. Even the sheriff came out; an older man with a big mustache and a large brimmed black hat. Probably the most people they'd ever seen at one time. Indians and Whites coming in together must have seemed strange. Carlyle, in his buckskins and beard, looked like he just came out of the mountains. They slowly rode up to the general store, got off their horses, stretched, and looked around. After some small talk, they tied up the horses and some went inside just as the mayor and sheriff came over to greet them. Frankie B., OK Bill, Red Fox, and Carlyle were just taking a few steps around the street.

"Hello there, are you with a cattle herd?"

"Hello. No, we were with a herd but we are on our way to the Comanche camp in the Chickasaw nation, a far piece from here."

"Okay, we were just wondering."

Frankie B. said, "Yes sir, I can understand your concern. We mean you no harm. We are a peaceful bunch, Sir."

"I'm the mayor and this is the sheriff. How long do you intend to stay?"

"Well, Sir, we'll probably be out of here tomorrow after we rest up a bit. Do you think we could get a good meal this evening?"

"I think so Mr., ah…,"

"Butler. I'm Frankie Butler. This is Carlyle Coeburn and this is Red Fox and OK Bill. The women will be out in just a little bit."

"I'm Mayor Cedric Tillman and this is Sheriff Bill Wasleman. See that building over there? That's the I Conquered Hotel. They have good meals. Or Sir, you can eat at the 'I Conquered Saloon.' They also serve a good meal."

"What's I Conquered?"

"That's the English translation for the Roman word Vici."

"Oh, that's different."

"Yes it is."

"Thank you, Mayor. We will talk later. Would it be alright if we bed down at the end of the street?"

"Sure, but they might give you a good rate for the bunch of you at the hotel. Why don't you ask them?"

"Thanks, Mayor. I think I will.

"Let's see what the women are buying and get our stuff."

"Okay, Frankie B. What do you think about the hotel and a bed?"

"That'd be fine if I didn't need a bath so bad."

"Well, maybe they got baths, too."

"Well, we can find out."

Everybody got their stuff and they headed for the hotel for a meal. Inside the hotel, they were welcomed. But the two ladies that took their orders were afraid of our Indian friends. Frankie B. assured them they had nothing to worry about.

"Prairie Flower, what would you like to eat? Look at what some of the other people are eating. Would you like that?"

"That look good. I want that."

"Okay, the rest of you do the same thing."

Carlyle asked them about rooms and a bath.

"Sure, we have rooms and if you want baths, we have tubs in the back."

"Okay, thank you, Ma'am.

"We might as well stay in the rooms tonight and anybody that wants a bath, here's your chance."

Mrs. Sikorski wasn't about to miss out on a bath. As it turned out, everybody ate good, had a bath, and rested on a bed for the first time in a long time. When morning came, they each headed downstairs.

"Let's eat breakfast so we won't have to mess with it later."

"Good idea, then we gotta get moving. Carlyle, are you really going with Mrs Sikorski?"

"I am. Why, you want to go, too?"

"No. I was just wondering, Carlyle."

"Like I said yesterday, I will see you all at the Comanche camp. Could be in about a month, I don't know."

461

"You need to take the pack horse, Carlyle?"

"Na, I don't think so. You just hang onto it.

"Well, I'm ready to go. Are you ready, Mrs. Sikorski and Antonina? Stuff whatever extra food you have in your saddle bags and let's get started." They went outside, hugged, shook hands, mounted up, and headed outta town in different directions. Frankie B., OK Bill, Red Fox, Prairie Flower, Angelina, and Like a Deer went east toward the Chickasaw nation. They hadn't gone far when Red Fox pulled up and everyone stopped.

He said, "I go with Carlyle and the women. I help fight bad ones."

"Okay, if that's what you want, hurry up. You can catch them. Be safe my friend," Frankie B. yelled to him as he turned and rode off.

Didn't take long to catch up to Mrs. Sikorski and the other two.

"I want go with you. Is it ok?"

"Sure, it's okay," Mrs Sikorski said. "Glad to have you with us, Red Fox. Let's ride."

They rode all day with very few stops till the sun was far west over the horizon, heading in a northeast direction. Hoping to wind up in southern Illinois at the little community of DuBois, Radom, and Ashley. That's where she could find her son staying with some relatives, on her dead husband's side. If not there, then with hers in the Nashville, Illinois area. They have about two weeks riding daylight till dark or more, if they don't run into trouble to get into the area. Red Fox, with his bow and arrow, killed two quail for the evening meal. Mrs. Sikorski peeled two potatoes.

Carlyle said, "Let me have those quail. I'll clean them and get them frying over a fire. Red Fox, can you keep a lookout for anything moving out there"?
"Okay, I do. You make good coffee, Antonina."
"Thank you, Red Fox, would you like another cup?"
"Yes, I like another cup."
The quail and potatoes were good with a little gravy. A little cleaning up and it's time to turn in. "Red Fox, wake me in a few hours and I'll take the watch."
"Okay, Mr. Carlyle."

Over at the other camp, Frankie B. and OK Bill, were taking turns on watch. The women were putting things away after their meal. Like a Deer gathered up all the wood she could find and put it close to the fire for the night. It was nice and warm close but cold a few feet away. While they didn't expect any trouble, they were not taking any chances. Just in case, Frankie B. and OK Bill would split the watch and make sure no one came up on them at night. Like a Deer's dog, Henna, picked up every sound from outside the camp. So they felt pretty secure.
Mrs. Sikorski woke up early. She heard a noise; turned out to be nothing. She got up anyway and started the coffee , and warmed up left over quail and biscuits. Wasn't long before Carlyle smelled the coffee and was up washing his face in the pan Antonina set up. Red Fox was sitting on a downed tree with a blanket wrapped around him with his

rifle in hand. Antonina took a cup of coffee to him. "How long have you been sitting here?"

"Maybe long time. I can sit like this long time— some sleep, some wake. Comanche learn when young to sleep like animals."

"I never heard of anything like that, Red Fox! So now, if you stay up all day you won't be falling asleep on horseback?"

"That right, haitse Antonina."

"What did you say?"

"I say friend. You are my friend— haitse."

"Yes, Red Fox, I'm your friend. Do you want something to eat?"

"Yes, I cold and want to eat."

"Come on over by the fire and get warm. I'll keep a lookout. You just go ahead and eat something. Soon as you get through eating, we'll move out."

"Alright, Mr Carlyle. Horses are saddled. Let's go."

"I'll put out the fire and we'll be on our way."

The sun was warming things up with very little wind. Just right. Looks like riders heading our way. "Let's keep moving and check your weapons. You know what to do. Red Fox, you and I out in front." Took a while but the closer we got to them, we could see there were six men, looked like farmers. They started to wave at us. We didn't expect any trouble from them. When we got close enough to shout back and forth, they said they were from Fairview and they're going to Chester to see about some cattle. We stopped long enough to talk. Carlyle asked, "You run into any trouble?"

"No, but we did hear about some gang running wild farther east: the Logan Belt gang coming outta southern Illinois. Someone needs to put an end to them. Word is they rob and kill a lot a people. We ain't seen them, just heard."

Carlyle said, "You shouldn't have any problems where you're going. We just came close by Chester and it was quiet as far as we could tell."

"Thanks, we'll be going."

"Okay, see ya."

"Mrs. Sikorski, you ever heard of the Logan Belt gang?"

"I have. Don't know anything about them though. Just heard some."

"Keep a sharp lookout. If we run into them, we don't want them to get the drop on us."

"Carlyle, I did hear they will hand women and young children over to the Comancheros for a price and do anything for money."

"I wonder how many there are."

"Carlyle, I think there are a lot but they work in smaller groups. So if you killed a few, you'd be up against the whole gang."

"That's alright. I'd still like to kill as many as we can. If they come down on us, I want us to be ready to shoot to kill as many as we can. Let's make sure none get away."

"Alright, that's what we'll do."

"Red Fox, do you understand?"

"Yes, Carlyle. We don't let any get away."

So day after day they rode, heading east northeast, being very cautious, bypassing all the little towns unless they needed something. Across the border from the Cherokee nation into the Joplin, Missouri, area, they stopped in for some supplies and were told by the storekeeper that there were some Logan

Belt's men at the saloon getting drunk and raising hell.

"Aren't they a little far from their base?"

"I guess, but I'm sure they don't give a damn. About a half dozen men or more."

"Okay, well, we're not looking for trouble so we'll just take our stuff and leave. Do you carry any whiskey?"

"Sure."

"Do you have any Deerhammer Whiskey?"

"No, but they do at the saloon. I happened to know they just got a shipment the other day. But you don't want to go in there, Mister."

"You're right, I don't. You got anybody that will go in and get me a bottle?"

"Sure. Any of the kids playing in the street will go if you give them some money."

Carlyle walked out on the boardwalk of the store and looked around. He saw the kids playing.

"Hey, you kids. Who wants to earn four bits?"

"I do, Mister." Several kids stood up. He picked one and sent him after a bottle of Deerhammer Whiskey. A few minutes later, the boy came out without the whiskey.

"Where's my bottle?"

The boy said, "Here's your money. They wouldn't give it to me."

"Okay, I guess I don't need it."

Mrs. Sikorski said, "I hope you're not going in after it, Carlyle."

"I thought about it but I guess I won't. It might cause trouble. Let's get our stuff and get outta this town. Wait a minute. I'm gonna get a bottle of whatever kind of whiskey the storekeeper has."

"Okay."

Carlyle went back in and bought a bottle and came back out and got on his horse and they slowly rode out of town. Passing the saloon, you could hear the noise from inside. All of sudden, a drunk man came out with a bottle and yelled, "Hey, you forgot your bottle."

They all stopped. The man staggered over to Mrs. Sikorski's horse, leaned against her horse, and held up the bottle of Deerhammer Whiskey.

"Okay," she said. "How much is it?"

"Here, it's free."

"Okay, thank you." She took it and stuck it in her saddle bags.

Another man came out through the swinging doors. "Hey, wait a minute, come on in and have a drink with us."

Carlyle spoke up. "I don't think so, we gotta be going."

"Well, why not? You're not being very friendly."

"We gotta get back to our camp. They're waiting for us."

"Okay," the one yelled. "Maybe next time."

"Okay, maybe next time," Carlyle yelled back. They started riding again. Carlyle said under his breath, "We will never get outta here without a shootout." By now, Carlyle had his pistol out and the hammer pulled back. Red Fox had his rifle across his saddle, hammer back. Mrs. Sikorski and Antonina both knew the drill and had pistols at the ready. Slowly, for what seemed like eternity, they moved till a loud voice yelled, "Hold it, hold it right there." Three more men came out of the saloon, one did the yelling. They were so drunk they could barely stand up.

"Don't you want your bottle?"

They swung their horses around and there was a drunk holding up a bottle.

"Thanks, but we got a bottle." Mrs. Sikorski pulled the bottle out of her saddle bag and showed them.

"Oh, okay, but if you want this one, you can have it, too."

"Thank you very much, but this one is enough. Thank you again."

They turned their horses and rode out of the town. They couldn't see the looks on the faces of the men but they would remember this day forever— how they came close to a shoot to kill over a bottle of whiskey. They talked as they rode that they might see these men again if they come after them.

"Let's get outta here in case they change their minds."

"Yeah but we're probably okay 'cause I don't think they could get on a horse they're so drunk and probably won't remember a thing about what happened when they sober up."

"Just in case, let's put a lot of distance between us and that town before we stop for the night."

When they finally did stop, Mrs. Sikorski and Antonina started a fire and got the coffee going.

"Red Fox, do you think you can find us something to eat besides these beans and bread?"

"I think so." Not long and Red Fox was back with a rabbit and a field grouse. He and Carlyle cleaned them and put the meat on the fire. Then they ate a very good meal. They were able to rest up quite well on full stomachs and got an early start the next morning.

As night was closing in, Frankie B. and OK Bill, with the other bunch miles away, were settling in for their evening meal. Angelina fixed a fire and got the coffee going. OK Bill killed a couple quail before they stopped so they had their beans and biscuits with quail. Prairie Flower fixed up an Indian recipe with baked quail drippings and made a delicious gravy. Dipping the biscuits in it was as good as it gets. After they got their fill and washed it down with coffee, a place to stretch out by the fire was all they needed. OK Bill didn't lay down for long. He heard the sound of pounding hoof beats, got up, and walked away from the fire and listened. Angelina asked, "What do you think it is, Frankie B.?"

"Well, it's either stampeded cattle or maybe horses spooked. I don't think it's riders coming our way." OK Bill jumped on his horse and rode out into the night to see if he could find out what it was. The moon was bright enough to see what looked like riders trying to catch up with cattle that had stampeded. The curious thing is what got the cattle spooked in the first place or are the riders rustlers that took them away from the owners. OK Bill was satisfied that they weren't in any immediate danger. He headed back to camp and told the others what he saw.

"We stay here, stay quiet. Six men ride after cattle. They can see pretty good, moon bright. We make noise, they find us. That not good. Then we have to fight. We don't want trouble. Frankie B., get rifle, come with me. We look in the dark. You see what I mean. Women, stay here with rifle. Get into dark spot away from fire. Okay, let's go."

The women did back away from the fire and waited. Frankie B. and OK Bill went out into the moonlit night and could see pretty well. They waited and, sure enough, the riders did come back with probably most of the cattle. They couldn't know if they had all the cattle. It was light but not light enough to see if any cattle were staying behind. "What in the world is going on? OK Bill, do you have any idea?"

"I don't know if they are the owners or rustlers. Let's get back to the camp, the women need to know we're alright."

The fire was burning bright, but no women. OK Bill did a bird call in the dark and in a low voice said, "Ohpitsa, (it means sweetheart in Apache.)"

"We're here behind the big rock," came a voice. Prairie Flower called out, "Yah-ah-Teh (meaning all is good in Comanche.)"

Frankie B. and OK Bill got hugs.

"Let's heat up the coffee."

Even Like a Deer gave them hugs.

"Okay, we'll get the coffee going."

"Now listen to me, a bunch a riders went past us in both directions chasing cattle and we don't know if they're good guys or bad guys. We don't think they saw us so I think we're okay for now. Soon as morning comes, let's move out. We wanna get as far from the riders as we can."

Morning broke. They had some coffee and left over biscuits and meat, mounted up, and rode.

"Let's see if we can get to Stillwater today and maybe Broken Arrow tomorrow, alright? We need to get to the Comanche camp before the weather gets really cold and snow blocks our travel. Prairie Flower, do you know how far the Comanche camp is from Broken Arrow in Oklahoma?"

"No, I do not know, maybe two days ride."

"Okay, that's good. I was hoping not more than two days. Let's see if we can get to Stillwater today. We can eat in the saddle and keep moving. We won't stop for the night till we get to Stillwater. Is that okay with everybody? Angelina, can you ride all day till we get to Stillwater?"

"I can."

"Prairie Flower, how 'bout you?"

"I can ride long time. Remember, I Comanche woman."

"Like a Deer, come over here and ride by me for a while."

"What do you want to say, Frankie B.?"

"We need to ride longer today so we can get to the town of Stillwater. Can you ride longer, maybe past dark?"

"I do what you say. I know it be right to do."

"Okay, everybody got enough water and a little something to eat?"

"Yep."

"Then let's keep pushing."

Hour after hour passed, no one complained. Little past dark, everyone was tired but glad to put those miles behind. They could see lights flickering in the distance.

"I don't know about you, OK Bill, but I'm damn glad to see this day over with. Let's see if they will cook up some food for us if it isn't too late."

Slowly making their way into town and riding up to the saloon, they got off their horses, shaking off some of the dust, giving their horses a chance to drink at a trough, then tying them up to a hitching post in front of the saloon. They went in and all eyes turned towards them: one White man and four Indians coming through the swinging doors. Even the piano player stopped playing and turned. It must have been a sight.

Frankie B. told everyone, "Don't worry, we're just here to eat, we're not here looking for trouble. Barkeep, you got any food cooked up for me and my friends?"

"Hang on, I'll see. Be right back… Yes Sir, got chicken and dumplings and fresh baked bread and butter and coffee."

"That will be just fine." Frankie B. looked at OK Bill and then at the three women. Each gave a nod. "We'll take five servings with extra bread and butter."

"Coming up. We don't usually serve Indians in here but I guess we can make an exception."

"Yeah, you make an exception," Frankie B. said.

"Been on the trail long," a voice said. They had to look around to see where the voice was coming from. It was a man sitting across the room in a big rimmed black hat and fine coat, flipping a deck a cards back and forth.

"Matter of fact, we have."

By then, they had their chicken and dumplings and were eating away. Been a while since they had a good meal. The man tried to engage them in a conversation but wasn't doing too well. They pretty much ignored him. When they walked in, they left their rifles on their horses. But they were well-armed. Frankie B. and OK Bill each had three pistols on them and several knives. The three Indian women had two or three pistols each and two knives each on them. They were also not afraid to blow his damn head off if he started something.

OK Bill looked up from his plate and said, "What is it you want from us? We don't know who you are. We not want trouble."

With that the man jumped up from his chair; the chair went flying back against the wall. "You do not belong in here," he said and threw his coat back revealing a low hanging, fast draw rig.

Frankie B. got up slowly, wiped his mouth with the towel on the table, set it back down, slid his chair back, and walked out into the middle of the floor. "We are not bothering you and I don't like what you are saying. We are paying for our meals and not hurting anyone so I would suggest you sit back down and leave us be or tell me what you want to do next."

The stranger turned like he was going to sit down, but pulled his pistol instead. Frankie B. was watching his every move and shot the pistol right out of his hand. The bullet went through his hand and grazed his side. Frankie B. went to the man and sat him in the chair, picked the pistol up from the floor, and stuffed it in the man's holster.

"Somebody get a doctor," he said.

Nobody moved— they were frozen. He said it again a lot louder and they came to. "Yes Sir. Right away." Several ran out the door and were back in a few minutes with Doctor Jim Clark and the sheriff. "Who wants to tell me what happened?"

Frankie B. went up to the bar and leaned forward, but didn't have to say a word. The bartender knew what he wanted. "One whiskey coming up." Frankie B. sipped it slowly, set the glass down, and turned to the sheriff.

"I shot him when he drawed on me."

The sheriff looked around. "Is that the way it was?"

"Yes Sir, Sheriff," several patrons said. "That's what happened."

"Can we go, Sheriff?"

"Yes, but give me your name before you go."

"Butler, Frank Butler is my name.

"Barkeep, how much do we owe you for the meals and the whiskey?"

"Five dollars will cover it."

Frankie B. paid the man and they walked out the door. The sheriff was right behind them.

"Hold on there a minute. Why'd that guy draw on you?"

"Because he said my Indian friends were not welcome in there. I told him to sit down and leave us be. That's when he drawed on me. That's all there is to it, Sheriff."

"Okay, Butler, you can go."

"Sheriff, we will head out a town a ways and make camp and leave the area at sunrise. We'll be heading towards Broken Arrow. If you need to talk to me more, that's where I'll be."

"Okay Butler."

"That's good what you did, Frankie B. I know you could have killed the man. But it's better you didn't."

"I know Angelina, the guy didn't need to die for being stupid."

"He won't look for trouble for a while."

"Yeah, I know OK Bill, and he won't be pulling a gun with that hand for a while either. Let's ride." About a mile out and in a wooded area, they made camp and turned in early so they could get up with the sun and get out of the area. When they got up, after a light breakfast, they were on their way. The next place to try for in two days was Broken Arrow. Frankie B., OK Bill, Prairie Flower, Angelina, and Like A Deer packed in enough food and water so they could keep going without too many stops.

Back with Mrs. Sikorski, Carlyle, Antonina, and Red Fox, they were going through Indian territory not expecting to run into bandits, but they did. Another part of the Logan Belt gang: seven approached them. Bad looking as hell. Their leader demanded they throw down their guns, get off their horses, and empty their pockets. Carlyle and the others already had their rifles in hand across their saddles. Carlyle made like he was going to get off with one leg but instead fired and the rest did too, killing five and injuring the other two.

"Now we will get off our horses. Mrs. Sikorski, Antonina, get all the guns and holsters. Red Fox and I will take care of these two. Carlyle questioned them. One died before he could finish saying the Logan Belt would find you. The other one wasn't saying much, like he knew he was about to die also. Carlyle asked him, "Where was Logan Belt?"

"We haven't seen him in days. He was last in the Mount Vernon, Illinois area. Said he was going to head for a cave in rock that same day. He had twenty men with him and a few captives he wanted to sell to the Comancheros."

"Are there any others around here?"

"There's another five men a few miles from here at Mountain Grove."

Carlyle said, "Okay, say your prayers you rotten son of a bitch and shot him dead.

"Let's get this bunch buried and get moving. We're taking these horses and gear. There's no brands on the horses so I say we sell them in the nearest town along with the saddles. What did you find in those saddle bags?"

"Nothing worth anything much. Maybe fifty dollars cash."

"Okay, Mrs. Sikorski, hang onto the money. We'll use it as we need things."

"Okay, Carlyle."

"Red Fox, help me bury these."

A quick prayer, "Lord have mercy on their souls." Mrs. Sikorski, Antonina, and Red Fox, take an extra rifle and anything else if you want. And if you want a different saddle on your horse, get it and divide up the pistols and extra bullets, too."

Carlyle was saying these men go around terrorizing people across a bunch of states, selling women and young girls.

"Somebody needs to kill them all. That's the only thing that will stop them. I feel like we just did a small part to at least bring some of them to justice."

"I know, Carlyle, that's a shame. Just like Antonina and I were taken by them earlier this year and my husband killed and my son, I don't know where my other son is. Constance and Antonina hugged each other and had a good cry. Red Fox came over to them and touched them, "We will find him." Mrs. Sikorski looked up. "I know, Red Fox. Thanks for helping."

"We should go, we don't want to waste any more time."

Without a word, they all mounted up and started to ride, taking the horses in tow. A few hours riding and the little town of Militia Springs came up.

"How 'bout we try to sell these horses."

"Okay, let's see if we can. They cautiously rode in looking all around as they went. Spotting the livery stable, they pulled up and the owner came out.

"Can I help you?"

"Yes you can. I'd like to sell these horses with the saddles."

"I, I don't know Mister."

"I'll take just $400 for all seven saddles and all."

"Mister, I hope they're not stolen and somebody will come along and take them from me."

"I don't know about that but they were not stolen when we got them. The owners were killed in a gun fight."

"You kill 'em, Mister?"

"Can't say. You wanna buy 'em?"

"Okay Mister, I'll give you $400. I can make some money on them."

"That's what I thought."

"Hang on, I'll be right back." He went in the front and out a back door. A few minutes passed and he did come back with the money. He handed Carlyle four one hundred dollar bills.

"Here you go, grab the reins. They're all yours. Is there a general store in this town?"

"Yes Sir, just over there a ways."

"Okay, thanks. Mrs. Sikorski, you need anything?"

"If I had some pie filling and flour, I'd make us some pies."

"Let's go in and look around. We'll think of some other things."

"Antonina, you want something? Now's your chance to get a few things."

"Okay Momma."

The storekeeper was a strange looking man: twitchy eyes and nervous. He kept looking at Antonina like she was a piece a meat.

"Mister, we're in here to buy supplies, not for you to drool over my daughter. So can you take your eyes off her and get me some canned cherries and apples and some flour and a half dozen eggs."

"Yes Ma'am, right away."

"Red Fox, you need anything."

"Candy. Sweet candy."

"Sure Mister, we got candy right over here. Is that Indian tame, Sir?"

"What you mean, tame? He's not a dog. I think you need to go back to school and learn how to be around people.

"Let's get what we need to get outta here before I beat the hell out of this storekeeper and get myself locked up in jail."

"Okay Carlyle, I got my pie ingredients. Let's go. Come on Antonina. Come on. You like that guy looking at you like you were candy?"

"No, I don't care about him, I just like to look at all the pretty things."

"Well then, let's go. We got daylight to burn. Good to get out of there. That storekeeper was creepy."

"Mrs. Sikorski, how about handing me that bottle in your saddle bag. The Deerhammer Whiskey."

"Okay Carlyle. Is that other one gone that you bought?"

"No, I just thought I'd have a drink of the good stuff."

"Here, don't drop it."

They rode on and bypassed Mountain Grove and kept going till dark. When they did stop for the day, Mrs. Sikorski made a couple of pies to go along with their quail and rabbit. Good hot coffee to finish off. After sitting around for a while and talking about what they went through, they bundled up by the fire in their blankets and were off to sleep and taking turns at watch. The night was over and morning came as always. A warm breakfast with leftovers and they were riding again. A few more days of heading east, a little north, and they had to find a way to cross the Mississippi River at Ste. Genevieve, Missouri. As luck would have it, there was a ferry boat landing and they were just in time. The boat was loading as they rode up. A big man with a French accent was motioning a wagon on and told Carlyle, "Maybe better to walk your horse on if it has not had a ferry boat ride before."

"Okay. Let's do as he says."

The horses were a little nervous, but made the long trip across without any problem. Once on the Illinois side, Mrs. Sikorski said, "We're getting close now."

Little did they know but they had another smaller river to cross: the Kaskaskia River. Not as wide or deep but too deep to walk the horses across.

"There has to be a ferry boat up or downriver somewhere. We'll have to find one or, otherwise, we're stuck. I'll go up river and look, you two go with Red Fox downriver and we'll meet back here in a little while. That's all we can do."

"Okay. Sure Carlyle."

They all came back without finding a crossing ferry boat.

"Now we pick a direction and all go till we find one. Red Fox, which way looks more likely?"

"I don't know, Mr. Coeburn. I not know what to look for."

They rode north till they came to a little town of Brewerville. The few folks that lived there had their own way of crossing the river. They had small boats but nothing for horses.

One of the men said, "You can take your saddles off and have the horses swim alongside the boats. That should work. We've done it that way a few times when we wanted our horses on the other side with us."

"Okay, we don't have a choice. Let's do it."

So they put all their saddles and gear in one boat to keep things dry and walked the horses around in the water for a while to get them used to it.

"You can hold onto the reins or let them swim by themselves. We've done it both ways. Either way, they will head for the other side to follow you."

Red Fox said, "I ride bareback my horse, others will follow."

"Okay, whatever you want to do."

It went very well. Red Fox got a little wet but he didn't care. On the other side, they put their saddles back on, thanked their new friends from the town of Brewerville, and rode off. It didn't take long and Sparta showed up in the distance.

"Mrs. Sikorski, you want more pie mix? We can stop in and look around."

"Yeah, that would be alright. They rode in and tied up in front of the general store. Carlyle and Red Fox sat down on a bench outside the store. Constance and Antonina went inside. The proprietors wife was glad to show off the latest fashions in women's wear.

"If you're interested, we have a bathtub in the back you can use." The woman said, "You both look like you could use a bath, no offense intended."

"None taken," Constance uttered. "I sure will."

"I will, too, Momma."

"Okay, you go first. I'll tell Carlyle. It won't take us long."

"Okay, Momma. We should get some new clothes."

"Sure. Pick something out and get it."

"Carlyle, Carlyle."

"Yes 'am. Did you call me, Ma'am?"

"I did. Can you come in here, please?"

"Yes 'am. I sure can."

"You think it would be all right if Antonina and I," (come over here so I can talk to you in private) have a chance to take a bath and we don't want to pass that up. And we'd like to buy some new clothes. You think that would be alright?"

"Mrs. Sikorski, Ma'am, I think it would be a great idea. Where do you have to go to take a bath?"

"They said they have a tub in the back room here in the store. Antonina is back there now. Will you check around the building outside? You know what I mean."

"Sure, Mrs. Sikorski. I'll do that right now." Carlyle walked slowly around the back of the building. There was one window and one door, nothing outta the ordinary. He tried the door and the window. They were both locked and the window had a shade. Satisfied, he went back around where Red Fox was on the front bench when two strangers walked up and asked Red Fox what he was doing in town.

"I wait for women. They in store."

Carlyle came back around just then and said, "Can I help you?"

"We were just asking what this Indian is doing?"

"He's not doing anything. He's with me and the two women in the store. You have a sheriff in this town?"

"Why yes. He's in his office over there."

"Okay, I don't need him. I just wondered if you folks had one."

Mrs. Sikorski and Antonina finished their baths, combed out their hair, and bought some new clothes. They said they felt so good.

"How much do we owe you, Ma'am," she asked.

"For the two sets of riding clothes, underwear, those soft socks, and the baths, twenty-five dollars would be just fine. They also had to pay the Chinese laundry for washing their clothes while they took their baths. Another two dollars.

"Carlyle, I'm so glad you suggested we stop. Now we can feel clean for a while."

"Well, okay, now I guess Red Fox and I are next. We'll get ours tomorrow when we get to Ashley."

Chapter 17

They spent the night outside of Sparta. The next day, a few hours riding brought them to the place were Constance and Antonina lived till last year when the bandits killed Constance's husband and run off her son and took her and Antonina captive. The house was still like when she left it. Plates still on the table. Everything dirty, full of cobwebs. Otherwise, everything looked the same. She wondered where her husband was buried. She began to cry.

"Momma, don't cry," Antonina said. "I don't want to stay here anymore, do you?"

"I don't know if I do or not. If we can't find where your father is buried, I don't for sure."

Carlyle and Red Fox started picking up things around the place. It was a real mess with no one living there for almost a year. Constance walked outside to see if there was a grave anywhere around.

"Carlyle, have you seen a grave?"

"No Ma'am, I haven't."

"Red Fox, you either?"

"No Ma'am."

"Two riders coming Ma'am," Carlyle said. "Get your rifles and wait. Mrs. Sikorski, will you and Antonina get inside just in case we have trouble?" Constance watched at the window. She thought she might know who was coming. Carlyle handed her a pair a binoculars to get a good look before they got too close.

"I know one. He's Sheriff O.P. Hallem. Good, he might know something about my husband's grave and my son."

When they pulled up, the sheriff asked, "Who are you people?"

"Sheriff, it's me, Constance Sikorski."

"If it is, you've changed a lot."

"It is me and I have changed. Do you know where my husband is buried and where my son Jacob is."

"Sure. Jacob is living with his uncle Leo and your husband Joseph is buried in the Radom cemetery. No one ever expected to see you or Antonina again after you both were taken by the bandits."

"You wouldn't if it had not been for these two here, Carlyle Coeburn and Red Fox, and a few others."

"Is that right?"

"Yes Sir, it is. They put themselves in much danger to save Antonina and I. We have learned how to stay alive with their help."

"Would you like to go see your boy now Ma'am?"

"Yes, I would. Carlyle, Red Fox, can you come along with me."

"Sure. Is it far?"

"No, not too far."

Jacob was so happy to see his mother and sister that he couldn't stop crying when he saw it was really them.

"Momma, I thought I'd never see you and Antonina again."

"If it wouldn't have been for some very special people, we wouldn't be here now. I want you to meet Carlyle Coeburn and Red Fox, two very special friends. I trust them with my life. There are more friends but only these two came with us to help out on the trip."

"Thank you both for helping my mother and sister."

"That's all right, Son. We think of your mother and sister as family. We have been through a lot together."

Red Fox put his hand on his heart and said, "We much family forever."

"Well, thank you so much."

Uncle Leo shook their hands. "Can we offer you some food and drink?"

"Yes, Leo," Mrs. Sikorski said. "That would be great. We haven't eaten much today. Then I'd like to see Joseph's grave."

"Okay, we can ride out to the cemetery after you eat something."

Leo's wife Darlene cooked up a quick meal with the help of some of the neighbors. It was like a feast: all the chicken and sausage they could eat. It reminded Constance of how things used to be.

"Momma, are you going to live in the home place?"

"I don't know Jacob. I guess for now. What would you like to do?"

"I kind of thought when I got older, I'd go back home and farm some. Uncle Leo said he'd help me get started."

"Jacob, I don't know if I can ever feel at home here anymore. Now that I'm back, I feel uneasy, nervous."

"I'm sorry, Momma. Daddy was killed and you and Antonia taken off like your lives were nothing."

"Yes, Jacob, I feel like it left a hole in my heart."

"I'm sorry for that but I can't help it."

"Leo, do you have any idea who any of the men were that kidnapped us?"

"No, but I know someone who might know. There is a man that don't live too far from here. He was questioned by the sheriff when you and Antonina, were taken. I don't know what he told the sheriff, but he might know something that might help. Everybody thinks that they were with that Logan Belt gang. Would you like to talk to him?"

"Yes, I sure would."

"I have to say Constance, you and Antonina look so different; your clothes for one thing. And do you both carry a gun all the time?"

"Yes, and there's more that you don't see."

"What do you mean?"

Antonina threw back her long coat revealing three pistols and two knives.

"Oh my God, really," Leo quickly said. "Constance, you too?"

"Yes, and we have used them. But don't be alarmed."

Leo looked at Carlyle and Red Fox. He could see Carlyle's three pistols and knives. Red Fox was also well armed, included with his pistols and knives, he had a bow over his right shoulder. His arrows were on his horse in a quiver made of leather. He was a very good shot.

"Leo, we are very capable of taking care of ourselves. And we will use them if we find the ones that destroyed our lives. You see, there is no way we can just come back here and live like nothing happened. You probably don't understand."

"Oh, I think I do. I was in the war and came back with a lot a demons and scars inside and out. It took me a long time to put those demons out of my mind and, sometimes, they still come back. Are you all going to stay at your place tonight?"

"Sure, I expect to stay there as long as we are here. It's still my place. Is that okay with you, Carlyle and Red Fox?"

"Yes Ma'am, if that's what you want to do."

Red Fox bowed his head and said, "Ma'am."

"Antonina, you don't have a problem with staying there, do you?"

"No Momma, this is still our home. We should be able to stay or leave it."

"Yes, we should, Antonina. Do we have enough time today to go see the man or should we wait till tomorrow."

"Let's wait till tomorrow, okay Constance?"

"Sure, that will be fine. Can you come by in the morning and get us?"

"Sure, that's what I'll do. Say about noon?"

"Okay, we'll see you then. Thanks for everything Uncle Leo, Aunt Darlene. Thank you for dinner and the extra food to take with us. We'll enjoy it for breakfast."

"You're very welcome."

Back at the house, the four of them did a little cleaning and they were able to sleep comfortably out of the weather. Antonina brought in a pile of wood and warmed the place in the very stove she had started a fire in many times before. They all slept later than normal. After a breakfast of leftovers and a little cleaning up around the place, they saddled up their horses. Leo was right on time. He brought along Constance's son Jacob.

"Let's go if you're ready."

"Okay, let's go."

About a half hour ride and they were at the man's place. As they pulled up, the man came out to meet them.

"Hi there, Leo. What brings you out here?"

"We want to ask you some questions about the bandits that took Constance Sikorski and her daughter Antonina and sold them to the Comancheros earlier this year."

"What do you want to know?"

"Well, do you know who they were?"

"I knew two of them from a trip I made to Centralia early this year. They were with the Logan Belt gang that robbed a bank there. George and William Byars from the Horse Creek area. They were working for the Reeves hardware and delivered five rolls of barbed wire to my wagon as I waited in front of the hardware store. They told me they were members of the Logan Belt gang and made no attempt to hide it. As a matter of fact, they were proud of it. The next afternoon, the bank was robbed. I saw the two of them in chains marched across the street to the jail. They were caught with two others coming out of the bank. They looked at me and smiled as they were walking by my wagon. Like the whole thing was nothing. Next time I saw them was here at the Mule Barn Saloon drinking with a wild bunch when I went in there for a whiskey. When Joe Sikorski was killed and his wife and daughter was taken, I knew it was them. I would bet on it being them."

"So, you think they would probably be back in Centralia if we wanted to find them?"

"Probably. Who are these people, Leo?"

Carlyle spoke up, "We're with a cattle drive south of here."

Constance and Antonina kept quiet. Red Fox said nothing.

"Okay, Chester, thanks. We'll be on our way. If you happen to see them, we would appreciate it if you didn't say you talked to us."

"Okay, Leo, you got it. See you."

"Let's go back to the house."

"What are you going to do with that information? How far is it to Centralia?"

"Not far. Less than a day's ride."

"Do you think we should look them up while we are this close to where they might be, Mrs. Sikorski?"

"Ah, you know I like that. Let's go see if we can find them. You think we should leave today or leave in the morning?"

"If we left today, we would almost be there tonight so I say we go now. What you think, Red Fox?"

"It not matter. I go where you go."

"Okay then, let's grab a bite of something and head out. We can get pretty close or maybe even get all the way today."

"Jacob, you better stay here with Uncle Leo for now. We'll see you when we get back. We shouldn't be gone long."

"What are you going to do if you find them and they are the ones that killed daddy and took you, Mamma?"

"We'll see."

490

The four of them are so used to riding long and hard, it don't bother them. Just another day. They did make it right to the outskirts of Centralia.

"Let's go in and find a place to eat while we make some plans."

The street was wide open: a few horses tied up here and there mostly at the two saloons. A lot of buildings were destroyed earlier in the year from a tornado, but not the saloons.

"Let's just go in both of them. We can ask around. Looks like the first saloon has the most horses, so let's try it. If you don't mind me saying, we should listen more and talk less."

"I agree, Carlyle."

Outside the saloon was a life size statue of an Indian. It made Red Fox laugh. They tied up and went in. It was so noisy you couldn't hear yourself think with the piano player banging away, somebody trying to sing, card players yelling for more beer, and an arm wrestling contest that was getting cheered on.

Red Fox said to Caryle, "I guess this is what White man wants Indian to be like."

"Yeah, Red Fox, aren't they great?"

Aside from the noise, they did get plenty a food and what they didn't eat, they would take with them when they left.

"I'm going to the bar and see what I can find out."

"Okay Carlyle, be careful."

At the bar, he was rubbing shoulders with both the Byars brothers, getting drunk and bragging about some of their crimes. Carlyle got a whiskey and headed back to the table.

491

"That's them bragging and drinking. I heard them say their names a few times. They ought to be easy to catch, if they're alone. We just follow them when they leave. If they're not alone, we follow them anyway and see how strong they are before we move on them. You all okay with that?"

"Yep, that sounds good."

"Ah, Mrs. Sikorski, you think you'd recognize a voice or Antonina, would you?"

"I don't know, Carlyle. I'm trying to think if there was anything that stood out in their voices. Antonina, anything?"

"I don't think so."

"Well, maybe when you hear their voices, it might help. Let's go outside. As long as we keep an eye on these two when they come outside, we can follow them."

"Yeah, I think we should. Let's go."

It wasn't long before the two came out almost too drunk to walk. They did manage to get on their horses. The two seemed to be alone. No one came out after them so, after a while they began to follow at a distance. Red Fox stayed back to keep a watch on their backs.

"We're going out of town in another direction than the one we came, so let's keep a sharp lookout. We don't know what's ahead."

A short ride and there was a camp with two men. No way to tell if there were more without doing a complete recon around the whole area. Red Fox was already off his horse and scouting around.

"You two women stay here with the horses and keep them quiet and I'll check around. Be right back."

"Okay Carlyle, be careful."

So Red Fox got back first and said, "No others around."

Then Carlyle gave the all clear. "Do we want to wait till morning or jump them now?"

"Let's wait till just before daylight."

Carlyle, Red Fox, Constance, and Antonina bedded down close but not close enough to be spotted or heard and did sleep as much as they could. And as soon as daylight broke, they moved in. All four poked a rifle under the noses and Carlyle woke them with the click of his lever action.

'What the hell is going on?"

Constance said, "This is the hell that is going on. Get up slow and if you make one wrong move, you're dead. Have you taken any women or young girls and sold them into slavery?"

"Ah, what do you care?"

"Yes or no? Yes or no? Come on, speak up."

"We work for Logan Belt, lady. He gives the orders."

"Well, then you can die for Logan Belt. All four of you get up, drop your gun belts, and take off your boots."

"What?"

"Take off your boots and hurry. The four of you are going to answer some questions and then we're gonna hang you."

"You can't do that, lady."

Red Fox collected the guns and hardware.

"Yes we can, just like you killed my husband and sold my daughter and I to Comancheros and all the other women and daughters and their husbands and sons that you killed. Start talking. You might work for Logan Belt, but he didn't shoot my husband in the head and laugh about it and stuff us in that wagon like we were nothing."

"Lady, it was nothing personal. It was just a job."

"You say it was nothing personal? That is a heartless thing to say. Then If I hang you and say it is nothing personal, how does that sound to you?"

"But lady, it is personal for you because you want revenge. We did all those things and we can't take them back, so do what you want to do."

"Are you at least a little sorry for all the lives you destroyed?"

"Can't say that I am."

One of the men said, "I didn't have anything to do with you being taken."

"That's probably true but you've taken others, right?"

"Well yeah, but…"

"But what? Did you kill anyone to take a woman captive?"

"Well, yeah."

"Well then," Carlyle said, "you are the worst of the worst. You can't even say you're a little bit sorry. It will be a pleasure to hang you sons a bitches. How 'bout the rest of you? You got anything to say?"

None had anything to say.

"Let's get it over with. That tree will do just fine. Antonina, you okay?"

"I'm fine. I remember my daddy on the ground with blood all over him when this man shot him in the head twice and laughed about it. Daddy was just trying to protect us."

They hung them and treated them better than they treated the people they killed. At least they buried them and put a marker over their grave with the names they went by. And left the area with their horses and gear.

"Mrs. Sikorski, you want to go back to your house?"

"For now I do, Carlyle. How far is that Comanche camp from my place outside of Ashley? You got any idea?"

"Don't know. I'd guess 'bout ten days ride."

"That far?"

"Yeah, I'd guess."

"Well, I'm not sure I want a stay around Ashley. Antonina, how about you?"

"I have mixed feelings. I could stay or go. But this is our home. Maybe we should give it a try, Mama. Our lives where changed so drastically and we didn't ask for it and now look at us. We probably look like outlaws ourselves."

"I know. But what we are Antonina is survivors. If it wouldn't have been for our newfound friends, we'd probably be dead in Mexico somewhere."

"I know, Mama."

"Carlyle, Red Fox, what you think?"

"I think I would miss you both dearly. But this is your home and maybe you should give it a try. If you change your mind after a while, you just get a hold of me and I'll help you leave."

"Red Fox, what are you thinking?"

"You stay here. I stay here, too, if you want. I help you and keep you safe. Bad Whites might find you and want to hurt you again. I not let that happen."

"Really, Red Fox, you'd stay here?"

"I stay till you say Red Fox to leave."

"Bless you, Red Fox, you are truly a friend. Antonina, what you think?"

"I like that he will stay and if we decide to go to the Comanche camp, Red Fox knows the way."

"Alright, I guess we'll stay. Carlyle, we'd be glad to have you stay, too, but we know you have a family waiting for you. You stay as long as you want."

"I'll find a place to take a bath in Ashley tomorrow, then I'll probably leave the next day unless you need me to do something."

"Can you and Red Fox fix that barn door and corral fence before you go?"

"Sure, I'd be glad to. I'll stay a couple days, then I'll go. Angelina is probably missing me by now. But I want to take a bath tomorrow first."

"What we gonna do with these four horses?"

"You keep them, Constance. You'll be needing them around the farm or you sell them if you want. I'll take the pack horse with me."

Into Ashley early next morning, Carlyle got his bath and clothes washed; even bought some new clothes to wear. By the time he got back to the farm, Red Fox was already working on the fence around the corral. Carlyle got off his horse, took the saddle off, put it in the corral, and started to help.

"Red Fox, what you need me to do?"

"We should get rails up and keep horses from getting out, then fix gate."

Mrs. Sikorski said, "Some hay is in barn for horses to eat. Straw, too, for ground. Carlyle, you look clean."

"I got washed after I fixed fence. Yeah, I feel clean, too, and bought me some new clothes. Got my old duds washed and sewed up. Red Fox, you should try the tub bath in town."

"They not like Indian come in town for bath."
"Maybe so, but the people doing the bath are not White, they're Chinese and they like money.
"What are Chinese?"
"They're people with different kind of eyes. I don't think they care who takes a bath. If you want, I will go in town with you and help you get your bath. They will even scrub your back if you want if you pay them."
"Okay, I go. You come with me."
"Sure, as soon as we get through with this fence. Like you said, we don't want the horses getting out."
It didn't take the two of them long to get the corral shaped up. Constance and Antonina were working on getting the inside of the house livable. It needed a lot of straightening up. Constance overheard Red Fox talking about a bath.
"You know, Red Fox, we have a tub in the barn. Why don't you and Carlyle get it set up in that little wash shed by the well. You can be the first to use it."
"Okay Mrs Sikorski, that better than me going into town."
As soon as they got through with the corral, they dragged the tub out of the barn and scrubbed it with lye soap. Wasn't long, it was ready with water in it. With a couple of buckets of hot water from the stove in the house, and the rest straight from the well. Carlyle was laughing. "Red Fox, you better get in there before it cools off."
"I will, if you keep those two woman away?"
"I will and I'll get you some soap and towels. Go ahead."

Antonina came out on the porch with soap and towels.

Carlyle said, "I'll take 'em to Red Fox. He's a little shy."

Red Fox was really having a good ole time singing in Comanche while soaking in the tub. After Red Fox had his bath and put on some clean clothes, they had a home cooked meal of chicken and mashed potatoes with plenty of gravy and sweet corn. And a cherry pie. And always plenty of coffee.

"Ma'am, you are spoiling us both with this kind of cooking. I need to leave and get back to the Comanche camp, but you'll never get Red Fox to leave if you're gonna feed him like this."

"Well, good, he can stay as long as he wants to. I feel safe with him here anyway."

"Ma'am, I'll be leaving in the morning. I want to say I have come to have a great affection for you and Antonina. I hope we can get together soon. Do you think your boy will come to live here, too, and help out with the work?"

"Carlyle, I don't know. He's staying away for some reason that I don't know about. He should be here now."

"If you two need me for anything, Red Fox will know how to find me, right Red Fox?"

"Right, Mr. Carlyle."

"For now, I'm gonna turn in. Do you mind if I lay by the fireplace?"

"Of course you can."

"Okay then, see you folks in the morning."

"Goodnight Carlyle. Red Fox, you can have that little room over there for yourself. Antonina and I will take that bigger room."

"That will do just fine, Mrs. Sikorski."

The fireplace and the stove kept the place warm through the night. The few chickens they had left were up early and the roosters were crowing at daybreak like an alarm clock waking up the whole house. Constance gathered up some eggs for a good ole breakfast with biscuits before Carlyle left. Antonina did the coffee.

Red Fox said, "That was a soft bed, I like it."

"Well, Red Fox, I'm glad you like it. You can sleep in that bed as long as you want to."

"Carlyle, we are going to miss you. Like a father, you have been good to us and we love you." Antonina threw her arms around his neck and cried. "I love you, Carlyle."

"I love you, too, sweetheart. Don't cry. We will be together soon. I tell you what, when I get to the Comanche camp, I'll send you a telegraph from the nearest town and let you know where you can send me a message. Would that be alright?"

"Yes, that would be alright."

"Okay then, I need to get going."

Carlyle and Constance hugged and they both wiped a tear or two. Red Fox gave Carlyle a big hug, too, and said, "You like Comanche father. I see you soon."

"Yes, Red Fox, we will be together soon, one way or another."

He got on his horse and rode off with his pack horse in tow. They watched Carlyle as long as they could and then went back to working on the place. Carlyle pondered all the things he had been through in the last year and all the wonderful people he had met along the way. He thought to himself how good God had been to him. He rode all day and then made camp by a creek bed. The first time he had been alone in a long time. He thought he was feeling the cold air more being alone, but he made do with a thick blanket and a hot fire. Some dried meat and a cold biscuit, soon he went off to sleep. His two horses standing nearby and one of his rifles within reach. Carlyle was up early as he usually was. After a face wash in the creek, a bite of the same old leftovers, and he was off. A few days of riding put him in the Fort Leonard Wood, Missouri, area. A stop in the fort store for a few things and he was off again. While he was in the store, he met a very interesting man: a black preacher by the name of Lefty. What was so interesting about this man was that he had worked for the government as a law man and now was a preacher, and he was no ordinary preacher. He had an army colt in a holster on his right side tied to his leg and a Henry revolver in his belt. He asked Carlyle if he'd mind if he rode along with him for a day or two.

"Sure, I don't care. I'm going to the Comanche camp just west of the Cherokee nation in the Oklahoma territory."

Preacher Lefty said, "Sure, I need to spread the message and that's as good as any place."

While they rode along, Lefty would get in a word or two about the Lord. Carlyle didn't care; that's about what you'd expect from a preacher. As they rode along to the rhythm of horses, Carlyle said, "I have to ask you how come you're called Lefty but not left handed."

"Pretty good with both hands, folks kinda thought I was left handed. Uh, Mr. Carlyle, you got any idea what's for supper?"

"Well, you could shoot us one of those rabbits or quail we see every once in a while, or you could pray up some manna and see what happens."

"Yes Sir, I could. Next rabbit or quail is sent by God. And we should not mock the Lord."

"I wasn't mocking the Lord, Preacher. I was just having a little fun with you."

As it turned out, they did have quail for their supper. Two jumped up at the same time. A quick draw, well placed bullet made the kill. Preacher Lefty whipped up some biscuits to go with the baked quail.

Carlyle said, "I don't know how you did it but it's alright with me if you want to do the cooking every day."

"Well, Mr. Carlyle, I may well do the cookin', that is if you put in a good word to the Chief. What's his name?"

"Bengalese, Chief Bengalese. He might just like you."

"Why is that?"

"Because he seems to like people that are different. If you go slow and not try to beat him over the head with all that religion at one time, he might just let you live."

"Oh really!! How come he let you live?"

"I guess he likes White people. I don't know about you. He might try to wash you off and see if you're really White. No Preacher, I'm just bull shitting you. The chief took me and my son in years ago and last year, my good friends, Frankie B. and OK Bill, came along and he liked them both; one's White and one's Apache. They're both wanting to marry Comanche women and the Chief don't seem to mind. I don't think you have anything to worry about. Preacher, we should be getting there in a couple days."

Meanwhile, Frankie B. and OK Bill, along with the three Indian women, had arrived at the Comanche camp. Chief Bengalese welcomed them with open arms and looked at the Crow girl named Like a Deer.

"You not afraid of Comanche?"

She answered back in Crow. "Grandfather say me be brave, not be afraid. Holy Spirit watch over me."

"Where my good friend, Carlyle Coeburn?"

Frankie B. spoke up, "Chief, he will be coming in a while. He and Red Fox went to Illinois with a woman and her daughter to keep them safe from the bandit, Logan Belt, and his gang."

"Okay, we much glad to see you and this Apache, Ahatahkakood."

OK Bill put his fist on his heart and said, "Good see you, Chief of the Comanche. We bring these women back like we said we would. And this Crow woman, too. Her grandfather died; she had no one."

"Good, she welcome here."

"Prairie Flower and Angelina ride and fight like warrior now. On cattle drive, we meet many that would kill us and take what we had. Indian woman and White woman would be taken as slaves. But they learned to fight and kill when they needed to. This young one, Like a Deer, will learn, too. Chief, you see all the guns they carry? They know how to use them and have used them."

"I see. Many moons have passed since you left with the two women. Do you know them now, and want to have them for wife?"

Frankie B. was the first to answer. "Yes, Chief Bengalese, Channanget and I would like to be married when her grandfather Carlyle gets here."

"I will think on it, Frankie Butler."

"Okay Chief, that's all I can ask."

OK Bill spoke next. "I wish to have Toh-Tsee-ah as my wife. What say you, Chief?"

"You are Apache warrior. Should you have a wife?"

"I would have this woman as my wife. I no longer warrior. I work on ranch for Mr. Dolphus Dickenson. I would take Toh-Tsee-ah, Prairie Flower, to Texas after we marry. Now we rest here for a time."

"Frankie Butler, you work on ranch, too?"

"Yes, Chief Bengalese, I would like to take this woman to Texas after we marry when my friend OK Bill goes. But for now, we just want to rest here with our Comanche friends if you'll have us."

"That is good. You stay here as long as you want."

"Chief, do all your people have enough food?"

"Most time we have plenty."

"While we are here, we will help with the hunt."

"Okay, Frankie Butler. For now, you and the Apache can stay together in a Comanche tent till you marry."

"That will be just fine, Chief."

Frankie B. went out on a hunt for deer with the hunters and they came back with two full grown deer hanging over a pack horse that will feed the thirty or more for a few days, along with the bread the women made with wheat and corn flour they trade for with other tribes in the area. When they rode in, the whole camp turned out to welcome them back with cheers. The work of cutting up the meat was done fast by many. Nothing was wasted; even the dogs got their share. The hides were hung up to dry. Tanning would come later. In the afternoon, two riders were spotted coming from the north. Frankie B. looked with his binoculars and said, "OK Bill, it's Carlyle and another rider."

Patiently waiting, they watched and after a bit they rode into the camp. Carlyle was the first to speak.

"It is good to be back among my friends, the Comanche." Looking around, he spotted Angelina. "I need a hug, Granddaughter."

As he got off his horse, she was right there for a big hug.

"I need to introduce you all to a good friend, Preacher Lefty Ledford. I met him at Fort Leonard Wood. We've been riding together since we met. He can bake a cake out of almost nothing."

"I see why you like it here."

The Chief made Lefty welcome with a feather to put in his hat. Lefty bowed and said, "Thank you, Chief Bengalese. May the Lord bless you and your people." He then put the feather in his hat for all to see.

Being near a waterfall, the Comanche people would regularly use the falls as a way to bathe. After Carlyle rested up a little, he was off to the falls for a cold bath: The Crooked Creek Falls. Lefty would soon follow. While at the falls, they washed out their clothes and put on something clean. As was usual, they kept their rifles at their side close by. "Taking chances is a fool's game," Carlyle has said. When they got back to camp, they could hear a lot of talk about a wedding. The people wanted to celebrate with a feast in honor of the up and coming wedding of Frankie B. and Angelina and OK Bill and Prairie Flower.

Frankie B. said, "I would like to have a Christian as well as Comanche wedding. Preacher Lefty might have arrived just in time to do the honors. That is, if he would be willing to do the wedding." "Yes I will, you just say when."

"Tomorrow would be good as far as I'm concerned. I don't know about the others."

Prairie Flower and Angelina both were willing and OK Bill was ready.

He said, "We need to marry and get back to our jobs with Mr. Dickenson in Texas. We will be riding through snow if we don't go soon, or we will have to stay here through the winter."

The four agreed. So, next morning before noon, the Chief had ordered two fires set with two different types of wood in each one with a feathered walk through in between. Preacher Lefty stood between two fires with the Chief. OK Bill and Prairie Flower held hands. Frankie B. and Angelina also held hands. The Chief held out his hands to welcome them and spoke an old Comanche prayer. In English, it would be, "God in heaven above, we honor you. Please protect the ones we love. We honor all you created as they pledge their hearts and lives together. May they always be as one."

Then Lefty spoke. Frankie B. and Angelina. OK Bill and Prairie Flower. Do you take each other to be husband and wife and promise to be true in good times and bad times, in sickness and in health, to love and honor each other, from this day forward till death do you part?"

They answered with, "We do."

Then they walked through the feathered walkway. At that, the whole camp started to dance around the four newlyweds as they went to the two separate teepees. Carlyle and Lefty sat down by a fire and toasted the four with coffee. And some of Carlyle's Deerhammer Whiskey. The marriages were complete and now thoughts of leaving with the winter coming on and hurry on to Del Rio or stay here and wait out the harsh weather that was sure to come to this part of the Oklahoma territory.

Frankie B. laid on a warm blanket with his hands behind his head thinking out loud. Angelina was laying close looking into his eyes. She was still in a state of mind that was different than Frankie B. They had just been in a wonderful new world and she had wanted to stay. But Frankie B. was already out of it thinking of things that needed to be done. He now had more than himself to worry about. The small fire crackling in the middle of their teepee kept it warm and cozy.

"Frankie B., I will go or stay, whatever you think best."

"Okay then. We can talk it over with OK Bill and Prairie Flower. We have to decide soon."

"OK Bill and Prairie Flower were still laying in an embrace under the blanket holding onto each other, talking of loving each other forever.

OK Bill said, "This is good. I'm a whole man. You have made me a whole man. When we go to Del Rio, everyone will know."

By evening, they came out for the meal to be eaten with the whole tribe. The four sat together and were sipping their coffee.

Like a Deer sat by Prairie Flower and asked, "What will become of me? Am I to go back to the Crow people?"

"Not unless you want to. It can be just like it was. No worry. When we go, you can go with us."

"Thank you, my mother." Like a Deer got a nod from OK Bill and Frankie B. Angelina got up and hugged her. "You are our family," she said, "and that won't change. We know what it is like to lose a family person. You come with us in our teepee, and stay warm by fire, my child, and bring your dog, Henna, if he wants to come in."

Like a Deer accepted the invitation to be like a daughter to Prairie Flower and OK Bill. Two days had passed since the marriages.

"While you are deciding on when to leave, I need to go into that little town and send a message to Mrs Sikorski. What's that town called?"

"Westville. It's Westville, Carlyle."

"I gotta send her and Red Fox and Antonina a message if they got wire going all that way into southern Illinois. I'll be back as soon as I can. "Preacher, you be okay here for a while?"

"Sure, take your time."

In the town of Westville, Carlyle found the telegraph office and sent his message. He thought he would go to the saloon and pass a little time; maybe if he was lucky someone might take his message to Mrs. Sikorski and somehow she'd get a message back to him. After a few drinks, he came to the realization that things just don't work that fast. So he went back to the telegraph office and told the operator if a message comes in either today or tomorrow, he'd gladly pay any charge if someone would bring the message to him at the Comanche camp west of here.

"Okay, if you don't hear from us here in a couple days, check back here."

"Okay, I will." And he headed back to the Comanche camp. By now it was getting dark. Just at the edge of town, he swung his horse around and thought, *I'm not going anywhere. I'll stay here some place and check back at the office before I leave tomorrow.*

Back at the saloon, he got a room upstairs and went off to sleep soon as his head hit the pillow. In the morning, everyone woke up to a light snow with cold wind. Carlyle got bacon and eggs for breakfast with cups of coffee. He checked at the telegraph office and there was a message for him. The message was, "Miss you, love you, wish we were with you, still undecided." He really missed them, too, but knew there was nothing he could do about it for now.

"I got to get back to the Comanche camp. It was so cold riding with the wind blowing snow in his face. He almost headed back into town for the second time, but he persevered for a while and then set up a camp in a cave cut into a mountain and stayed put till the next day when it warmed a little. His fire made him so warm, he said, "I ain't leaving this place till spring." With plenty of firewood and water nearby, rabbit to eat on, and sleeping on and off, he thought, *I got it good. Bet OK Bill and Frankie B. won't be going to Texas till spring.*

The weather at Comanche camp wasn't any better and they did change their minds about going to Del Rio, Texas.

"We can wait," Frankie B. said. "Let's wait it out. We've got nothing to rush for anyway, do we OK Bill? If it was just you and I, we might see how far we'd get and hold up for how long it might take for the weather to warm up. But with the women, we better not chance it."

It did clear up enough where Carlyle was. At least, enough for him to leave the comfort of his cave and make it back to the Comanche camp. He came straggling in about noon all bundled up and cold. The camp scouts saw him coming from a long distance. So they all knew. Everyone was glad to see him. After settling in and warming up in his and Preacher Lefty's teepee, Frankie B. and OK Bill wanted to have a talk with him about staying here till the spring.

"Come in, Frankie B. and OK Bill. Come on in. I'm fine. I gotta tell you, I had the best place you could ever imagine when I left Westville. I was freezing and stumbled into a cave and had fresh water, all the wood I needed to keep a fire going forever, a rabbit I killed, and my bottle of Deerhammer. I'm a telling you, I didn't want to leave but I knew I had to get back here. So, here I am. What you want to talk about. Oh, before you start, I need to say I contacted Mrs. Sikorski and seems like they'd leave there and come here in a heartbeat. I guess it doesn't feel like home anymore. I guess what I mean is they'd go with us to Del Rio if we go."

"That's what we want to talk to you about. Do you feel like you'd ever leave here and go on to Del Rio with us and the women and do you think the Chief would be willing to move the whole camp to Texas? You know they would be better off there."

"And just how do you figure they would be better off in Texas."

"Well, the fact that there are a lot more Comanche there and the weather is better. No harsh winters. The Comanche living in Texas are doing pretty well and Dolphus Dickenson makes sure they have plenty to eat if need be. Besides, if they want to work for the ranch, they can."

"I can see what the Chief thinks." He had a short conversation with the Chief and his advisers.

"They said yes, here not good, too many other tribes. Sometimes they must fight for deer meat and grass for horses to eat."

Frankie B. and OK Bill already decided with Prairie Flower, Angelina, and Like a Deer that they would wait out the bad weather and leave sometime in spring. So, if the tribe wants to go, we can all go together when the weather starts warming up. They will need to get the people ready, make sure every family has at least one horse to pull their sled with all their belongings and clothes.

"How 'bout you, Preacher? You want to go to Del Rio in the spring?"

"Don't know. Maybe, if I ain't got any better offers."

"You know, Frankie B., that gives Mrs. Sikorski and her daughter and Red Fox time to decide if they want to go, too. They can be here in a few weeks. For now, we just settle in from the cold and snow, stock up on food, and help each other . When spring comes, we'll be ready."

Frankie B. and OK Bill are the best of friends from two different cultures and this has been their story in the old west in the year of our Lord, 1888.

www.ingramcontent.com/pod-product-compliance
Lightning Source LLC
Chambersburg PA
CBHW052352020726
47503CB00001B/209